THESE
INFINITE
THREADS

BOOKS BY TAHEREH MAFI

This Woven Kingdom

An Emotion of Great Delight

A Very Large Expanse of Sea

The Shatter Me Series
Shatter Me
Unravel Me
Ignite Me
Restore Me
Defy Me
Imagine Me

Novellas
Destroy Me
Fracture Me
Shadow Me
Reveal Me

Novella Collections
Unite Me
Find Me

Furthermore
Whichwood

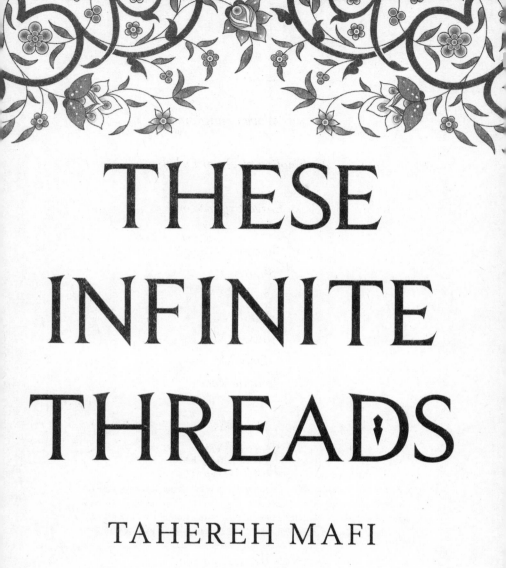

THESE
INFINITE
THREADS

TAHEREH MAFI

HARPER
An Imprint of HarperCollinsPublishers

Library of Congress Control Number: 2022943680
ISBN 978-0-06-297247-7 — ISBN 978-0-06-329272-7 (special ed)
ISBN 978-0-06-330669-1 (intl ed)

Typography by Jenna Stempel-Lobell
22 23 24 25 26 LBC 5 4 3 2 1

First Edition

Why did fate indulge the prince in luxury and ease
only to abandon him at the hands of his cruel slayers?

The wise know there is no justice in this valley of tears.

—Abolghasem Ferdowsi, *Shahnameh*

Tell me about my end.
When is it written for me to leave this world?
Who will inherit my throne?

—Abolghasem Ferdowsi, *Shahnameh*

THESE INFINITE THREADS

ONE

"DON'T!" KAMRAN SHOUTED. "THE FIRE—"

The words died in his throat.

He watched Alizeh charge toward the thigh-high blaze with an astonishment so complete he sank to the ground, the cold of the stone floor seeping through the tattered silk of his trousers. Kamran had the benefit of heavy layers and jewel harnesses at least; the fire had been unable to devour him with any speed. But Alizeh—Alizeh wore little more than a whisper, so fine was the fabric of her gown.

The fire will melt the flesh from her bones.

He thought it even as she crossed the blaze without care, her gossamer dress inhaled in an instant by the fiery ring, an abomination magicked to life by the young Tulanian king. Cyrus, the monarch in question, stood just opposite Kamran, sword still held aloft in anticipation of a fatal blow, his hand stayed only by the sight of Alizeh, who headed toward him now. As if from outside himself Kamran watched as she batted away flames from her dress with bare hands, snuffing the fire as one might a light. He stared down at the remains of his own disintegrated garments, then at the blood dripping between his knuckles. Slowly, he looked back up at Alizeh, possessing clarity of mind enough to register that she'd emerged from the inferno unscathed, even as her gown suffered. He blinked at the impossibility of it; he was either dreaming or deluded. He could not make sense of her.

No, he could not make sense of anything.

Alizeh, who'd nearly tripped over the king's fallen crown in her haste, had sent the weighty heirloom spinning toward Kamran as she ran. He stared at that crown now, stared at it as a sudden tremor seized him, shock and cold combining, reminding him—

His grandfather was dead.

King Zaal was supine before the world, blood pooling beneath his lifeless body in the imperfect oval of an open-mouthed scream. His grandfather had bargained with the devil to extend his life—and in the end Death had devoured the king swiftly and without dignity, the sovereign and his sins withering in unison. The limp, corded muscle of twin white snakes still soldered to the pale shoulders of a beloved king painted a scene so grotesque it inspired in Kamran a sudden impulse to heave; he braced his unsteady hands on the icy floor and wondered, with increasing horror, how many street children had been sacrificed for his grandfather's serpents.

It was an imagining too monstrous.

Kamran was ill with disillusion, with denial. He willed himself to remain calm, to marshal his thoughts, but an unidentified agony clawed at his consciousness, the pain seeming to emanate from his left arm. He wished to be someone else. He wished to turn back time. Above all he wished, without a mote of hyperbole, that Cyrus had been allowed to kill him.

The whispers of their heretofore silent audience had been growing steadily in the interlude and now built to an alarming crescendo, the din awaking in Kamran years of training and awareness. His mind sharpened against the gossip, duty piercing the fog of grief and replacing it with anger, focus—

A sudden clatter.

Kamran looked up in time to see Alizeh toss Cyrus's sword to the floor, the young man flinching as glinting steel struck marble. The foreign king stared at Alizeh with an astonishment to rival Kamran's, fear torpefying his features as she rounded on him.

"How dare you," she said. "You horrible cretin. You useless monster. How *could* you—"

"How—how did you—" Cyrus fumbled back an inch. "How did you walk through the fire like that? Why are you not—burning?"

"You despicable, wretched man," she cried. "You know *who* I am, but you don't know *what* I am?"

"No."

Alizeh struck Cyrus across the face with the force of a bludgeon, the impact so violent the young king staggered, audibly striking his head against a column.

Kamran felt the shock of it in his bones.

He knew he should rejoice in this moment—knew he should celebrate Alizeh's actions against the depraved royal—but his mind would not submit to relief, for the scene unraveling before him did not align with reason.

Cyrus appeared entirely too unnerved.

The trepidation in his eyes, his astonishment at

her approach, the blind steps he took backward as she advanced—it made no sense. Alizeh had insisted to Kamran but moments ago that she did not know the southern king; yet Cyrus, who'd more than proven his ruthlessness, displayed every sign of alarm in her presence. If they were truly strangers, why would he cower now at the unarmed advance of a girl he did not know? She'd tossed his sword to the floor, insulted him repeatedly, and slapped him in the face—and the young king who'd minutes ago buried a blade in Zaal's heart hadn't so much as lifted a hand in his own defense. He'd only stood there and stared at her and all but *allowed* her to strike him.

Almost as if he feared her.

Kamran dared not breathe as a terrifying suspicion dawned in his mind, the thought provoking in him a spasm so acute he thought his chest might crater.

From the first, Kamran had been mystified by Alizeh's transformation at the ball. In a matter of hours her injuries had miraculously healed, she'd discarded the iconic snoda of her servant's uniform, and her drab work dress had been replaced by an extravagant gown no maid could ever afford—and still he'd denied the truth, so desperate was he to absolve her of artifice. Finally, he understood.

He had been deceived.

His eyes flickered again to the fallen figure of his grandfather.

King Zaal had tried to warn him; he'd begged Kamran to see how Alizeh was tethered to the prophecy, to the end of Zaal's life—and only now that his grandfather was dead did

Kamran understand the magnitude of his own folly. Every foolish word he'd spoken in her defense—every stupid, childish action he'd taken to protect her—

Without warning, Cyrus laughed.

Kamran looked up; the southern king appeared pale and disordered. From where he knelt, Kamran could not see Alizeh's face; he saw only the horror in Cyrus's eyes as he looked her over. The young man had killed his own father for the throne of Tulan; he'd newly murdered King Zaal, the ruler of the greatest empire on earth; he would've killed Kamran, too, had he been granted but a moment more to accomplish the task. Now the copper-headed tyrant steadied himself slowly, blood seeping from his lips, smeared across his chin. Of all the adversaries they might've encountered, it seemed they'd both been cowed by the poor, gentle servant of Baz House.

"Damn the devil to hell," the Tulanian king said quietly. "He didn't tell me you were a Jinn."

"Who?" Alizeh demanded.

"Our mutual friend."

"Hazan?"

Kamran recoiled. He'd not been prepared for the blow of yet another betrayal, and the impact of that single word lanced through his body with a ruthlessness against which he had no defense. That she was somehow allied with Cyrus was torture enough—but that she'd gone behind his back with *Hazan?*

This was more than he could bear.

She'd playacted at fear and innocence, had outmaneuvered

him at every turn, and worst of all—*worst of all*—he had fallen, madly, for her manipulations. In all the time he'd known her, Alizeh had clung to her snoda, fighting to hide her identity even in the midst of a rainstorm; now she stood unmasked before a sea of nobles, glowering at the formidable sovereign of a neighboring nation, declaring herself to the world.

All this time, Alizeh had been making plans.

Already Kamran had been attacked by grief and anger; he struggled even then to digest the magnitude of the last moments, could hardly piece together his discordant thoughts about his grandfather—but now— Now he was expected to make sense of this? He, who prided himself on the strength of his instincts—he, who believed himself to be a capable, intuitive soldier—

"Hazan?" Cyrus laughed again, his hand trembling almost imperceptibly as he wiped blood from his mouth. "*Hazan?* Of course not *Hazan*." Cyrus locked eyes with Kamran and said, "Pay attention, King, for it seems even your friends have betrayed you."

Alizeh turned suddenly to face him—eyes wide with panic—and her obvious flush of guilt was all the evidence Kamran required. Just hours ago he would've sworn an oath that her desire for him was as palpable as the press of satin against his skin; he'd tasted the salt of her, had felt the exquisite shape of her body under his hands. Now he knew it had all been a lie.

Hell.

This was hell.

But to say that this revelation had broken his heart would be to misrepresent the truth; Kamran was not heartbroken, then, no—he was incandescent with rage.

He would kill her.

Any naive, lingering softness in Kamran's heart evaporated. He'd been seduced by a siren while being deceived by his own friend—and had all but spat in the face of the only person who truly cared for his well-being. King Zaal had sold himself to evil in the pursuit of Kamran's happiness—and the man was repaid with only disloyalty and treason. This dark night had been wrought by Kamran's actions alone; he understood that now. The entire Ardunian empire had been left vulnerable because he'd been frail of mind and body.

Never again.

Never again would he allow a woman to own his emotions; never again would he be made weak by such base temptations. He swore it then: this monster from the prophecy would die by his hand—he would drive a blade through her heart or die trying.

But first, Hazan.

Kamran caught the eye of a guard hovering—awaiting orders—and with a single glance he issued his first decree as king of Ardunia: Hazan would hang.

Kamran experienced no victory as he watched his former minister seized, then dragged away; he felt no triumph at the sound of Hazan's feeble protests ringing out through the astonished silence of the room. No, Kamran suffered only the ascent of a terrifying madness as he forced himself upright, daring to bear weight on his injured arm in the process, and realizing only in the excruciating effort that his legs, too, had been badly burned. His skin and clothes were sticky with blood; his head felt leaden. It was a truth he was loath to admit: that he did not know how much longer he could stand here without the aid of a surgeon. Or a Diviner.

No. The royal Diviners were dead. Slaughtered by Cyrus.

Kamran's eyes squeezed shut at the reminder.

"Iblees."

His eyes flew open at the sound of her soft, traitorous voice. Kamran's heart began pounding anew, startling him with its intensity. He couldn't decide then what disturbed him more: to realize that she and Cyrus shared *a mutual friend* in the devil, or to discover that his body still wanted her, still heated at the mere sound of her voice—

She had disappeared.

Panicked, Kamran searched for her and was unsuccessful; instead he saw Cyrus, still staring intently at what could only be Alizeh, who'd a moment ago been speaking—

Without warning, she materialized.

Alizeh stood in precisely the same spot, except now she appeared hazy, oscillating in and out of focus with a dizzying consistency.

Was she doing this to him? Had she access to dark magic?

Where once was Alizeh stood now a milky blur of movement, her voice warped and waterlogged, reverberating as if she were speaking from inside a glass jar.

"Ssssttt you you sspeakthe the the vvvvil . . ."

Kamran dragged bloody hands down his face. As if each revelation weren't already more annihilating than the last—he was now blind and deaf, too?

"Sssssendyyou you iiiinterest heeeee my my lllllife?"

His injured legs failed as his mind fractured; he trembled, hands grasping at air as he sought purchase, and fell hard onto one badly burned leg. He nearly cried out in agony.

But then, a mercy—

The Tulanian king spoke, his words lucid: "Is it not obvious? He wants you to rule."

A terrible thunder filled Kamran's head. There was no time to rejoice in the restoration of his hearing. The demon-like monster with ice in its veins had been foretold to have formidable allies, and here was further evidence of the Diviners' wisdom, of his grandfather's warnings—

The devil himself was assisting her.

The crowd was growing louder now, and he could hear *them*, too, whispers having evolved into shouts and hysterics. Kamran was reminded once more that all the nobles of Ardunia were collected in this room; the highest ranking officials from across the empire had been brought together for an evening of decadence and celebration; instead, they would bear witness to the fall of the greatest empire in the world.

Kamran did not know how he would survive it.

He heard Cyrus laugh again, heard him say clearly: "*A Jinn queen* to rule the world. Oh, it's so horribly seditious. The perfect revenge."

Again, Kamran attempted to draw himself up. His head pounded with a vengeance, his eyesight still an uncertain thing. The room, the floor—Cyrus himself—were all

perfectly clear, but Alizeh remained more nimbus than person, a series of halos stacked in the general shape of a body.
Then again, just knowing where to aim might be enough.

This evening's admissions had more than proven his
grandfather's every warning about the girl—and Kamran
would die before he failed the man twice. His sword lay a
few feet away, and though the distance seemed insurmount-
able, Kamran would force himself to clear it. He might be
able to bury the blade in her heart now, kill her now, end this
tragedy tonight.

He'd just managed to take an agonizing step toward his
sword when the haze of her shifted away from Cyrus; then,
in a flash of kismet, Kamran could see Alizeh's face.

She looked terrified.

The sight speared him through the chest at the precise
moment the cataracts in his eyes seemed to clear; her figure
came suddenly into sharp focus and, oh, this was a cruel fate,
indeed. Alizeh was an enemy possessed of a power he never
could've imagined. Even now her shining eyes glittered with
an emotion that destroyed him. Her guile was so graceful, so
natural; she searched the room as if she were truly frantic.

Kamran cursed the wretched organ in his chest, then
pounded a clenched fist against his sternum as if to kill it.
In response, a terrible anguish ripped through his body, so
brutal the sensation it took his breath away; it was as if a tree
had planted in a single shot at his feet, the trunk suturing to
his spine, tremendous branches pushing violently through
his veins.

He doubled over, gasping, almost missing the moment

when Alizeh glanced up in his direction and then bolted without warning, exiting the inferno once again unscathed.

Had she seen him reaching for his sword? Had she gleaned his intentions?

Alizeh was a maddening sight even as she fled, the gauzy layers of her gown having now been incinerated twice. She flew past in little more than scraps of transparent silk; he could see every lush curve of her body, the lithe shape of her legs, the swell of her breasts, and he hated himself for wanting her, even now. Hated himself for the hunger he felt as he watched her go, hated the instincts that screamed at him, despite all logical evidence to the contrary, that she was in danger—that he should go to her, protect her—

"Wait— Where are you going?" Cyrus shouted. "We had a deal— Under no circumstances were you allowed to run away—"

We had a deal.

The words rang in his head, over and over, each syllable striking his mind like a scythe, drawing blood. By the angels, how many more blows need his body survive tonight?

"I must," she cried, the agitated crowd leaping apart to let her pass. "I'm sorry, I'm sorry, but I have to leave— I need to find somewhere to hide, somewhere he won't—"

At once Alizeh doubled over, as if struck by an invisible force, and was promptly jerked upward, into the air.

She screamed.

Kamran reacted without thinking, a rush of adrenaline propelling him upright, dregs of stupidity compelling him to cry out her name. He pushed as close to the edge of the flaming bastille as he dared, the anguish in his voice no doubt betraying him to the world, if not to himself—but he could not think on it then. Alizeh was being launched higher and higher in the air, twisting and screaming, and Kamran condemned himself for his tortured response to her suffering; even then he couldn't fathom the battle being waged inside his body.

"Make it stop," she screamed. "Put me down!"

Sudden understanding forced Kamran to look Cyrus in the eye. "*You*," he said, hardly recognizing the rasp of his own voice. "You're doing this to her."

Cyrus's expression darkened. "She's done it to herself."

Kamran was prevented from responding by the sound of yet another tortured cry. He spun around in time to see Alizeh spiraling toward the rafters—she was without a doubt in the grip of a very dark magic—and promptly lost his battle with sense. He could not fathom this chaos into order, could not answer the multitude of questions that hounded him.

Kamran felt unmoored as he watched her.

Alizeh was a force so powerful she claimed the devil as a friend, knew the sovereign of an enemy nation as an ally. She'd used dark magic to create illusions so compelling he'd truly believed she'd suffered physical blows to her hands, her throat, her face. She'd tricked even King Zaal into believing she was a helpless, ignorant servant girl. And yet, she sobbed then with a hysteria so believable that even he—

"You can see her."

The statement startled him. Kamran turned back to

Cyrus, assessing in an instant his enemy's copper hair, his cold blue eyes. Of all the things Cyrus might've said, *this* was particularly strange, and Kamran was too discerning to dismiss it as meaningless. That Cyrus appeared surprised Kamran could see her seemed to point to a simple inverse—

Perhaps others could not.

It was a theory that explained nothing yet seemed somehow vitally important. Kamran wondered then about the source of his temporary blindness, and renewed fear branched up his back.

"What," Kamran said carefully, "did you do to her?"

Cyrus did not answer.

Lazily, the southern king pushed himself off the column before bending to pick up his sword. He walked toward Kamran with affected unconcern, dragging the blade behind him like a dog on a leash, the eerie exhalation of steel against stone briefly overpowering the sounds of Alizeh's screams.

"I thought she broke through the fire to punish *me*," Cyrus was saying. "I see only now that she did so to protect *you*."

There was a flicker in those blue irises, and for a second Cyrus betrayed himself. Beneath his placid surface was something desperate and unrestrained, if not broken. Kamran cataloged the moment as a kind of mercy, for he realized then that the young man was a king weaker than he appeared.

"You know her name," Cyrus said softly.

Kamran felt a pulse of trepidation but said nothing.

"How," Cyrus demanded, "did you come to know her name?"

When Kamran finally spoke, his voice was heavy, cold. "I might ask you the same question."

"Indeed you might," said Cyrus, who was lifting his sword by inches. "But then, it's my prerogative to know the name of my bride."

A sharp pain exploded in Kamran's chest just as an ear-splitting crash broke open the room. He fought back a cry, clasping his ribs as he fell once more to his knees, heaving through the brutality of the blow. Kamran had no idea what was happening to him, and there was no time to hazard a guess. He could only force his eyelids open in time to witness not merely the destruction of his home but the arrival of an enormous, iridescent dragon, the sight of which seemed to drain the blood from his body.

The Diviners would never have allowed a foreign beast to enter Ardunian skies.

But the Diviners were dead.

Kamran watched the dragon catch Alizeh just as she began a sudden, dizzying descent, the monstrous creature seating the young woman firmly on its back before launching upward once more. The animal gave a stalwart roar, flapped its leathery wings, and, in a blink, both beast and rider were gone, vanishing into the night through the cavernous hole newly blown through the palace wall.

In the proceeding chaos, Kamran could no longer deny the devastation of his mind.

The grief of losing his grandfather had only just begun to penetrate, and each subsequent betrayal had broken him not unlike a series of other small deaths, each one a violent injustice, each one demanding a period of mourning.

Zaal had been false. Hazan had been false. Alizeh—

Alizeh had *ruined* him.

Somehow he still heard the uproar of the crowd, felt the oppressive heat of his cage, the insistent cold of the marble floor under his knees. He lacked the strength to stand; pain was streaking relentlessly across his body in a steady rhythm that showed no signs of abating. Slowly, Kamran lifted his head, looked Cyrus in the eye. He felt so raw his throat seemed to bleed as he spoke.

"Is it true?" he asked. "She's really going to marry you?"

Cyrus stepped forward, his sword at the ready. "Yes."

Kamran would not recover.

He grimaced as fresh pain exploded up his neck, across his shoulders. The action was so unrehearsed even Cyrus frowned.

"Fascinating," said the Tulanian king, who then lifted Kamran's chin with the tip of his sword. Kamran, who could hardly breathe through the torment, still managed to jerk backward, the movement provoking a fresh deluge of suffering. "You appear to be dying."

"No," Kamran gasped, bracing his hands against the stone floor.

Cyrus almost laughed. "Unless you intend to follow in your grandfather's footsteps, I don't believe you have a choice in the matter."

From where he drew the strength, Kamran did not know, but he heaved himself up off the floor with the kind of fortitude borne only of a broken man, a reckless one.

Kamran had been hollowed out.

In the space of an hour the threads of his entire life had come apart. He felt mad and feverish in the aftermath; a bit like he was moving through a nightmare. Somehow, the horrors had fortified him. He felt he had nothing left.

Nothing to lose.

He reached for his sword as if his arm wasn't still bleeding out, as if the flesh of his legs had not been recently charred. It seemed a miracle at all that he managed to lift the blade, face his opponent.

He heard a storm of footfalls then, a chorus of concerned voices as a brigade of guards surged closer to the fiery ring— but Kamran stayed them with a single hand.

This was his fight to finish.

Cyrus glanced at these armed onlookers, then considered the prince for what felt like a long time.

"Very well," the southern king said finally. "Never say I'm not merciful. I'll make this quick. You will not suffer."

"And I," Kamran said, the rasp of his voice like gravel, "will make certain that your torment is never-ending."

A flash of anger and Cyrus's sword cut through the air in a single, blinding strike, which Kamran met with surprising force, even as his broken body shook in the effort. His legs trembled, his arms screamed in anguish, but Kamran would not capitulate. He'd rather die fighting than surrender— and it was this thought that heated his chest, that generated within him a second life, a terrifying adrenaline.

Happily, he would perish in the effort.

With a guttural cry he managed to push against his opponent, launching Cyrus backward, freeing his sword. Kamran advanced without delay, moving now with shocking swiftness as he lunged, as Cyrus parried. For a time all Kamran heard was steel; he saw nothing but the sheen of metal, waves of blades crashing, escaping.

Cyrus feinted, then sprang forward with surprising alacrity—and too late, Kamran felt the burn of his injury. He heard the panicked shrieks of the crowd, but he couldn't see the laceration; in fact he was hardly able to identify which aspect of his body had been injured.

There was no time.

Kamran moved to stave off a second attack, experiencing a brief moment of triumph when Cyrus fell back with a muttered oath. The southern king rallied without delay, meeting Kamran blow for blow in a series of strikes so precisely choreographed even Kamran was not immune to the beauty of it. There was a rare pleasure in fighting a worthy adversary; in testing, without restraint, the potential of one's power. But this evidence of Cyrus's prowess—and lightning-fast reflexes—only cemented Kamran's certainty that the southern king had earlier allowed Alizeh to overpower him. To the prince, this behavior pointed to one of only two explanations: either she was his superior in their arrangement, or he hadn't wanted to hurt her. Perhaps both.

Maybe they really were betrothed.

This shattering thought brought him alive with an alarming strength, the breadth of which remained unfamiliar to him. He knew only that his instincts were sharper than he'd ever felt them, and he soon saw a faint strain in Cyrus's face, the sheen of sweat at his brow no doubt mirrored upon his own features. Both were breathing hard, but even as blood dripped down Kamran's hands, his every motion staining the marble underfoot, he did not tire.

Again, he advanced—

The young men crossed swords in a movement so violent Kamran felt the tremor move through his entire body. They were trapped in a herculean standstill; adversaries locking eyes through the glimmer of their blades.

Then, for no fathomable reason, Cyrus faltered.

It was only a fraction of a second that the Tulanian king frowned, that his focus was distracted, but Kamran did not misuse the opportunity; with brute force he bore down, compelling Cyrus to fall back into a crouch. Kamran had the advantage now—all he had to do was break his opponent. There would be great satisfaction in spearing Cyrus through the heart; Kamran already knew he would have him disemboweled. He would display the bloody organs under a glass cloche in the town square, let the maggots find them and feast freely.

"I feel you should know," Cyrus said heavily, the fatigue of exertion apparent on his face. "That something is happening to you. To your skin."

This, Kamran ignored.

Cyrus was trying to unsettle him, and he would not allow it, not when he was this close to victory. With a sudden cry, Kamran propelled his opponent back a final time— and Cyrus fell to the floor with a harsh exhale, his sword clattering as it struck marble.

Kamran wasted no time, approaching his fallen rival with a ferocious determination. One final time he raised his sword—

And froze.

A breathtaking paralysis took hold of his body where he stood, so severe the sensation that Kamran could hardly breathe. He watched, as if pressed between panes of glass, as Cyrus clambered to his feet, sheathed his sword, retrieved his staff, and searched for his hat. Once the strange article was settled firmly on the tyrant's head, he walked up to Kamran's statue and smiled.

"There is very little honor left in me, Melancholy King. Certainly not enough to die when I deserve it."

In the distance, someone screamed.

Kamran thrashed against the prison of his own body, but he felt his lungs weakening by the second, his organs being compressed from the outside in.

Cyrus's smile did not waver.

"Unfortunate as it is," he went on, "a flicker of humanity persists in animating my flesh. So I will leave you tonight with a beating heart. Anyway, it's better if you live, isn't it? Better for you to suffer consciously, to grieve your vile grandfather, to live every day with the knowledge that you have been betrayed not only by those you loathe, but by those you love—and to fail, tremendously, while trying to lead a pathetic empire."

Kamran felt his heart seizing in his chest, his eyes burning with the threat of emotion.

No, he wanted to cry. *No, no—*

"I look forward to fighting you again," said Cyrus softly, tipping his hat. "But first, you'll have to find me."

Then he vanished.

TWO

"

FOR A LONG TIME, ALIZEH did not move.

She felt paralyzed by fear and disbelief, her mind assaulted by a tumult of uncertainty. Slowly, sensation returned to her limbs, to the tips of her fingers. She soon felt the wind against her face, saw the night sky drape itself around her, a midnight sheet studded with stars.

By degrees, she began to relax.

The beast was heavy and solid, and seemed to know where it was going. She took deep lungfuls of air, trying to clear the dregs of her panic, to convince herself that she would be safe for at least as long as she clung to this wild creature. She shifted, suddenly, at the feel of soft fibers grazing her skin through what was left of her thin gown, and looked down to examine it. She hadn't realized she was in fact sitting on a small carpet, which—

Alizeh nearly screamed again.

The dragon had disappeared. It was still *here*—she felt the beast beneath her, could still feel the leathery texture of its skin—but the creature had gone invisible in the sky, leaving her floating on a patterned rug.

It was deeply disorienting.

Still, she understood then why the creature had disappeared; without its bulk to blind her, she could see the world below, could see the world beyond.

Alizeh didn't know where she was going, but for the moment, she forced herself not to panic. There was, after all, a strange peace in this, in the quiet that surrounded her.

As her nerves relaxed, her mind sharpened. Quickly, she yanked off her boots and chucked them into the night. It gave her great satisfaction to watch them disappear into the dark.

Relief.

A sudden thud shifted the weight of the rug, startling her upright. Alizeh spun around, her heart racing once again in her chest; and when she saw the face of her unwelcome companion, she thought she might fling herself into the sky with the boots.

"No," she whispered.

"This is *my* dragon," said the Tulanian king. "You are not allowed to steal my dragon."

"I didn't steal it, the creature took— Wait, how did you get here? Can you fly?"

He laughed at that. "Is the mighty empire of Ardunia really so poor in magic that these small tricks impress you?"

"Yes," she said, blinking. Then, "What is your name?"

"Of all the non sequiturs. Why do you need to know my name?"

"So that I may hate you more informally."

"Ah. Well, in that case, you may call me Cyrus."

"Cyrus," she said. "You insufferable monster. Where on earth are we going?"

Her insults seemed to have no effect on him, for he was

still smiling when he said, "Have you really not figured it out?"

"I'm entirely too agitated for these games. Please just tell me what horrible fate awaits me now."

"Oh, the very worst of fates, I'm sorry to say. We are currently en route to Tulan."

The nosta burned hot against her skin, and Alizeh felt herself go rigid with fear. She was stunned, yes, and horrified, too, but to hear the king of an empire denigrate his own land thus—

"Is Tulan really so terrible a place?"

"Tulan?" His eyes widened with surprise. "Not at all. A single square inch of Tulan is more breathtaking than all of Ardunia, and I say that as a discernable fact, not as a subjective opinion."

"But then"—she frowned—"why did you say that it would be the very worst of fates?"

"Ah. That." Cyrus looked away, searched the night sky. "Well. You remember how I said I owed our mutual friend a very large debt?"

"Yes."

"And that helping you was the only repayment he would accept?"

She swallowed. "Yes."

"And do you remember how I told you that he wanted you to rule? To be a Jinn queen?"

Alizeh nodded.

"Well. You have no kingdom," he said. "No land to lord over. No empire to lead."

"No," she said softly. "I don't."

"Well, then. You are coming to Tulan," Cyrus said, taking a quick breath. "To marry me."

Alizeh gave a sharp cry, and fell off the dragon.

She heard Cyrus unleash a torrent of foul language as she fell—the wind rushing up against her feet—and found, to her surprise, that though she actively pitched toward what could only be certain death, she could not summon the appropriate response.

Alizeh did not scream; neither did she experience fear.

This unusual reaction to a sudden plummet from the heavens was in part precipitated by an ambivalence toward the direction her life had recently taken—for Alizeh had thought, in absconding with the dragon, that she would at the very least be running away from the machinations of Iblees. She'd not realized that her actions, inadvertent or otherwise, had in fact delivered her directly into his diabolical plans. Alizeh did not think of herself as a particularly maudlin person, but just then she couldn't bring herself to care whether she survived.

Then again, her uncommon calm was perhaps a result of a far simpler reasoning:

Alizeh knew she would be saved.

She'd hardly generated the thought when she heard the diminished roar of an inconvenienced dragon, the flap of its heavy wings funneling fierce gusts in her direction. This was twice in the same hour that Alizeh had fallen from a great height, and as the frigid wind tore at her body, chapping her skin, she realized with a detached sort of amusement that her yards of black curls had come loose of their pins entirely. The midnight locks lapped at the air around her like strange tongues, several restless tendrils curling around her eyes, her mouth, her throat, her shoulders. Alizeh was blinded by her own body, thoroughly windswept, downhearted, and quite possibly frozen solid.

True, Alizeh was always cold; the ice that marked her as heir to an ancient kingdom ensured that she rarely, if ever, enjoyed a bout of warmth. Couple this with the brutality of the winter night, the unrelenting winds that walloped her now, and the fact that she wore mere scraps in place of a gown—

It was a surprise to Alizeh that she was not yet a corpse.

Still, she made no response at all when the dragon came up underneath her, registering only a muted shout before Cyrus's warm hands circled her waist, plucking her from the air as if she were an itinerant flower. He drew her firmly onto the carpet beside him, where she landed with a teeth-chattering thud, and after which he drew away from her with unflattering haste. She took note of it all as if watching through fog, for Alizeh seemed suddenly incapable of emotion. She felt not unlike a rag doll, unable to animate.

All seemed irretrievably lost.

Hazan would hang. King Zaal was dead. Kamran—

Kamran was in danger.

Ardunia's royal Diviners had been murdered; the palace had been attacked. Kamran had been injured when she left—how would he receive swift treatment without the Diviners? How long would he be left vulnerable before they were able to gather a new quorum of priests and priestesses? Even Alizeh, who'd witnessed the devastation of her own life in the last hours, could see clearly that Kamran had suffered a series of similar travesties.

As if the death and disgrace of his grandfather had not been enough to endure, Alizeh could still picture the look on Kamran's face when he realized Hazan had betrayed him, when he seemed to think that she, too, had been disloyal—

No—no, she could not bear it.

Every hope she had recently, privately clasped to her chest—every effort she had made these last several years to build herself a quiet, protected life—every backbreaking labor to which she had submitted herself in hopes of securing a quiet future—

She shuttered her mind against the thoughts.

There was an unconscious part of Alizeh that seemed to understand that if she unlocked the pain in her chest, she might not survive it. Much better, she thought, to keep it leashed.

In any case, it was the devil who'd done this to her— who'd designed grand plans of torture for her—and here, here was proof.

His disciple sat beside her.

"Will you not say something?" said Cyrus, his voice uncharacteristically subdued.

Alizeh felt as if her lips were numb. "I will not."

"You will not speak?"

"I will not marry you."

Cyrus sighed.

The two sat in a terrible silence, darkness inhaling them both. The magnificent skies were her only consolation then; for even as she clenched her teeth ever more desperately against the glacial atmosphere, Alizeh refused to be immune to the midnight sea upon which they appeared to sail, nor to the resilience of stars burning holes in the heavens.

This was a habit Alizeh had mastered long ago.

Cataloging moments of grace even in the midst of disaster often helped steady her mind; indeed there had been days in her life so bleak that Alizeh had resorted to counting her teeth if only to prove she still owned something of value.

Just then she forced herself to listen to the susurrations of the wind, to appreciate that she'd never seen the moon so close, in all its unobstructed glory. She drew in a deep breath at the thought, tasting pure cold on her tongue, and lifted a searching hand to the night. The skies passed under her fingertips much like a cat, demanding to be pet.

"Abandon the idea," Cyrus said sharply, wrenching open the silence. "Your efforts will be futile."

Alizeh did not look up. "I'm sure I don't know what you're talking about."

"Fling yourself into the sky as many times as you like. There will be no escape. I will not allow you to die."

"Do you speak to all young women with such ardent affection?" Alizeh asked steadily, even as her bones shook with cold. "If I swoon and fall off the dragon again, you will have only yourself to blame."

Cyrus made a sound, something that was almost a laugh, and which quickly evaporated. "Your first attempt has already cost us precious minutes. Should you insist upon throwing yourself over and over you will only put us behind schedule and irritate my dragon, which she doesn't deserve. It's well past her bedtime; you need not torture her."

"Careful now," Alizeh said to him. "You're in grave danger of suggesting you might care about this dragon."

Cyrus sighed, looked away. "And you appear to be in grave danger of freezing to death."

"I am not," she lied.

Without a word he removed his heavy, unadorned black coat—but as he leaned forward to drape it over her shoulders, Alizeh stayed the gesture with a single hand.

"If you think," she said carefully, "that I will ever accept an article of clothing from you again—then you, sir, are deluded."

She saw the uncertain movement in his chest, the sudden tension in his jaw. "There is no danger to be derived from this garment. It was only the gesture of a gentleman."

She felt a spark of heat near her sternum just as surprise widened her eyes. "A *gentleman*? Do you often confuse yourself for such a man?"

"With what ease you insult me," he said, his eyes mocking. "Were you anyone else, I'd have you executed."

"Goodness, more poetry. Are these tender declarations meant to endear you to me?"

He fought a smile at that, running a hand through his hair as he looked up at the stars. "Tell me—is it too much to hope for our future that you will not make it a habit of slapping me in the face?"

"Yes."

"I see. Then married life will be exactly as I imagined."

"Let me be plain: I detest you. I would sooner ingest poison than marry you, and I am astonished to discover that you think I'd even consider submitting to such a horror when it is clear your every action is predicated upon the demands of the devil himself. You are an incorrigible reprobate; how you could ever hope to be a gentleman I will never understand."

Cyrus was quiet for a beat too long.

He did not meet her eyes when he spoke, not even when he forced a smile. "Do let us cast aside decorum, then. I promise to never again endeavor to be a gentleman in your presence."

"Is there any point, sir, in setting a goal for an accomplishment already achieved?"

Cyrus tensed before turning suddenly to face her, his eyes glinting in the moonlight with something like fury. He said nothing as he allowed his gaze to travel, too slowly, from her eyes to her lips, down the column of her neck, the curve of her breasts, the narrowing line of her barely there bodice, then lower—

"You really are a terrible scoundrel," she whispered, hating the way she flushed under his attentions.

For all the darkness that enveloped them, there was a great deal of illumination, too. She could see Cyrus quite plainly in the glaze of starlight, the luster of the moon. It could not be denied: his was an objectively striking face, so much so that Alizeh could not decide whether it was the wicked copper of his hair or the piercing blue of his eyes that proved his greatest asset. Then again, she did not care to decide, for not only was she unmoved by his beauty, she nursed a private hope that, given the right opportunity, she might be able to kill him.

"That dress was meant to protect you," Cyrus said bitterly. "I wasn't expecting you to set it on fire. Twice."

The nosta warmed against her skin, and Alizeh drew a sharp breath. She'd never been more grateful for the nosta, the marble-sized magical orb that sorted truths from lies. She'd tucked it deep into her corset before Cyrus's abrupt arrival in Miss Huda's bedroom, but after her most recent spiral from the heavens, she'd nearly forgotten its existence. Remembering it was with her did a great deal to fortify her heart, for she'd now acquired enough key information to know, unequivocally, that Hazan and Cyrus had not worked in tandem to assist her—which meant that Cyrus need never know that she possessed the powerful object. No matter the horrors ahead, at least she would always know whether he lied.

Alizeh experienced a pang of heartache at that realization, for it was Hazan who'd gifted her the nosta, and it seemed a categorical fact that she would never see him again.

He would no doubt hang at dawn.

It was Hazan who'd brought hope back into her life, whose existence inspired her to imagine an end to the wretchedness of her days. Hazan was proof that there remained any Jinn who still searched for her, believed in her. Alizeh had not known his true identity—that he was in fact a minister to the crown, that he worked alongside the prince every day. He'd risked his life in the attempt to transport Alizeh to safety, and he would pay the price for it now. It was a sacrifice she would never forget.

"Had I known you'd incinerate the gown I might not have wasted so much magic in its making," Cyrus was saying, shaking his head. "Much good it did you, in the end. That dress was meant to hide you from any who wished you harm; instead, you destroyed it, exposing in the process both your identity and your undergarments to all of Ardunian royalty. You must be well-pleased with yourself."

"I beg your pardon?" Alizeh looked up at him in horror. "My *undergarments?*"

"Surely you possess a pair of eyes," he said, staring intently at her face. "You are practically naked."

"How dare you."

In a fluid motion Cyrus draped his coat over her shoulders, surprising her so completely she'd no chance to protest before she was rendered powerless by relief. The lingering warmth of the wool garment was crossed with the heady, masculine scent of its owner, but Alizeh could ignore this; the heavy coat enveloped every inch of her folded, huddled body, its silk-lining caressing, then soothing, her wind-chapped skin. Alizeh tried to resist this luxury, but no matter her silent castigations toward herself, she could not animate her arms enough to shrug off the article. The satisfaction was in fact so painful that treacherous tears sprang to her eyes, and she had to bite her lip to keep from making a sound of pleasure.

When she finally looked up, she found Cyrus watching her, bewildered. "You've been truly suffering," he said. "Why did you say nothing?"

She was unable to meet his eyes when she confessed quietly: "I am always suffering. The frost lives with me much like an unwanted limb; it does not diminish. I seldom dwell on it."

"Then the frost is a real, lived experience?" Cyrus seemed to frown as he spoke. "I've heard mention of it, of course, but I'd assumed it was meant to be a poetic turn of phrase."

She'd forgotten: Cyrus had known only a little of her heritage.

Alizeh squeezed her eyes shut and exhaled, grateful her body seemed to be losing the worst of its tremors.

"The ice marks me as heir to the lost Jinn empire. The brutal cold is meant to prove my mettle," she explained. "Those who cannot survive the ravages of the frost in the body are not expected to survive the ravages of the throne."

Softly Cyrus said, "You really do exist, then. You're not merely a fairy tale."

Alizeh's eyes flew open. "What do you mean?"

"I'm not ignorant of Jinn folklore," he said, turning away. "This world has many failed royals. I assumed you'd be some coddled, uncrowned queen from a collapsed empire too small to be remembered. But you're the one they've been waiting for, aren't you? The one, it seems, even the devil has been waiting for. It would patch the holes in the many riddles he's fed me. And it would explain why he covets you so desperately."

"Yes," Alizeh whispered, feeling more like a fraud in every moment. *She* was meant to be the savior of her people? She, who'd spent the last few years of her life scrubbing floors and toilets? "I suppose I am."

In response, Cyrus only sighed.

When Alizeh finally dared to look at him, she found him staring into his black hat, his fingers tracing the brim.

The sight of it made her wonder.

"Earlier tonight you used magic to transport us to the ball," she said. "Why not do the same to deliver us to Tulan? The dragon seems a bit much."

Cyrus's hands stilled. He looked up slowly, his eyes glittering in the radiance of the firmament. There was no censure—only surprise—when he said: "You really know nothing about magic, do you?"

She shook her head. "Very little."

"And yet"—he frowned—"I have been informed that you require it. That in fact you possess inside yourself its most essential elements, somehow. Are you truly ignorant of your fate?"

Alizeh felt a bolt of fear at that, a familiar thrum as her heart began to race in her chest. It was only now occurring to Alizeh just how much the devil might've divulged about her life to this veritable stranger. It put her at a terrible disadvantage.

"What else has he told you about me?" she asked.

"Who? Iblees?"

Alizeh breaths were coming faster now, dread mounting. His was an inane question, one she would not answer—and Cyrus, who was not stupid, soon sighed.

"As I said, he intimated only that you were a queen from another empire. One who'd lost her throne and sought a

kingdom elsewhere. He did not tell me you were a Jinn." A
beat, and then: "Or if he did, it was not clear."

The nosta sparked warm.

"His asinine riddles make it damn near impossible to
understand him sometimes," Cyrus muttered, his expression
souring. "Then again, it all seems to work out to his advantage. Such convoluted communications appear to be quite
effective at fleecing susceptible humans."

"Yes," Alizeh said, surprised to experience an alignment
of sympathies with the southern king. "I know the feeling
well. He's been haunting me since I was born."

Cyrus met her eyes, studying her with something like
caution. "I cannot magic myself—or others—across great
distances. The half-life of the mineral is too short."

Alizeh did not understand this explanation, but just as
she was deciding whether to expose her ignorance, a violent
gust did its utmost to unseat her. She clutched desperately
at her borrowed garment, pulling the lapels more tightly
around her body—and her fingers met with something wet.

Alizeh drew her hand away sharply, inspecting the moisture under the moonlight before pinning Cyrus with a look
of abject fear. "There's blood on your coat," she breathed.

Cyrus's cool stare gave no indication of his feelings on the
matter. He said only, "I'm certain you boast intellect enough
to imagine how difficult it is to kill a man without soiling
one's clothes."

Alizeh looked away and swallowed.

Only now did she realize that Cyrus and Kamran had been
left alone for some time in the wake of her unceremonious

departure—before which Cyrus had been poised to deliver Kamran a fatal blow. She knew better than to betray her emotions on the matter, but how would she ever be at ease if she did not ask? She had to know—she had to find a way to determine whether he'd finished the task—

"How had the crown prince come to know your name?"

Alizeh started, so unnerved she nearly dropped the coat. "What?" she said, turning slowly to face Cyrus.

Anger flared to life in his eyes. "Come now; we've been doing so well. Let's not evolve backward, insulting each other with exhibitions of ignorance. You've proven far more clever than that."

Alizeh felt her heart fail. "Cyrus—"

"How does he know your name?" he demanded. "It was my understanding that you lived in hiding as a laboring servant. What reason might have an empire's heir to intimately acquaint himself with a maid?"

Alizeh touched trembling fingers to her lips. "You did kill him, didn't you?"

"I see we're both eager for explanations as concerns the nascent king of Ardunia."

"You astonish me," she whispered. "First you entrap me in this poisonous scheme, then you demand an admission of my private thoughts, as if you have any right to my honesty—"

"As your betrothed, I have a right to know of your history."

"We are *not* betrothed—"

"You misunderstand me," he said, cutting her off, "if you think I arrived at this degrading juncture in my life on the basis of honor and goodwill. I bound my life to yours before I even knew your name—before I had any idea who you were or what you looked like. Why you seem to derive so much pleasure from thinking my interest in marrying you has some sordid, personal motivation, I cannot imagine.

"Tell me," he said viciously. "Is it terribly thrilling to imagine yourself the sole object of my thoughts and desires? Do you purposely deny me ownership of basic dignities, excluding from your memories the essential fact that I was forced into this situation just as you were—all in the pursuit of feeling sorry for yourself?" He shook his head. "My, but it must be exhausting to be a narcissist."

Alizeh laughed at that, the sound bordering on hysterical. "You accuse *me* of narcissism when your every action has been in the interest of your own protection—the lives of others be damned?"

"And you," he said, tilting his head at her. "So preoccupied with your own personal dramas it never once occurred to you to ask *why* I might be yoked to such a despicable master—"

"Am I meant to feel sorry for you?" she snapped. "You, who no doubt suffer now the consequences of your own sins, lured a sacrificial lamb into this reprehensible arrangement like the most hateful charlatan. You sent me magical garments under the guise of friendship. You led me to believe that you were helping me—that you cared—"

"I did no such thing," he said, looking away. "You drew the conclusions that best suited you, and these are the results. Your naïveté is no fault of mine."

Alizeh was dumbfounded. "How? How can you feel no remorse for what you've done?"

He turned to face her. "Why do you continue to act as if I had a *choice?*"

Alizeh drew back, but Cyrus was undaunted.

He closed the inches between them, his glittering eyes assessing her face now with a renewed fervor. "Do I appear to you a free man boasting of free will? Or perhaps you thought that, after lowering myself to execute the obscene demands of the devil himself, I might take one look at your wide, doe-like eyes and experience a change of heart?"

"No," she whispered. "That is not what I—"

"Yes," he said softly, his gaze dropping, briefly, to her mouth. "You are well aware of your beauty, I think. Much as I am well aware of the maneuvers of the devil, and the weakness of human flesh. You think me so ignorant of his schemes? From the very moment I saw you I suspected his game—I knew he'd sent you to *me*, specifically, to torture me—as if I might be so tempted by the sight of you that I would bend in but a moment to your wishes, abandoning in the process an oath I signed with my soul, ensuring I am bound to him forevermore. *No.* I will not be moved by you—and you have underestimated me if you think I will succumb to your charms."

"Sir, I fear you have lost your mind," Alizeh said, her heart racing wildly in her chest. "You misjudge me terribly—"

"*And you take me for a fool,*" he said angrily, the movement in his throat briefly distracting her. "This story is both odious and familiar, and I already know how it ends; indeed, I have already seen the consequences of your seductions. Just tonight you snapped in half the spine of one sovereign. I will not be the next."

"What on earth can you mean?" she breathed, panic intensifying. "You sentence me for crimes I wouldn't even know how to commit—"

He leaned in, so close she could feel his whisper against her lips as he spoke. "Try to weaponize those eyes against me again and I will have them permanently sewn shut."

The nosta flashed hot against her skin, and Alizeh gasped, horror briefly paralyzing her in place.

Cyrus drew back.

"If you wish to ingest poison after we exchange our vows, I will not stand in your way. But I *will* marry you," he said sharply, "for you do not know what I stand to lose if this arrangement goes awry. You cannot even begin to imagine. So spare me your tears. You have confused me for your melancholy king, and you will suffer for the delusion."

As if in direct violation of his command, tears threatened her vision, blunting the stars beyond his head, blurring the sharp planes of his face. The magnitude of this impending horror was cementing more in every moment, and Alizeh was surprised to discover the depth of her fear. A single tear escaped her then, and she saw Cyrus track its progress down her cheek, toward her mouth, and she swiped at the moisture before the salt of it touched her lips. The abrupt action appeared to startle him.

"I truly hate you," she whispered, her voice thick with emotion. "With my whole heart, I hate you."

Cyrus held her gaze for what seemed a brutally long time before he finally tore away. He said nothing.

That Alizeh heard the slight tremor in his breath when

he finally exhaled, or that she noticed the unsteadiness with which he touched his fingers to the brim of his hat, did not rate mention.

She would not feel compassion for a fiend.

Then—in the distance—

Alizeh gasped.

"Do prepare yourself," said Cyrus, his tone softer than she expected. "It can be a little startling when you see it for the first time."

She sat up straighter, wiping her eyes. "See what?" she asked. "What am I looking at?"

"Tulan."

THREE

THE FIRE HAD EXTINGUISHED UPON Cyrus's exit, leaving in its wake a charred impression of a circle several feet in diameter, the stain of which no amount of soap or toil would eliminate. Of a certainty, the floor itself would have to be demolished and replaced—but then, this work could not take precedence.

Prior to fixing the floor there were other, more pressing issues in the palace to contend with; there was, for example, a dead king sprawled at Kamran's feet, a vermeil stain still spreading under his limp figure while, at his shoulders, the flaccid faces of twin snakes rested delicately upon their own unfurled tongues. The hulking crown of this once illustrious sovereign now glinted upside down in a plash of red, the glossy floor sticky with slipshod streaks of blood, evidence of regicide everywhere. Prominent gashes and abrasions could be cataloged around the perimeter of the imposing ballroom where the dragon's studded tail had whipped through not merely the stonework but glittering sconces, heavy drapery, and priceless artwork—all of which would need to be discarded, their substitutes promptly sourced. Still, the physical destruction most distressing was perhaps also the most obvious.

There was a massive crater in the palace wall.

It was a cavity so large it brought to mind the perpetually shrieking mouth of a newborn babe; it gaped unabashedly open, an eclipse of moths fluttering in and out of its crumbling aperture not unlike a horde of dithering idiots.

The detritus of the evening's chaos would be a task of its own to manage; debris littered all and sundry, heavy dust powdering the hair and shoulders of scandalized nobles, all of whom stood around now, shock briefly muzzling their aristocratic mouths, hands clasped to cheeks and hearts as their heads swiveled between horrors.

The dead king, the destroyed wall, the ossified heir—

Yes, there was a great deal of work to be done. The wreckage alone would take days to sweep up, and Kamran would have to charge Jamsheed, the palace butler, with the task of contracting stonemasons to repair all else with celerity. There was too much at stake; already there would be a week of mourning before Kamran could be crowned king in an elaborate ceremony, after which he would finally carry out his grandfather's most impassioned command and choose a damn bride—any bride—and only then, only when that grim business was sorted could he move on to the most important task, which was to officially declare war against Tulan. He would avenge both his father and his grandfather. He would have Cyrus's head. He would bring Tulan to its knees. And Alizeh—

No. He would not think of her now; not when the very thought of her tore open fresh wounds inside him. He could not reconcile so many horrors at once.

First, he would have to cease being stone.

There were swarms of people drawing near him now, all of them staring, speaking about him like he might be dead—which struck Kamran as a terrible taunt, for death seemed a far more pleasurable fate than this:

"Is it the light, dear, or does he look disfigured to you?"

"By the angels—what a terrifying sight—"

"First the king, now the prince—"

"Who was the girl? Does anyone know?"

"Too soon to tell—"

"The fate of our empire—"

"Will someone touch him? To see if he moves?"

"An ugly business, terribly ill-bred—"

"You cannot simply touch the prince of Ardunia!"

"Anyone understand what she was saying? I only—"

"But—"

"Thought she was helping until she ran off with the dragon—"

"Could be dead, really—"

"Why can't we do something about the king? This is so distasteful—"

"We could throw a sheet over him!"

"Or *move* him, you idiot—"

"Dark magic! Oh, dark magic to be sure—"

"He say something about a Jinn queen? To rule the world?"

"I, too, struggled to hear the girl—"

"Are you suggesting I touch those snakes? Are you really suggesting I touch those snakes?"

"*Where are the servants?*"

"Complete nonsense—Jinn royalty died out ages ago—"

"But you were able to see her, then? Sometimes she really seemed to blur—"

"The servants? They appear to have run away—"

"Look, he's still bleeding!"

"Ha! It's more likely you've had too much wine—"

"Am I meant to call for my own carriage, then?"

"Appalling, really—simply appalling—"

"What on *earth* do you think is happening to his face?"

True, there existed no criterion for managing the present situation—Kamran had sympathy enough to understand that—but this stream of insipid, unproductive commentary was punctuated by random shrieks and shouts, all of which so aggressively thrashed his frayed nerves that he wished, with great passion, that the mass of imbeciles might drop dead.

It required every bit of his energy to keep his mind sharp as pain battered his body, electric spasms seizing his chest, his neck—even aspects of his face—so much so that Kamran didn't know how much more he might withstand. He was well aware his body was bleeding out, his lungs compressing under the ever-increasing weight of this magic.

Still, he dared hope he might not die.

It was Cyrus's parting words that kept him calm, kept his mind from unraveling; for it seemed clear that if the southern royal had meant to kill him, surely he would have.

But Cyrus had wanted him to live.

The demented king had claimed a desire to see Kamran survive if only to watch him suffer; indeed, Cyrus seemed to look forward to his survival, and to the inevitability of their next skirmish.

How, then, might Kamran be released from this prison?

Without a doubt there were living Diviners capable of undoing such magic, but they were scattered across Ardunia; it would take weeks to collect enough of them to form the necessary quorum at the Diviners Quarters—but with an urgent summons, it was possible to deliver to the palace whichever Diviner was nearest.

Even *one* might do just fine.

Perhaps if Hazan hadn't proven an unfaithful bastard, he might've already issued such a summons; doubtless Hazan would've handled every detail of this horrific night with aplomb, stepping gingerly over pools of blood only to usher home the affronted nobles with a smile. Even Kamran, who intended to kill his former minister, could acknowledge this truth—and experienced at the thought a resulting pang in his chest. Nevertheless, Kamran would not allow himself to dwell on Hazan's betrayal; there was no point, and there was no time.

If only he could speak, Kamran would direct the masses himself; he would right now be shouting commands into this sea of gaping halfwits, some too busy proving their delicate constitutions by repeatedly fainting into the arms of their escorts, others too accustomed to the softness of peacetime to remember how to react in a crisis.

Kamran would not refute it: he loathed his peers.

He hated their pretensions, their obsessions with frivolity, their quiet competitions to crush each other with displays of imagined superiority. He resented that he belonged to their circles at all, resented that his new role would force him to spend more time in their company, resented his birthright altogether.

It was then—in an extraordinary moment—that the impending king of Ardunia realized he wanted his mother.

She had been here.

He knew she'd been here, for much earlier in the evening he'd seen her sitting in a throne adjacent to his grandfather. Surely she'd not abandoned the party before witnessing the night's devastations? Surely she still owned a fraction of a heart, a lingering ounce of maternal affection for her only child?

Why, then, had she not come to his aid? Had she not been bothered to watch him suffer?

Would that he might search the room for her, but Kamran could not shift even his eyes. His mother's ominous last warnings began to pound in his head, reminding him that he'd treated her poorly, startling him to realize how she'd predicted his future just hours ago.

Soon, she'd said, *I will be all you have left in this palace.*

You will walk the halls, friendless and alone, and you will search for me then. You will want your mother only when all else is lost, and I do not promise to be easily found.

She'd been wrong on one important count—Kamran could not at the moment walk the halls of this castle—but if he survived the night, there might be time yet for that, too.

How easily Kamran had dismissed her warning.

Now his mother was absent, his grandfather was dead, his minister was shackled in the dungeons. Even his aunt—with whom he'd been speaking just seconds before identifying Cyrus in the crush—was conspicuously truant. The truth of his situation bore down on him with a chilling awareness:

He had no one.

There was a sudden moment of shoving before a familiar, greasy figure was revealed in his attempt to part the throng, his forceful actions rippling through the swarm of spectators, the lot of which went abruptly silent upon sighting him. The defense minister—whose name was Zahhak—was a slight, balding man of average height, whose face was more often than not a reflective surface, for it retained always a slick sheen. Tonight his skin seemed to glister more than usual as he pushed forward, the blue-green whirl of his robes representing the colors of the noble House of Ketab. He forged a path through the assemblage with an air of authority so desperately required of the situation that every head turned to track his movements, all awaiting with bated breath a pronouncement that might allow them to finally exit this tragic stage and retire to their beds.

Dread coiled in Kamran's gut.

Zahhak was a character he heartily detested. Just yesterday, Kamran had unapologetically insulted the aristocrat in a room full of his peers. Hateful as the defense minister was, Kamran's actions had been foolish—and it was only as the oily figure examined Kamran's unflinching face now, his beady black eyes gleaming with something like triumph, that Kamran realized the depth of his error. Zahhak was a truculent man, and yet too craven to lift a sword in his own defense; instead he carried into every conversation the poison of passive aggression, the preferred weapon of cowards.

No doubt he would land a ruinous blow now.

"I'm afraid," Zahhak said calmly, his voice ringing out in the silence, "that we've no choice but to declare the prince dead."

The crowd gasped, then drew back in unison.

So shocking was this pronouncement that Kamran felt it as a physical electrification inside his heart—and then, just as swiftly, this feeling was displaced by shame, for the magnitude of his astonishment struck him only as a reflection of his own stupidity. His grandfather had tried to warn him of such machinations—and Kamran had given the words no weight.

As if conjured from the ether, he heard Zaal's whisper:

My child, do you not understand how precarious your position is? Those who covet your position would invite any reason to deem you unworthy of the throne—

Kamran had never thought himself naive, and yet—he'd not endured much more than an hour in the absence of his grandfather's protection and already he'd been filleted open, the infantile contents of his mind exposed, the truth of his sheltered life laid bare. Kamran was the very definition of a fool; he'd anticipated none of the betrayals he'd suffered tonight, so comfortable had he been in his role, so certain had he been of his authority in the world. Now he was a caged animal for the world to gawk at, stripped of all that ever defined him in but a matter of moments.

Never had he felt so powerless.

The murmurs of the crowd had grown only more frantic in the interlude, and Kamran raged within the prison of his body, his blood heating even as his lungs continued to compress.

Zahhak, meanwhile, preened as he faced the people, imitation grief coloring his voice as it carried across the room.

"My dear nobles, this has been a grave night indeed. To have lost both our emperor and our heir in the same hour, and under such ghastly circumstances"—someone sobbed, loudly—"but I stand before you tonight to offer this assurance: Ardunia is too great an empire to be felled even by these great tragedies.

"Even so," he went on, "the unpalatable particulars that led to the murder of our beloved king will require immense scrutiny. A council of House leaders will be assembled on the morrow, during which time we will decide whether retribution is befitting of the situation—and begin a search to select a worthy inheritor of the throne. Until then, as dictated by Ardunian law, I shall assume temporary ownership of the crown, and forthwith sue for peace with Tulan so that we might, without delay, return our empire to the state of tranquility we've come to enjoy—"

A ferocious pain detonated without warning in Kamran's shoulder, the unmistakable weight of a blade piercing his flesh in a moment that struck him only as surreal. The puncture awoke inside him an unnatural cold, a unique torment that flashed through his veins with such severity he cried out in anguish. He was unaware the sound had escaped his lips until he heard the shattering clang of his sword, steel striking the floor as it fell from his unfrozen hand, his knees knocking stone when his legs gave out, his thawed body trembling with abandon.

By agonizing degrees, Kamran lifted his head.

The din of the room had silenced in an instant, astonishment rendering all mouths immobile for the length of a miraculous moment. Kamran, in his bewilderment, did not hear the bumbling stupefaction of the defense minister, now desperately backpedaling; nor did he bother to parse the whispers of the crowd, now regenerating around him. No, Kamran was too preoccupied by the piece of evidence buried in his muscle:

He had been attacked.

He reached up with one shaking arm to pull free the ruby dagger planted in his left shoulder, the action so excruciating he nearly lost consciousness in the effort. He felt himself begin to convulse even as he examined the decadent weapon, the room appearing to swim before him.

This blade— He *knew* this blade—

Kamran turned his head with difficulty, his skull swinging with the grace of a pendulum as he searched the room for his assailant. At least the miracle of his release had a clear enough explanation: the glittering scarlet dagger had cut through his enchantment, which meant the weapon had once been fortified by the Diviners, the better to empower its owner against an enemy whose armor might be coated in magical protections.

In and of itself, this was not a notable discovery, for such fortifications were common in the reinforcement of royal weapons; Kamran's own swords boasted the same benefits. Far more interesting was the near assassination itself; for in his mind there existed but one person alive who would risk killing Kamran in the pursuit of his survival.

The dagger had belonged to his mother.

Unsuccessfully, he scanned the room for her face, increasingly perplexed by her actions. His mother had saved him. Why, then, had she abandoned—

Kamran went deathly still.

It was not magic this time, but fear that paralyzed him anew, for he'd glimpsed his reflection in a bank of shattered mirrors gracing an adjacent wall. Dumbstruck, he lifted an unsteady hand to his chin, his cheek, the delicate lid of one eye.

Earlier, the decorative mirrors had adorned the ballroom at intervals to great effect, enhancing the flicker of crystal and fire and the fractured light of a hundred glimmering chandeliers—elevating, in the process, the ambience of a dignified evening to dizzying heights.

Now the broken glass cast back only monstrous scenes, chief among them a likeness of himself he was not yet ready to fathom into words. He lacked the privilege of time even to process the transformation, for it was but an instant later that Zahhak fell, theatrically, to his knees.

At once, the sheep encircling him followed suit.

"Your Highness," Zahhak cried. "We'd not dared to hope for such a miracle! There can be no doubt but that our empire has been blessed by the heavens!"

Kamran studied the sea of nobles kneeling before him with a vague disgust. Even now their duplicity was on display; these sycophants bowed without a word, motionless as glass even as their uncrowned king failed to stand upright, his broken body bleeding. They did not rush to his side, call for a surgeon, order a litter to carry him to safety—

No, they did not seem to care that he was dying.

And Kamran was indeed dying.

The restoration of his movements had returned him to himself, yes, but the rewiring of faculty and flesh had awakened, in the process, every brutal devastation his body had sustained this night; Kamran could feel that something was irrevocably wrong with him. It was more than the grisly transformation of his face—his lungs rattled when he inhaled; galvanic pain pulsed in his eyes; his vision faded in and out as bright, white light overexposed his sight with increasing frequency. His charred arms and legs still bled profusely, and worse—would no longer obey a command to desist shaking. There was something the matter with his chest, too; his heart felt both fast and sluggish, an ache like bones breaking where a soft organ was meant to beat.

He'd lost too much blood, perhaps—or sustained a blow to his lungs—or maybe he'd been frozen for too long, his many injuries growing only more gruesome in the interim. Whatever the reason, his death seemed now an inevitability. Without the immediate application of a powerful, restorative magic, Kamran knew he would soon lose the ability even to speak, for it was growing only more difficult to breathe. That he maintained his composure at all was a result only of violent determination, and it was a miracle that he managed to speak clearly when he said, breathing hard—

"Fetch me the nearest Diviner. With all possible haste."

"Yes, sire. Right away, sire."

Compelled into motion, Zahhak barked at a footman to ready a team of horses, snapping orders at gaping servants who'd materialized from the shadows only in the wake of Kamran's reanimation. If he survived this infernal night, the gossip alone would be hell to endure.

"The rest of you," Kamran said, staring blearily into the genuflecting crowd, "go home."

When the petrified mass made no move, Kamran grew light-headed with anger.

"*Now*," he bellowed, his lungs seizing in the effort.

The horde unfolded with a series of shrieks before bolting for the exits, silk and tulle shuddering as the ballroom was evacuated in a single exhalation.

Finally, he was alone. Or at least, appeared to be.

Kamran suspected there lingered wide-eyed servants in the wings, still watching him, but he could neither move nor risk raising his voice again, for his last attempt had so diminished his intake of air that every breath felt like pulling gasps through a pinhole. There was nothing for it; Kamran finally sagged to the floor, grimacing through the relentless pain still ravaging his body. The room tilted as he collapsed, supine in a sea of devastation, his only companion the body of a dead king, the cold blood of his beloved grandfather pooling ever closer to his own shaking limbs.

Were Kamran a different sort of man, he might've acqui-
esced then to a terrifying compulsion. He felt in that moment
nothing greater than an ancient impulse to cry, valiantly
resisting the instinct even as a flare of grief tore through
him. He had never felt more desperately alone in the world
than he did then, trapped in the set piece of a nightmare,
in the failing flesh of his own body. His mother had done
him a mercy, but she'd promptly vanished. There was no one
left he might trust, no one upon whom he might rely. The
thought threatened to break him, and he vehemently refused
it residence in his mind.

He would not die.

Dying would mean he'd failed his king twice—and this,
Kamran could not allow. He fought to stay conscious even as
violent spasms wracked his bones; he had to live long enough
to murder those who'd wronged him; to avenge his father,
his grandfather. He would survive this barrage of murders
upon his soul; if he had to, he would lift this broken empire
upon his own shaking shoulders—

"Sire?"

Kamran's heart seized. His every instinct screamed at
him to pull himself upright, but his limbs would not obey.
He could only lay there, his chest cratering, until without
warning his line of sight was crowded by a mop of red curls
hanging over a cowed, freckled face. Omid Shekarzadeh, the
street urchin whose attempted thievery had set in motion
every recent, horrific turn of Kamran's life, stared straight
into his eyes.

"*You*," Kamran managed to gasp.

He noticed the tears staining the child's cheeks, eyes bloodshot and swollen. The boy, Omid, studied him warily, fear and fascination warring in his expression. Neither said another word as Omid bent carefully beside the dying king, and with a trembling hand withdrew from his pocket a glittering blue sugar cube.

Kamran stiffened at the sight.

"I think they knew, sire," Omid said in Feshtoon. "The Diviners. I think they knew what was going to happen. I think they knew they were going to be murdered."

Kamran felt his heart pounding in his ears. The object Omid held in his hand was a magical ration called *Sif*; the legendary blue crystals were compressed into bite-sized cubes that had historically been provided to Ardunian royals on the battlefield. So valuable were the lives of emperors and their heirs that the Diviners had always sent them to war with these single-use reinforcements. The final blade of fatality, once delivered, none could overcome; but there was a great deal to be done for those even inches from death.

Just one Sif was enough to undo even the worst injuries.

"Bengez," the child whispered. *Take it.*

"No— I—I cannot—"

"They gave it to me after I began to recover," the boy said quietly. "Told me to keep it with me always, that I'd know when to use it." He swallowed. "I thought they gave it to me to save myself in the future, see. I didn't realize until just now that maybe I wasn't supposed to use it on myself."

"*No*," Kamran said again, this time sharply. He was seeing

stars, bright lights sparking and fading behind his eyes. "If the Diviners blessed you with such a gift"—he wheezed— "you should not— You cannot give it away—"

"I'll do as I please," said Omid, anger edging into his voice. "You saved my life, sire. Now it's my turn to save yours."

FOUR

چھار

IN THE DISTANCE, ALIZEH SAW stars.

Tens of thousands—or perhaps hundreds of thousands—or thousands of thousands—

It was impossible to tell, and she seemed incapable of conjuring an estimate large enough to account for them all. She knew only what she saw, and what she saw was a seemingly infinite expanse of densely assembled celestial bodies, all of which appeared to tremble upon approach. They had been sitting in a bleak silence for hours now, and with each flap of the dragon's enormous, leathery wings, their small party drew steadily closer to the spectral sight, the distant lights rearranging themselves repeatedly, shifting in erratic patterns.

Finally, Alizeh frowned.

It was very unlike a star to act in such a manner.

She turned to her companion for an explanation but was brought up short by the sight of him. Cyrus sat beside her with a palpable discomfort made apparent in the unnatural stiffness of his body: head up, shoulders back, spine straight. His eyes were fixed firmly ahead, his hair rippling in the wind, longer strands occasionally obscuring his vision—and still he did not move.

It was impossible to know what tormented him the most,

and Alizeh could not bring herself to care. Her eyes still itched with the remnants of tears; she despised this black-guard, and yet, until she could figure out a plan of action, she would need a great deal from him: his answers about the devil's plans for her, his guidance in navigating Tulan, the offer of a safe place to stay while she gathered her wits and decided her next move. It was a hateful situation, one she would have to manage with all possible caution, and Alizeh was still considering this, still examining his stoic features when his jaw suddenly tightened.

"Enough," he said sharply. "I don't welcome your analysis. Cease studying me."

Something bitter prompted her to say, "You are not my master."

Cyrus turned at once to look at her, staring into her eyes with an intensity that bordered on alarming. "Do you aspire to be mine?"

This question was so shocking, Alizeh drew back in response.

Cyrus leaned in. "Relinquish the dream," he said softly. "You have no hope of mastering me."

Alizeh tensed. "I could kill you right now."

He only looked at her, a slow smile spreading across his face. "Go on, then," he said. "Kill me. I will not intervene."

Her eyes narrowed. "I do not dispose of that which is still useful to me."

"Useful? Is that what you've decided I am?" He almost laughed. "And do you lie to yourself often?"

Alizeh felt a flash of heat at that; an anger that compelled

her into silence as the two locked eyes then in a vicious contest. Alizeh did her utmost to remain still under Cyrus's now
ruthless inspection, but the full weight of his scrutiny—at
such close proximity—was indeed too much to bear. He
seemed to devour her with a single look, his blue gaze holding hers without mercy before cataloging every inch of her
face, the angle of her jaw, the column of her neck. His eyes
were charged with something both electric and devastating,
the unbound energy of his entire body diverted to this single avenue of connection. Alizeh felt the heat of his slow
appraisal in her bones, in the tips of her fingers; her heart
sped up in response, understanding even as he frightened
her—that he was trying to frighten her.

Too soon, Alizeh averted her gaze.

"As I thought," he whispered. "You're too soft even to bear
the weight of my attentions."

Alizeh laughed quietly as she pressed a finger to the wind,
felt the current curl under her touch. "The sky, too, is soft,"
she said. "Yet all who fall into its arms will perish."

She felt him stiffen beside her.

"You," he said finally, "are not who I expected."

Alizeh did not reward this with a response, choosing
instead to resume her study of the night. They were beginning to descend into Tulan—she could feel it—and as they
drew closer to what seemed an endless celebration of jittery
lights, her eyes grew wide with wonder.

"Tell me," she said. "Why do these stars move? Is there
magic in the heavens here?"

"Those are very different questions," said Cyrus, whose

eyes she felt fixed on her face. "As for the first: they move because they are not stars."

She glanced at him, eyebrows high.

"You will soon learn that Tulan is crowned by a series of protective skies," he explained. "The fireflies live in our third atmosphere, where they gather in such large numbers they present almost as small galaxies, or even terrifying ghosts, from afar. It can be a little disconcerting to the unaccustomed eye."

"*Fireflies*," Alizeh said, turning fully to face him. "How—"

There was an unexpected swell of sound then, a mellifluous harmony that crescendoed as she went suddenly weightless, suspended in midair for the length of a single breath before they plummeted at breakneck velocity through a bloat of clouds. Alizeh grasped desperately at nothing, nearly losing her seat as strong gales pushed open the flaps of her borrowed coat and promptly tore the oversized garment from her body, tossing the article in the sky. Alizeh heard Cyrus's cry of frustration even as she nearly screamed in pain; the cold bit into her uncovered flesh with an unexpected brutality, and in a moment propelled by nothing more than desperation did she finally find purchase at the nape of the dragon's neck, holding fast as they bore down with increasing speed. Wind barreled relentlessly against her exposed body, battering her over and over as her hair spiraled in a storm of its own, loose tendrils occasionally snapping with static.

It was only after they were wrung from the clouds and released back into the open air that Alizeh felt the shimmer of dew on her skin, the damp press of her tattered dress against her body. The landscape below her came into a vague focus, the hush and roar of that distant resonance growing only more deafening. Howling squalls still thrashed her face, an unnamed crash and clamor rising to a decibel level nearly incalculable—until finally, Alizeh understood.

What she heard was water.

They had to be above the ocean—this much *had* to be true—but then the smell of wet soil filled her head, confusing her, and she was at once consumed by the bracing scent of rain and the heavy cloak of mist, the latter promptly obscuring her vision.

Alizeh struggled to stare through the fog at the scene below, condensation settling in her hair, vapor clinging to her eyelashes. She climbed closer to the head of the dragon—deaf to the sound of Cyrus calling her back—and locked her arms as best she could around the beast's neck before pressing her face deeper into the fog. In the shattering moonlight she saw the faint outline of what appeared to be the end of the earth.

A colossal sequence of staircase waterfalls had been born at the top of towering cliffs, the cataracts emptying into the ocean from varying, and terrifying, heights. The scene was in fact so sublime that Alizeh experienced an inexpressible, joyful fear in its presence; she'd never seen such steep bluffs nor such devastating cascades, and she was still trying to digest the magnificence of it all when she remembered, suddenly, to look up.

Her face was met with an exhalation of mist, ocean spray glazing her body as her lips parted in awe, then exhilaration.

She distinguished the stark lines of turrets in the night sky, the formidable outline of what could only be a royal palace balanced upon the cliff's edge, its foundations planted at the base of hundreds of falls so majestic her breath caught at the sight.

Water.

She could hardly believe it.

Jinn's bodies were forged from fire, yes—but water was their true mainstay in life; unlike other living creatures, Jinn did not require food for survival. It was this precious elixir alone that had allowed Alizeh's ancestors to survive eons of a frozen, sunless existence on earth, and it was no surprise, then, that Alizeh felt most alive only when she drew nearer to water—when she drank it, bathed in it.

When she lifted her face to the rain.

Alizeh closed her eyes, felt the spindrift wash over her. They were approaching the castle with great determination now; the closer they drew, the more intensely she experienced the unrelenting drizzle—and she made no effort to take cover. Instead, Alizeh leaned in only farther, licking the water from her lips, inhaling the scent of sodden earth, damp moss, wet pine. She was soon drenched and frozen half to death, shivering uncontrollably and still undeterred. Her long curls were heavy and dripping, rivulets snaking down her face, her neck, running along her collarbone.

Alizeh paid these discomforts no attention.

She couldn't remember the last time she'd experienced such heady relief. Her daily baths at the local hamam were nothing compared to this—to the magnificence of an overwhelming ocean, to the fervor and mercy of the sea.

It was as if she'd been returned home.

This dream was crudely interrupted by an ungentle-manly word released by a familiar voice; Cyrus's arms came suddenly around her waist, too easily plucking her off the dragon's neck and planting her back onto their shared seat, the patterned rug beneath them now damp with ocean spray.

He drew away from her at once.

"Good Lord," he said, shaking out his hands. "You're soaking wet. Why are you acting as if you've never seen water before?"

Alizeh hardly heard him. She was too overcome with exhilaration and as a result did not think before she smiled at Cyrus, turning the full force of her joy in his direction, eyes squinting, cheeks dimpling, chest heaving with excitement.

Cyrus went inhumanly still, then turned sharply away.

"You act as if you've never met a Jinn before," Alizeh said breathlessly. "I love the water. I live for it."

"On the contrary," he said flatly, still avoiding the sight of her. "I've met thousands of Jinn, and I've never seen a single one of them nearly fling themselves into the ocean."

Alizeh was offered no opportunity to respond; the dragon made its final descent without warning and without grace, wings clipping the falls as they approached land, dousing them both with fresh water in the process. Alizeh heard Cyrus swear as the animal hit the ground hard, forelegs first, then back legs, stomping to a halt in a series of drunken thumps, the reverberations of which made Alizeh's teeth chatter.

"She's very tired," Cyrus muttered by way of apology.

Alizeh said nothing.

It was a moment before she was even able to shake herself free of whiplash, carefully collecting her mind in the midst of this current astonishment. They'd come to an abrupt stop on a stretch of flat, mossy land upon one of the higher cliffs, where the roar of the water grew so loud the two of them would have no choice but to cease speaking or else scream at each other, granting Alizeh the quiet she needed to survey her new surroundings. It was a shame, then, that they had arrived in the dark, for she could make out only faded impressions of the royal grounds.

Even so, she was thunderstruck.

The jagged, staggering castle appeared to be fashioned from glittering stone, for the smooth exterior glinted under the undiluted glow of starlight, casting constellations upon her skin, the scattered trees, even the leathery beast still kneeling beneath her. No doubt it was the late hour, her extreme fatigue, and the emotional obliteration of the evening that were to blame for her disorientation, but Alizeh was so affected by the surrealism of the moment that she felt a bit out of her mind. Her own bones seemed foreign to her; even when she shivered she felt as if she were experiencing it from afar. Frost had begun to crystallize along her eyelashes, upon the stiffening tendrils of her hair. She was so numb with cold she could hardly feel her extremities anymore, but neither could she bring herself to hurry indoors into the arms of an unknown fate.

Cyrus, meanwhile, stared a beat too long at what was

ostensibly his own home—and released a heavy sigh.

He disembarked in a brisk, fluid motion, landing firmly on his feet and not bothering to look back, leaving Alizeh to topple off the dragon in an inelegant heap. She drew herself up and looked around, trying and failing to take in the magnitude of this new setting. The air felt fresher here—crisp and delicious in a way that reminded her of childhood—and she couldn't get enough of it. She inhaled over and over in quick succession, and soon grew light-headed.

Feeling delirious, she peered up—and gasped.

Where the royal palace in Ardunia was an arresting work of art sprawled leisurely upon hundreds of acres, this Tulanian stronghold was forced to fashion its palatial size upon a modest plane offered by a steep cliff. Alizeh supposed it was for this reason that the castle was so dizzyingly vertiginous.

Then again, it might've been done simply to intimidate.

Gilded spires pierced the heavens above her, impaling stars, grazing the moon—and disappeared fully into the clouds, a herd of which crowned the palace like a halo. Alizeh was unable even to see the top, so tall was the edifice, and she lifted a frozen hand to her mouth, astonishment forcing her eyes wide.

The sky, meanwhile, was beginning to show telltale signs of dawn.

The heaviness of night drew back in an unhurried reveal, inches of dark pleating away not unlike curtains on a stage. An audience of one stood impatient before the sight, waiting with bated breath for the set dressing of the next scene, the next act in her life.

Alizeh felt a terrible sense of foreboding.

Nevertheless, a golden radiance soon illuminated the world, fingers of light touching trees and birds as if counting its children.

Alizeh thought to search for Cyrus then, and found him tending to the dragon, first dropping a massive bucket of water at the creature's feet, then procuring from nowhere a single apple, which he polished against his shirt before holding under the animal's nose. The beast opened its mouth with a pitiful whine, curls of smoke puffing from its nostrils before it snatched, in a terrifying bite, the offering from Cyrus's open hand.

Alizeh thought she might've seen the demented king smile.

The king in question stroked the dragon's head with the tenderness of a child before leaving the beast to its water. He walked briskly toward a steel chest—which appeared to have been delivered in anticipation of their arrival—and threw back the heavy lid, withdrawing from the trunk's belly an enormous platter heaving with dead animals.

Alizeh turned away.

She need not watch the dragon eat a grisly meal; she felt she'd been served more than her fill of bloody images this night. In any case, Cyrus's current preoccupation was a mercy she would not squander; Alizeh's mind was spinning with a multitude of pressing complications, and she was grateful for the solitude—for the moment to think.

She still hadn't decided what to do.

Outrunning the devil was hopeless, she knew that, but

participating in this twisted game felt equally impossible.

She would not marry Cyrus, at least; this first step seemed clear enough. It was what came *next* that confounded her. Alizeh had been exposed, actively hunted by two empires— and while she'd managed to outrun one, she'd been easily caught in the maw of another, forced now to play a role in the devil's schemes. This web was now too intricate; her existence too well-documented. She didn't think she could return to a life of obscurity until she'd felled her enemies— and hers were formidable indeed.

Alizeh clenched her shaking hands.

Oh, she had never feared death. No, it was life that scared her, life that scarred her. It was the slow torture of conscious-ness that had done its utmost to crush her. Alizeh was meant to be the salvation of her people—destined to save the Jinn of this world from the horrors they'd endured for centuries. How could she not carry the weight of this failure with her always? The burden had been hers to bear and she'd borne it badly. Now she was trapped between a deranged king and the devil himself, and she feared, for a terrible moment, that she might fail to overcome this, too.

A wave of panic seized her body.

Alizeh's legs shook, her knees suddenly giving out; she staggered back a step, the heels of her bare feet striking the trunk of the nearest tree. She braced herself against its heft, her head filling with the scent of pine. She'd grown used to the sound of the rushing water now—experiencing it more as a comforting hum than a distracting noise—and as her heart steadied, she was better able to discern the sounds of leaves fluttering, a charm of birds chirping melodies into the sunrise.

Alizeh drew a deep, steadying breath.

She reminded herself to take comfort, as she always had, in the strength she carried in her body, in her mind, in the faith she'd always had in herself. She was not stupid enough to think she could find her way to safety in her current state—bedraggled, destitute, and ignorant of this foreign landscape—nor was she delusional enough to trust anyone she might encounter in Tulan. Instead, she thought she might take a day or two to assess her new circumstances, bide her time until she could form a plan. Besting Cyrus, at least, would be the easier task—for she knew he was but a pawn in this scheme.

It was *Iblees* she'd need to outmaneuver.

Alizeh was still contemplating this when she heard the soft, unexpected voice of a stranger calling her name. She stiffened at once, fear bolting through her afresh.

Carefully, she turned to face the new arrival.

FIVE

ﺣﺞ

KAMRAN STOOD BEFORE THE LOOKING glass with a grim expression.

He'd been in his dressing room long enough to witness the sun rise, and still his valet, Sina, had not finished with the details of his regalia. Early golden light poured through a bank of narrow windows along one wall, casting a gentle radiance upon the uncrowned king. From collar to boot, Kamran had been styled in accordance with Ardunian tradition; he wore varying shades of dark blue, a color only the heir to a newly vacated throne might wear in mourning, symbolizing to all the empire that though they grieved what was lost, they were not without hope.

A leader still lived.

Or at least clung to life, according to the morning's headlines.

Kamran's jaw clenched in sympathy with his fist, a copy of Setar's morning journal, *The Daftar*, crushed in his right hand. The crumple of paper was the only sound to break the strained silence. Kamran was known by his valet to be taciturn, but the prince had been unusually quiet this morning, unable to speak aloud more than a few furious words in the wake of so many devastations.

He felt he could either say nothing, or scream.

The choice seemed clear.

Painstakingly, Sina pinned the last few military insignias to Kamran's breast pocket, then carefully tugged through the shoulder loop a satin sash so liquid it fell at once into elegant folds across his chest, the tails pinned neatly along the side seam of his field jacket with a series of silver-blue pearls. Sina then attached a collar chain at the base of Kamran's throat; large, hexagonal amethysts were clipped on either side of the placket, the gems anchoring between them three strings of glittering black diamonds, which hung in gentle arcs across his sternum.

There was a sharp snap of fabric.

His valet had conjured from nowhere a cape of midnight-blue velvet, which Kamran felt billowing at his back; Sina fastened the cloak to the prince's shoulders before crowning the ensemble with a set of weighty, scale-mail epaulets that had been forged in an imitation of dragon hide.

That Kamran owned these articles at all pointed directly to his mother; she alone would've had the foresight to order such garments, the details of which would've been arranged months ago. Never would it have occurred to the prince to prepare his wardrobe in anticipation of the king's demise— which reminded him not only of his mother's conspicuous disappearance, but of how very alone he was in the world now.

His hand trembled without warning, and he flexed his fingers in response, closing a fist once more around the day's news.

The paper had not been delivered to Kamran on a silver tray alongside the hot breakfast he'd left untouched—it had been hand delivered. It was a snoda who'd cowered before him, the man all but bent in half in obeisance as he'd held out a copy of *The Daftar*, its dusty green pages unmistakable.

"Forgive me, Your Highness," he'd whispered. "We felt you should know."

Kamran could hardly process his shock.

Never in his life had a palace snoda dared speak aloud in his presence, much less act as a mouthpiece on behalf of the others—whose opinions should not have mattered to him. Any other royal of Kamran's caliber would've had the servant hung for his audacity alone, but the prince could not quell a certain measure of curiosity.

He'd had no intention of reading any articles this morning, for anything printed so early would almost certainly be old news; there'd not been enough time last night for any paper to have detailed the evening's travesties. Even so, he'd felt compelled to study the servant for a full minute before finally accepting from his outstretched hand the proffered newspaper, after which the snoda fell to his knees with a muted gasp, hand clasped to his mouth as he crawled backward out the door.

Kamran had promptly cracked open the paper.

The headline was crammed above the fold, bold letters as black as death and just as damning:

LONG LIVE THE KING, AT WHAT COST

The pages had nearly fallen from his hands, his heart pounding viciously in his ears. The Ardunian empire was the largest on earth, spanning a third of the known world; that the news had been already released meant that it had by now spread like seed, no doubt disseminated via second- and thirdhand gossip that would inevitably invent details in the retelling—fomenting widespread hysteria in the process.

The people would riot.

The King Is Dead, the Diviners Are Dead, the Prince Is Unwell

SETAR—*The Daftar* declares with profound regret and confusion the brutal murder of King Zaal. It was announced from the royal ball last evening, at approximately 11:43, that the young sovereign of Tulan, King Cyrus of Nara, slaughtered His Royal Highness without contest. It has been widely reported by attendees that the king was crudely exposed in the moments before death, leaving unchallenged an accusation that he'd sacrificed the lives of countless orphans to feed a dark magic keeping him unnaturally alive.

The prince and heir was present upon the king's death, though it has been confirmed by more than one bystander that Prince Kamran suffered severe injuries upon engaging the Tulanian king in single combat, in satisfaction of honor.

"There was a ring of fire," a breathless partygoer, who wishes to remain anonymous, said of the bloody clash between royals. "The prince fought valiantly, but he was badly burned. We all thought he was dead until he screamed at us to go home."

As yet, the state of Prince Kamran's health is unknown.

Further reports indicate that due to the ghastly circumstances surrounding the king's death, the noble houses of Ardunia will begin talks today to decide whether retribution against the southern empire is necessary. Should they decide in the affirmative, their decision would mark the end of an unprecedented seven years of peace time, launching what officials say could be the bloodiest war in recent history. . . .

There was more.

More about Alizeh, described as a mysterious blur of a young woman whose name he'd cried aloud—"The prince was rumored to be but days away from selecting a bride"—for all the world to memorize. There was more about historical precedents, stories of other failed kings who'd succumbed to the dark magic of the devil and paid dearly. Most horrifying, though, were the inches dedicated to Cyrus's altercation with Miss Huda, the latter having apparently found time to give an interview to the press, describing in excruciating detail all that she knew of Alizeh, and taking care to add that she'd heard the southern king refer to Alizeh as "Your Majesty," leading Miss Huda to speculate on record that perhaps the two had been betrothed for some time.

Kamran wanted to set it all on fire.

It was not among his responsibilities to know the names of every guest attending a ball—it was Hazan who would've possessed such a list—but there must've been at least one journalist in attendance, for how else would they have been able to write and print such defamations before dawn?

The timing of it all seemed calculated to throw his days into tumult; he'd hardly had a chance to catch his breath and already he'd need to manage a chaos that could've been easily avoided. Had he only been given an opportunity to address the people directly, he might've soothed their fears with a show of strength—instead, their minds had already been taught to panic, fertilized by a garbage article. No doubt they'd all cough up their coin for the next printing of horseshit that would profit from his pain.

Startled by a sudden motion, Kamran tore his eyes away from the mirror, where he'd been staring blankly at his own reflection.

Sina had bowed before him.

His heart still thudding painfully in his chest, Kamran compelled himself to be calm, staring just a beat too long at the top of the older man's head, his graying brown curls. The valet had been with him for years now; always quiet, always thin, always in custody of impeccable manners. With great deference, he presented Kamran with a pair of dark blue kid-skin gloves.

"If you wish, sire" was all he said.

As if in response Kamran flexed his left hand, staring down at the shimmering gold veins splitting open the skin along his fingers, then snaking up his wrist, under his sleeve, where he knew they continued branching up his arm—

Briefly, he closed his eyes.

Never had the prince been particularly self-admiring,

but neither had he been willfully blind. It was but a simple fact that he'd been a royal who boasted more than just a title; a single glance around any room was enough to confirm that Kamran possessed an uncommon beauty, that he was orders of magnitude more handsome than his peers and elders. Too, Kamran had been well-fed and well-formed; he'd been wielding swords, riding horses, and training in full battle armor since childhood. He was as a result honed to something resembling perfection—so much so that he'd in fact never been much impressed with his reflection, for he'd grown accustomed to the splendor of his face and body.

Now, he hardly recognized himself.

There still remained the template of a handsome young man: his powerful body still stood tall and strong, his olive skin still gleamed, his dark hair remained thick and lustrous. But upon the foundations of his exquisite beauty now lay a grisly veneer. Gone was the gloss of a charming, noble prince; Kamran looked more like someone who might roast children on a spit, set fire to a village in the dead of night, feast upon the entrails of his enemies.

Slowly, the prince lifted his ruined hand to his ruined face.

Just last evening he knew that most women would happily consent to be his wife; even had they disliked him, he did not think they'd be revolted by the prospect of sharing his bed.

Now, he wasn't so sure.

His fine clothes hid a figure that looked as if it'd been struck by a strange lightning; the gold streak he'd been blessed with at birth—a mark placed upon him by the Diviners themselves—had once intersected his chest and torso in a tidy, elegant line. It was tradition for an heir of the Ardunian empire to be touched by magic, to own evidence of their birthright on their skin, announcing them forevermore as a true inheritor of the throne.

Never before had this magic been known to mutate.

Now the burnished gold stripe had all but shattered along his skin, glowing branches snaking tremulously up the left side of his body, the glimmering veins growing thinner as they braced the side of his neck, his cheek, and finally pierced straight through his left eye, rendering his iris an inhuman color.

He now possessed one dark eye and one the exact color of gilt, the sight so disorienting it cast doubt upon the original magic itself, which appeared, by all accounts, to be rejecting him.

"Your Highness?"

The tentative sound of Sina's voice shook the prince from his reverie; he met the valet's eyes without hesitation, pretending not to notice when the older man flinched.

"No gloves," Kamran said.

Sina bowed his head once more. "As you wish, sire."

The valet fluttered around him minutes more, using a coarse brush to remove any lint from his ensemble. The steady *hush hush* of the bristles against fabric nearly lulled the uncrowned king back to sleep.

To note that Kamran had hardly slept the night before would be to remark upon the roundness of the earth; stating the obvious would not help the young man's mind clear any more quickly. He was presented, in any case, with evidence of his own exhaustion by the sight of his haggard, disfigured reflection: crescents of darkness were smudged beneath his eyes; the cords of his neck were visibly tense; his jaw was set in a perpetual clench. Grief, exhaustion, betrayal—he couldn't decide which was the worst aggressor.

Without warning Kamran felt his body flash hot and cold, nerves prickling not unlike a colony of ants stretching their legs under his skin. It was a discomfort that made him want to jerk out of his own body. Kamran's impatience, then, was a symptom of inaction; his need for action a consequence of controlling his fear; his mounting fear a direct result of a conclusion his mind had recently drawn:

He was running out of time.

He could not explain *why* he was so sure of this fact; he could cobble together only feeling and memory as evidence: a sea of nobles speaking callously about his paralyzed body; Zahhak pronouncing his death without substantiation; the lack of action proceeding his reanimation.

Perhaps it was enough that, upon Zahhak's eventual return to the castle with a Diviner in tow, the defense minister had been able to hide neither his astonishment nor his anger upon discovering the heir to Ardunia was still alive. Kamran had bid the man fetch help with all possible haste; instead, hours and hours Zahhak had taken to return to the palace, during which time the hateful minister had no doubt convinced himself that Kamran would've succumbed to death.

Instead, he'd discovered, with an unmistakable shock, the

prince reclining leisurely in a copper tub, rinsing the night's travesties from his body.

Inexperienced Kamran might've been, but he was seasoned enough to know when enemies were conspiring. Too soon, he feared, the nobles would assemble an argument strong enough to steal his crown, his empire, his *birthright*—

Unable to stand still any longer, Kamran cleared his throat, and Sina drew back at once.

"Your Highness," said the valet, bowing his head. "Forgive me. I was forced to dispose of yesterday's garments, though I've pressed and scented all else you wore earlier in the day. Should you require it, your cloak awaits you in your chamber."

Kamran merely nodded, never looking away from his own reflection, not even when Sina moved soundlessly to the exit, the door snicking shut behind him.

Only when he was sure the valet had gone did Kamran close his eyes, allowing his shoulders to fall for the length of a single heartbeat as he drew a deep, bracing breath. There was a great deal to be done in the hours ahead, and every bit of it was urgent.

There was one week before he could be crowned king.

One week, during which he knew he'd be fighting the machinations of his own officials in addition to all else—and he intended to devote his days to righting the disasters that had befallen his home, his throne, his life itself. But first, there was a lingering matter to address.

He had to kill Hazan.

SIX

شش

ALIZEH'S INSTINCTS SHARPENED AS A distinguished older woman appeared as if out of nowhere before her, floating down a dew-touched path with an elegance she instantly admired. The stranger's powder-blue gown was adorned with fringed epaulets constructed entirely of sapphires, layers of decadent satin rippling gently around her ample curves in the morning breeze. Her hair was the color of fire itself, a shocking wave of red and gold sparingly streaked with gray, the silky locks swept over a single shoulder and clasped at intervals with diamond rings.

Her beauty was breathtaking—irrefutably so—but it was in the woman's eyes that Alizeh found reason for true astonishment, for there lived in her expression an unguarded enthusiasm that surprised Alizeh so completely she took a step back. A terrifying suspicion had risen up inside her, but even as Alizeh glimpsed the diadem atop the woman's head, she reasoned with herself that she might be wrong—that the lady drawing toward her now could be anyone, and certainly wouldn't be—

"Mother, wait—"

Alizeh's body seized at the sound of Cyrus's voice, panic causing her heart to pound furiously in her chest.

Cyrus came crashing between them—one hand raised

as if to intervene—when he abruptly recoiled, as if struck, upon sighting Alizeh. His eyes widened in something that could only be described as alarm.

Heat exploded in her body.

Rarely did Alizeh blush so deeply as to feel true warmth, but this humiliation was acute indeed—for she'd nearly forgotten what she looked like.

Moments ago she'd taken inventory of herself and dismissed the results, comforting her pride with the assurance that she'd meet with no one new at this early hour. Now, the burgeoning rays of heat had melted the frost from her hair and eyelashes, sunlight painting her so completely there was no hope of escaping scrutiny.

Alizeh looked like a woman of ill repute.

She was soaking wet; the scraps of her twice-incinerated gown were now entirely see-through, the translucent silk suctioned to her dripping body in a manner so scandalous it was somehow more shocking than a display of nudity. It didn't help that her stockings had disintegrated in the fire, or that the loose, drenched locks of her hair were so heavy they now grazed her waist, lapping at her curves and emphasizing the gentle swell of her hips, her glistening legs exposed up to her thighs. Little else was demanded of the imagination when her breasts were all but bared to the world, spared only an inch of modesty by a corset so scorched and waterlogged it had slipped to a dangerous degree, one unfortunate movement away from exposing her in an imitation of something so erotic Alizeh thought she might expire on the spot.

Instead, she seemed paralyzed.

Alizeh could only stand there, frozen in a nauseated sort
of humiliation, as Cyrus—and the woman Alizeh had to
assume was his mother—silently appraised her. Rationally,
Alizeh understood that the opinion of this unknown woman
should not matter to her, but it was no use; her dignity
chafed.

The older woman quickly recovered, her smile wavering
only a moment before it came back stronger; in fact, of the
two who stood before her, it was Cyrus who appeared truly
disturbed.

Alizeh chose to focus instead on his mother.

The latter soon cleared the distance between them, taking Alizeh's hands with a confounding familiarity.

"You must be Alizeh," she said, nearly blinding her with
a pair of familiar blue eyes. "I am Sarra. I can't tell you how
happy I am you've finally agreed to come."

Alizeh blinked, shock rendering her silent a moment
before she was able to falter, "I— That I *agreed* to come?"

Sarra's smile deepened. "I've been so anxious to meet
the young woman who is to become my daughter-in-law.
Cyrus has talked of little else these last few months, but he's
kept the details such a secret I was beginning to worry you
weren't real."

The nosta awoke without warning against Alizeh's chest,
heat flaring across her skin and provoking her heart to beat
harder.

Very slowly, Alizeh turned to look at Cyrus, who was now
staring determinedly into the distance. She all but bore holes
into his head with her eyes, and he would not face her.

Still staring at the king, Alizeh said angrily: "Cyrus has talked about me? *For months?*"

Finally, he did look at her—his eyes narrowed in warning. This only made her angrier.

"Odd, isn't it," Alizeh went on, "that he's known about me all this time and yet"—she glanced at Sarra—"did you know, I only met him for the first time tonight?" She hesitated, then frowned at the sun. "Or I suppose it was last night. Regardless, I can't help but wonder why he never bothered to introduce himself any earlier—or even to ask whether I wanted to be here before *tricking me into coming*—"

"You must be very tired," said Cyrus flatly. "This is hardly the time—"

"On the contrary," Alizeh said, meeting his eyes with a fire that would've made a weaker man flinch. "I find that this is the perfect time to tell your mother that I have absolutely no intention of becoming your wife—"

Sarra laughed loudly and without warning, the hollow, inauthentic sound drawing Alizeh's attention at once.

The lady had not let go of her hands.

There was something desperate about the way Sarra squeezed Alizeh's fingers now—with a pressure that bordered on painful—that screamed all manner of things unspoken. Alizeh couldn't be sure, but as she blinked up into the woman's strained eyes she was struck by a vague suspicion that Sarra was afraid.

Of what, she didn't know.

"You and I will get on just fine," the lady said urgently, her focus still locked on Alizeh's face. "I've been so eager to meet you, and now I know that we are to be the best of friends."

Again, the nosta flashed hot, and Alizeh went a bit slack
with astonishment.

Very well, then.

The situation seemed to demand a more direct approach.

"Your son," she said, carefully enunciating each word, "is
a liar. A scoundrel. And a criminal. Just earlier he murdered
the king of Ardunia, no doubt ensuring your empires will
soon go to war. And while I do not mourn the loss of the
Ardunian king, I do mourn the countless innocent lives that
will soon be lost as a result of your son's stupid decisions. In
the short time I've spent in his excruciating company I've
already been exposed to his rudeness, his cruelty, and his
disgusting arrogance, and if I'd not decided he might prove
useful to me in the short term, I would've killed him already.
You, on the other hand, strike me as quite kind, but let me
be clear: I have absolutely no intention of becoming your
daughter-in-law, nor would I recommend leaving me alone
with your son, who I'm liable to murder without warning—"

"So much to discuss!" Sarra cried, gripping Alizeh's hands
now with a fervor she found frightening. The woman beamed
at her, a sheen of emotion glazing her eyes as she exuded
what could only be described as unadulterated joy—so much
so that Alizeh was forced to wonder, in a moment of panic,
whether Sarra might not be as demented as her own son.

"What a delight you are," the lady said gently, a single tear
tracking a clean path down her cheek. "What happy conversations we're sure to have."

Alizeh blanched.

"All that matters is that you're here," Sarra said softly, never relinquishing Alizeh's hands, not even to wipe her eyes. "You're finally here, and now all will be well."

Something was wrong, upside down. Wasn't it? This woman was out of her mind. Wasn't she? Or was Alizeh so very delirious that she merely *felt* delusional?

Alarmed, she looked around, instincts urging her to escape, to identify all possible exits—but there were none. Alizeh stood atop a treacherous cliff at the base of a terrifying castle in a foreign empire, where the rising sun glittered mercilessly across the palace grounds. Paces away a tired dragon fell unceremoniously onto its haunches, rattling the earth beneath them as it fell asleep, the silent and sudden exhalations of its deep breaths rippling the rainbows cast in the spray of so many waterfalls.

The obvious way out of here, she reasoned, was through Tulan itself.

The heart of this empire was no doubt accessible only through—or beyond—the castle, but Alizeh doubted she could take a single step toward the palace without being intercepted. Which meant she could either fight to the death—

Or jump.

She would have to fling herself into the water, into the arms of frenzied, thrashing cascades that, if she even survived, would only dump her into the legendary Mashti River, a body of water so vast and violent its whitecaps were legendary, known for devouring on more than one occasion the ships that dared venture through them. This, she knew she'd never survive, but even the slim chance that she might was pointless: overcoming the river meant she would be emptied into the sea, which would only leave her adrift in the middle of nowhere.

Surreptitiously, Alizeh took a bracing breath.

She'd not slept in what felt like days; she was delirious, frozen, almost entirely naked, and still dripping slowly in the morning light. She stared down at her bare feet, then at her makeshift shackles, the iron grip Sarra kept upon her hands. Were it not for the adrenaline coursing through her veins, Alizeh doubted she'd be able to remain upright for much longer. She was at a terrible disadvantage.

Steeling herself, she said softly: "Very well."

Cyrus's gaze sharpened at that, his eyes betraying a flicker of surprise. With a small cry of pleasure, Sarra finally released Alizeh's hands, clapping her own together in delight.

Alizeh drew back at once.

The southern king followed, stepping cautiously toward her, watching Alizeh with the wariness of a hunter approaching a rabid wolf.

"You will come willingly?" he asked, his brows drawing together. "You will marry me without protest?"

They were close enough then that Alizeh could touch him had she wanted to. She could lift a finger to the silky copper lock curling across his forehead, his golden skin gleaming in the reflected light. His blue eyes were luminescent and somehow frigid, and for the briefest moment Alizeh thought she sensed in him what she still carried within herself—

A vast, bottomless grief.

She stood on tiptoe, asking with her body that he come closer—which he did, drawing toward her then without seeming to realize what he'd done, not until she nearly grazed the shell of his ear with her lips, when she whispered, for all the world as if they were playful lovers, "Choose your weapon, sire."

Cyrus drew back so suddenly he nearly stumbled, newborn anger flaring to life between them. His chest heaving, his jaw clenched, he looked as if he might implode with fury.

"This is terribly inconvenient for me," she said, drawing her shoulders back, planting her feet firmly beneath her. "But I'll have to kill you now."

Alizeh heard Sarra laugh.

SEVEN

KAMRAN STRODE DOWN THE HALL much like a stallion finally allowed to bolt. He moved with a swiftness that almost betrayed his nerves, his steps ringing out in the silence, his presence met only by occasional scurrying snodas, all of whom stopped in place at the sight of him and promptly fell to their knees, nearly dropping copper trays in the process, the sounds of crystal clattering between them.

The prince strode past these strange displays without betraying his surprise, but he was made uncomfortable nonetheless, for he was unaccustomed to this level of servility. It would be another week before he was crowned king; in the interim, he didn't know whether this behavior was normal.

Once again, his mind drifted to Hazan.

Hazan, upon whom he'd always relied to keep him abreast of precisely such things; who'd always been there to correct and inform and guide him. Surely it had not *all* been a lie?

No, Kamran was too perceptive.

He trusted his own instincts too much to believe such a feat was even possible. Hazan's betrayal had to have been a recent development. What Kamran couldn't understand was *why*.

Why, after years of loyalty, would Hazan turn on him—turn his back on an empire his own family had been serving for decades? Had he somehow known of King Zaal's crimes? Had Hazan been exacting revenge upon his grandfather by assisting the monster foretold to destroy him?

"Hejjan?"

Kamran bristled at the sound of the familiar voice.

"Hejjan, septa—" *Sire, wait—*

He did not wait.

The prince felt his cape billowing about his shoulders as he moved, the steady knock of his boots against the green marble acting as a metronome against which he kept pace. Hazan was shackled in the dungeons waiting to die, and Kamran wanted to get the hateful business over with as soon as possible, for he was plagued by an uneasiness that made him feel ill. In an honest moment he might even admit that he did not, in fact, desire to kill the only person he'd ever called a friend, and if he failed to execute the traitor straightaway, he feared he'd lose the will to do it at all.

Omid jogged to keep up with him, slightly out of breath when he said, in Feshtoon, "Lotfi, hejjan, septa." *Please, sire, wait.* "There's something I need to tell you."

Kamran did not slow his pace. "Is he ready?"

"Han, hejjan. Bek—" *Yes, sire. But—*

"Then I must get on."

"Bek—"

"Surely you have other things to do," said Kamran, cutting him off for the second time. "As I recall, I gave you the list myself."

More lunacy from the uncrowned king: Kamran had made Omid—former street rat, aged twelve—his new home minister. Kamran had made the pronouncement upon Zahhak's return to the palace, citing the child as the reason for his recovery. The defense minister could hardly shut his gaping mouth long enough to stammer out a single word of astonishment, and when he finally did, he all but accused the prince of losing his mind—which seemed, to Kamran, entirely plausible.

He *felt* a bit mad, in any case.

In Kamran's opinion, the former street child had proven himself fully capable of the role Hazan had failed to perform, and it did not matter to him that the boy was only twelve. When Kamran was twelve he might've been crowned king of Ardunia, if only his elderly grandfather—aged well over a century at the time—hadn't made a bargain with the devil to live longer. He felt certain that Omid, too, could rise to this lesser occasion.

"Well— Yes, sire, and I've been doing other things, honest I have," the boy said in breathless Feshtoon. "But if you're going to see him, sire, you should know that he's real angry."

Kamran glanced at the child. "Hazan is often angry."

"I don't think so, sire. I never seen him angry. Certainly never seen him like this."

"You never knew him."

Omid boggled. "But I did. He was the one who gave me the tickets to the—"

"*Enough.*"

The unpalatable truth was that this irritating child was the only person Kamran could think of who'd never lied to him. What's more: the child had possessed one of the most powerful pieces of magic known to man—he could've sold the Sif for a small fortune on the black market, earning enough money to live comfortably for years into the future. Instead, he'd chosen to give the precious ration to someone who'd treated him with nothing but disdain, anger, and unkindness. Kamran could not imagine a finer litmus test of character.

Still, it did not follow that he had to *like* the boy.

"But does he really have to hang right away?" Omid pressed on, undaunted. "Without even a trial? You haven't asked him a single question—you're just going to kill him because of something King Cyrus said, and we hate King Cyrus, sire, so it doesn't really seem fair to take such a man at his word—"

Kamran came to a sudden stop, his cape whipping around his chest as he turned, looking Omid in the eye. "It is precisely *because* I am fair," he said sharply, "that I intend to put Hazan out of his misery this morning."

Omid frowned. "Is that meant to be a joke, sire?"

"Far from it. I am teaching you something vital." He studied Omid a moment, noting for the first time that the boy looked ridiculous in the serviceable, oversized clothes he'd been given by the Diviners. Omid would need a new wardrobe if he were to represent the crown in such a capacity. "Confine a guilty man to a dungeon with only the company of his own conscience," he said quietly, "and you prolong his torture. It is because I care that I intend to be merciful now."

"But, sire," Omid said, his frown deepening. "Can you be merciful later? I came to tell you that Miss Huda is here, and she's hoping to speak with you without delay. You remember Miss Huda, don't you, sire?"

Kamran bristled at the mere mention of the young woman's name, revulsion raising bile in his gut.

The eagerness with which Miss Huda had disgorged the contents of her mind to a bloodthirsty journalist struck him as the action of a person desperate for attention, which in Kamran's estimation was both an incurable condition and a terrible crime. The illegitimacy of her birth having already been known to him, he could not help but wonder whether the affections withheld from her in childhood had led to her becoming the kind of young woman who'd do anything for a pat on the head. He felt, as a result, that she might loan out her loyalty to anyone in exchange for favor, which meant he could not trust her—and the words of a liar, no matter how entertaining, were useless to him.

"Send her away."

"But— Sire, Miss Huda says she has important information to share with you about King Cyrus," Omid pressed. "She says she has to speak with you on a matter of great importance to the crown. Do you— Do you remember her, sire? How the southern king had trapped her in a fiery ring? And how she screamed?"

Kamran shot the boy a scornful look.

"Do I *remember?*" he asked. "Do I remember the events of a few hours ago? Do I remember witnessing my grandfather's murder, my minister's deflection, the destruction of my home, the disfiguration of my body?" He almost laughed. "Goodness, but I pray for your sake that you are not yourself

as stupid as the questions you ask, otherwise this arrangement will see its end before sundown."

Omid flushed scarlet.

"I have no interest in talking to anyone who might divulge
sensitive intelligence to a newspaper before offering to share
such knowledge with the crown. Tell her to go home."

"But, sire," Omid insisted, still flushing past his hairline,
"she says she has a bag. A carpet bag that belonged to Miss
Alizeh. She says that Alizeh accidentally left her belongings
at Follad Place, and that you might want to go through them,
see, on account of there might be something of interest—"

Kamran had frozen in place.

He'd felt like someone had shot an arrow through his head
at the mention of her name, pinned him to a tree. His heart
had begun pounding in his chest. His mind felt suddenly full
of fog, something like mist clouding his eyes.

He felt cold.

"Sire? Should I allow her to bring the bag?"

"Yes." The prince blinked, shaking himself free. "Yes.
Have her escorted to the morning room at once."

Omid grinned, clearly pleased with himself, and bolted
down the hall.

Kamran remained where he stood, his mind reeling.

He hated the way his body reacted to the mere mention of
her; to the sound of her name, spoken aloud.

Alizeh still had this hold over him, and he couldn't fathom
why. He'd known the girl but a matter of days—and then
she'd proven herself to be the worst kind of monster. Why,
then, did some pathetic part of him protest the assassination

of her character? Why did he feel as if he were missing something—lacking some essential piece of information?

Without a doubt she'd bewitched him.

Why else would his heart beat this hard at the prospect of discussing her? Why else did he feel a strange flutter in his chest, a terrible joy at the thought of looking through her things?

Kamran remembered her carpet bag.

He remembered watching her stuff the small luggage to its limits, jamming every article she owned into its depths. Her entire life had fit inside that bag; these were the most essential items she owned; the possessions she cherished the most. He felt almost light-headed at the prospect of unraveling her secrets.

He expected he would only ever be rid of these feelings once she was dead.

EIGHT

هشت

CYRUS MADE NO MOVE.

He only stared at Alizeh, hatred flashing in his gaze with a fervor that—for a moment—nearly scared her.

It was a good thing, she reasoned.

Cyrus had been vicious with his tongue, true, but he'd been otherwise docile, presenting no threat of physical harm—which had lulled her into a false sense of security. This was dangerous; were Alizeh to underestimate him she'd pay dearly for the oversight—as Cyrus, she would take care to remember, could be quite frightening indeed. She'd not allow herself to forget how easily he'd murdered Zaal; how casually he'd suggested killing Miss Huda; how confidently he'd lifted his sword to slay Kamran.

Kamran.

She still didn't know whether he was dead.

A sharp pain bore through her at the realization, steeling her resolve anew. If he'd killed Kamran, she'd gouge his eyes out. She'd gouge his eyes out and force them down his throat.

"*I said choose your weapon,*" Alizeh repeated angrily.

Still, Cyrus did not move. "And you? From where will you procure a weapon of your own?"

"I do not require one."

He actually laughed at that, a dry sound that inspired no change to his stony expression. "Of all the trials I've recently endured," he said, turning his face up to the sky. "You are by far the most excruciating."

"I'm pleased to hear it."

"It's not a compliment," he said with some heat, meeting her eyes again. "And I will not fight you."

"Then let me go."

He made a small bow, a faint gesture with his hand. "Go."

Alizeh stared at him a beat, then spun around, taking in the landscape to which he'd gestured, the sights she'd already seen: the cliffs, the waterfalls, the devastating drop to the river below. He was all but suggesting she die to escape him.

Heavens, but she was dealing with a madman.

Cyrus shook his head at her, almost smiled. "Is the fall not worth your freedom?"

Her anger only intensified. "You are despicable."

"And you are the worst coward," he said. "Even while you pretend at bravery."

"How dare you," she said, her fists clenching. "How dare you slander my person when you know *nothing* about me—"

"A hypocrite, too, how divine," he said lazily. "Meanwhile, I was forced to listen to you disparage me at length in front of my own mother, and still I managed not to take up arms against you."

"Perhaps because you found it difficult to disagree with my assessment of your character."

"Character?" He raised his eyebrows. "Oh, yes, do let's discuss your character. You've been threatening to kill me

for hours—despite having had ample opportunity to do so—
and now you're picking a fight when you know full well that
I won't lift a finger against you—that I *can't*, even if I'd love
nothing more than to see your smart mouth shut forever.

"You think you're so cunning," he said, stepping toward
her now, "but these last few hours have already taught me
everything I need to know about your *character*."

Alizeh wanted to throttle him.

"*Choose your weapon*," she said again, but he was still striding forward, his eyes catching intermittent rays of light as he
moved, the flash and flare constricting his pupils at different
rates. The effect on his eyes was strange; his irises seemed
incapable of deciding on a color, vacillating between shades
of blue and making him appear occasionally inhuman. It
caused Alizeh to wonder whether that was how people saw
her, as well.

The fraction of a moment would cost her.

Too late, Alizeh realized that Cyrus was not slowing down.
She was forced to stumble back as he stalked toward her—
his forward strides increasingly confident, her hasty retreat
ever more fumbling. Only when she became suddenly, desperately aware of the fact that she was mere inches from the
edge of the cliff did her instincts reassemble; quickly she
halted him with her hands, staying his march with a firm
shove he met with strength of his own, pushing valiantly
against the force she exerted and somehow conceding only
inches in the process.

Alizeh didn't understand. She was much stronger than
him—she should've been able to throw him back—

But Alizeh was weak, too.

She still trembled with cold, with the deliriousness of one who'd hardly slept in days, with the fatigue of a mind that had been all but shattered. Alizeh did not need food, but she still required sustenance—and the taste of mist in her mouth upon arrival had been her only drink of water in several hours. Adrenaline was losing its effect on her; she was beginning to buckle under these myriad pressures, and worse: Cyrus was confusing her senses. He no longer wore a coat, for the article he'd lent her earlier had been tossed into turbulent skies, and in fighting her strength now he was only pressing himself more firmly into her hands, the thin sweater he wore doing little to mask the firm musculature of his body, the soft strength of his chest. The distracting heat and sensation of him was proving altogether too intimate an experience. She did not want to know him like this.

"What are you doing?" she practically gasped. "I told you to choose—"

Unexpectedly, Cyrus smiled.

For the first time since she'd met the reprobate, he truly smiled. He grinned like a boy, not a man, the infinitesimal flash of his white teeth rendering him almost childlike, softening him into something more mischievous than vengeful. The sight was distracting enough that she failed to notice her hands had fallen from his chest, that *his* hands had wasted no time landing at her waist. He gripped her firmly, stepping so close their bodies nearly aligned in all the wrong places; he was crowding her with his heat, with his height, with his unrelenting stare. She could hardly fuse together the wires in her brain; she was too tired, too unaccustomed to such closeness, too overwhelmed by the scent of him, the stubble along his jaw, the strength she felt in his hands, on her hips, his fingers sinking into her flesh. It was but a moment that she froze, confusion costing her the opportunity to regroup, and she knew two things then with absolute certainty: First, that she had failed.

Second, that he had lied.

How had the nosta failed to sense this? *He was going to kill her.* He was laughing when he lifted her off her feet, laughing when, without warning, he tossed her off the cliff.

Alizeh screamed.

"I choose dragons," he called after her.

Her arms and legs pinwheeled as she fell backward into the sky, hands fumbling in vain for purchase as she cried out in fear, in rage, plummeting all the while from a terrible height for the third time in less than a day.

She didn't understand why this kept happening to her.

Alizeh, who had enough experience now for comparison, could say with confidence that *this* was the most terrifying fall of the three, made worse by the fact that she was falling in the wrong direction, growing only more disoriented as she tumbled, her limbs tangling as she struggled to right herself. The drop was so immeasurable she could hardly make out the river below, and she braced herself for the force of impact, praying she'd at least die instantaneously upon hitting the water. It'd be far worse to survive the fall, she knew, and sustain injuries that would kill her slowly. Either way, she could look forward to excruciating pain.

Oh, Alizeh was tired.

Tired of feeling she had no control over her life, tired of being manipulated by the devil, tired of living in fear, tired of fear itself. The dark truth she seldom revealed even to herself was that sometimes she wanted nothing more than to break, to be weak, to tear off her armor and give in.

How long would she be forced to fight for her life? More important: Was her life really worth so much effort?

It troubled her that she had no answer.

Her emotional and physical exhaustion were in fact so acute she almost welcomed the idea of closing her eyes forever, and with a terrible shudder, she squeezed them shut.

Alizeh had no idea whether she would die, but she knew she could expend no more energy fighting gravity. She let her limbs be flung akimbo, let her hair snake around her face, listened to the tatters of her dress rap relentlessly in the wind. She was finally surrendering her life to fate when she heard an unmistakable, deafening roar.

Alizeh's eyes flew open.

She stared, thunderstruck, as a flight of dragons broke from the waters below, a starburst of behemoths rising up to meet her. Another earsplitting roar, then a fifth and sixth joined the chorus, and Alizeh set aside all thought of relenting to the skies. Death by water was one thing, but she was determined she would not be eaten alive by dragons.

It was fresh terror that inspired her to summon the lingering strength she possessed; and through nothing short of

a miracle she managed to flip herself into a position remi-
niscent of an exclamation, her head pointing to the water.
She hoped to descend more rapidly this way, to escape the
dragons and, with any luck, break the surface with less
brutality—but she'd hardly a moment to celebrate her success before one of the shimmering creatures swooped toward
her with a terrifying screech, its enormous mouth yawning
open upon approach.

It was no use.

Alizeh screamed, pulling her knees up and cradling herself like a child, as if the cold comfort of her own arms would
make any difference. The dragon snapped her up into its
jaws with a violent jerk, and in the second Alizeh expected
to be devoured, the animal only soared upward with astonishing speed, the sudden motion throwing her back against
its teeth, which pierced her skin with a violence that tore the
breath from her body. Alizeh felt the excruciating burn of
the injuries, the telltale moisture of her clear blood oozing,
and grew suddenly light-headed. The whiplash of descension
and ascension had wrought havoc upon her mind.

Through layers of distorted awareness, Alizeh grew cog-
nizant of her own confusion; she didn't understand why she
was not yet dead. She felt the graze of a fresh breeze against
her skin, so different from the humid mouth of an animal,
and was abruptly released; her body rolled to a gentle stop
onto damp ground, her fingers catching blades of grass.

Alizeh groaned.

With a whopping flap of its enormous wings, the dragon

took off into the sky, releasing a screech as pain lanced viciously through her body. For a worrying moment, Alizeh thought she might throw up.

It was with great bitterness that she realized she'd just experienced Cyrus's idea of a joke.

She wondered why she didn't hear him then, why the degenerate did not show himself, applaud himself for a job well done. She wondered, as she forced herself up, nearly biting through her tongue to keep from crying out, what Sarra would think of this performance of her son's affection.

Alizeh prepared herself to ask, swinging around tipsily for a glimpse of her captors—when she realized she was alone.

The dragon had deposited her somewhere new.

Alizeh stood at the open mouth of a monumental structure, a series of stone archways closing around her like a set of ribs, the gaps between them lashed by golden rays. The soft grass underfoot was dense and springy; tiny orange flowers bloomed against her toes. Birds tittered, fluttering between arches as they sang, their colorful plumage glittering in the morning glow. A gentle wind pillowed her weary face, the gust at once strong and soft enough that she let herself rest against it, just until it pulled away, coaxing her to look right, where she was presented with a sight so breathtaking she went slack, almost forgetting about her injuries.

The stupendous waterfalls appeared both smaller and calmer from this vantage point, the stone columns providing a frame through which the magnificence of the scene was presented in all its glory. Alizeh had collected enough visual information by then to deduce she'd been deposited somewhere high up in the castle, and she couldn't help but wonder whether this secluded, heavenly garden was meant to be hers.

Surely Cyrus had meant to toss her in a dungeon instead?

As she followed the path, she came upon a small table and chairs, the three of which were positioned just so under a specific trio of arches, where flowering vines had snaked up the stone, braiding natural shade across the tops. The decadent fragrance of the blooms scented the air so completely Alizeh felt compelled to stop; for a long moment she closed her eyes, inhaling the perfume as a flurry of air caressed her cheeks, stung her wounds, curled her hair.

When she opened her eyes she spotted a set of doors in the distance. Alizeh approached these cautiously, the grass underfoot disappearing under a series of silky, patterned rugs, their vivid colors standing out in stark contrast to the green path.

Inside, Alizeh discovered an oasis.

A soaring, domed ceiling crowned the central room, marble tiles arranged in geometric patterns along the floors, over which ran yards of lush red rugs that spanned the room. Massive windows had been thrown open to let in the light, the welcome breeze ruffling the sheets of an enormous bed that sat, silky and decadent, in the center of everything, quilts folded down in invitation. Alizeh walked through it all as if in a daze.

Was this meant to be hers?

If this was meant to be hers, she thought she could understand why someone might make a deal with the devil. For the space of a single moment, something like this might seem worthwhile.

But then, there was more.

There were more rooms beyond this one: an opulent sitting room; separate rooms for the bath and toilet; a small courtyard with a dining table—

It was only as Alizeh wound her way through these spaces that she realized she'd been delivered here in reverse. The entrance to this wing was not through the bedroom; it was in fact just ahead of her. An imposing wooden door seemed to wink at her from where it stood, daring her to open it.

She would not.

Not yet.

She stole into the bathroom instead, locating a stock of bed linens in a cabinet and quickly tearing a sheet into strips. Half of these she used to mop and stanch the blood of her wounds, the remainder she repurposed as bandages, wrapping them neatly around her injuries. With a heavy sigh, she slumped against the wall. All she desired in the world at the moment was to take a warm bath, swaddle herself in clean clothes, and sleep for an eternity.

The first two seemed impossible in her current state; she didn't think she'd survive the time it would take to draw a bath, and neither did she know where to find a change of clothes. But if she could only make her way back to the bed, she might yet accomplish the third.

She peered through the wrong doorway in her search, discovering inside a luxurious dressing room, which, as curiosity coaxed her forward, she found to be fully stocked with garments so fine she was afraid to touch them. She only dared graze the articles with the tips of her fingers, the sight of such superb textiles sparking to life a slumbering part of her brain; Alizeh suddenly itched for her sewing supplies. Without thinking she patted herself down, reaching for pockets that did not exist, looking about herself for a luggage she no longer owned.

With a terrible fright, Alizeh froze.

Comprehension dawned by aching degrees, dread flooding her body as memories filled her head, the chaos of the last twelve hours trying desperately to sort itself into chronological order.

Alizeh clapped a hand over her mouth.

Only then did she realize where she'd left her carpet bag.

NINE

MISS HUDA WAS WAITING FOR him inside the morning room, unmistakable and severely out of place, clothed in an ensemble so hideous that even Kamran, who did not know the difference between a ruffle and a petticoat, could not help but condemn.

The situation was dire, indeed: she was a broad young woman, the sharp slashes of her chin and cheekbones hinting at a regal bone structure one could only imagine was repeated in the lines of a figure presently swathed in the skin of a deflated sun. She wore yellow from ruff to hem, the billowing folds of her gown inhaling her, occasionally pinching in places he took care not to study. Aside from the tragedy of her costume, the miss looked well enough despite being visibly nervous, her eyes darting around and unable to settle. Kamran watched her a moment from the doorway, noting, with a start, the bulging carpet bag at her feet, the sight of which sent a bolt of feeling through his chest.

Quietly, he cleared his throat.

Miss Huda sprang up at once, curtsying with a grace that contradicted the inelegance of her dress. "Your Highness," she breathed, her eyes pinned to the floor. "You must know how grateful I am that you made time to see me this morning. I know we've never been formally introduced, but after

the events of last night I felt I must breach propriety in the
hopes of pressing into your arms an item of great— That
is, not that I would ever press it directly into your arms, I'd
never dream of taking such liberties, I only meant that I
wished to deliver you— I wished— *Oh*—"

Kamran had by then already crossed the room and
retrieved the carpet bag from the floor. Only when he
stepped back did Miss Huda finally look up, after which she
gaped at him, her mouth hanging open like a codfish.

"Your face," she gasped.

"Thank you for the bag. You may go."

"But what happened to your face?" she insisted, astonishing him with her rudeness. "Was it that terrible king? Did he
do this to y—"

"Miss Huda," he said, jaw tensing, "if you would please—"

"Oh but never fear, sire, you are still quite desperately
handsome," she assured him in a breathless rush, her hands
fluttering about her waist. "I didn't mean to imply you'd
lost your appeal, only that you've a much more tragic look
about you now, something some might even consider *more*
attractive—depending, of course, on their individual tastes,
but then I—"

"*Miss Huda.*"

Like a tractable child's toy, she suddenly snapped shut.

Her mouth closed, her hands clasped, her heels clicked
together. She straightened as best she could in that travesty
of a yellow gown, and pinned him with a look of intense
mortification.

"Yes, Your Highness?" she whispered.

"Unless there is anything else of note you wish to impart about the young woman to whom this bag belongs"—he nodded to the small luggage he still held—"I'm afraid I must be on my way."

"Anything," she said nervously. "I'll tell you anything you'd like to know. I've already looked through the bag, sire, and while I wasn't able to discern anything of great significance, I did find a few medicinal salves stamped with the seal of the local apothecarist, who I thought might prove a worthy lead should you choose to pursue an investigation—"

"I already know about the apothecarist," Kamran said curtly.

"Right." Miss Huda took a sharp breath. "Well. I suppose all that remains is to ask whether you might return me my gown, which I can't imagine is of any relevance to your interests, but which I was hesitant to remove from the luggage for fear of tampering with what might be considered a body of evidence—"

"Return you your *gown*?" Kamran cut her off, dropping the bag to the floor before pinching his nose between thumb and forefinger. First she had the audacity to give him investigative advice, and now she had the nerve to ask him for clothes? Lord, but this woman was giving him a terrible headache. "Are you feeling ill, Miss Huda? What business might I have with your wardrobe?"

She went slack a moment, still as a pillar of salt before she laughed in a sudden, terrible burst, clutching a hand to her chest as she assured him, with not a small bit of hysteria, that she did not think he would have any business with her wardrobe, that she was only referring to the unfinished garment still stuffed into the carpet bag, and "which I'd dearly love to have returned, sire, for the gown is still pinned quite neatly in all the right places, and I think I might be able to convince my maid to finish the job Alizeh had started—"

Kamran flinched.

Her name struck him like a stone when she spoke it, filling his head with the sound of wind and birdsong and a sharp, blistering pain that forced him to turn away. He pressed the heel of his hand against a sudden spasm in his neck, along the fissures snaking up his skin, trying in vain to understand what the devil was happening to him.

"Forgive me, sire," said Miss Huda, misinterpreting his abrupt motion. "I didn't mean—"

"I don't understand a word you're saying," he managed to get out, turning once again to face her. "She was a servant, not a seamstress, and you indicated to *The Daftar* that you'd only met her shortly before the ball, so it doesn't follow that she'd even have time to alter a gown for you, and never mind the fact that she'd have no reason to do such a thing."

"I see," she said, surprise widening her eyes. "So you've already read the article."

Kamran scowled in response.

"I am grateful," she said carefully, "to understand now why you're so reluctant to speak with me, though I fear you've formed a terrible impression of my character, and I must now assure you, sire, that I spoke to *The Daftar* only briefly, sharing only a small part of what I know, and only because I was accosted by a journalist not long after that odious king released me from his fire. I was feeling vulnerable and was caught quite off guard, you see, but I swear to you I told them but a fraction of the truth, for even if you will not accept that I acted on principle, you might believe that I'd withheld the whole story in the pursuit of protecting my own interests— for the truth would've landed me in a great deal of trouble with my parents, sire, so I could not have risked the lot of it being printed in a paper for all to read."

At long last, the exasperating miss had piqued Kamran's interests. He regarded her carefully. "Get you into trouble how?" he asked.

Miss Huda took a bracing breath. "Well, I'd quite stealthily engaged the services of Miss Alizeh—"

"*Don't,*" he said sharply, clenching his fists through a fresh bolt of pain. "Don't say her name."

Miss Huda took a startled step back. She blinked at him a moment, then studied her hands. "Very well, sire. I won't say her name. But I had engaged her services," she said, swallowing, "to design me several new gowns, for Mother is always forcing me to wear some monstrosity she's commissioned, and as I have a little pin money from Father, I thought perhaps I might circumvent these little tortures inflicted upon me by finding my own modiste."

"Once again, Miss Huda, I will remind you that the young woman in question worked as a snoda, not a seamstress."

"Oh, but she did, sire," Miss Huda said eagerly. "She did both."

"That's impossible. She worked, at minimum, twelve-hour shifts at Baz House—she was in the employ of my own aunt, I saw her working there—"

"Yes, sire, quite true. But she came to me at night, after her shift was done."

Kamran stared at her, dumbfounded. "If that is true, when did she sleep? When did she eat?"

These were such strange questions that even Miss Huda fell silent. She stared curiously at the prince, and Kamran, realizing too late that he'd exposed something essential about himself, quickly appended his questions with another, this one more damning:

"When did she find time to conspire with the Tulanian king?"

The spell broke.

Miss Huda nodded, her eyes lit now with a new fervor. "That's just it, sire. She—that is, the young woman I shall not name—could not have conspired with him. She didn't even know who he was."

Kamran's spark of interest evaporated.

"Not only is what you allege impossible," he said unkindly, "it also contradicts what you yourself told the paper—for you claimed on record that she'd been betrothed to the Tulanian king for some time."

"I did think it possible, yes," said Miss Huda, taking a step toward him before remembering herself and drawing back. "She did confess to be some manner of forgotten nobility, and often such matches are made in infancy. Royals are all the time betrothed to people they do not know."

"Not in this case," he pointed out. "The two were well-acquainted."

Miss Huda shook her head vigorously. "I was there the first time they met—I saw the way the two looked at each other, and they were strangers."

"Where was this?"

"In my room, sire, the night of the ball. Aliz— That is, *she* was meant to have finished the aforementioned gown— which you will discover buried in her luggage—ahead of the festivities, but had come to me that evening in a bit of a panic, claiming she could not complete the job in time. Only after I pressed did she admit she was running for her life from some unnamed entity—shortly after which the southern king all but magically *appeared* in my room, and, Your Highness, she hadn't the faintest idea who he was. Neither of us did. He wouldn't even tell us his name; he insisted she call him *Nothing*—"

"What a convenient way to protect his identity," said Kamran, leveling Miss Huda with a dark look. "Yes, I'm sure they both did a fine job pretending not to know each other in your presence."

Miss Huda paled. "Oh, no, I assure you, even when she opened that strange box of shoes—which had been delivered to me ahead of her arrival—she was entirely shocked, you must believe me, her manners were quite unrehearsed—"

"What strange box of shoes? What on earth are you talking about?"

Miss Huda bit her lip; wrung her hands. "I do apologize, sire. I'm more than a little nervous and I fear I'm telling the story entirely out of order . . ."

Kamran was forced to listen then, with mounting

irritation, as Miss Huda described the delivery of a mysterious package, which had only revealed its contents to Alizeh
herself, and had contained in its depths a disappearing note
and a beautiful pair of shoes, whose matching gown Alizeh
had already possessed upon arrival at Follad Place.

"Enough."

The prince squeezed his eyes shut, his headache threatening now to split open his skull. The proof of Alizeh's
traitorous behavior was almost too much to bear. He felt
sick at the revelations, at the descriptions of her thoughts
and movements prior to the ball. While he had been replay-
ing their stolen moments together, dreaming of her like a
lovesick fool, she'd been plotting all the while against him,
no doubt laughing at how easily he'd been brought to his
knees by her beauty, her charm, her performances of grace
and compassion.

Kamran hated himself then, hated himself so thoroughly
he thought he might make himself ill.

With tremendous effort he composed himself, saying
calmly, "The series of events you describe to me now present
a trail of evidence so clear—and so incriminating—I cannot
imagine how you might misunderstand it. Altogether these
details paint the very *picture* of an elaborate scheme and,
contrary to what you might believe, the young woman was—
is—conspiring with the king of an enemy nation who wishes
to destroy me. There can be no questioning this fact."

"I do question it, sire— Forgive me, but I do question
it, for I spent many hours in her presence and I am uncon-
vinced she is, as you imply, an evil young woman. In fact, I

am convinced of quite the opposite, for she was terribly kind to me; she all but offered to defend me with her life, sire, even in the midst of her own life-threatening trials, which I'm sorry to say is a generosity no other person has bestowed upon me, and I cannot now in good conscience abandon her, not when I fear she might be in great danger, and if there's any chance of finding her, I'd love to be able to assist—"

"Your inconstancy is maddening," Kamran cried, no longer able to control his anger. "First you out her to the papers, then you demand to save her? Have I not made it clear that she is a traitor to this empire?"

"Forgive me, sire, I don't mean to be maddening—Mother is always telling me how maddening I am, and I see now that there might be some merit to her claims, but I confess I'm also confused by your anger, for I'd hoped— You see, I heard the way you called after her last night, and I'd thought maybe you, too, would worry about what that terrible man might do to her—"

"You trouble yourself for no reason." Kamran was furious, and he fixed the young woman with an unrelenting stare. "I am not concerned about her well-being. In fact, your confessions this morning have only cemented my certainty that she should be hanged, drawn, and quartered. That she was wise enough to prey upon your emotions is proof only of a tactical manipulation, and certainly not evidence of a generous heart. You have been exploited, Miss Huda. Accept this fact. She is not your friend."

This last line seemed to strike Miss Huda with a powerful force, for she took a step back, trembling a little as she looked away. She met the prince's eyes only briefly before averting her gaze again, her own eyes glinting with emotion.

"Quite right," she whispered. "Yes, I hear it now—I hear how it sounds when I say it aloud. What reason would she have to show me kindness if not to mock and abuse me? It would certainly align more closely with all my other experiences. I am hard-pressed, you know"—she looked up, attempted a laugh—"to find friends among my peers. I was perhaps too eager to believe she meant the kind things she'd said to me. Forgive me, sire, I am terribly stupid."

Kamran did not know what to do with this watery display. He felt frozen in the face of it, uncertain what to do with his hands, where to rest his eyes. He thought perhaps he should deny the unkindness she'd leveled against herself—but he, too, thought Miss Huda was terribly stupid.

"Thank you for the carpet bag," he said quietly. "You may go."

"Yes." She took a sharp breath, struggling to pull herself together. Then she unlatched the carpet bag on the ground between them, withdrew an armful of wrinkled green fabric from its depths, and bundled it in her arms. "Thank you, sire, for your—"

A small insect shot up from the inside of the open luggage with a speed that startled them both. Miss Huda gasped and swatted at her face, but the pest launched itself across the room, knocking itself against tables and lamps as if it might be drunk. Its tiny body ping-ponged off nearly every surface before it suddenly bopped Kamran in the forehead, triggering a flash of memory from the night before.

Hazan.

The insect was disoriented. It was trying to escape, now throwing its hard body against the closed door over and over in a failed attempt to find the keyhole. Cautiously, Kamran moved closer to the exit, and in a swift motion, trapped the tired insect under his hand. He felt the bug struggle against his skin, and carefully scooped it into his palm, where it pelted the inside of his hand with the frenetic motions of a small firework.

"What on earth?" Miss Huda wondered aloud. "How strange—I've been trying to catch that little thing all morning."

Kamran turned to her with a frown. "This bee came from your house?"

"I found it buzzing around my room when I returned home from the ball." She wiped at her damp eyes. "I tried to catch it several times, but it was too fast. And it's not a bee, sire, it's a firefly. I saw its little bottom glowing in the dark. I can only imagine it snuck into the carpet bag when I opened it."

"A firefly?" Kamran frowned, then froze, the gears in his mind spinning wildly. Why did this revelation seem so significant? Why did it sound so familiar?

"Sire?" said Miss Huda, her brows furrowed in dismay. "Are you quite all right?"

But Kamran did not hear her.

"That lying *bastard,*" he said softly.

TEN

"DARLING? DARLING, YOU MUST WAKE up."

Alizeh felt the press of a delicate hand against her forehead, skin so soft the sensation was almost bizarre. Her nose filled with the scent of something decadent and floral; she heard the rush of silk, the soft clatter of jewels, bracelets stacking and retreating with each caress of her hair. For the length of the most divine moment, Alizeh thought she'd been reunited with her own mother.

She was delirious.

She seemed unable to move even a finger; her limbs were leaden, her body cemented to the rug. Alizeh had never made it to the bed; soon after registering the price she'd pay for leaving her carpet bag behind, any lingering adrenaline had drained from her body. Alizeh, who'd already been struggling with exhaustion, was reduced to a faint, trembling husk. Her knees gave out; she collapsed to the floor, her fatigue so acute she could no longer stave off the thirst for sleep; she faded in and out of consciousness, her mind braiding the sounds and scenes of reality with dreams until she could no longer tell the difference.

It was a delicious sleep.

She'd drifted off in a shaft of sunlight that baked her slowly as she slept; and though Alizeh had no idea how long she'd dozed, it felt as if she'd spent only a few minutes unconscious, and already someone was demanding she wake.

Just then, she could imagine nothing crueler.

"My dear, we haven't much time, and I must speak with you." Another stroke of a soft hand, this time against her cheek, and Alizeh nearly drifted off all over again. She was groggy and disoriented and desperately did not want to wake. She wanted to lie here forever, or at least until the sun had cooked her frozen flesh evenly.

"No," she croaked.

There was the sound of a soft laugh. "I know you're very tired, my dear, but so long as Cyrus thinks you're sleeping, he'll not suspect us of conspiring. You must wake, darling, for I must speak to you quickly."

The nosta awoke, flaring against the delicate skin of her breasts, a reminder that it was still tucked away in her damaged corset, and a warning of the truth in Sarra's words. Only fear was strong enough to compel Alizeh to consciousness, and even then the effort was agonizing. Her eyes were so dry that they burned as her lids peeled apart, her head pounding with exhaustion and dehydration even as her slumbering heart rate began to spike.

"What's happened?" Alizeh asked, blinking through a sting of tears, her gritty eyes attempting to lubricate. She tried to sit up and gasped instead, her muscles seizing as a searing pain awoke along the left side of her body.

"Oh dear," said Sarra uneasily.

Alizeh tensed as the woman looked her over with what appeared to be sincere concern; she took Alizeh's injured

arm in her hand, gentle fingers probing the homemade bandages, then pressed lightly against a stretch of Alizeh's leg,
which triggered an unexpected wave of torment.

The girl bit back a cry.

"I see," Sarra said softly. "These are teeth marks, aren't
they? Dragon bites."

"To be fair," Alizeh said, still wincing, "I don't think the
dragon meant to bite me."

"No, it wouldn't have." Sarra frowned. "Don't be deceived
by their size; they're quite dear creatures, actually."

"Well." Alizeh attempted to breathe through the agony,
comforting herself with the reminder of a recent discovery:
that her body had some ability to mend itself. "Little to do
about it now. I've cleaned and wrapped the wounds. They'll
heal eventually."

Sarra raised her eyebrows. "I take it you didn't see the line
of bites along your leg, then."

"What?" With some difficulty, Alizeh heaved herself up
into a seated position and studied the leg in question. She
still wore only the remnants of her twice-destroyed gown,
which meant Alizeh was fairly exposed, her bare thigh dis-
playing a neat sequence of puncture wounds, which, she had
to assume, were repeated somewhere along her abdomen as
well. The visible lacerations had bled and messily clotted, her
clear blood making it look as if her skin was slathered in a
crusty, translucent jelly.

Alizeh's stomach turned at the sight.

"He really is quite the monster, isn't he?" said Sarra quietly.

Startled, Alizeh looked up at the woman. "Who?"

"My son," she said, her expression grim even as she smiled. "He's an unforgivable brute."

Even as the nosta warmed, it felt like a trap.

Alizeh said nothing; she only studied Sarra warily, wondering what to believe. From the first, Cyrus's mother had been hard to understand, her actions always straying from the path of an obvious logic. Alizeh didn't know what to do with the woman now. She certainly didn't trust her.

"What was it you needed to speak with me about?" Alizeh said instead, careful to keep her face placid. "You made it sound as if something was wrong."

"Oh, everything is wrong, my dear. Everything is wrong." Again Sarra smiled; again the effect was tragic. "I had hoped, upon your arrival, that together we might change the course of things, and I'd come here to speak with you about just that, only I see now that you do not trust me, which means we cannot even think of forming an alliance until you do."

"You and I form an alliance?" Alizeh nearly laughed. "You can't be serious."

Sarra shot her a hard look before rising to her feet, outstretching a hand. Alizeh studied the woman with a guarded expression.

"Don't be daft," Sarra said with a slight shake of her head. "I'm not going to hurt you."

"Then what will you do with me?"

"I'm going to help you up, and then draw you a bath."

The nosta glowed warm at the statement, hope burgeoning in Alizeh's chest. A bath sounded *divine*. "That's all?"

Sarra gave her a dry smile. "That's all."

Alizeh accepted the woman's hand and gingerly levered herself up; once she'd found a measure of balance she hobbled along behind Sarra, who led the way to the tub. The woman turned taps until the sound of rushing water filled the room; the sight and promise of it all was enough to calm Alizeh's senses almost at once.

As the jet sloshed reassuringly against the porcelain, Sarra reached for a tray of small wooden bowls perched along a mounted ledge, and measured out precise scoops of what appeared to be multicolored herbs, which she then emptied into the water.

Steadily, the basin began to fill.

"These are medicinal," Sarra explained, nodding to the tray she was now returning to its shelf. "When the water touches your wounds it'll burn like hell itself, but if you can endure a bit of pain, there's little better for helping calm and clean your injuries quickly."

Alizeh bristled.

She didn't know why, but the woman's words felt almost like a challenge. "I assure you," she said, limping toward the sink. "I can endure a bit of pain."

Alizeh grabbed a length of toweling from a lower shelf and ran it under the faucet; she intended to clean the mess of her neglected injuries while the tub filled. Gritting her teeth, she gently patted at the congealed blood along her leg, careful lest she cause the lacerations to reopen.

All the while, Sarra watched her with an undisguised curiosity. "You know, I had no idea what to expect before you arrived," she said, perching along the edge of the tub. "Despite everything Cyrus told me about you, I wasn't sure what you'd be like." She paused. "Then again, I wasn't even sure you'd come."

Alizeh froze at that, then straightened. She tossed the soiled towel in the sink. "When, exactly, did he start talking about me? And what did he say?"

Sarra waved a hand, dismissing her own words as she said, "Oh, it was a few months ago. He strode into the dining room unannounced one day, and, with no preamble, declared in front of all the servants his intention to marry. He told me to begin preparing your rooms; he said you wouldn't have the right clothes—or even a trousseau—upon arrival, and that I was to begin assembling such items, and never mind that he never offered me a clue as to your measurements.

"Naturally, I had thousands of questions, but his answers were bloodless. He told me your age, that you resided up north. He said that you'd been orphaned but that you were descended from a forgotten royal line, insisting you had noble blood despite lacking a proper upbringing, and that you might present as a bit uncivilized as a result of your incomplete education—"

Alizeh's eyes widened in outrage. "I *beg* your pardon—"

"Oh, I wouldn't take it to heart, my dear," Sarra said, a wry smile curving her lips. "It's clear to me that you're well in possession of your faculties. Then again"—her eyes glittered with mirth—"you did make a rather unorthodox first impression, and I found I was grateful for the warning. Had I not been prepared to meet with a rather wild young woman,

I might've been too shocked to proceed."

Chastened, Alizeh's mouth snapped shut.

"Nevertheless," Sarra went on with a sigh, "it was obvious even then that he had no idea who you really were, for his descriptions gave me no indication of your character or personality. In point of fact, whenever I forced him to discuss you he did so with palpable revulsion. *Several* times he spoke aloud his hope that you weren't stupid, and never once did he spare me a detail about your physical attributes, despite the fact that"—she looked up, giving Alizeh an appraising glance—"well, even bedraggled as you are now, you're quite astonishingly lovely, aren't you? You'd think he'd have mentioned such an obvious detail. Instead, his most pressing concern was that you'd turn out to be an incurable idiot."

Alizeh blinked at the woman, stunned. Sarra had not lied once. "I take it he didn't mention, then, that he was being ordered to marry me by decree of Iblees himself."

"Of course he did," said Sarra, cutting off the water.

Alizeh's stupefaction at this answer would have to wait to unfold, for the tub had filled to its limit. The added herbs caused the water to bubble and froth, the fragrance of eucalyptus and jasmine scenting the humid air. Alizeh's heart soared at the sight, the familiar smells.

Sarra stepped into the doorway, presenting Alizeh with the back of her red head in an offering of privacy.

Alizeh, for her part, did not delay; she stripped off the remains of her gown with pleasure, hesitating when she remembered the nosta, which had so far been hidden expertly away inside her corset. Thinking of no other alternatives, she first glanced at the back of Sarra's head to make certain she was alone, then retrieved the little marble and popped it quickly into her mouth, where the orb fit easily inside her cheek. She piled her destroyed corset and her tattered undergarments in a neat little heap atop the dress, all of which she studied with a vivid feeling of disorientation.

It was still surreal to her that she was here.

She stood stark naked in the belly of a foreign empire, trapped in a bathing room with the mother of a ruthless king unapologetically tethered to the devil, and hadn't the slightest clue what horrors awaited her here.

It was almost too much to hold in her mind at once.

Even as she carefully lowered herself into the foaming, frothing bath, Alizeh wondered whether she was mad for trusting Sarra not to have filled the tub with poison—but then the water touched her wounds and Alizeh's pain grew so loud she could think of nothing else. She didn't know whether to moan in relief or cry out in anguish.

"Give it a few minutes," Sarra said from the doorway. "The pain will ebb, I promise. And then it will feel much better."

Alizeh squeezed her eyes shut, muscles tensing as the medicine seeped into her flesh. "I don't understand," she said, speaking slowly so as not to dislodge the nosta from her cheek. "You mean to tell me you know about Cyrus's alliance with the devil? That he's told you everything?"

Sarra laughed. "I never know *everything*."

"But you know the details of your son's treachery—that he's determined to marry me against both his will and mine, all in the interest of fulfilling some terrible debt owed to

Iblees? You know this and yet—you do not seem to care."

Sarra's voice took on an eerie stillness when she said, quietly, "It's not that I do not care. It's that I no longer believe him. For the last several months, my son has blamed all his bad decisions on the devil. Never does he take accountability for his actions. He's always begging me to understand that he has no choice—even as he makes demands of me, of his own people—he insists he does so only because he's shackled against his will."

"But"—Alizeh frowned, her eyes still closed—"he confides in you, then? He comes to you with the truth? I'd not expected so tyrannical a young man to seek out his mother's counsel."

Again, Sarra laughed darkly. "He does not seek out my *counsel*. He only unburdens himself in what I have discovered to be the deluded pursuit of my absolution. He is still young and foolish enough to think that confiding in me will earn him my compassion, but I've become inured to his self-pity. Of course I *tried*," she said with a sigh. "I tried, initially, to guide him, but I learned quickly enough that he only talks—and never listens. I've had to accept that I no longer have any influence over him; that in fact no one does. He might blame Iblees, but in the end Cyrus acts as he wishes; it is clear enough that we are all but pawns in his schemes."

Alizeh opened her eyes.

It was a strange sensation, to feel the nosta flash its heat inside her mouth. Stranger still that Sarra's confounding revelations were true, for Alizeh had not imagined Cyrus to be so forthcoming with his mother. And while she had no interest in defending the loathsome king, Alizeh was herself too well-acquainted with Iblees to deny the pressures of his influence. It seemed unreasonable to deny that Cyrus might be acting under extreme duress.

"To be fair," Alizeh said quietly, "the devil has ways of tricking even the smartest among us. And I'm sure you know that the only way to withdraw from a deal with Iblees is, at minimum, to forfeit your life in exchange. Cyrus would have to willingly die should he wish to walk away."

"One might counter," Sarra said sharply, "that the best course of action would've been to never make a deal with the devil in the first place. Iblees approaches every newly crowned sovereign with the bait of a disadvantageous bargain; Cyrus has known this his whole life, and he was forearmed to face it—to walk away from such temptations as all others did before him." She shook her head. "His excuses have grown tedious in the retelling, my dear, and my patience has worn thin."

The woman's anger surprised her.

Alizeh studied the lady framed in the doorway: her flashing eyes, her pursed lips, the tension she carried in her shoulders.

Rather than being comforted by the woman's fury, Alizeh found the conversation alarming. Sarra railed against her son, condemning him for his actions and demands—even as she fulfilled them. Alizeh had sympathy enough to imagine why Sarra might *stay* in the palace; perhaps she remained on principle, not wanting to be forced out of her own home— or maybe Cyrus had taken control of her assets, leaving her with nowhere to run. Having experienced it herself, Alizeh could not recommend destitution as a worthy alternative to a warm bed.

No, it was not that Alizeh lacked insight to understand the difficulty of the woman's situation; it was the matter of Sarra's inconstancy that scared her—that insisted something was amiss. These rooms, after all, were by Sarra's own admission a result of her efforts; the wardrobes stocked with gorgeous garments were evidence of orders executed.

How could she rage against her son while doing his bidding? How could she not see that by building Alizeh this beautiful prison, she was complicit in her son's crimes?

Still, there was some comfort to be derived from the woman's company, for Sarra had proven that she was not a liar. As promised, the pain in Alizeh's wounds had begun to subside and, finally, she unclenched; she allowed her body to float a moment in the warm water, her hair surging against her face, dark tendrils like tentacles streaking across the foamy surface.

Carefully, Alizeh reached for a bar of soap set neatly in a cove above her eye line and began lathering her aching limbs. Her head soon filled with the decadent scent of star jasmine. "Why did you come to me?" she asked, glancing at Sarra. "Why did you think we could form an alliance?"

Sarra studied her, saying nothing for a long moment. "You're certain you don't want to marry my son?"

Alizeh returned her assessing gaze. "You doubt me?"

"I am not blind to the beauty of my own child," she said, arching a brow. "There are thousands of young women across

Tulan who would marry him in a trice. It might shock you to hear it, but he has quite a dedicated army of admirers. They don't yet know about you, of course—but they'll be very sorry, indeed, when your betrothal is announced."

"There will be no such announcement," Alizeh said angrily, "as I will not be marrying him. Why are you even telling me this? You think my opinion of your son might be swayed by the passing fancies of a deluded mob?"

"Not at all," Sarra said, rewarding her with a blinding smile. "You were tricked, as you said, into coming here. You told me yourself that you loathe him. You've already tried to kill him. And you proved in the first minutes of your arrival that you are both brave enough to stand up to him—and strong enough to challenge him. I have no expectation of you marrying my son."

Alizeh went uncommonly still.

Sarra was closing in on her, taking careful, measured steps into the room, and Alizeh couldn't shake a fear that she was being slowly outwitted—swindled, somehow, by the character she'd least suspected.

The problem was, she didn't know why.

Or how.

"What do you want from me?" Alizeh said, reaching for a nearby towel. She snapped open the cotton as she stood, somehow managing to protect her privacy while bandaging herself in its warmth, clinging to the cloth as if it were a suit of armor. "You vilify your son at great length, and yet I haven't heard you offer me an avenue of escape. If you hate him so, why will you not help me break free of him?"

"Because I need you," she said, retrieving a robe from a hidden cabinet, which she then offered to Alizeh. "Because we need each other."

"I need *nothing* from you," said Alizeh, even as she snatched the robe from Sarra's hands. She stepped out of the tub, her heavy curls dripping water everywhere. "But I see now that you, as with everyone else, seem to want something from me."

"I only want justice."

Alizeh scoffed at that, discreetly swapping her towel for the soft robe, which she tied, with angry motions, at her waist. "You remain complicit in my capture—and yet you expect me to trust that you have any idea of justice?"

"You and I are both captive here," Sarra said softly. "I only play my role differently than you."

"How can that be true?"

"You seem to forget, darling, that Cyrus killed my husband."

At that, Alizeh went still.

Very slowly she looked up, studying the woman before her as if for the first time.

Indeed, Alizeh had forgotten.

She'd heard the rumors of course; there'd been all kinds of stories about Cyrus the Ruthless, the child who'd murdered his own father for control of the crown. This news was as recent as several months ago; Alizeh had not yet arrived in Setar then, where the conversations surrounding the bloody exchange had no doubt been louder—but it had not mattered. The massive headlines had been plastered across the front page of every local paper for weeks on end, for the savage transfer of power had seemed ominous to all the world. If the young king was willing to murder his own father in the pursuit of glory, whose throne might he try to overturn next?

Well. They knew the answer to that now.

"It's not fashionable for a mother to hate her own son," Sarra said quietly. "No matter their ills and evils we are expected to go on loving them, forgiving them even when they mutate before our eyes into murderers."

"I'm so very sorry," Alizeh whispered.

Sarra canted her head. "When Cyrus killed my husband, I didn't believe it. Not at first, of course. I gave my child a chance to deny these horrors, to confess it had all been a terrible accident—or even to tell me he'd been framed. He did none of those things. Instead, Cyrus looked me in the eye and told me he'd murdered his father—a man who'd loved him more than life—because he was unfit to be king. He showed no remorse. He did not regret his actions."

Horrified, Alizeh clapped a hand over her mouth.

"One day," the woman said softly, "Cyrus was my son. The next day he was not."

"Why do you stay?" Alizeh asked, her hand falling away from her face, disbelief coloring her voice. "Does he threaten your life? Do you have nowhere else to go?"

"Motherhood is complicated," said Sarra, turning away. "In nearly every way, I have disowned him in my heart. I will never forgive him. I cannot love him. But I've learned that there are some things I can't bring myself to accomplish. In vain I've tried to do the deed myself, but I've found that this is the line I'm unable to cross." She met Alizeh's eyes then. "I need you to stay because I cannot do this on my own."

"I don't understand," Alizeh said, even as her heart pounded in her chest, her instincts screaming at her to keep quiet, to ask no further questions. "What can't you do on your own?"

"Kill him, darling. I need your help to kill him."

ELEVEN

یازده

THE SMELL OF WET STONE filled Kamran's head, the dark path before him illuminated by a series of torches affixed to the dank walls, their collective glow casting flickering shadows across the filthy stone floors underfoot, occasionally throwing into stark relief the scuttle of spiders fleeing the light. His footfalls echoed in the tall, narrowing passage, the sharp sounds and smells of his surroundings inspiring in him a deep dread and a desire to escape. Earlier he'd been in a hurry to get here, to finish this ugly business with Hazan and move forward with his life, but now he found he'd rather be anywhere else, anywhere but following the same circuitous path to the dungeons he'd walked just two nights prior—the dingy, dripping walls closing in on him as he went.

His grip tightened around the handle of the carpet bag.

Memories haunted him as he moved, his emotions clouded, complicated. Two days ago his grandfather was still alive; two days ago they'd walked this track together, and yet—it was one of his worst memories of the late king, who'd accused him that night of treason, and who'd been ready to lock him in the dungeon, threatening to behead him if he resisted the sentence.

A single day his grandfather had been dead, and of all the

better memories they'd shared, *this* was the recollection that besieged him.

It was a tragedy of the current chaos that Kamran hadn't been afforded more than minutes to mourn the loss of King Zaal. He'd been unable, as a result, to sort out his feelings about the man. He wished someone might simply tell him how to feel, or at least teach him to make sense of the unspeakable horrors his grandfather had committed.

How was Kamran meant to condemn someone who'd debased himself in the interest of his own protection? How, when he'd known eighteen years of love and devotion from his grandfather, was he supposed to compartmentalize his feelings now, when his mind was battered by grief, when he lacked the tools necessary to hack apart the chambers of his heart? Was it possible, he wondered, to love and detest a parent simultaneously?

As a child his convictions had been stronger; the world had seemed simpler, his opinions more absolute. He'd thought with age and experience his ideas of the world would grow only more certain; instead, the opposite had proven true.

The more he lived—the more he endured—the more convinced Kamran became that he knew nothing at all.

It was impossible to unbraid the many pains and horrors tangled in his head just then; impossible when his trek was nearly at an end, when the dungeons and the lone young man trapped within them were now nearly in sight. It was humbling, indeed, to realize that the last time he'd walked this path he'd lacked the perspective to understand that his problems had been minuscule—even as they'd loomed so large.

What he wouldn't give to turn back time now.

Kamran strode past the guards stationed at the mouth of the main chamber, all of whom shouted something he didn't bother hearing. In one hand Kamran clutched Alizeh's modest carpet bag; in the other, a small, sealed jam jar, the thin lid of which he'd speared several times with his mother's dagger, poking holes so the insect inside might be able to breathe in its confinement.

Finally, he came upon the man in question.

The dim outline of Hazan's body was legible through the wrought iron bars of his cage: his back rested against a filthy wall, his long legs outstretched in front of him, his face obscured. Hazan's head hung low over his chest, a mop of dirty-blond hair occasionally glinting in the tremble of firelight. His former minister moved not an inch, not even when a fleet of guards followed Kamran into the chamber, falling to their knees at his feet as they encouraged him, breathlessly, to leave the inmate alone.

"We didn't know he was a Jinn, sire—he's already destroyed two of the other cells—

"Took twelve of us to restrain him—"

"He's been violent, Your Highness, you shouldn't be alone with him—"

"We had to knock him senseless—"

"Put him in shackles, made specially for his kind, but he's like a beast, out of his mind—"

"Unbelievably strong one, sire—best if you let us deal with him—"

"*Get out*," Kamran said, his voice like thunder. "All of you.

I can handle him just fine."

The cluster of guards froze, stood upright in unison, bowed en masse, and rushed out the door, which closed with a violent clang behind them. Only when he was sure they were alone did Kamran draw closer to the rusted bars of the cell.

"Hazan," Kamran said into the silence. "Look at me."

He did not.

"Hazan," Kamran said again, this time angrily. "I bid you rise."

Without lifting his head, Hazan said, "With all due offense, sire, please fuck off."

Shock provoked Kamran to make a sound, something like a laugh. He'd never heard Hazan use foul language, and somehow it only fed his curiosity.

It seemed Hazan had been hiding a great many things about himself; and Kamran, who suddenly had numerous questions for his old friend, made no preamble.

"Why did you never tell me you were a Jinn?" he asked.

"I thought it none of your concern."

"None of my concern? We've known each other since childhood, and you didn't think I had a right to know that your loyalty, all this time, was to another empire? To another sovereign? You didn't think it was my concern that my home minister was only biding his time, using me, no doubt, to feed information to his people, hoping to one day lead an insurrection?"

"No."

Kamran almost smiled. There was nothing to celebrate

here, and yet he felt strangely invigorated. All pretenses between he and Hazan had evaporated; stripped of the deference his rank once demanded of their interactions, Hazan had betrayed more about his true self in the last minutes—and in his time in the dungeon overnight—than he had in a decade.

There was something fascinating about the discovery: this irate, belligerent, devil-may-care iteration of his former minister was somehow refreshing. Hazan was neither afraid of him, nor was he invested any longer in the maintenance of his good temper. They met now as equals—if not in status, then in emotional aptitude and physical prowess. Though why this revelation offered Kamran any measure of comfort, he could not articulate into words.

He only felt the rise of an inexplicable relief.

Kamran had realized the truth about Hazan's heritage only when Miss Huda had earlier identified the insect as a firefly; Kamran was not entirely ignorant of Jinn history—he knew what their fireflies meant to them—and he was grateful for that education now. Had he not been able to piece together Hazan's motivations for dissembling, he might never have been inspired to imagine a more complex explanation for the young man's crimes. The possibility that Hazan had been loyal only to *Alizeh*, and not Cyrus—well, that changed everything.

"I have your pet," he said.

Hazan straightened at that, studying Kamran with a wariness that said he didn't believe him. "My *pet?*"

Kamran held up the jam jar for inspection, elevating the

container to Hazan's eye line. Upon sighting him, the dispir-
ited insect took flight with a terrible frenzy, flinging itself
desperately against its prison, its abdomen illuminating at
intervals, the small body striking the glass with a series of
dull, steady pings.

"Will you attempt to deny that this belongs to you?"

It was a while before Hazan said, reluctantly, "No."

"I assume you want to keep it."

By way of response, Hazan only sighed. He tilted his head
back against the wall, crossed his arms against his chest. The
tense line of his mouth all but screamed an unspoken irritation.

"It's not an *it*," he said darkly. "It's a *her*."

"And I will give her back to you after you've answered my
questions."

Hazan shot him a bleak look. "You think too highly of my
relationship with an insect if you think I'd divulge sensitive
information for so small a reward."

"I see. So you wouldn't mind if I were to crush her under
my boot."

"You wouldn't."

"I would."

Hazan shook his head, turned away. "You really would,
wouldn't you? You faithless rotter."

Kamran's expression was grave. "Hazan," he said. "I need
to know what you did for her."

"Why?" Hazan laughed bitterly. "Lost her again, have
you?"

"Yes."

Hazan looked up at that, a ghost of a real smile grazing his lips. "Then you've delivered me joyous news indeed. I'm quite ready to hang now, for I may die peacefully knowing she's escaped."

"I need to know what you did for her," the prince said again, this time angrily. "Did you intend for her to overtake my throne?"

"*Overtake your throne?*" Hazan said, his eyes incredulous. "Overtake the throne of the largest empire in the world, you mean? She and what army?"

"So you did not intend for her to attain power?"

"To what end do you interrogate me now?" Hazan scowled. "You thought I'd attempt to resurrect an old empire? To sentence my own people to death by inciting a war they lack the numbers to win? An innocent young woman was being actively hunted by your grandfather for the terrible crime of *existing*, lest you forget. I wanted only to situate her somewhere safe, somewhere far from the reach of mercenaries. She has no interest in overthrowing you, in any case. She is a tenderhearted young woman who wishes only to be left alone."

Kamran clenched his jaw. "There, you are mistaken."

Hazan went silent, taking a moment to study the prince with renewed curiosity. "You flaming idiot," he said. "Don't tell me you've had a change of heart in the wake of your grandfather's death? After I had to endure the hours of you moaning on and on about saving her, you've now decided to fulfill the man's final wishes and lop off her head?"

Kamran flinched.

That Hazan had been able to read him so easily was a disconcerting revelation, one he didn't know how to digest.

"If you think I will tell you anything about her," Hazan said darkly, "you are quite deluded. Now either kill me or fuck off."

"Hazan."

"*What?*"

"She is betrothed to him."

"Who?" Hazan appeared distracted, staring intently at the carpet bag still clutched in Kamran's hand. "Betrothed to whom?"

"The girl. She is betrothed to Cyrus."

Hazan's head lifted sharply at that, his eyes fathomless, dark as pitch. "*Cyrus?* You refer to the sentient piece of human excrement responsible for murdering our Diviners? The man she accused of being a monster just before striking across the face?"

"The very one."

Now Hazan looked murderous. "What is your game? Do you slander her hoping I might be inspired to kill you, spare you the mess you've made of your own life?"

"Upon my honor, I swear it to be true," Kamran said sharply. "Cyrus told me himself that they would soon marry. She escaped the ball last night on the back of a Tulanian dragon. No doubt they are together now."

Hazan unfolded his body slowly, rising to his full height before stepping forward, the orange glow of torchlight gilding the lines of his face, emphasizing the broken slope of his nose. Hazan studied Kamran with a familiarity the latter had always taken for granted. Fifteen years they'd known each other and never had Kamran realized the value of his old friend, who'd been the closest thing he'd ever had to a brother.

"Your face," Hazan whispered. "The magic has changed."

"Yes."

Hazan closed his eyes a moment, drew a deep breath. "And has no one spoken of it? Have they not come for you yet?"

"What do you mean? Who would come for me?"

"The Diviners," he said quietly, before meeting the prince's eyes. "You are in danger, Kamran."

"You know what it means, then?" Kamran felt his pulse pick up. "You know why the magic has changed?"

"Yes."

"Will you not tell me?"

"First, make one thing clear to me right now." Hazan drew away from the bars and began to pace. "Have you come here to kill me, or to make me a deal? Because if I'm going to die anyway, I fail to see the point in assisting you."

"I need you to live."

Hazan stopped moving.

"I sentenced you to death," Kamran explained, "because I thought your alliance with the girl meant you were conspiring with the Tulanian empire. I thought you assisted in my grandfather's murder, in the assassination of the Diviners. I assumed you were trying to overthrow the crown, and that you were working in tandem with the Tulanian king."

"I suppose I should be flattered you thought me so

enterprising," Hazan said coldly.

"I see now," Kamran went on, "that your entirely inde-
pendent acts of stupidity managed to become entangled in
this chaotic web, and I was only this morning able to discern the disparate role you played. I don't have to condone
your actions to understand them—and I still think you're an
unalloyed bastard for lying to me—but I can appreciate the
instinct you felt to spare her; for I, too, felt the same instinct,
as you well recall."

"Then you *are* offering me a deal."

"I need your mind, Hazan. I need whatever knowledge
you have about the girl. I know you feel immense loyalty
to her—I realize you find yourself in this dungeon precisely
because you pledged your life to her—but she's deceived us
both, and I fear we will only understand why when it is far
too late."

"You want to wage war against Tulan."

"I do."

"And you are asking me to assist you in murdering the
young woman who is meant to be the salvation of my people."

"I am."

Hazan stepped closer to the door of his cage, wrapping
his hands around the iron bars. His eyes flashed with fury. "I
would sooner die."

Kamran leveled Hazan with a glare of his own, rage sim-
mering too close to the surface. With impressive control he
managed to say, quietly: "She is working with the devil."

Hazan froze. He fell back a step, his hands releasing the

iron bars, his face going slack.

"What?" he breathed.

"You weren't there. You didn't hear them speak. She has a formidable ally in the Tulanian king, yes—but her biggest supporter is Iblees."

"That's impossible," said Hazan. "Iblees is responsible for the ruin of our entire civilization— She would never—"

"Think of all that has happened since she entered our lives, Hazan. It is just as the prophecy foretold—the Diviners are dead; my grandfather is dead; Ardunia is unprotected—"

"And your face," Hazan said, seeming to surprise himself as he spoke. "The magic has changed."

"How is that connected to this?"

The former minister was silent too long. He was staring into the distance, his eyes vacant.

Lost.

"The distortion of the magic," Hazan said finally. "It means your right to the crown is no longer absolute. It means there might live a worthier inheritor of the throne."

Kamran felt his heart rate spike. It was with great equanimity that he managed to say: "So she intends to take my empire."

"She will not need to," Hazan said, dragging a hand down his face. "As if the nobles didn't have enough reason to deem you unfit to rule—they are no doubt assembling a halo of Diviners from across the empire as we speak. They'll want a validation of the magic, which you will not receive, and once you're declared an uncertain heir, they will oust you from the palace. If you do not take swift action now—"

"Then you agree I have no choice—I *must* kill her—"

"No," Hazan said, cutting him off. "There are other ways. But if you're going to accept my help, you will also accept my judgment on this matter. *I* will be the one to decide whether she has betrayed her people—which means you will not disturb a hair on her head unless I give you leave to do so."

Hazan lifted his shackled hands, and in one swift movement, tore the iron manacles apart. He used his teeth to pry the cuffs off his wrists, after which he tossed the metal to the floor, where it landed with a heavy clatter.

And then he ripped the prison door off its hinges.

He set the iron gate against the wall before crossing the threshold, where he met the prince eye-to-eye.

Kamran, to his credit, showed no surprise.

"All this time you could've walked free," he said, staring steadily at his friend. "Why let the guards think they'd subdued you? You couldn't have known I would come."

"I didn't," Hazan said quietly. "I fought the guards because they treated me like an animal, and when they realized I was Jinn, their behavior toward me grew only more reprehensible. I remained here because I thought I deserved to die, for I thought I'd failed her. Now I've learned I must live, if only long enough to understand what's happening."

Kamran was quiet for some time, absorbing this. "It's astonishing," he said finally, "how long you managed to hide your true self from me. I always suspected you were holding back; I never realized how much."

"And are you horrified," he said, "to discover the truth?"

"No. I think I prefer the real Hazan."

"I fear you might regret saying that," he said, even as he almost smiled. "Be warned, Kamran. The terms of our agreement are nonnegotiable. Lift a finger against her prematurely and I won't hesitate to kill you myself."

TWELVE

دوازده

ALIZEH WATCHED AS A SMALL bee landed atop a lavender bush, the chosen sprig swaying under its buzzing weight. Birds chirped and tittered all around her, for the most part unseen from their assorted perches upon assorted branches, their cheerful songs never ceasing long enough to allow a moment of silence. The breeze was warm, the sun divine upon her skin, the heat of it filtering through her airy dress.

Though Sarra had selected a wealth of gorgeous articles for Alizeh, she'd not known the girl's measurements, and as a result, most of the pieces were ill-fitting and would have to be altered. There were, however, a few in her size, alongside a wide array of undergarments of various dimensions available to her, and she'd been happy indeed to don fresh, clean things before finally stepping into the comfort of a soft, tissue-thin gown with long sleeves, hoping to protect the healing wounds along her left arm. She'd chosen an ivory number, the ethereal layers of chiffon offset by a weighty collar forged from a single gold cable that circled her neck and shoulders in cascading orbits, the precious metal halting its revolutions just below her breastbone. The neckband obscured an otherwise scandalously low neckline, where the delicate fabric crisscrossed firmly around the bodice before nipping in at her waist, below which it billowed out into a full skirt that fluttered in the wind.

Her hair she'd tied up in her usual style, a mass of glossy curls pinned haphazardly atop her head. It was Sarra who'd insisted she choose something from the prearranged allotment of jewels, and the options were so stunning it had taken little indeed to convince Alizeh to do so. Still, she'd chosen to wear only a simple circlet in her hair: three whisper-thin gold bands hammered into a fine crown, a rainbow assortment of gems embedded throughout.

Alizeh glittered as she moved, as she pushed through the double doors that led to the lush green path she'd discovered upon arrival. It felt good to be clean, to reset.

With the exception of her magical ball gown, it had been many years since Alizeh had worn anything but the drab, serviceable garb of a servant, and despite the tragic circumstances, she was immensely grateful for the finery. Always she'd appreciated an artfully woven garment, but there was an even greater pleasure to be derived from the textile itself; here, at least, her gowns would be fashioned from cloth so fine they'd never chafe or itch, never leave angry marks where the coarse seams scraped painfully against her skin during endless hours of labor. In a situation so bereft of mercies, she clung to this small gift, let it feed her starving heart.

Alizeh sighed, taking a sip from the cup of hot tea she'd carried with her into the garden.

Earlier, Sarra had summoned a servant to deliver a tray of comestibles and an assortment of beverages, and Alizeh, who'd gratefully drunk her fill of water, had been surprised to discover that here, too, the servants wore snodas—masks of tulle that wrapped around the eyes and nose, softly blurring the wearer's features without impeding necessary vision. She'd been unable to look away from the young man who'd appeared, wraith-like, at the door; Alizeh had been too mesmerized by the reminder of who she herself used to be, by how much in her life had changed in so short a time. As a servant Alizeh had always been grateful for her snoda—for the anonymity it provided—but she'd never forget how cruelly her caste had been treated, nor the injustices they were forced to endure. Alizeh had whispered hello to the young snoda when he'd arrived, had offered him an encouraging smile; the boy had made a frightful sound in response, nearly dropping the tray as he hastened to set it down.

After that, Sarra had given Alizeh leave to rest.

The older woman had reasoned that if Alizeh stayed in her rooms, Cyrus would grow anxious to check on her, for he awaited her downstairs with great anticipation. Alizeh should wait for him to come to her, Sarra had said, whereupon she should take advantage of the private moment—away from the wide eyes and perked ears of watching servants—to tell Cyrus she'd had a change of heart and to accept his proposal.

Thinking it over now, Alizeh felt a bit sick.

It had been with a shocking reluctance that she'd agreed to Sarra's morbid arrangement. Shocking, because, as Cyrus had so boldly accused Alizeh earlier, she'd indeed been threatening to murder him for hours. That Alizeh vacillated at all about killing him now was strange, for it should not have been so difficult a choice to make, certainly not under the current circumstances.

Still, had Alizeh decided to follow through with murdering the loathsome king under her own advisement, she'd never doubt the decision, for she trusted her judgment. But there was something about being *asked* to do it—something about being all but *threatened* to do it by decree of the young man's mother—

It unnerved her.

Something about it didn't sit right, and yet, by her own admission, Alizeh thought Cyrus a terrible, hateful king. His list of crimes was long and foul; she need not hesitate now, not because his mother had asked her rather aggressively to do what she'd already been planning to do anyway.

No, surely not.

If she killed Cyrus, she'd be free.

She might flee; Kamran might be safe; the world might be spared another needless, bloody war; and she might yet wriggle out of the devil's grip. Sarra had not lied when she'd made the girl a series of promises—Alizeh had the nosta to prove that—so why had the entire business left her so uneasy?

Alizeh's mind was muddled.

She needed to assemble herself—to prepare for a tactical maneuver that would make her deeply uncomfortable—for Sarra had assured her that the easiest path to a man's murder was not forged with a weapon, but with unimpeachable kindness.

"Forgive me, darling, but you'll never best him in battle," she'd said sympathetically. "I shouldn't try it, if I were you."

Alizeh had protested at that, preparing to defend her many strengths, but Sarra only lifted a hand dismissively.

"Oh, I'm sure you're quite capable. Noble, too. My son, on the other hand, will not fight fair. He's been studying sorcery and divination since he was old enough to toddle. He's exceedingly clever, rather deceptively strong, and lacks a basic standard of virtue. He's also very, very angry, and suspicious to a fault. He trusts no one. He won't take even a sip of water without having a servant taste it before him." She'd looked Alizeh over. "Your unchecked anger makes you a clear threat, my dear, and for as long as you persist in this attitude, Cyrus will remain on guard.

"We must approach this from a position of strength," Sarra had said firmly, "and I believe your greatest strength might be something unexpectedly quiet. Convince him you *genuinely* wish to marry him, and once he ceases to suspect you of standing against him, you might then poison him over breakfast."

Alizeh had raised her eyebrows. She understood well the extenuating circumstances, but it was still hard to believe Sarra could discuss her son's murder with such nonchalance.

"Or, you know, anything, really," Sarra had gone on, misunderstanding the look on Alizeh's face. "You don't have to use poison. There are a number of ways to do it, all of which we can sort out after you've convinced him you mean no harm. This is the most important step, and we must get it right."

Oh, it was too much.

Alizeh briefly closed her eyes now, rubbing at the tightness growing at the base of her neck. She sat down heavily at the table positioned just under the shade of a bower, her

brows pulled together in frustration. Her head and heart felt
heavy, her worries mounting.

She was trapped in a foreign land, charged with a strange
task by a strange woman. It seemed all who met Alizeh possessed ulterior motives, whether to maim or manipulate or
lie. Kamran, too, cherished as he was by her, had been dis-
honest from the start; and while of course she understood
his reasons, it troubled her nonetheless that even the posi-
tive relationships in her life—Omid and Miss Huda and even
Deen, the apothecarist, among them—had all been born in
some manner of unkindness.

Alizeh was grateful for the good in her life, really she was,
but sometimes she longed for a joy undiluted; she wanted
to know what it was to smile unhampered by darkness, to
laugh without knowing the drumbeat of pain, to see friends
without the shadow of uncertainty.

What was uncomplicated happiness?

She dearly wished to know.

In all the years since her parents had died, there had been
only one soul who, from start to finish, had been truly in her
corner.

Hazan.

From the moment they'd met, Hazan had been steadfast,
and now he was dead.

The sudden heat in her eyes surprised her, even as the
need to release this pain seemed somehow inevitable. She
made a terrible sound, clapping a hand over her mouth to
stifle the sob even as tears fell fast down her face. With
shaking fingers she swiped at her cheeks, thinking of how

Hazan had given up his life in the unmitigated pursuit of her protection, had taken chances for her without even knowing whether she was worthy. Even now she benefited from his generosity, the nosta having proven over and over to be the greatest gift she'd ever received, for without its guidance she'd have been well and truly lost.

She sniffed and sent up a whisper of gratitude, wishing, as she struggled to fight back another wave of tears, that she'd had the chance to thank him while he was still alive.

Hazan had *believed* in her.

He'd offered up a blind faith in all that she was meant to be, in the queen her blood had crowned her, in the salvation promised her people—and in all that she'd never achieved.

Were there others, Alizeh wondered, who lived with the hope that she might save them? And if so, did she not owe it to them to give up her life in the unmitigated pursuit of *their* protection?

How she wished her parents were still alive.

If only they were here to help her, to show her the way. More than anything, Alizeh found she wanted two things simultaneously: to go into a deep hibernation from which she might never emerge; and to rise up and become all that her people had ever hoped for. The problem with the latter option was both simple and tragic.

She didn't know how.

It was a general ignorance of the path she was meant to follow that had forced her into hiding in the first place. Prior to her eighteenth birthday—the event having occurred only several months ago—the power she'd been promised wouldn't have even opened to her, and now that she'd finally come of age, she couldn't access that which was hers. Five souls had to be willing to die for her before the magic would even reveal itself, and prior to that she'd have to *find* the glorious substance, the location of which was a lost secret. All she knew was that the volatile minerals were buried deep in the Arya mountains of Ardunia—and the only object that might've helped her pinpoint the precise location was now gone.

When the fire had destroyed her family home and killed her mother, she'd managed to save her parent's handkerchief, which she'd tucked into the protection of her fireproof fist. Nothing else appeared to have survived; metals and gold had been mutilated, all else had been reduced to ash. And yet, the morning after the horrific event, she'd seen a slim volume glinting in the rays of a rising sun, beckoning her close even as her heart shattered in her chest.

It was no book she'd ever seen before.

This one object had endured the blaze entirely on its own; and, much like Alizeh herself, the object in question had proven impervious to fire. Alizeh had known, unequivocally, that the book was meant for her. It had seemed to *beckon* her.

She'd approached the gleaming hardback cautiously, understanding even then that her parents must've hidden it from her on purpose. Alizeh had been but thirteen when her world had gone up in flames, and though her mother and father had by then told her who she was meant to be—had prepared her in so many other ways for the role—they hadn't wanted to burden her in childhood with the weight of every truth. They'd told her their intentions, that they meant to withhold certain information so that she might enjoy her youth awhile longer. They'd promised to tell her everything when she came of age, at eighteen.

They'd never had the chance.

In their absence all these years, that enigmatic book had been her only guide. It was a tattered, unspectacular object that didn't draw attention to itself, but which was quietly magicked; it offered what appeared to be but the first clue in a cryptic puzzle, one Alizeh had long ago memorized, but as yet had been unable to decipher. Still, she'd clung to this small offering, protecting the enchanted volume as best as a destitute servant was able to protect their few possessions. Not until this moment had Alizeh allowed herself to think about the misplacement of her carpet bag, the important artifacts of her entire life lost, no doubt forever. That she'd lost her mother's handkerchief was hard enough, but this . . .

It was yet another blow, another devastation.

Alizeh wiped again at her damp face, clutching the cup of tea like a lifeline. She'd left the drink untouched for so long it was likely cold now, but she didn't mind. Flowering vines released a heavenly fragrance into the air around her and she did her utmost to focus on the delicious scent, closing her eyes as she steadied her breathing, taking a sip of the luke-warm tea and savoring it.

"You changed."

Alizeh startled so badly she spilled the drink down the front of her clean white dress, gasping as the liquid soaked through the thin fabric, cold tea dripping steadily down her chest.

She shot to her feet in a fury.

Cyrus, on the other hand, was sitting calmly in the chair across from her, his iconic black hat nowhere in sight. His eyes shone a bright, mesmerizing blue against the golden warmth of his skin, the waves of his coppery hair glinting in errant streaks of sun, the resultant sheen making the locks seem almost metallic. He was infuriatingly beautiful, and she nearly threw her teacup at him.

"You absolute heathen," she cried. "Why did you not *knock—*"

"I did," he said, and spoke his next words slowly, as if she were a child. "But you couldn't have heard, because you were sitting all the way out here."

Alizeh's grip tightened around the empty glass in her hand. "And it didn't occur to you that perhaps I wished to be alone?"

"No." He tilted his head, a strange little smile touching his lips. "My mother told me you were waiting for me. She said you wished to speak with me on a matter of great importance."

Alizeh had to close her eyes then, pressing her lips firmly shut lest she say something brutal about Cyrus's family and ruin this new, kinder approach she was meant to take. Sarra was proving to be a real trial, and Alizeh thought she might hate them both.

"Forgive me," said Cyrus quietly, "but do you intend to make it a habit of wearing transparent garments in my presence? Do tell me now, I beg you, so that I might blind myself in anticipation."

Alizeh opened her eyes, a quiet rage building in her chest even as her battered dignity demanded she blush. "How dare you," she whispered.

"It's only that I can see straight through the front of your dress," he said, gesturing vaguely at her body. "And I'm beginning to see that this is a pattern with you."

It demanded everything of her self-control not to clobber him over the head with her teacup. Alizeh welcomed the feeling, stowing it away as ammunition for the unsavory task of murdering him at a more opportune time. She summoned all that Sarra had said to her, reminding herself that this madman had killed his own father, murdered a team of Diviners, slaughtered the king of Ardunia, and heavens knew what else; he'd likely committed any number of truly heinous acts.

Alizeh presented all this as evidence to her unshrinking mind, assuring herself quite firmly that she ought to be afraid of Cyrus. She ought to treat him with the utmost caution, not shout at him as if he were some mutton-headed boy, for he was in fact a powerful, forbidding king that might lop off her head with little inducement.

And yet.

Even as she scolded herself, she failed then to *feel* the terror the situation demanded.

The problem was, she did not feel unequal to him.

It was perhaps a dangerous conviction, but Alizeh felt quite certain she could manage him. Too, Cyrus did not strike her then as truly monstrous, which should've been alarming in and of itself, but it was hard to maintain such a position when she failed to feel fear in his presence. None of this made sense, of course—for when she listed his evils in her head, he cut a truly despicable character.

It was possible, she allowed, that the excruciating events of the last twenty-four hours had irreparably addled her mind.

In any case, her task was to kill Cyrus, quite literally, with kindness—a stratagem that, however distasteful, might save her *and* spare innocent lives by avoiding a bloody war. This tactic would not work if she allowed herself to be so easily riled by him; and if she did not cease these childish, angry reactions to every minor provocation, she would no doubt live to regret it.

So she smiled.

She sat back down in her wet dress, dropped an elbow onto the table, her cheek into her hand, and smiled. She put a great deal into the effort, too, recalling her happiest memories until the smile was no longer forced, but genuine.

"No," she said politely, all trace of anger gone from her voice. "I do not intend to make it a habit. And I'm glad you've come. There's a great deal we must discuss."

Cyrus did not hide his surprise.

She thought he might look away from her unbridled smile; instead he studied her with visible fascination, turning fully in his seat to face her. He said nothing even as his eyes fairly glimmered with mirth, watching her for so long she nearly gave up the effort, all the while ignoring the way her heart reacted to the full force of his attentions. It was impossible to deny: there was something physically potent about Cyrus, a powerful presence he carried with him into every moment. He looked at her then with a focus so complete she felt she might buckle under its weight, and tried not to think about why her breaths seemed to come a bit faster, her heart pounding a bit harder when his lashes lowered, his gaze falling to her lips for a moment too long.

She felt trapped.

"Alizeh," he said softly. "Have you been a wicked girl?"

Abruptly she drew away from the table and hugged herself, her wet gown chilling her anew in the breeze.

"No," she said too quickly, realizing that, in fact, she might've underestimated the southern king.

Never averting his eyes, Cyrus mirrored her earlier movements. He dropped an elbow onto the table, his cheek into his hand, and blinded her with a smile so sincere it unsettled her, inciting an unexpected, detestable flutter of feeling in her chest.

"No?" he said, still smiling.

Not trusting herself to speak, she shook her head.

"God, you're so beautiful," he said, his smile vanishing. "Even when you lie to me."

His admission awoke a flare of heat in her veins, a reaction she didn't understand and was afraid to analyze. She knew not why he'd say such a thing to her, nor why his words had made any impact, and she didn't want to think on it. She knew only that Cyrus's eyes had darkened with an emotion she was afraid to name; and she had no idea what he was going to say next.

She was realizing she never did.

Cyrus stood up suddenly, stepped closer, towered over her. He all but blotted out the light with his height, casting her in shadow, causing her to shiver in the absence of the sun.

He touched her then, shocking her with a tenderness she wasn't expecting, tracing the line of her jaw so lightly her lips parted on a sudden breath.

She couldn't seem to move.

Her body had betrayed her. *Her body had betrayed her,* even as her mind screamed.

"Wicked girl," he whispered. "You've been making deals with my mother."

THIRTEEN

سیذده

"YOU GAVE MY JOB TO the *child*?"

Hazan threw open the door to the war room with an unchecked anger that was beginning to feel familiar. The former minister had bathed and changed; he'd not been imprisoned long enough to have lost his rooms and belongings, so it was with some efficiency that he was able to return to a semblance of normal.

With one great exception.

"Omid saved my life," Kamran said without looking up. He sat in the war room alone, drinking tea as he paged through a fresh stack of reports from the different reaches of the empire.

"Yes, so you said. Though I'd not realized he'd relieved you of your good sense in the process."

"Did you know," Kamran said, lifting a sheaf of paper as he scanned it, "that in recent months there've been a dozen reports of unexplained avalanches—in three different mountain ranges across the empire?"

Hazan ignored this as he strode into the room, slamming the door shut behind him. "You hired an uneducated twelve-year-old to succeed me, and you expect me not to take offense? As if my job were so simple—and I, so easily replaced?"

Kamran put down the papers. "Do you not think it strange?"

"*Strange* is too gentle a word—I think it verifiably crackbrained—"

"Not the situation with the child, you fool, the unexplained rockslides." Again, Kamran glanced at the report. "Four in the last month alone, though our troops have found nary a trace of explosives. By all accounts, the occurrences— in the Istanez, Pouneh, and Sutoon mountains—are random disturbances of nature, which I was happy enough to accept until this morning, when, just as I was contemplating the astonishing devolution of my life," he said with a wry smile, "two more were reported. With the recent inrush of Tulanian spies I can't help but wonder whether there's more to this than we previously considered. Perhaps they've been hiding out in the mountains, making a bit of a mess in the process; perhaps there've been other rockfalls in more remote regions with no witnesses—making the real number much higher. What do you think?"

"I think you're a righteous ass."

"Throw a fit if you like," Kamran said, setting the papers aside to take another drink of his tea. "But I'm not firing the boy. In the last several hours he's already proven quite capable."

"Capable?" Hazan's eyes widened. "Capable of what? Snatching purses? Emptying out the treasure houses? Have you even thought to make certain your gold is still there?"

"I will allow," said Kamran, lightly clearing his throat, "that I was perhaps not entirely in my right mind when I made the decision. Still, I would argue that your judgments of the child are too reductive; in my estimation, Omid has proven a great deal less conniving than the members of our own parliament. The nobles of the Seven Houses will likely never change, but with proper guidance, the boy might yet make something of himself."

"And I? What am I meant to make of myself?"

"I intend to confer knighthood upon you."

Hazan scoffed in anger, preparing to argue—when he realized, with a visible shock, that Kamran had spoken in earnest.

"You wish to make me a knight?" he said, stunned. "But I'm not even a soldier."

"I have proof enough of your valor, Hazan."

The former minister fell back, fell silent. He stared for a moment at the floor as a rare heat burned across his cheek-bones, the tips of his ears.

"And I have full confidence," Kamran said, returning to his papers, "in your ability to storm a battlefield."

"You are not yet king." Hazan looked up, his tone still betraying a stubborn skepticism. "Do you even have the power to do such a thing?"

"Are you trying to offend me?" said Kamran, a shadow of a smile touching his lips. "I've always possessed such a power. Though as imminent heir to an empty throne, I do have more authority now than I did yesterday, and I find I'm eager to exercise these rights before they're taken away."

"And what does that entail?"

"First, I must tell you that you were right," Kamran said,

rising from his chair. "In your absence I learned that the nobles have already assembled a new royal court of Diviners, who should be arriving steadily throughout the day. The last of them will be here by nightfall. They are to stay here at the palace while their rooms are readied at the Diviners Quarters; they won't be leaving until after all the funerals take place over the next couple of days."

"Zahhak told you this?"

Kamran's eyes narrowed. "Zahhak wouldn't tell me if a sword were inches from my throat. He still thinks me an ignorant child unworthy of my father's throne."

"A shame, isn't it? That you've never given him reason to think otherwise."

"Shut up, Hazan."

Hazan only smiled.

"The lords of the Seven Houses did all this in relative secrecy," Kamran went on. "I only found out from Jamsheed, who needed my sign-off on the repairs for the palace, and who wished to express aloud his pleasure that the protections around the empire would be back in place as soon as our quorum of Diviners had fully settled. You will also be fascinated to hear that Jamsheed, our dear palace butler, is better informed than I on more than one salient issue, for when I asked him whether he'd seen my mother, he rather cheerfully told me she'd be home in a matter of days."

Hazan blinked. "But— Your mother has fled the palace? When? Not after she buried her dagger in your arm?"

"Impeccable timing on her part. I'm afraid she has a fantastically warped idea of what constitutes maternal affection."

"And you don't know where she's gone?"

"I haven't the faintest. When I asked, Jamsheed claimed she'd gone to fetch me a gift in honor of my impending coronation." Kamran then raised his eyebrows at Hazan.

Hazan mirrored the expression. "A vial of poison, then?"

"My thoughts exactly," said the prince, a reluctant smile tugging at his lips. "It really is a great comfort to me that you are not dead this morning, Hazan."

"It is a great comfort to me as well, sire," Hazan said drily.

Kamran began stacking his papers, moving things aside to make room on the table, and though his smile diminished, it did not fade altogether. His life was falling apart at the seams, but he'd managed to prove wrong his mother's last ominous words. If Zahhak were to have his way, Kamran might never haunt the halls of this palace again—but at least, wherever he landed, he would not walk alone. He'd come to the stunning realization that he'd rather be falling apart with friends, than living a decadent life of isolation.

"Whatever my mother's gone to do," he went on, "I cannot begin to imagine, for the turns of her mind are impossible to predict. The only thing I know for certain is that she will be sorry indeed to return, for upon arrival she will discover the palace is no longer her home. I've concluded I have at most a day before the Houses cobble together reason enough to strip me of my title, and less than a week before Zahhak usurps my throne. Which means we must work quickly."

"*We?*" Hazan balked. "You and I are meant to save the Ardunian empire all alone, then? And where is the child who stole my job?"

"The child is occupied."

"With what?"

"Bringing me witnesses."

"*What for,* you exasperating halfwit?" Hazan threw up his hands. "Are you so incapable of anticipating that I might want more than the paltry, monosyllabic responses you serve?"

"Heavens, you sound almost hungry."

Hazan sighed, searching the room as if for patience. "Do you know," he said finally, "it's just occurred to me that I no longer have to pretend to own an appetite at regular intervals. A small but rather delightful gain of all this perfidy, for I find eating meals an exhausting waste of time."

Kamran raised his eyebrows. "Speaking of Jinn I don't understand," he said, reaching underneath the large table and unearthing the forgotten carpet bag. "I take it you know who this belongs to."

The prince dropped the luggage onto a newly cleared section of the polished wood, still managing to send papers scattering in the process.

Hazan only stared at him.

"In the dungeons earlier," Kamran explained. "I saw you studying it, as if it looked familiar to you."

Hesitantly, Hazan said, "I'm not certain of the owner. I have only an unsubstantiated theory."

"Go on."

"I think it belongs to Alizeh."

Kamran gripped the table, anticipating pain, and instead he felt only a gentle heat, a flutter in his chest, a heavenly fragrance filling his head. He hadn't realized he'd squeezed his eyes shut until he forced them open and was met with a look of astonishment on Hazan's face.

Slowly, Kamran released the table. "How," he said, clearing his throat, "do you know it belongs to her?"

Hazan only gaped at him. "What just happened to you?"

"Nothing." He sighed. "I don't know. Just don't say her name again."

"Who? Alizeh?"

"*Bastard*," Kamran muttered as renewed feeling lanced through him, birdsong filling his head, a warm, not unpleasant sensation sparking along the disfigured lines of his neck, his cheek, his changed eye. "You did that on purpose."

"I swear I didn't," said Hazan quietly, studying Kamran closely now. "I don't understand. You can't hear her name without experiencing . . . what? Pain?"

The feeling was slowly abating, and Kamran drew a steadying breath as he shook his head. "It's not always pain. I feel . . . different things each time, and it only started this morning. You don't happen to know what's wrong with me?"

"I'm afraid not," said Hazan, concern etching his forehead. "But if she has some kind of hold on you from so far away, only a powerful magic can be involved. I know little more than that."

Kamran fell silent, recalling the way he still felt when he thought of her—the way some chamber of his heart thrashed against his better judgment, demanding to see her, to speak with her despite everything—and could not help but agree.

He took a sharp breath. There was no use in thinking of their time together. If he thought too long about the tears she'd shed in his presence, the fears she'd exposed, the smiles she'd shared—

No.

Some baser part of his mind wanted desperately to find reasons to exonerate her, and he refused to be so weak. The only way to armor himself was to forget the brief moments they'd had; he refused to remember the softness of her lips; refused to recall the way she'd surrendered to his touch, the sound she'd made when he'd kissed her. She'd looked into his eyes like he was worth something, had touched him like he might be precious. Her soft curves had fit perfectly in his hands, against his body. He'd wanted to unravel her slowly, strip her down to nothing, press his face to her heated skin and live there, devour her. He'd never admit aloud that he'd done as much in his dreams, losing himself in her over and over, only to wake in a fevered, painful state of frustration. She had gouged a hole in him from which he feared he'd never recover. Not once in his life had he felt such a powerful attraction to anyone. He'd never even known a kiss was capable of such power.

"Kamran?"

"Yes." The single word was breathless.

"Where did you go?"

"Nowhere," he said unsteadily. He took another ragged breath, his body tense. When he looked up, he stared only at the wall. "Let us focus, for the moment, on the questions we *can* answer. How did you know this bag belonged to her?"

"I saw her carrying it," said Hazan, "the night she was to be murdered by the king."

That cleared Kamran's head in an instant.

He looked sharply at Hazan, his brows pulling together. "So my grandfather was right," he said. "She did have help. It was *you* who assisted her in defeating those ruffians."

"Not at all." Hazan laughed. "She did that entirely on her own. I only watched her from the shadows, waiting to intervene should she need assistance, which she never did." He shook his head. "Your grandfather was so convinced she'd had access to a complex arsenal, when in fact she'd murdered those men with little more than her own sewing supplies."

"These, you mean?" Kamran turned the bag on its side, dumping its contents in a contained scatter across the table. Among them was a small silky pillow and matching quilt; cases of pins and needles; scissors; spools of thread; salves and strips of linen from the apothecary; small bags containing various notions; gilded scrolls inviting her to the royal ball; a number of heavy, faded garments—

"Where did you get this?" Hazan said, dumbstruck. He stared at the table, then at Kamran, then back again. "How did you get your hands on her things?"

"Miss Huda delivered the luggage to me this morning."

"The daughter of the Lojjan ambassador?" Hazan frowned. "The screaming one from last night? With the candelabra?"

Kamran nodded. "She thought its contents might be helpful to me in my search." He relayed to Hazan the information Miss Huda had shared with him that morning: all about the magical shoes; the dress; how Cyrus had appeared as if from nowhere in her room at Follad Place; how he'd threatened to kill her before whisking them all away to the ball without notice, where Miss Huda had arrived terrified and without a voice. "Your queen left behind her bag by accident," Kamran said archly. "She hadn't time to take it with her."

Hazan, who'd gone silent during the explanation, was now frowning. "But I thought the two of them were on good terms. Why would Miss Huda wish to assist in the capture of her friend?"

"So you knew, then," said Kamran, irritated in a flash. "You knew she worked as a seamstress in addition to being a snoda?"

Hazan shot him an imperious look. "Naturally," he said. "When I learned of her existence, I uncovered all I could about her."

"And you didn't think to tell me?"

"As you will recall, sire, I was at the time withholding a great deal of information from you."

"For the love of God, Hazan," he said with a sigh. "Do cease being useless to me."

"I promise to consider it."

"Miss Huda only wants us to find the girl," Kamran pressed on, "because she thinks the Tulanian king might do something terrible. She claims to be worried about her."

Hazan raised his eyebrows. "I see I have an unexpected ally in Miss Huda, then."

Kamran wanted to make a quip, to name them allies only in idiocy, but he found he could not make his mouth form the necessary words. He'd never wanted to hate Alizeh, and he'd be lying if he said the collective opinions of those around him were not beginning to destabilize his convictions on the matter. Still, the evidence stacked against her was damning.

And confusing.

"Very little of note inside," he muttered. "I've already searched everything thrice, broken open the seams of the pillow and quilt, turned pockets inside out, studied even the most minuscule items for evidence . . . of anything." He looked up, his apprehension spiking as he spoke, recalling the many discrepancies in her character, her actions, the prophecy itself. "She doesn't own a single weapon."

"As I've already told you," Hazan said flatly. "She has no aspirations to topple any empire. What reason would she have to stockpile weapons?"

"The inconsistency is not lost on me, Hazan," he said quietly. "But then, there is something else, too."

From within the depths of the overturned bag, Kamran retrieved a slim, clothbound volume the rough size and shape of a novel, which he slid across the table, toward Hazan.

"What do you make of this?" said the prince.

The cloth cover was worn and faded; what was once a bright blue was now washed out, nearly gray. The blank pages were stiff and waterlogged, the book warped by time and moisture.

Hazan studied it without a word, looking grim about the mouth as he did, and when Kamran flipped the book over so his friend might read the inscription on the back, Hazan drew a sharp breath.

In faded gold letters, it read—

MELT THE ICE IN SALT

BRAID THE THRONES AT SEA

IN THIS WOVEN KINGDOM

CLAY AND FIRE SHALL BE

FOURTEEN

پچھارہ

ALIZEH REMEMBERED HERSELF A MOMENT too late, jerking away from Cyrus's hand with the shock that she'd allowed him to touch her at all. She studied him warily in the intervening silence, his eyes as startling as her own, her heart pounding in her chest with a delayed fear. Alizeh had been wrong; she could not manage him. She had been wrong, too, to underestimate him.

Always Cyrus seemed to be one step ahead of her, and somehow she knew it would not do to lie to him now, for he seemed preternaturally attuned to deception.

It made her wonder whether he owned a nosta, too.

"What did my mother convince you to do?" he said quietly, tilting his head as he took her in. "Did she ask you to kill me?"

Alizeh could hardly mask her astonishment.

The fact that he might guess at Sarra's dark, decidedly unnatural intentions was alarming, and crowded her head with only more confusion. How twisted was the tale of his family, and what was this trap she'd walked into? How many players were in this game?

"Or did you think," he said, impatience edging into his voice, "that I was unaware of my mother's barely concealed hatred for me?"

Oh, she'd been so sure of herself only moments ago, so certain she was not afraid of him.

She felt terrified now.

"*Alizeh.*"

"Yes," she said breathlessly. "I agreed to kill you in exchange for my freedom."

Something flashed in and out of his eyes at her admission, and she could've sworn it was something like pain. But then he took a sharp breath and straightened, his sardonic smile firmly back in place as he looked over her head, stared into the distance.

Alizeh took that opportunity to bolt.

She shot up from her chair and dashed down the path with supernatural speed, trying to form a plan as she went. She wasn't sure what purpose it might serve to flee, but she couldn't imagine he'd take kindly to her confession, and while she wasn't sure what he planned to do about it, she could only imagine his mind would resolve to do something bloody. If his mother was right about him—and it appeared that she was—and Alizeh would certainly lose to him in a fight of force—which she suspected she might—then she had no choice but to run.

"*Alizeh,*" he cried.

She barreled through the double doors that opened onto her bedroom, but only after slamming them shut did she discover they didn't lock, and in the moments she spent trying to bolt the blasted doors, she saw him fast closing the distance between them, his long legs carrying him along the grassy path at an impressive clip. She abandoned the door just as he tore it open; he was right behind her now, following as she darted uselessly through the serpentine space, preternatural swiftness proving useless to her as she turned in circles, realizing too late that she still didn't know the layout of this room well enough to locate the exit with efficiency.

"I'm not going to hurt you," he called out, frustrated. "How many times do I have to tell you that I *can't* kill you before you actually believe me?"

She halted at that, her crazed mind devouring the reminder as the nosta burned against her skin. It was no wonder she couldn't decide whether to fear him; it was obvious now why she wavered so much on the subject, why she struggled to feel danger in his presence. Her instincts were not addled; it was only that he'd been ordered by the devil not to harm her.

She had some kind of immunity.

Alizeh spun around, the movement so fast that Cyrus, who'd been chasing after her, didn't have time to process the change. He abruptly crashed into her, sending them both hurtling before they finally slammed together, him pinning her to the wall so hard she gasped, air leaving her lungs in a rush.

Alizeh froze.

She was trapped under the unexpected weight of him, the crush of his hard body, the column of his throat a mere inch from her mouth. His closeness was so overpowering it dulled her senses, slowed her mind. He was a heavy wall of heat, his dark, masculine scent overwhelming her, activating some ancient response that made her heart race. At least he, too, appeared stunned, and in the milliseconds during which their minds caught up to their bodies he'd lowered his eyes, nailing her in place with a look that liquefied her bones. She didn't know if what she felt in his presence was fear or anticipation, but either one seemed cause for concern. She only knew that the anger he conjured a moment later belied the hitch in his breath, the tremble in his body. She watched him swallow as he slowly drew away, his hands sliding off the wall where he'd planted them.

He moved back, but not nearly enough.

"I hate you," he whispered.

Alizeh blinked, her heart pounding too hard in her chest. "I know."

He leaned in then, his throat working, his gaze fixed entirely on her mouth. "I hate everything about you. Your eyes. Your lips. Your smile." His words grazed her skin when he said, softly, "I find your presence insufferable."

The nosta flared hot against her sternum.

"Okay," she said again, her pulse skyrocketing. "That's okay."

He was still breathing hard, his chest heaving between them. "But I'm not going to hurt you."

Again the nosta verified his words, and Alizeh felt some of the pressure ease in her lungs.

"Do you believe me?" he asked.

Alizeh nodded.

He was so close, his eyes so firmly fixed on her face that she wasn't sure she'd have noticed the surprise flit in and out of his features otherwise. It was clear he hadn't expected her to agree, to trust him. He couldn't have known that he'd been right to doubt her, for what she trusted was not him, but the nosta.

Still, a degree of tension seemed to leave his body, relief prompting him to finally step back. He looked shaken as he turned away, staring at the wall, the ceiling, the floor—anywhere but at her face.

When he met her eyes again, his were bright with unvarnished feeling.

"I need you," he said roughly. "Don't run away from me."

"How can you expect me not to run from you," said Alizeh, still trying to shake off her apprehension, "when you threatened just hours ago to have my eyes sewn shut?"

He looked sharply away from her then, a muscle jumping in his jaw. "I shouldn't have said that."

"And then you threw me off a cliff," she said, her voice a bit breathless even to her own ears.

"You wouldn't stop threatening to kill me," he said angrily, turning back to face her. "I was merely trying to change the subject."

"By having me devoured by dragons?" she nearly cried.

Cyrus scoffed at that, arching a brow. "You were never devoured by dragons."

"I was, too," she shot back. "Your little joke resulted in some nasty bites all along my left side. Your mother was kind enough to mix me a medicinal bath."

Cyrus studied her then with an inscrutable expression. She thought he might demand to see proof of her injuries, but he said only, "Dragons are gentle creatures. They don't bite unless provoked."

"Well," said Alizeh, averting her eyes. She was feeling pet-
ulant, and there was only so much eye contact with Cyrus
she could handle. "I don't think the animal *meant* to bite me.
But I was rolled onto its back teeth with rather gruesome
results."

She felt, rather than saw Cyrus go suddenly still, and for
the length of a wild, charged moment she thought he might
do something unhinged, like apologize.

Instead, he said, "You seem well enough now."

"I'm fine," she said, irritated.

"Good."

"And I'm not sorry," she added bitterly, turning to face
him. "I'm not sorry I made a deal with your mother to murder you."

His lips twitched, his eyes flashing. "I'm not sorry I threw
you off a cliff."

"Excellent," she said, matching his anger.

He only smiled in response.

Alizeh tried to steady herself, to calm her chaotic heart.
She didn't know what was happening here, between them,
but whatever it was, it was making her wary. She and Cyrus
were no longer speaking to each other like mortal enemies;
instead, they were tolerating each other with an ounce of
civility. It was almost as if they'd—inadvertently—initiated
a reluctant truce.

She didn't trust it.

Still, she was beginning to believe there had to be more
to Cyrus than the stories she'd heard—than even the horrors
his mother had described—for it was becoming clearer by the

minute that he was a character more complicated than she'd expected. She studied him as he began to pace, as he dragged a hand through his hair, mussing the copper locks in a show of agitation, and was forced to wonder why someone so young and intelligent and capable—someone who, by his mother's own admission, had grown up beloved by his parents, and had the beauty of Tulan and its people at his disposal—

"Cyrus," she said suddenly.

He halted at once, meeting her eyes.

"Why, exactly, did you make a deal with the devil?"

Cyrus blinked slowly, visibly thrown by her question. "I thought you didn't care," he said. "I thought you said I was *no doubt suffering the consequences of my own sins.*"

"And are you not?"

This, he didn't answer, not at first. He seemed to be assessing her, deciding whether she was worth an honest response before he said, quietly, "I was desperate. And stupid."

The nosta agreed with this, and Alizeh took a tentative step closer. "Why were you desperate?"

Cyrus laughed, but there was an ache in it, a tension in his smile, in the lines of his body. He locked eyes with her, holding her entirely in his thrall before he said, in a softly lilting voice—

"Should you choose to tell her why, you'll only ruin all my fun. Soon thereafter you shall die, bit by bit and both are done."

Alizeh felt the grip of a familiar terror. "Iblees," she breathed.

"Yes," he said quietly.

"What does he mean—*bit by bit and both are done?*"

Cyrus only shook his head.

"Right," Alizeh said, wringing her hands. "You can't say."

She searched the room then with a vague panic, as if it might offer her answers. Alizeh understood too well how awful it was to be trapped by the devil, and her intimate knowledge of such a situation inspired in her a begrudging commiseration. Cyrus's actions were being choreographed by a master planner; he was but a useful puppet in a larger scheme. The difference was, Cyrus had *summoned* the beast into his life, while Alizeh had only ever been a luckless victim. No doubt some weakness of the flesh had prompted Cyrus to bring these tortures upon himself; she could only imagine what he'd wanted in exchange.

His pains, she reminded herself, were not her problem.

His mess was *not* hers to manage.

"I realize," she said calmly, "that you're in a terrible predicament. I think I can understand why you need me. And while I empathize—more than I'd like—with your situation, I cannot and will not wittingly become a pawn in the plans of the devil. He is the most abhorrent of living beings, and personally responsible for the ruination of my people—for the pain they continue to endure today. I've spent my entire life trying to outrun his abiding interest in me, and I don't intend to stop now.

"And while, yes, you might need me," she went on, "I feel it necessary to point out here that I require nothing from you. I derive no benefit from helping you; only harm."

"What if"—he took a deep, measured breath—"what if I made it worth your while?"

"What? How?"

"My mother offered you a deal, which you accepted," he said. "I'll offer you a better one."

She gaped at him. "You're asking me to double-cross your mother? Heavens, but you're a very strange family."

"Marry me," Cyrus said, a spark of heat in his eyes. "Become my queen just long enough to sate the devil's demands. Once he's satisfied, he'll discharge me of a tremendous debt, and I'll be that much closer to my freedom. When I'm finally free, I give you leave to kill me at your leisure and take Tulan for yourself."

Alizeh stiffened, disbelief roaring through her, even as the nosta burned hot against her chest.

"You can't be serious," she breathed.

"My kingdom," he said softly. "For your hand."

FIFTEEN

پانزده

"DO YOU KNOW WHAT IT means?" Kamran asked.

Hazan shook his head. He picked up the book with a reverence evident in his eyes, his hands, in the stillness of his features. Carefully he flipped through its blank pages, then studied the cover with his fingers, searching its skin for something—

"There," he said softly, pressing down on something along the spine. "Just there."

"What is it?"

"A faint embossing," he said. "It's a symbol. Quite old."

Kamran took the book in his own hands, searching the spine. When he found the mark in question, he frowned. It was the outline of two triangles side by side and interlocked—a third triangle forming where they overlapped—with a single, wavy line underscoring it all. "What does it mean?"

"*Arya.*"

Kamran froze, then slowly lifted his head, meeting Hazan's eyes. "Like the mountain range? In the north?"

Hazan nodded, his eyes inscrutable. "Have you ever been?"

"No."

"It's brutal up there. Blistering cold like you've never experienced and a snowfall that never ceases, reducing visibility

near to nothing. It was the home of my ancestors," Hazan
said quietly. "It was where the Jinn built their first kingdom
after the fall of Iblees. It's been whispered among us that the
Arya mountains hold a powerful magic accessible only by
the true sovereign of the land—but most think it's only an
old story, for no one in documented history has ever found
evidence of such a magic."

"And you?" Kamran tensed as he studied his friend. "Do
you think it's an old story?"

Hazan hesitated, taking a breath before saying, softly:
"No."

Kamran dropped the book on the table, watching it land
with a dull thud. "Heavens," he whispered. "*That's* what
they've been doing here. All these Tulanian spies. All these
months." He shook his head, looked up. "I was wrong, Hazan.
War will not solve our problem with Tulan. In fact, I'm start-
ing to think it will make things worse."

"How do you figure that?"

Kamran briefly squeezed his eyes shut, muttered a foul
word under his breath. "Because," he said, "it seems so obvious now that war is what they want. All this time, they've
been goading us."

"I don't follow your logic. Why would they goad us into
war? If they want war, they might launch a preemptive strike
of their own—"

"If they were to invade our borders," Kamran said, frustrated, "they'd be fighting us on our own land. An ant
challenging a lion to a duel. Ardunia is enormous, our bases
spread generously across the empire, our soldiers numbering

in the hundreds of thousands. It'd be a suicide mission."

Hazan visibly tensed, understanding dawning in his eyes. "But if we were to engage in a land war on their territory—"

"Exactly," said Kamran. "Our soldiers would be compelled to leave their posts. Ardunia's forces would be fractured; our priorities rearranged, our troops diverted, our empire far less guarded as a result. Tulan would take full advantage of our distraction to plunder the Arya mountains at their leisure, striking us where we'd least expect it. They'd sustain great losses in the process, but if this magic you speak of truly exists, their reward would be great indeed. Several thousand lives lost in exchange for untold, unknown magical power? It would certainly be worthwhile to someone like Cyrus."

Hazan looked a bit shellshocked.

"All these recent offenses"—Kamran shook his head— "Hazan, you know as well as I do that neither of our empires is allowed to use destructive magic at the border—and in all our years of discord with Tulan, they've respected this, never breaking the Nix convention. But during the last water journey our ship was nearly overturned upon impact with a magical barrier. This alone should've been cause for retaliation, but despite my protests our officials would not see reason—"

"Yes," said Hazan drily. "I can imagine how they struggled to see your point when you convoluted the issue by insulting them, suggesting that our exchanges with Tulan had become as familiar to them as their own *bowel movements*—"

Kamran silenced Hazan with a dark look, choosing to ignore this proof of his recent stupidity. "In the last two years," he said instead, "we've detained sixty-five Tulanian spies, more than half of whom we intercepted in the last eight months alone. But spies have been infiltrating our borders for centuries. Did they suddenly forget the definition of stealth? Why would they be so sloppy now? It's almost as if they *wanted* to get caught."

Hazan took on a shrewd look. "And then, of course, there is the small matter of your grandfather."

"Precisely," Kamran said, his own eyes narrowing. "It was you who pointed out that never, in all these years of peacetime, had a Tulanian king accepted an invitation to one of our balls."

Hazan drew a deep breath, releasing it slowly before he said, "It goes without saying that killing and disgracing the sovereign of a neighboring empire are grounds for immediate retaliation."

"And yet." A muscle ticked in Kamran's jaw. "Our officials continue to hesitate."

"It doesn't compute."

"Hazan," said the prince. "I smell a rat."

"A rat?" Hazan looked up, surprised. "But wouldn't a rat aim to fulfill Tulan's desires? If, as you posit, Tulan is goading us into war, would not the guilty official have pounced eagerly upon any one of these opportunities to strike back?"

Kamran hesitated. "Maybe our rat is awaiting new intelligence."

"Who? Zahhak?"

"I don't . . . know," Kamran said, his focus drifting as he remembered something his grandfather had told him just yesterday—he couldn't believe it was yesterday. But Zaal had confessed to putting off war with Tulan all these years only for *Kamran's* benefit, to spare him the loss of another parent, an immature ascension to the throne, a childhood forged in war.

But the late king was also the first to confirm—despite the reticence of all the other nobles—that war with Tulan was absolute. It was in fact one of the last things King Zaal had said to the prince.

War is coming, he'd whispered.

It has been a long time coming. I only hope I've not left you unprepared to face it.

Kamran found his nerves would not settle after that; some unspoken unease had come alive in his body like a warning, as if the last of his grandfather's betrayals had yet to reveal itself.

"I'm not sure," Hazan was saying, his steady voice pulling the prince free of his reverie. "I'd like to believe Zahhak is a rat—he fairly looks like one—but I've also known him too long. He's been brutally loyal to Ardunia for decades." He paused, his brows pulling together. "When did you say we began to intercept the bulk of the spies? Several months ago?"

Kamran took a sharp breath, regrouped, and nodded. "I was on a tour of duty the first time we brought a cluster in for questioning. It was fairly unprecedented to capture so many at once, and we'd foolishly congratulated ourselves on a job well done. This was seven, eight months ago—"

"Cyrus took the throne eight months ago."

The prince's jaw clenched. "You think they were under his orders to be captured? Or do you think Cyrus has been doing reconnaissance?"

"Both. The other rockfalls you've been reading about—perhaps they were distractions. Decoys to divert our attention from their true aim." Hazan shook his head. "Perhaps Cyrus was deluded enough to think he'd be recognized as the true sovereign of the land, that Arya would open its arms to him. But if he's spent months searching the mountains with no success, it follows that he'd then seek out someone who might be able to possess it—and if the stories are true, there's only one person alive for whom the Arya mountains will give up its secrets."

"The lost queen of Arya," Kamran whispered.

Hazan stilled. "Where did you hear that?"

"She told me," Kamran said, remembering. "She said her name was Alizeh of Saam, daughter of Siavosh and Kiana. That I might know her better as the lost queen of Arya."

Hazan took a step closer, studying Kamran now with a renewed focus. "Why would she tell you that?"

"Because I asked her. I'd wanted to know her name."

"Was this when you went to Baz House? When you were meant to search her rooms—and claimed you'd found them empty?"

Kamran, who was perturbed by the look on Hazan's face, considered lying but didn't see the point. "Yes," he said.

"Angels above," Hazan said quietly, horror awakening in his eyes. "You kissed her, didn't you?"

Kamran felt uneasy now. "Why does that matter?"

Hazan turned sharply away, pressed the heels of his hands to his eyes. *"How can you not understand?"* he all but exploded as he spun around. "She is the hope of an entire civilization—she is not some girl to be trifled with, to pass the hours on a dull day—"

"You misunderstand me," Kamran said sharply, "if you think I ever—"

"I should call you out right now, you arrogant bastard, for treating her so poorly—that you'd ever dally with her and discard her—"

"I did *not* dally with her—"

"You speak of killing her!"

"I would've married her," Kamran cried.

Hazan stiffened at that, his features frozen in a strange shock. "You lie."

Kamran laughed, laughed like he'd lost all reason. "I only wish I were. I wish I felt nothing for her. I wish I could rip this useless organ out of my chest for all the trouble it's caused me. I was so deluded—so disgustingly besotted—I even named her as a possible bride to my grandfather. I had the gall to propose as my queen the young woman *prophesied to be his downfall*, and he nearly chopped off my head in response.

"I'd asked her to give me hope, Hazan. I asked her to wait for me. It was *she* who didn't want me, who didn't want to be with me. I never trifled with her. If she'd given me even a little encouragement I would've laid down my life for her— happily, I would've made her my queen, I—"

"Wait."

"No— You accuse me without evidence—"

"I said *wait*," Hazan cried angrily.

"What on earth for?" Kamran shouted back.

"Just—shut up a moment." Hazan swiped the book from the table, scanning the inscription on the back once again. When he looked up, he appeared confused. "Maybe," he said, his frown deepening, "maybe you *are* supposed to marry her."

"What?" Kamran blinked; his anger vanished; his heart wrenched in his chest. "What do you mean?"

"*Braid the thrones*, it says." Hazan studied the book again, touching his fingers to the embossed letters. "This is a clear message to the chosen sovereign. The last Jinn kingdom existed a millennia ago, and the empire comprised only Jinn; it was a purely homogeneous contingent for a number of reasons, namely in the interest of our safety. But here"—he tapped the book—"this message is both evident and unprecedented. She's not meant to lead the Jinn in an isolated empire—she's meant to braid us all together. *In this woven kingdom, clay and fire shall be.*"

"That may well be true," Kamran said, still struggling to calm his racing pulse, to quash the hope blossoming inside him. "But you're thinking of the wrong thrones. You forget that she is betrothed to the Tulanian king."

Hazan pushed a hand through his hair. "I cannot accept that," he said, frustrated. "You've leveled accusations against her that do not withstand reason. She would never betray her people. She would never accept assistance from Iblees. And she would *never* agree to marry Cyrus."

"You don't actually know her, Hazan," Kamran said

quietly. "You only know who you want her to be."

Hazan swallowed. "Well, then," he said. "There's only one way to have our questions answered."

"What's that?"

"We go to Tulan."

SIXTEEN

شانزده

"WHAT ON EARTH," SHE SAID, blinking, "could be worth both your life *and* your kingdom?"

"Alizeh," said Cyrus quietly, and for a moment he looked quite desperate. "Please."

Oh, she was not made of stone.

She was not unaffected by the sound of his voice nor the tragedy in his eyes. She understood, rationally, that Cyrus was a shameless brute, but she also knew the devil too well to dismiss the terror that accompanied his whispers, the way his riddles pierced a soul and lingered, clawing at a mind until one could think of nothing else.

She couldn't help it; she pitied him.

"Cyrus," she said, shaking her head. "What am I to do with your kingdom?"

A flicker of irritation animated his features. "You might do the obvious thing and fulfill your destiny. You are meant to lead your people, are you not?"

"Yes," she said, subdued. "In theory."

"Well, if you take my kingdom, you might put that theory into practice," he said. "You saw our fireflies— You must realize that Tulan is home to one of the largest populations of Jinn. Our numbers aren't huge, but it could be the start of something."

"But isn't that exactly what the devil wants?"

"Isn't it what *you* want?" he countered. "As far as I can tell, you've never bartered with Iblees, so any power you attain will be yours to do with what you will. He can only manipulate you through the will and actions of others."

"As he is now," she said wryly. "Through *you*."

"Right. Well." Cyrus cleared his throat. "I'm afraid the devil's wishes are a great deal more complex than this, in any case."

"And I suspect you're not allowed to tell me more?"

He laughed; the sound was bleak. "I will only say that arranging our unhappy marriage is but a fraction of what I've been commanded to do, and yet it's the scheme he cares most about. He wants me to help you attain power first and foremost, and I'd be surprised indeed if he isn't making deals with other unsuspecting fools, tethering their freedom to your ascension much as he has with mine. I pity them all," he said sullenly. "Dealing with you has been the simplest and by far the most punishing of all his demands."

"*By far the most punishing?*" Alizeh echoed, almost smiling. "Come now, you don't really find me that unbearable."

"You think I exaggerate?" he said tersely. "Being forced into your company ranks high on the list of the most abhorrent experiences I've ever had."

The nosta flared hot at that, and Alizeh was thrown by the heft of the insult. "You really mean that," she said, astonished. "But what crimes have I committed to earn your unyielding censure?"

"Are you giving me permission to insult you?"

She felt a flash of anger. "I didn't realize you needed permission."

"Alizeh," he said, his expression both grave and impatient. "Do you have any idea how many people would leap at the opportunity to overtake my kingdom and kill me? Your hesitation is unnerving."

"But what if I don't want to kill you? What if I can't bring myself to do it?"

"What on earth would prevent you?" he shot back. "My overwhelming charm and charisma? You've been so eager to off me all this time, but now, suddenly, when I *ask* you to do the godforsaken deed, you refuse to take direction?"

"Heavens. You talk almost as if you want to die."

"And you would judge me?" He took an alarming step closer. "For relishing an exit from this brutal consciousness we call life?"

"Not really," she answered honestly, inching backward. On more than one bleak occasion she, too, had wished for a fast finish to her life—for an escape from the agonies that oppressed her—but she'd never dreamed of saying so out loud, much less to another person. "But you're terribly morbid."

"I fear your presence inspires me."

Alizeh's anger sharpened; she was growing tired of his childish jabs at her pride. "If you're so keen to die," she said, "why not let the devil do it?"

"Oh, I don't know," he said, attempting a smile. "I watched you kill five mercenaries with an assortment of sewing supplies. I think I prefer your creativity."

"Wait— What?" She blinked, alarm awakening her pulse, which fluttered fast now against her throat. "You were there?"

"I was there to protect the devil's darling," said Cyrus, his eyes darkening. "Clearly, he underestimated you."

"But—if you'd seen me," she said, her mind buzzing, "why did you later mistake me for Miss Huda?"

At the mention of Miss Huda, Cyrus's expression soured only further. "You were always wearing your snoda," he said. "And I never saw you in daylight. I stood watch that night, but only from afar. Had I been able to get closer without exposing myself, I might've been able to better hear the scandalous whispers of your next assignation; but then, I saw enough of your meeting with *Hazan* to piece together the more unsavory aspects of your life."

Alizeh was too astonished—too outraged—even to speak.

"Tell me one thing," Cyrus said bitterly. "Just how many men do you have wrapped around your finger?"

"None," she breathed, shaking her head. "Why—*why* do you continue to misjudge me? Why would you assume the worst of me based on a single scene you witnessed without context—"

"You stunning little hypocrite," he said angrily, "I might ask you the same question."

She looked up at him then, rendered briefly speechless, for she knew not how to respond. It was true: most of what she knew of Cyrus—even the shocking tale of his father's murder—had been pieced together entirely by hearsay and speculation. It was just that so many people seemed to agree that he was a vile person, and the story of his rise to king was so incontrovertibly horrific that she—

Alizeh hesitated, then frowned.

"Wait," she said suddenly. "Cyrus, you murdered your own father for your crown."

His face cleared of expression at that, his eyes going vacant and cold. "That wasn't a question," he said.

"You committed patricide," she went on, "in the pursuit of domination and glory, for control of a formidable empire. You went to such lengths for power! It couldn't have been a small thing to kill your own parent. So why would you then toss your spoils at my feet, as if your title means nothing to you?"

Cyrus visibly swallowed. It was a long moment before he said: "I'm quite desperate."

The nosta warmed at this, but Alizeh's irritation only intensified. "No," she said, shaking her head. "It doesn't follow reason. There's something you haven't told me."

"There are all kinds of things I haven't told you."

"What kinds of things?"

"Oh, I don't know," he mused. "I didn't say a word until I was three years old. I don't like eggplant. And you have a single little freckle in the hollow at the base of your throat."

Alizeh clasped a hand involuntarily against her neck, almost surprised when her fingers met with the heavy gold collar of her dress, which all but obscured her throat from view. "How did you know that?"

"I have eyes," he said flatly.

"You're lying to me."

"About my eyes? I assure you, they're quite firmly affixed to my skull."

"Cyrus—"

"Even if I *could*— You think I'd tell you, of all people, my sorrows?" he said, turning away. He sounded suddenly bored. "Did you think I brought you here against your will because I was in want of a sympathetic ear?"

"No."

He looked up at her, a strange emotion flitting across his face. "No," he echoed softly. "And you should take care to remember that. Should you marry me, it would be in title only. I have no interest in your companionship."

The nosta went cold.

Alizeh fought both her shock and the impulse to flinch against the icy spark, her heart thrumming in her chest as she held Cyrus's gaze, her alarm escalating. Was he lying about having no interest in her companionship? Or was he lying about their marriage being in title only?

"You won't"—she swallowed—"that is, we won't— I mean, it's understood, isn't it, that in the off chance I agree to this arrangement, there won't be any physical aspect to the relationship—"

"No," he said sharply. "I won't touch you."

The nosta warmed.

Breathing a little easier, she said, "Very good. But there's still one thing I *must* know. Before I can make any decision, you must tell me, once and for all—"

"Ah, here we are," he said darkly. "I was wondering when you'd bring this up again. You want to know whether I've killed your melancholy king."

"Why do you continue to press this point? He's not *mine*."

"I have a hard time believing that."

"Truly, he isn't," she said, irritated. "It was— What transpired between us was so brief, and we never— That is, he did try to make me some promises, but it was never clear, really, and I did tell him that it couldn't—that he and I—"

"Never mind." Cyrus cut her off. "I don't care to know the dizzying particulars of your relationship with the idiot heir of Ardunia."

This made her angry. "What reason could *you* possibly have to malign *him*, when you're the cretin who barged into his home and killed his grandfather?"

His eyebrows went high. "Don't say you mourn the loss of the heinous King Zaal?"

"Oh, just answer the question, you infuriating fool—"

"Which question? About whether he's dead, or why I hate him?"

"I don't care if you hate him," she said. "I only want to know whether he's alive."

"And will you cry," Cyrus said quietly, "if I tell you he's not?"

Alizeh felt the blood drain from her face at that, horror forcing her voice to a whisper. "Did you kill him?"

"No."

At the flash of heat from the nosta, Alizeh nearly lost her footing. She closed her eyes and drew a deep, shuddering breath, involuntarily clasping a hand to her chest. Her eyes pricked with feeling and she fought it, not recognizing until just that moment how much tension she'd been holding in her body—nor how much hope she'd held that Kamran might still be alive. Only then did she see how thoroughly she'd compartmentalized her feelings on the subject.

"I must say, I find your reaction shocking," said Cyrus, who affected a look of surprise. "It's hard to believe you truly cared for him when you were all the while going behind his back with his home minister."

"Hazan is my *friend*, you terrible halfwit!" she cried, and then looked sharply away, emotion threatening to disorder her. "Was my friend. Hazan *was* my friend."

"I warn you," said Cyrus. "If you weep, I might vomit."

Alizeh managed a watery laugh even as her heart broke, as the nosta warmed, as her vanity was wounded. The reminder of Hazan—of his sacrifice for her—made her think of her own resolution to step out of the dark, to rise up and be more for all the others who'd maintained a silent faith in her.

After all, she'd been born for this.

She'd been raised from infancy to lead her people, to free them from the half-lives they'd been forced to live, to fight against the injustices they'd been served for so long.

She wondered then, in a moment of inspiration, what her parents would say—and when she heard a responding whisper in her heart, she felt closer to an answer.

She looked up, studying Cyrus with a renewed appreciation. "You will willingly die? Cede the throne?"

"Only," he said sharply, "after the devil releases me from my arrangement."

"And how long will that take?"

"I don't know."

Alizeh took a steadying breath, and considered him a moment. "Cyrus, there's something I still don't understand."

"What?" he said with disdain.

"If you're so unafraid of death, why does it matter what the devil wants you to do? Why suffer under his command, carrying out his orders, only to be murdered regardless?"

Cyrus's cold expression grew somehow icier. It was a long moment before he said, finally, "I must die on my own terms."

"Why?"

He smiled, and there was anger in it. "If you're unable to imagine why I can't risk an untimely death," he said, "then you, like all others, have built your understanding of me upon a faulty foundation."

"What nonsense." Alizeh felt a flash of irritation. "Are you being intentionally cryptic?"

"Yes."

"Oh." Her irritation vanished. "Because of Iblees?"

"There's precious little I can say on this matter," he said with a swift shake of his head. "So I will say only this: if I'm careful with my life now, it's because I must live long enough to accomplish something crucial. Beyond that, my beating heart is of no consequence." He hesitated. "You have no idea what's at stake. My life is the least of it."

The nosta warmed at this admission, and Alizeh felt a spike of fear.

"I see," she said softly. "So you mean to imply that you act now not in your own self-interest but for the benefit of other—"

"*Do not speculate.*" He cut her off, his voice taking on a note of panic. "Do not theorize out loud."

"Okay," she said, and swallowed. "All right."

Heavens. This confusing web grew only more tangled by the moment. Alizeh could not then even wonder at what might be motivating Cyrus's actions. She didn't know enough about his life, his weaknesses, or his wants to hazard a guess.

"You appear to be in quite a predicament," she said quietly. "Will you not tell me what you received in exchange for your bargain with the devil?"

He laughed in response, but the sound was soulless.

"I will take that as a no," she said, and frowned.

Cyrus sighed. "And I take it you will not accept the terms of my offer."

She lifted her head, meeting his heated eyes. "No," she said. "But I can promise you this: I will sincerely consider it."

Cyrus went briefly still.

Relief hit him slowly, then suddenly, so much so that he looked as if he'd been knocked back a step. He closed his eyes as he exhaled, reaching unsteadily for the wall to support his weight.

"Thank you," he whispered. "Thank you."

"I've not promised you anything yet," she said, approaching him with some caution. When still he didn't move, she gently prodded his chest with one finger. "You shouldn't be so pleased."

Cyrus opened his eyes, and for the first time since she'd met him, he looked almost happy. It turned back time on his face, made him look more youthful. His eyes were bluer, brighter. He smiled, and it was real.

She had to fight the urge to smile back.

"Come with me," he said, straightening, and held out his hand.

Alizeh eyed his outstretched hand warily, biting her lip as she hesitated. "Why? Are you going to throw me off a cliff again?"

"Maybe later," he said lightly.

"Then what?"

"I thought you might like to see Tulan."

SEVENTEEN

هفده

"WAIT— WHERE ARE YOU GOING?"

Hazan charged after the prince, who'd bolted out the door of the war room without warning and was then striding down the hall clutching the strange book with a speed indicative of only one of two things: eagerness or anger.

Kamran wasn't sure which he felt more powerfully.

That they would go to Tulan *now*—that he might evade the tedious political route, circumvent the fruitless, circular discussions of the nobles who'd no doubt spend days, if not weeks, debating the merits and demerits of waging war—

This was astonishing to him.

He'd never considered that there might be benefits to the current, nightmarish state of his life.

Kamran had grown so accustomed to the shackles of royalty and the endless rigamarole that defined their international affairs that he'd not realized what freedom he might possess in the wake of all this recent personal devastation. If he were stripped of a title, if he continued to be sidelined by Zahhak, if the nobles refused to include him in their discussions— Well, then, he might become his own master.

He would go to Tulan as a man, not a prince.

He would avenge his grandfather's murder on a personal mission, not an order. He would finally, after eighteen years of unfailing service to the crown, do whatever he damned well pleased.

Oh, he had plans for Cyrus.

He would not merely kill the young man—he would first destroy him. He would make the southern king pray for death, and only then would he be merciful, fulfilling Cyrus's wishes by driving a blade through his heart.

"Kamran, you *ass*— Wait—"

As was his wont, the prince did not wait. Only when Hazan had caught up to him did he answer his friend's question—but quietly, so they wouldn't be overheard—

"There are an untold number of things we must do before we can leave," said Kamran, "and if we don't start now, we'll never make it in time."

"In time?" Hazan stared at the prince. "In time for what?"

"I don't know. I only feel that we're going to be late."

"Kamran, I'm going to ask you something, and I want you to know that I ask it sincerely—"

"What?"

"Have you lost your mind?"

The prince laughed at that, the sound hollow. "I lost my mind the moment I met her, Hazan, and you were there to witness my fall from reason, so don't feign surprise now."

"I swear, sometimes you scare me."

"Sometimes, Hazan, I scare myself." Kamran continued moving at a steady clip, even as he glanced down at the book in his hands. "We'll set sail tonight, at midnight, under the cover of darkness."

"Sail?" Hazan's eyes widened, nearly missing a step as he

kept pace. "You mean to enter Tulan via the Mashti River? We might not survive such a journey in daylight, much less—"

"Our dragons are under heavy guard in Fesht province," Kamran said, "which you know as well as I do is a month's journey by coach. I can't summon the beasts without drawing unwanted attention, and there's no faster way to get to Tulan. Our fleet, however, have the benefit of being bolstered by magic; water journeys often take months, not only because of the amount of work required at every stage but also because of the immense cargo we haul. Without the added weight of metric tons of water, we'll move much faster—and by the time anyone notices our absence in the morning, we'll be gone. I've done enough water journeys to know the way well enough; and I can sail any ship myself. So long as we avoid major delays or turbulent weather, we might be able to clear the distance in under a week."

Hazan fell silent at that, even as his eyes were troubled. "Very well," he said finally. "What will you tell the boy?"

"Omid?" Kamran frowned. "Nothing. The fewer people who know of our whereabouts, the better."

"And why must we keep our journey a secret?"

"Because I'd rather they didn't know where to find me."

"Who?" Hazan said, brows furrowing. "I didn't realize you were being hunted."

"No, but I soon will be." Kamran rounded the corner and rushed up the grand marble staircase, the staccato knock of his boots echoing in the massive hall. "I intend to empty out the treasure houses before we go, and I'd rather not leave an

easily followed trail, else the nobles will sort out my execution with impressive speed."

"Wait"—Hazan hurried up the stairs alongside him—
"what need do you have of the treasure houses?"

"Gold. Weapons. Horses." Kamran came to an abrupt stop
at the landing and turned sharply to face Hazan. "This task
I leave to you: open our stores while we still have access and
take a great deal more than you think we'll require. If I'm to
be ousted from the palace, I'll need a place to land upon our
return. Find us somewhere safe—purchase property from an
unsuspecting farmer if you must—then organize a team of
the finest riders and fighters, and compensate them hand-
somely for a period of six months. We will require our own
armed force."

"Tell me you jest."

"You are more than capable."

Hazan stared at him in stupefaction. "You want me to
raid the coffers of the crown, travel north to the country,
chase down a farmer, buy his broken home, scour the empire
for its best mercenaries, and form a covert militia—all in the
same day?"

"You are possessed of supernatural speed, strength, and
invisibility, Hazan. I grant you full permission to use your
powers for good."

"And if I'm stopped by a magistrate?"

Kamran reached into his pocket, retrieved a coin, and
flipped it in the air, watching as Hazan easily caught the
piece in one hand.

"Show them this," said the prince. "It has my seal upon it."

"Which they will believe is forged."

"I feel confident you will figure it out," Kamran said with some finality.

Hazan shot him a dark look, but still he gave Kamran a deferential nod. "You are very lucky, then, that I already have a trusted team upon whom I rely. They'll make a fine militia."

Kamran, who'd been about to resume his walk, turned fully to face his friend. He was unable to leach the surprise from his voice when he said, "You have a *team*?"

"I've never worked alone," said Hazan quietly. "I'm not the only one who's been searching for her, you know."

The prince looked away at that, subdued. For over a year he'd been reading about small revolts in Jinn communities throughout Ardunia. He'd thought they were merely unhappy—seeking change—he'd not known then that they might've sought solace in the idea of a lost empire, that some might've even been searching for an unknown leader around whom they might rally.

"No," he said finally. "I suspect you're not."

"Kamran."

The prince looked up, the question in his eyes.

"What will you do?" Hazan asked, watching him closely. "When you see her?"

At the mere suggestion, Kamran's heart reacted. Until this very moment he'd managed to avoid visualizing this part; some protective instinct in his brain had prevented him from focusing too much on the aspect of the journey that might injure him most. But that he might see her again—speak with her again so soon—

It was almost too much.

He felt the grip of a terrible anxiety close around his throat, experiencing an inexplicable pain in the aftermath, a searing heat along his breastbone he could not fathom into words. She'd betrayed him, punched through his sternum with the heft of it, and he didn't know what he'd do when he saw her again, for he couldn't know what he'd uncover in Tulan. Either he'd discover he'd been a faithless jackass to have doubted her, or he'd be dealt a final, obliterating blow he feared would break him. He might fall to his knees before her; or he might be forced to kill her.

The possibility left him sick.

His voice was an unrecognizable rasp when he said, finally answering Hazan's question: "I don't know."

"For what it's worth, sire, I don't believe she betrayed any of us."

"Enough," Kamran said, turning away. "We've much to do. You will meet me at the docks at midnight."

Hazan stared at him a beat.

Then, with a nod, his former minister was gone, and in his wake, Kamran found he could not move. He stared into the middle distance, clutching the book in his hand ever more tightly. Her handkerchief he'd tucked into his pocket much earlier, telling himself he'd deliver it to her himself one day, not knowing then how soon he might face her.

Kamran had never known how muddy grief might be; it had never occurred to him that the death of a loved one might prove difficult to mourn, or that a heart might continue to beat long after it was broken. He'd not been taught to navigate this misty, middle track of uncertainty; no, Kamran had lived always with the luxury of absolutes. Even in childhood he'd known the delineated position he was meant to occupy in the world, had known the rules that corralled his life. He'd stepped from one gilded milestone to another with a confidence so complete it had never occurred to him, not until Alizeh tore open his life, to doubt the course laid before him.

Now he stood at the mouth of an indistinct, untraveled path; his role, his title, his tomorrow—all unknown.

"Hejjan? Hejjan—" *Sire? Sire—*

Very slowly, Kamran turned toward the desperate sound, catching sight of the long-legged child struggling up the stairs, two at a time. Kamran had been on his way back to his rooms to manage a bit of correspondence; he meant to send a letter to his aunt Jamilah—whose conspicuous silence in the aftermath of Zaal's death had struck him as deeply unusual—and ask if she'd welcome a visit from him on the morrow. He did not intend, of course, to actually pay the dear woman a visit; he was only hoping to leave a paper trail that might convolute the details of his disappearance.

It seemed this would have to wait.

When Omid finally reached the landing, he doubled over almost at once, bracing his hands on his knees, trying to catch his breath.

"I've been looking for you," he panted, "everywhere—"

"Yes, and what took you so long?" Kamran said quietly. "Are they here yet?"

Omid tried to stand up and nearly made it, squinting one eye as he breathed, reinforcing the effort to be vertical with one hand placed firmly on his hip. "They won't come, sire," he said, gasping in Feshtoon. "They don't believe me when I say they've been summoned by the crown."

Kamran closed his eyes and sighed.

This morning—grieving, delirious, and, admittedly, not quite in possession of his faculties—Kamran had thought he'd no one else to trust. In the wake of one heroic act, the boy had seemed an obvious choice for a role meant to prioritize the prince's safety and protection above all else. Now Kamran was beginning to wonder whether Hazan had been right.

This had perhaps been a terrible idea.

"We should've gotten you a new wardrobe," Kamran said, opening his eyes to study the boy's oversized, ill-fitting clothes anew. "Of course they don't believe you; you don't look as if you come from a royal household." He looked askance at the child. "Why did you not take the carriage as I instructed? The royal seal would've been proof enough for anyone."

Omid shook his head, hard. "I tried, sire, honest I did. But he wouldn't let me take the carriage."

Now Kamran frowned. "Who wouldn't let you take the carriage?"

"The coachman. He told me he'd whip me if I so much as touched one of the coaches, so I been runnin' round on foot, you see, which is why it took me so long—"

"Dear God."

The boy flushed a bright red. "I *am* terribly sorry. And these"—he stared down at himself, tugging at the hem of his too-long tunic—"well, these are all the clothes I've got, sire, and I don't know what to do about them, but I'd hate to toss them because they were gifts from"—his eyes filled with tears—"well, from the Diviners, see, and they were ever so kind to me—"

Kamran held up a hand to stop the boy from blubbering.

He himself had not shed a single tear since the night prior, and while there was an aspect of his consciousness that suspected, on some base level, that this was probably strange, there was a much larger, louder, and unhealthier part of him that took pride in his ability to keep his emotions constrained.

"This is my fault," Kamran said to the child. "I should've seen to your clothes before sending you off on an errand. And it didn't occur to me that I might have to make introductions to the staff. You are not to blame on these counts." He sighed. "In fact, I see now that I made a larger mistake in giving you so much responsibility. You're clearly a poor fit for this role—"

"*No, sire*—" The boy threw out a hand as if to stop Kamran from speaking, realized too late that he'd nearly touched the prince, and recoiled in horror. "I'm sorry—I mean, forgive me—"

"Omid—"

"Please," the boy said, wiping desperately now at his damp face and straightening to his full height. "I can do it, sire, I promise I can. I want this job more than anything—my ma

and pa would be so proud if they could see how I'd turned
things around—and I promise I'll show you what I can do.
On my parents' graves, sire, I swear it."

Kamran narrowed his eyes at the boy, who was standing
now at attention, his red-rimmed eyes no longer leaking. In
any other situation, Kamran would've dismissed the child
without question. But the stakes were admittedly low at this
juncture; come tomorrow morning, Kamran would be gone.
Too, he was anticipating trouble from the nobles, taking
for granted that the distorted magic snaking along his body
would all but guarantee his expulsion. He felt uncertain only
about *when* he'd be asked to leave, for he'd so far managed
to evade what seemed an inevitable encounter with Zahhak
himself—

As if he'd conjured the man with his mind, Kamran saw
out of the corner of his eye the slinky retreat of the defense
minister, who'd appeared down the hall as if out of the ether.
He was moving with some haste in the direction of the king's
wing of the palace—though what Zahhak hoped to do in his
grandfather's rooms was a mystery, one Kamran was eager
to unravel. If the defense minister's darting eyes were any
indication, the answers were bound to be bleak.

"Sire?"

Kamran returned his gaze to the boy, his mind working
double-time, assessing the situation from all possible angles
in the space of a millisecond. As Zahhak's treacherous figure
grew fainter in the distance, Kamran grew certain he'd know
more about his fate in the palace very, very soon.

In which case there was little point, he reasoned, in

breaking the boy's heart. He might as well let the child dream a day more.

"Very well," Kamran said stiffly, lowering his voice. "But if they're not here by nightfall, I'm placing you elsewhere in the palace. I'm sure we could use a new stable boy." He paused, assessing the child. "Are you any good with horses?"

Omid was shaking his head so hard Kamran feared he might shift things around in there permanently. "I don't like horses, sire, and they don't like me. I'll get it done—you won't need to place me elsewhere. They'll be here by nightfall, I swear it."

And as Omid darted away, dashing down the staircase at a dangerous clip, Kamran changed course, too, following Zahhak's trail toward his grandfather's rooms.

EIGHTEEN

هجده

"I BEG YOUR PARDON?" ALIZEH blinked at Cyrus. "You want to show me Tulan?"

"Aren't you curious?"

"Very," she said. "It's only that I didn't think you'd let me leave the palace."

Cyrus laughed at that, then frowned. "Why wouldn't I let you leave the palace?"

She matched his look of confusion. "Because," she said slowly. "I would run away, you see. And you need me to remain here and do your bidding, or else the devil is going to kill you."

"Ah." He grimaced. "Right. *Well*. In that case, I must get on. I suppose I'll see you at dinner, should you choose to join me." He gave her a nod, turned on his heel and, with a purposeful stride, headed to the door.

Alizeh watched this happen with undisguised disappointment. "Wait," she called out, crestfallen. "Are you really leaving? Are we really not going to see Tulan?"

Cyrus hesitated, but didn't turn to face her. She saw only the tense back of him, his copper hair a brilliant contrast to his simple black coat. She was again struck by the cut of him, the space he commanded even now, when she couldn't see his face.

He said softly, "It was rather foolish of you to mention the bit about running away."

"I know." Alizeh bit her lip. "I'm quite sorry for it now."

Slowly, he turned around. "Are you saying you're *not* going to run away, then?"

Alizeh prevaricated.

She was torn but also distracted; the sun had changed positions in the last hour, and shafts of golden luminescence were flooding the room through the glass doors and open windows, anointing all in their path. Even Cyrus was caught in this tempest of light, the hard lines of his body limned around the edges, a diffuse glow dancing across his face, painting his eyes. He squinted against the brightness, his pupils contracting to pinpoints, blowing out the blue of his irises; she watched him watch her a moment, his confusion apparent.

Alizeh didn't mind.

She let her gaze wander as she mulled over her warring emotions. She felt less inclined to flee this castle than she had upon arrival, not only because she'd been made two rather robust offers in that time, but also because— Well, the truth was, she had nowhere else to go. Here, at least, her favor was being courted by both mother and child; and Alizeh, who'd been forced to sleep too many brutal nights in the gutter, her cheek pressed to the filth of a city street, did not take for granted the luxury of a warm bed. She could not deny that this was a lovely place to rest awhile—and to sort through the myriad disasters strewn before her. In fact, she could still hear the birds chirping outside; the hush of the waterfalls in the distance; the efforts of the wind pushing apart branches, rattling leaves. It was, in a word, lovely.

And she did dearly wish to see Tulan.

Unfamiliar as she was with the manipulation of magic, Alizeh was aware enough to understand that there was some kind of enchantment in the air here, for the season was entirely wrong. True, Tulan was farther south than Ardunia—which was in the midst of a ruthless winter—but the two empires shared a border; some variation in temperature would not have been amiss, but *this* was practically summer.

Alizeh would be lying if she said she didn't prefer it.

She lifted her eyes, finally meeting Cyrus's impatient gaze. Hesitantly, she said, "Perhaps I won't run away *today*."

His agitation gave way to visible bemusement. "Is that so? Having a good time, then, are you? Enjoying my hospitality?"

Quietly, Alizeh cleared her throat.

"You may choose to poke fun," she said, clasping and unclasping her hands. "But I *am* deciding, after all, whether or not to marry you, and I think I should be allowed to see the land you intend to leave me before I make my choice."

Cyrus stiffened at that.

He stared at her, unblinking, the light dying in his eyes as he turned slowly away, lapsing into silence. In fact, he said nothing for so long that Alizeh felt forced, in the mounting discomfort of the moment, to speak.

"Cyrus?" she said uneasily. "Are you all right?"

He looked up. "Ever?"

She frowned.

"You know," he said attempting a laugh, "I realize you

might not believe this, but I never dreamed I'd one day be forced to take a wife in this manner." He shook his head, turned away again. "I'm trying to give you Tulan—a jewel among empires, a land that is my home. I stand here begging you to marry me—to *kill me* and take my nation, my crown, my legacy—and you won't even say yes." He closed his eyes and swore. "I really thought I'd already hit rock bottom, but this— This is a shade of wretchedness I've never known."

The nosta warmed at this sad speech, and Alizeh's pliable heart felt a rush of pity, which she hated. She hated that she could not unceremoniously loathe him, hated that she could not shift the levers that ruled her emotions, hated that she was unable to power off compassion when the feeling was inappropriate.

With a sigh, Alizeh approached him.

Cyrus's head shot up at her advance like he was being hunted, and he watched her with increasing wariness until she met him where he stood, halfway across the room. She then surprised herself by doing something that was either stupid or bold; she couldn't decide.

She touched his arm.

Or at least, she tried. Cyrus caught her hand before she even made contact, his reflexes so fast she hardly realized what'd happened until she saw, with some astonishment, that he held her limb upright before her eyes. His hand enveloped hers in both size and warmth as he studied her, his own eyes wild and wondering. Alizeh felt she couldn't move; she was still as stone, marveling that she could perceive slight calluses against his skin when his fingers slid, in a stuttering pattern, down the undersides of her knuckles, inspiring a slow burn of sensation so unexpected she nearly gasped.

Awareness quickened through her.

He drew his hand slowly downward, grazing her palm until he'd clasped her wrist like a bracelet, his fingers pressing tenderly against her racing pulse. She wondered if he was counting the beats there, cataloging her reaction.

"Alizeh," he said, his voice low, heavy. He was looking at her like she might've been about to stab him through the heart. "What are you doing?"

"I wasn't"—she shook her head, found her voice—"I swear I wasn't going to hurt you."

Cyrus dropped her hand like it had burned him, stepping farther away from her. He was breathing just a touch too fast, his eyes heavily guarded. "Then what were you going to do?"

She hesitated, deliberating over whether to admit the truth, and then feeling too stupid to do so. Again, she shook her head. "Nothing, I swear—"

"Alizeh." He sounded angry now. "Why did you try to touch me? What is your game?"

"I was just"—she sighed—"oh this is *ridiculous*," she said in a frustrated burst. "I was only trying to be sympathetic."

He blinked at her, even as tension visibly fled his body. "You were trying to be sympathetic?" he echoed, his incomprehension palpable. "You mean—you were trying to console me?"

"Yes."

He pointed at himself. "*Me.*"

"You know what?" An angry blush burned across her cheeks. "Never mind."

Cyrus stared at her for a full second before he finally broke, and laughed out loud. "I tell you a single sad story and your defenses weaken that easily? Against *me*? You lovely little fool, you're going to get yourself killed."

"Oh, shut up." She crossed her arms.

He shook his head slowly, closing the distance between them again, his eyes analyzing her carefully, lingering along the lines of her face. For a moment he almost looked as if he might touch her, though he never did.

"Humor me," he whispered. "What were you going to say? How did you intend to comfort me?"

"I don't— I wasn't going to say anything—"

"Were you going to tell me not to worry?" he said, still smiling. "Were you going to remind me that, though my life is essentially worthless, I should keep my chin up and look on the bright side?"

"No," she said, hearing the breathless sound of her voice and hating it. "I had no intention of feeding you such nonsense. I don't see any bright side to this."

He took a deep breath, his chest lifting with the effort. It was a long moment before he said, "You know, neither did I."

Alizeh's heart was pounding too hard. She didn't know how the two of them kept finding themselves in these charged moments, and as a result she didn't know how to escape them. There was something decidedly fascinating about Cyrus; something potent and complex, and prodding him for truth felt a lot like prodding a sore muscle; the results were both painful and pleasant. She pitied him even as she detested him, understood him even as she scorned him. He was a series of mystery boxes she wasn't certain she wanted to open, and whose hidden depths tempted her even as they scared her.

She didn't know what she wanted from him—or whether she wanted anything at all—

And then he touched her.

He lowered his eyes and touched her, breaking the trance between them so abruptly Alizeh drew a sharp, unsteady breath. She watched him smile at the sound she'd made, laughing quietly to himself as he dragged his fingers lightly down the front of her gown, from just under her breasts to the apex of her navel.

She tore away, but too late.

"What are you doing?" she said, trying to call upon anger and struggling. Her head grew cloudy when he stood near, and she made a silent note to herself to keep distance between their bodies.

"I was fixing your dress," he said, taking a step back. "I didn't think you'd want to keep the stain."

Alizeh looked at herself as if emerging from a dream, absently patting down the bodice of her frock. The brown spatter of tea that'd so thoroughly soiled the gossamer layers was now gone. Her dress was restored entirely.

"How did you do that?" she whispered, staring up at him with wide eyes. "How do you cast spells so easily?"

"Aren't you meant to wield great power?" he asked, brows

furrowing in confusion. "How is it you're so unschooled in the workings of magic?"

She flushed lightly under his questioning, feeling self-conscious. "My magic, should I ever possess it, is meant to come to me without formal education. It's meant to be intuitive."

"Fascinating," he said, his frown only deepening. "And you know nothing else? You don't know what it is?"

"No," she said, suddenly uncomfortable. She couldn't tell whether his was an honest, casual question, or whether he was deftly mining her for information. Either way, she proceeded with caution. "As far as I'm aware, no one does."

"Why not?"

"Because in all of recorded history, it's never before been accessed," she said briskly, then changed the subject. "As to more ordinary enchantments, I know only rudimentary things. Ardunia is too large an empire to rely upon magic to thrive. For us it is a very limited resource, and thus it's used only sparingly. It's also owned and regulated entirely by the crown. We're not allowed to use it as we wish."

"Yes," he said quietly. "I've heard that Ardunians teach magic only to those interested in joining the priesthood."

She nodded. "The same isn't true in Tulan, though, is it? Your mother told me you've been studying divination and sorcery since you were a child, and it takes but one working eye to deduce there's nothing even remotely priest-like about you."

He froze, briefly surprised by the insult, and then laughed with his whole body, his shoulders shaking, his eyes crinkling at the edges. "Heavens," he said. "Tell me how you really feel."

"Take care, Cyrus," she chided him. "If you keep laughing like that, I'm liable to think you have a heart."

"Oh, you needn't worry," he said, his smile fading. "I most certainly don't."

The nosta went cold.

Alizeh's own smile faltered at that, some essential armor crumbling inside her. She suddenly didn't know what to say.

"Come along, then," he said, quite literally moving past the moment as he strode to the door. "If you're really so uninformed, I'll show you how it works."

"How what works?" She stared at him, unmoving. "And where do you mean to take me? Are we going into Tulan now?"

Alizeh saw only the back of his head when he said, "Yes."

"Really?" She hurried after him. "And you're no longer worried I'll run away?"

"No."

"Wait— Why not?" Alizeh stopped in place. "You should be a little worried, at the very least."

"I'm afraid that's not possible," he said, finally turning around to face her. "For I've recently deduced that you're quite charmingly pathetic."

Alizeh stiffened, shock and outrage awakening in her body. "How dare you," she said, drawing herself up to her full height, her fists clenching. "I am *not* pathetic—"

"I have a theory," he said, cutting her off as he walked

backward to the door, "that if I were badly wounded, you would help me. True or false?"

"False."

His smile widened. "Liar."

"I wouldn't," she said ruthlessly. "I'd leave you there and run for my life."

He was fighting a massive grin now, his eyes glittering with barely suppressed delight. "You would save me."

"I'd absolutely let you die."

He shook his head. "You wouldn't be able to leave me behind."

"I would, too," she insisted.

"You certainly *should,*" he said softly. "For it'd be terribly stupid to save me, and I didn't think you were stupid."

She couldn't believe she'd ever felt sorry for him. She wanted to pummel him now. "I'm not stupid," she said angrily.

"I never said you were stupid." Cyrus was at the door, gripping the handle. "I'm merely pointing out that all signs seem to indicate you *might* be."

"Oh, you're truly awful," she said, glaring at him even as she stalked to the door. "You're mean and awful and I regret ever feeling bad for you."

He raised his eyebrows. "Your first mistake was ever feeling bad for me."

"It's a mistake I won't make again."

He stared in silent amusement as she pushed him aside, turned the knob, took a single step over the threshold—and screamed.

There was no ground beyond the door.

Alizeh pinwheeled backward, teetering violently until Cyrus caught her, steadying her flailing body against his chest. She'd plummeted from the sky too many times in the last twenty-four hours to stomach another such fall so soon.

Her poor nerves were frayed.

"Why is there nothing out there?" she practically cried. "Why is this castle so strange?"

"Alizeh—"

"Is this actually a prison?" Her panic was escalating now. "Have you locked me in a tower? Am I never meant to leave?"

"*Alizeh*—"

"No"—she pushed at him, pushed at him until he let go of her, until he stumbled a few steps away from her—"I *don't* like you, and I *don't* trust you and I *wouldn't* save you, you despicable, good-for-nothing, unprincipled reprobate—"

He grabbed hold of her shoulders anyway, tried to look her in the eye. "Alizeh, you infuriating girl, listen to me—"

"I certainly will not listen to you— And how dare you call me stupid *and* infuriating—"

"*The stairs are made of glass.*"

Alizeh went suddenly still. She reanimated by degrees, mustering what was left of her dignity as she adjusted her dress and stepped gingerly away from him, after which she peered through the open door and over the threshold, this time looking more closely.

"Well," she said, taking a sharp breath. "I suppose they are made of glass." She crossed her arms, unable to look at him. "But that's a foolish idea, you know, having stairs made of glass. It's quite dangerous."

Cyrus was silent for so long she eventually dared to look up at him, and found him staring at her with the oddest expression on his face. He appeared both pained and confused; she couldn't quite define it, and she didn't know what it meant.

Feeling sheepish, she lowered her eyes again, wondering whether he'd changed his mind about showing her magic and seeing Tulan.

"Alizeh," he said finally.

She did not look up, choosing to stare instead at her feet, which she'd earlier tucked into a very pretty pair of boots. "I do realize I just called you a fair amount of terrible names, but I'd still very much like to see Tulan."

"Why are you refusing to look at me?"

"Why should I?" she said quietly. "I've already seen your face."

"Alizeh—"

"You know, you say my name a lot."

"I say your name," he said tersely, "a perfectly normal amount."

"Do you really think so?" She peeked up at him, and he looked mad about it.

"Yes."

"Well, I suppose that might be true," she said. "It's been so long since anyone has spoken to me in earnest that I fear I've lost perspective."

He hesitated. "What do you mean?"

She shook her head, wincing as grief caught her, the way

it always did, at the most inopportune moments. It had been years and years since her parents died, and for so long since then she'd only ever been commanded, never acknowledged. Mrs. Amina had never even *asked* her name.

"Nothing," she said brightly, even as she sniffed, suddenly, against a swell of feeling.

"What are you— Oh, for heaven's sake, are you going to cry again? I'll take you to see the blasted city, Alizeh, I'll show you the bloody magic, you don't have to cry about everything—"

"I'm not crying," she said irritably. "I'm *thinking*. Sometimes I get emotional when I'm thinking—"

"When you're *thinking*? You mean all the time, then?" He pushed his hands through his hair and swore under his breath. "The devil really is trying to kill me."

She wiped at her eyes. "I thought you already knew that."

"All right, that's quite enough out of you," he said, and then he took her hand without warning, and tugged her out the door.

NINETEEN

نوزده

ALIZEH STARED, WONDERINGLY, AT THE piece of bread she was holding, turning it over in her hands. Cyrus had earlier ripped in half a larger round, and the share she held was, as a result, an unconventional shape, something like a crescent moon.

It was still warm, too.

They'd been walking past a bakery when Alizeh had smelled the familiar scent, and after she'd commented aloud that in her life she'd only ever walked past bakeries, never stepping inside of one, Cyrus had expressed surprise. He'd asked her why she'd never been inside of a bakery, for "surely Ardunia was not so pathetic an empire as to lack such establishments," to which she'd responded that Ardunia was "quite thick with bakeries, thank you very much," it was only that she'd never had the time to visit one, for she'd always worked, at minimum, twelve-hour shifts, though even if she'd had the time, she'd reasoned, she'd "invariably lacked the money to purchase anything from such a place," and as a result hadn't seen the point in torturing herself with even the possibility of such decadence—

Cyrus had abruptly taken her by the arm then, given her a strange look, and guided her toward the shop in question, into which they disappeared for a wondrous few moments, and emerged, shortly thereafter, with bread.

Bread that Cyrus had purchased for her.

She'd not thought they'd actually buy anything, not only because Alizeh had no money but because in all her life no one but her parents had ever bought her anything. The entire experience of being out with Cyrus, from the moment they'd said goodbye to a smug Sarra—who'd seen their clasped hands and given Alizeh a sly, encouraging nod—to the current moment they occupied now, had been so unfamiliar and strange that Alizeh hardly knew what to do with herself. If she tried to think about it all in full, she thought her head might fall off.

For now, she focused on the bread.

With a bit of guidance from her unlikely—and surprisingly patient—companion, Alizeh had chosen a small, humble disk of the baked good. It was fairly thin, visibly hand-kneaded, and had been sprinkled generously with sesame seeds. It was brown and crispy on the outside, but—she poked its insides now with one finger—light and springy within. This accomplishment struck her as functionally impossible.

"Did they make this with magic?" she asked Cyrus, still poking the soft interior. There were many little holes inside and she couldn't imagine how someone might've scooped out bits of dough from the middle without disturbing the perfect, crunchy shell.

Cyrus, who was actually eating his piece of bread, was still chewing when he looked over at her, staring at her now like she might be touched in the head.

He swallowed. "Please tell me you're joking."

"Well, if you're going to be rude about it," she said. "I'll just keep my questions to myself."

"Alizeh."

She pretended not to hear him.

Instead, she picked cautiously at the crust, attempting to break the shell away to fully expose the soft, spongey inside. She crunched on a piece of the crust first, her voracious senses savoring the mild taste and crisp texture, and then bit into the pillowy middle, which was—she raised her eyebrows—surprisingly chewy.

Alizeh decided she liked bread very much.

They were wandering down a bright, delightful avenue finished with gleaming ivory pavers, the street hemmed in on either side by colorful shops of all kinds. Alizeh had already looked around a great deal, but just then she was looking *up* as they strolled, mesmerized by the majesty of the stratospheric ceiling above them, and which was not a ceiling at all, but an unfathomable number of wisteria vines stretched across the width of the road, crisscrossing from the top of one building to another. The purple flowers, Cyrus had explained, had been bewitched to bloom in perpetuity. They hung in astonishing masses from on high like ripe, decadent grapes, their otherworldly, honeyed scent infusing the air around them while loose, fallen petals decorated all in a surreal confetti. Occasionally a strong gust of wind blew through and shook the vines, resulting in a soft shower of wisteria petals, the sight and smell of which were so heavenly—so overwhelmingly beautiful—that Alizeh thought she might lie down in the middle of the road and happily die of delight.

"Alizeh," Cyrus said again.

"Hmm?" She was still staring at the flowers, picking apart her bread methodically.

"What are you doing?" he said, audibly frustrated. "The crust is not a skin. You don't have to peel it off to eat the insides."

"I wasn't peeling it," she scoffed, finally turning to look at him. "I was studying it. I *was* wondering, though— Could you tell me how the bakers poked all these little holes in the middle without breaking the shell? It seems terribly clever."

Cyrus came to a sudden stop. "My word," he breathed. "Have you never eaten bread before?"

She frowned. "Of course I have."

"You haven't, have you? You've never eaten bread before."

"Not true," she said, pointing a finger. "Once, in one of my previous positions working in a big house, I was clearing away the dishes in the breakfast room, and there was still so much food untouched—an entire tray of perfectly good toast, can you imagine?—and I was so curious I actually took a small bite."

Cyrus only stared at her. "When was this?"

"A couple of years ago."

He searched the skies then as if for strength, and turned back to her with a sigh. "Once, a couple of *years* ago, you had a single bite of toast? That's it?"

"Well, I couldn't bring myself to do it again," she said, worrying her lip. "One of the other servants saw me do the shameful deed and snitched straightaway to the housekeeper, who promptly dismissed me from my position. I tried to point out that I'd not been *stealing*, as she'd so unfairly described it, for we'd been ordered to toss all the bread straight into the trash, which seemed to me a shocking waste—"

"Heavens, Alizeh." Cyrus had gone completely slack. "You might be the strangest girl I've ever met in all my life."

"Are you insulting me?"

"Without question."

She shot him a dirty look, but Cyrus only laughed.

Just then came a series of shouts; a team of men were unrolling a massive rug from a high balcony, the intricate piece unfurling in the sun like a newborn leaf. Suspended only by their efforts, it hung in the wind like a magnificent flag, its silk threads shimmering as one of them shouted rather aggressively from the balustrade about good prices and discounted delivery.

Despite her irritation, Alizeh smiled.

There were aspects of Tulan's royal city—*Mesti*, Cyrus had called it—that reminded her very much of Setar, but there were rather glaring differences between them, too.

First, they spoke a duo of languages in equal measure here. Tulan was positioned just beyond Fesht province, the southernmost territory of Ardunia, and as a result there'd been quite a bit of blending along borders; the Tulanian people spoke Feshtoon *and* Ardanz—though Alizeh occasionally thought she heard people speaking a third, unofficial dialect that sounded like a slapdash mix of both.

Second, and most obvious: while both royal cities were stunning feats of color and architecture, only one had been built with an abundance of magic. Tulan being but a fraction the size of Ardunia, its royal city was a great deal smaller, giving it a cozier quality where every inch felt cleaner, more closely cared for, and delicately enchanted. Alizeh had been taking it all in with the enthusiasm of an ingenue, absorbing the life and bustle of the atmosphere not unlike a child discovering wind for the first time.

"What other essential things must I know about you?" Cyrus was saying. "Have you never had a glass of milk, for example? Have you never eaten a piece of cake? Do you need me to teach you how to use a knife and fork?"

Alizeh felt her face heat at that last question, for she'd almost certainly require such lessons. She'd only ever fumbled poorly with utensils, because she'd never had any use for them. As a servant she'd tried, on many occasions, to familiarize herself with their many uses, but whenever she lingered too long watching people eat, she was either punished or sacked.

"You," she said finally, turning away to hide her embarrassment, "are being intentionally mean. You know full well that I'm not like you, that I don't need to eat food to survive—"

"Oh, don't you dare blame your strangeness on your own people," he said, cutting her off. They'd started walking again. "There are many thousands of Jinn in Tulan who don't *need* to eat, and yet they patronize the local grocers and bakeries with gusto."

At the mention of Jinn, Alizeh faltered a moment.

She'd be surprised indeed if Cyrus hadn't noticed the many strange looks she'd been getting—he was too discerning to miss such a thing—but he hadn't said a word about it, which led her to worry she might be imagining things. Still, she struggled to deny outright what seemed increasingly obvious.

Jinn here seemed preternaturally attuned to her.

Their heads lifted as she passed, looks of confusion crossing their faces. They frowned at her as if they were supposed to know her, as if her face belonged to an acquaintance whose name they struggled to recall. More than once someone did a double take as she went by, only to turn and whisper urgently to their companion, saying something she couldn't hear.

It was the fireflies that gave them away.

Were it not for the cheerful insects bobbing alongside their owners, Alizeh might not have been able to discern the difference between Clay and Jinn residents, who swarmed about town with an ordinariness unseen even in Ardunia. Back home, Jinn were legally free to go about their days as they wished, but they lived always with a caution that defined all aspects of their existence. They kept their heads down, spoke little, didn't mix much with Clay, and retreated to their own circles whenever possible.

For reasons unknown, Jinn seemed happier here.

Nevertheless, Alizeh felt the rise of a familiar apprehension in her chest—something she'd felt many times in her life, and that suggested she was being followed. She and Cyrus had only resumed walking for a minute now, and already she was noticing more and more eyes in her direction. She glanced around nervously, likely giving herself away in the process, but it couldn't be helped. Someone was there.

"Cyrus," she said quietly.

"No—I don't want to argue about it," he said, gesticulating with his unfinished bread. "It's my business to know the consumption habits of my own citizens, and I swear to you, Jinn eat all the time—"

"*Cyrus,*" she hissed, tugging on his arm.

"What?" He turned to look at her, and in an instant his frustration gave way to concern. This reaction was in and of itself something to wonder about, though perhaps some other time.

"What is it?" he said, stopping abruptly. "What's wrong?"

She ducked her head and whispered, "Is it too late to put an illusion on me?"

Cyrus's concern morphed into alarm. Immediately he looked up and down the street, then searched higher, scanning the sky. She realized he was looking for assailants.

"I don't think anyone is trying to kill me," she said lightly, trying for a bit of levity. "But I do think someone is following us."

He swore under his breath.

Earlier, Cyrus had used magic to render an illusion around himself; as a result, people who saw him registered only a forgettable face, one they instantly put out of their minds. He'd explained that it was the only way he could walk freely about Tulan, for he'd once caused a riot even heavily obscured in a mask and hooded cloak. "It's my bloody hair," he'd muttered with no small amount of bitterness. "This color is a curse."

He'd insisted upon drawing an illusion about her face as well, but Alizeh had adamantly refused. She didn't trust Cyrus enough to allow him to use magic on her, and for obvious reasons: the last time she'd trusted one of his enchantments to protect her, she'd been unceremoniously dragged up into the air, dropped onto the back of a dragon, and delivered directly into the devil's trap.

No magic, she'd maintained.

While all of Ardunia's nobles had seen something of her face—and her undergarments, apparently—she'd since fled, and entered a completely different empire. It'd seemed unlikely that anyone in Tulan would know who she was. Cyrus had relented begrudgingly, though only because she'd agreed to wear a rather large hat, which she'd pulled low over her eyes.

A useless hat, apparently.

"If someone is already watching," Cyrus said, still furtively scanning the street, "they'll see the illusion take effect, which means they might yet be able to track you. First, we need to go somewhere relatively deserted. Did you see where this person went?"

Alizeh shook her head and then, as surreptitiously as was physically possible, glanced over her shoulder.

There was a young woman there.

She was wearing a bright red dress, standing stock-still in the middle of the avenue, staring at Alizeh with wide, unblinking eyes.

"She's just there," Alizeh whispered. "Right behind us."

Cyrus echoed her earlier movement, glancing cautiously over his shoulder, but then he turned all the way around, making no secret of his search.

He frowned.

"What lady?" he said, not bothering to lower his voice. "There's no one here."

"You don't see her?"

"I don't see anyone," he said. "Maybe it only seemed like she was following us."

Feeling a sense of relief, Alizeh sighed. "Yes," she said, pivoting to survey the street. "Maybe she—"

Alizeh had lifted the brim of her hat as she turned, hoping for a better look, when the young woman fell, without warning, to her knees. She pointed a shaking finger at Alizeh and screamed. She *screamed*, crying out so violently Alizeh was excoriated by the sound, by the weight of it, the wildness. She couldn't move even as she trembled, as her face paled.

She felt bolted to the ground.

"Alizeh?" said Cyrus urgently. "What's wrong? What's happening?"

"You can't hear that," she managed to whisper, her heart pounding furiously in her chest. "Can you?"

"Hear what?"

The woman in the street was still screaming, sobbing hysterically and shrieking.

"Alizeh?"

"*Cyrus.*" She was breathing hard, and reached for his arm without looking, clenching a fistful of his shirtsleeve. "Why didn't you tell me that Jinn in Tulan were allowed to use their strengths openly?"

"You"—he looked down, confused, at her death grip—"you never asked. And we've had a number of other things to . . ."

Cyrus inhaled sharply.

His eyes went wide as—Alizeh could only imagine—the screaming girl came suddenly into view. The young woman had likely lost control of her invisibility in the furor, and her screams echoed through the avenue now, as people of all kinds came running from every direction. They tried to help the girl up, but she wouldn't be moved. She shook off their assistance, alternately pointing at Alizeh and dragging her hands down her face.

Alizeh could feel Cyrus panic.

"Let's go," he said, "right now—"

"No— I can't— I can't just leave her—"

A crowd was gathering now, eyes following the direction of the young woman's outstretched finger, and as the shouts and whispers reached a stunning crescendo, the screaming woman broke somehow further, a tortured expression overtaking her face—a mix of something like joy and grief—tears still streaking down her cheeks. She finally managed intelligible speech.

"It's true," she cried. "They said you were here— I didn't believe— But it's true—"

"Who?" someone else called out. "Who is she?"

"The servant boy from the palace," a man shouted, "he said—"

"No— It can't be—"

"Alizeh," Cyrus said urgently, "I know you asked me not to use magic on you, but please, let me get you out of here—"

"In the Ardunian newspaper, from last night—"

"No, long before that, we've been hearing whispers for days—"

"I can't leave," Alizeh said desperately, her pulse sky-rocketing. "Can I? These people, they're—they're my responsibility—"

Cyrus tugged her sharply back as the crowd surged forward, and her hat fell to the ground with a dull thud. There was no time to retrieve it. The mass wasted no time swarming her as one, trying to get a better look.

"Her eyes!"

"And her hair! She wears a crown!"

"It's just as they said—"

"My wife's cousin in Setar sent her a letter, swore it was her, said it had to be—"

"Heard she was in hiding all this time—"

"I remember those rumors—nearly twenty years ago—"

"Angels above, I heard it, too, but I didn't believe—"

"Our prayers have been answered!" cried an older woman, who was weeping into her hands. "It's finally happened, and in my lifetime—I never dared to hope, even as my brother has been jailed in Forina for seventeen years—"

"And my mother, in Stol province, they cut off her feet—"

"*Justice!*" someone screamed. "Justice will come to this rotting earth!"

Alizeh lost her footing then, nearly falling over until Cyrus caught her and turned her firmly in his arms, hiding her face in his chest.

"Please," he whispered against her hair. "Please let me get you out of here— You're not ready for this, and they're not ready for you—"

"You must start with the prisons, Your Majesty!" another woman cried. "Our brothers and sisters are treated worse than animals in the Soroot empire—"

"And in Zeldan—"

"They still bury the children in Sheffat—"

Alizeh absorbed each blow, each statement gutting her, every sentence cutting deeper, these reminders of her purpose, her duty, snatching the breath from her lungs.

"Does she not speak? I don't understand—"

"The snoda from the castle, he said she'd spoken to him—*smiled* at him—"

"I thought he said she was here to marry the king—"

Alizeh gasped, her chest heaving.

"Our king? King Cyrus?"

"For months he's been preparing rooms for a bride—he's made no secret of it—"

"But you're sure it's her?"

"Servants said she arrived this morning! That she moved into the palace—"

"Who's she with, then? I can't see his face—"

"Is that the king, you think?"

"The king? In the middle of broad daylight?" Someone laughed. "I think not—"

"Hear he killed Zaal? In his own home?"

"Yes, and I heard the depraved monster deserved it—"

"Long live King Cyrus!" a voice rang out. "Long live our queen!"

Alizeh's heart was beating too hard in her chest. She felt

dangerously light-headed. She was dizzy with emotion, with panic, and plagued by a disorienting suspicion that she might be dreaming.

"Alizeh, please, stand up— *Alizeh*—"

"Why do they like you?" she whispered, her lips moving against his throat, even as her head filled with static. "I thought they would hate you—"

"Please, Your Highness," a man shouted. "Say something— we beg you to speak—"

"Forgive me," Cyrus whispered, holding her tighter. "I know you didn't want me to, but I won't wait any longer—"

"Cyrus," she breathed, closing her eyes against the spinning world. "I think I'm going to faint."

"My queen!" screamed the first woman, whose voice Alizeh suspected she'd remember for the rest of her life. "My queen, you've finally"—she gasped, still sobbing hysterically—"you've finally come for us, after all this time—"

Quite suddenly, they disappeared.

TWENTY

پیست

THEY'D SHIFTED THROUGH SPACE SO smoothly that Alizeh hadn't even realized they'd left the chaotic avenue until they materialized, a moment later, in the middle of an expansive flower field. Neither had she realized she was silently crying, not until she felt the wet of Cyrus's sweater under her cheek.

With painstaking care he let go of her, drawing away in cautious movements before helping her to the ground, where she sank with a grateful sigh for only a moment before tipping slowly over. She curled onto her side, crushing a bed of tulips under her body, and experiencing all the while a physical reaction she didn't understand. Her limbs felt dead and leaden. She was colder than she'd ever been, more exhausted than she'd ever felt, and her head seemed impossible to hold upright. Her numb fingers could hardly manage to unclasp the heavy collar from around her neck, which felt now like it was choking her, and with a final, exhausting effort, she tore it away from her throat and tossed the glittering piece to the ground.

She took a deep, shaky breath.

Alizeh could still feel those people—she still heard their voices—her lungs compressing under the weight of their hopes, her ribs cracking under the heft of their dreams.

She'd never longed for her parents more than she did in that very moment, wishing for guidance, for someone to tell her that she was strong enough, that she was worthy. That she should rise, now, more than ever.

That she would not fail if she did.

"Alizeh," he whispered. "You're scaring me."

She heard his familiar voice and opened her eyes at the sound, searching for his face. Instead, everywhere she looked were flowers. She smelled grass, the welcome scent of over-turned soil, the freshness of dew. Her wet cheek was pressed against the velvet petals of many tulips; a trio of bees were buzzing near her nose. She felt she might live here forever, might rest her weary head upon this flower bed and pretend, for a moment, that she was still a child.

"Please," said Cyrus. "At least tell me you're okay."

"I'm afraid that's impossible," she said, sniffing softly. She closed her eyes again, let the flowers dry her tears.

"What do you mean?" he said, alarmed. "Why impossible?"

"Well," she said, "because I've recently deduced that you're quite charmingly pathetic."

He sighed. "Really? You're choosing this moment to insult me?"

"And I have a theory," she went on, "that if I were badly wounded, you would help me. True or false?"

He went silent.

He was silent so long Alizeh had time enough to watch a drop of dew drip off a glossy green leaf.

"True or false, Cyrus?"

She heard his uneven exhale, the raw edge to his voice

when he said, irritably, "*False.*"

The nosta flashed cold.

"Liar," she whispered.

"I don't care for this game."

"Where are we, by the way?" she asked, her eyes landing on a particularly purple tulip, the color so vivid it seemed imagined.

In response, Cyrus did not say what was obvious, which was that they were in a flower field; instead he answered the more specific question she'd failed to ask, and said simply, "Somewhere safe."

"Safe?" she said, managing a small smile. "Even with you here?"

It was a moment before he said, quietly, "Yes."

The nosta warmed.

Alizeh still hadn't seen him. She *couldn't* see him. The tulips were tall, her head was heavy, and she felt no inclination to move. She wondered whether Cyrus was sitting just to the side of her, and tried to picture him in his austere black clothes, perched in a sea of flowers, his long legs pulled up to his chest like a boy. His hair, she thought, would look very nice against all the green.

"And is there magic here, too?" she asked.

"Yes."

Alizeh reached a tired hand toward a wilted bloom, stroking its broken neck and sleepy petals, and the flower wriggled under her touch, straining to stand upright. She realized then that the blooms would pop straight back up once she left.

"Someone would have to walk for miles to find you here," he said, answering another question she hadn't asked. "There's no direct path to this field."

"Then what purpose does it serve?"

"What do you mean?"

"The flower field," she said. "I don't think it's a wild field—for it seems planted intentionally—but you say there's no way to access it. And if it's been enchanted to bloom always, I have to assume the stems aren't meant to be sold at market. So why is it here? Who put it here?"

"The field exists simply to exist. There are thousands of different types of flowers here," he explained. "It's meant to be a kind of living painting; an experience with beauty meant to invigorate the tired senses."

Alizeh nearly lifted her head, she was so surprised. "That's why you brought me here?"

"Yes," he said quietly.

"You mean, you were trying to console me?"

"Bloody hell, Alizeh, knock it off."

"All right, okay," she said with a sigh.

"Good."

"*Me?*" she said again. "You were trying to console *me?*"

"You know what, you can walk back to the castle—"

"I'm sorry, I'm sorry, I promise I'm really done this time." She bit the inside of her cheek, and then—very, very softly—she said, "I do hope you know how grateful I am that you brought me here. It's absolutely beautiful."

"Yes, well," he said, taking a sharp breath. "You strike me as precisely the sort of maudlin person who would appreciate the company of flowers while crying."

She sat with that for a moment, trying to decode it. "Do you know," she said finally, "I think that might be the nicest thing you've ever said to me."

"It wasn't a compliment."

"Yes," she said, smiling. "I think it was."

He laughed quietly at that and she did, too, and the two of them fell into a companionable silence, studiously avoiding the most obvious topic of conversation. Alizeh didn't know what Cyrus was doing where he sat, but if he had any idea how ardently she was now mulling over the prospect of taking over his empire, he said nothing about it.

Alizeh, for her part, was tickling the stems of tired flowers, watching them squirm while she deliberated. She was grateful for the moment of quiet, for her mind was a distorted mess.

If ever she'd doubted her place in the world before, she knew now unequivocally that there were people waiting for her—people who would follow her—and to whom she was tethered by birth and fate, duty-bound to lead and unify.

And yet, for years this had seemed impossible.

It had been easy to tell herself that she could do nothing about so large a problem when she lacked a crown to make her queen, an empire over which to rule, and resources to help her people. But now—how could she willingly walk away from her responsibilities when an easy answer was sitting right there next to her, offering up his castle, his title, his land, and his people?

She'd be a fool to say no.

Then again, the obvious answer to so many of her problems was also entangled in the wishes of Iblees, who'd orchestrated this circus from its inception. He'd likely nudged her into this exact moment through devious means, having found ways to bend her emotions to his will without ever saying a word. Her parents had once warned her that her heart, if tuned precisely to compassion, would become a two-pronged tool: it would be her greatest strength *and* her greatest weakness.

She'd never really understood what they'd meant, for it had been difficult to imagine how empathy, so necessary in an emotional arsenal, might prove a weapon of destruction. But now she knew—now it was clear to her that the devil, who was a master of pinpointing and exploiting a person's greatest weakness, had struck her target straight and true, and would use her compassion against her until she broke.

What would happen, she wondered, if she accepted Cyrus's proposal—if she fulfilled her destiny?

How might the devil intervene?

She sighed and the sound carried, awakening a rustle of movement in her neighbor.

"Cyrus?" she said softly.

"Yes?"

"Can I ask you a question?"

She could almost feel him stiffen in response. "I'd really rather you didn't."

"Yes, I realize that, but may I ask anyway?"

He sighed.

"Why do you always wear black?" she said. "It doesn't suit your coloring at all."

"Pass."

"You're not going to answer?" said Alizeh, taken aback. "But it's such a gentle question."

"Oh, and you have less gentle questions for me, do you?" He didn't sound happy about it.

"A great deal, in fact."

"Once again, I'll pass."

"Cyrus," she said patiently, "you can't just ask a girl to marry you and then decline to answer a single question about yourself."

"Try me."

"Fine. Do you have any brothers or sisters?"

He cleared his throat and said, quietly, "Pass."

"You *do* have siblings? Really? Where do—"

"Next question."

She hesitated, feeling dejected, and resolved to ask him something a bit meaner. "All right, then. Maybe you can explain to me why the people of Tulan don't seem to hate you."

"Hate me?" He laughed at that. "Why should they hate me?"

"You're surprised," she said, more a statement than question. "That's interesting. But you took the throne in such a bloody, violent manner— It was in fact so brutal a takeover it was talked about all over the world. There was also a great deal of speculation as to your mental state and your ability to rule—"

"I was not the first in history to claim a crown in an unsavory manner," he said coldly, "and I will not be the last. In the end, citizens care most about clean water, fair wages, good harvests, and a carefully managed treasury. I take care of my people. I give them no reason to hate me."

"But people in Ardunia really seem to hate you," she pointed out quietly. "A lot."

He laughed again, this time with some anger. "They hate me only because they fear me."

"Should they fear you?"

"Yes."

The nosta warmed at that, and Alizeh's heart beat a little faster. "Very well," she said, bracing herself. "I'm going to ask you possibly the harshest question now."

"What?" he said sharply.

Alizeh held her breath and waited, just until she heard him sigh.

Gently, he said, "What is it?"

"Was your father— Was he a terrible man? Is that why you killed him?"

Cyrus fell silent for so long that the sounds of the world around them came into brighter focus. The hush of a restless wind grew fiercer, the chirps of busy birds grew louder; flowers swayed as clouds parted and passed, making paths for the setting sun to glimmer through leaves and branches, dappling all in a heavy, golden light. She heard crickets and bees, parted her lips to draw breath, tasted the chill before it pressed against her skin.

Most of all, she could hear him breathing.

"Cyrus," she said finally. "Will you not answer me?"

"I don't want to talk about my father."

"But—"

"I won't discuss it."

"How am I supposed to trust you," she said, "if I can't understand why you did such a gruesome thing?"

"You don't have to trust me."

"Of course I do." She frowned. "You're making me enormous promises, and I have to believe that you mean them—that you'll fulfill your end of the bargain—"

"I'll make you a blood oath."

Alizeh went very, very still. "No," she said, exhaling the word. "Absolutely not."

"Why not?"

"Because— Cyrus—"

"If you kill me, as we've agreed, none of it will matter."

"But you'll be *bound* to me—possibly forever—"

"Only if you don't kill me."

"And until then?"

He took a deep breath. "Well. Yes. Until then it'll be fairly uncomfortable. Mostly for me."

She shook her head against the flowers. "I won't do it. It's not humane. You'll have no free will."

He laughed bitterly. "And I suppose you think killing me is the more humane option?"

"Killing you was *your* idea!"

"This, too, is my idea. I don't see why you're being so obstinate—"

"Why won't you just tell me your reasons?" she countered, frustrated. "Your mother said you did it because you claimed your father wasn't fit to rule. Is that true?"

"My mother," he said stiffly, "talks too much."

"Cyrus—"

He stood up without warning, and Alizeh saw him come into view with a start, as if she were seeing him for the first time. She turned slowly until she was no longer on her side but on her back, her curls catching loose corollas as she moved, her motions sending into chaos a tiptoe of tulips. She picked a loose petal off her cheek and stared up at him through a kaleidoscope of color and stems and leaves, and for a moment she saw nothing but sky and the blue of his eyes. Then his hair, gleaming in the dying light; the elegant lines of his face, gilded by the golden hour. Alizeh did not like to admit to his beauty, which was hard enough to deny under ordinary conditions, but here, standing in an ocean of flowers, tall and somber in his simple black clothes, Cyrus was fairly magnificent.

He was looking at nothing in particular, his body turned away from hers, but the tension in his limbs—and the rigidity in his stance—belied the placid look on his face.

Softly, she called his name.

He turned his head, saw her there, and visibly flinched. Of all the things Alizeh thought she might find in his gaze, she hadn't expected fear.

She watched his throat work as he looked at her, taking in every inch of her languid body with care. His eyes lingered in places, darkening with something she'd come to recognize as hunger. He regarded her then with an expression that came dangerously close to weakness, as if he couldn't decide which part of her to savor longest, and his attentions, so intense, made her feel both desperate and unsteady, like she couldn't breathe.

"You took off your necklace," he said with some difficulty.

"Yes."

"Why?"

"I felt it was choking me."

"Right," he said, and dragged a hand down his face. Abruptly, he turned away.

"Cyrus," she said after a moment. "Are you afraid of me?"

He almost laughed then, but his expression was strained. "What an absurd question."

"Will you answer it anyway?"

"No," he said drily. "I'm not afraid of you."

The nosta went cold.

"You are," she insisted. "You think I'm going to hurt you."

"No. I don't."

Again, the nosta went cold.

"Cyrus—"

"Stop." He was breathing harder than usual. "I don't want to talk anymore."

"But—"

He made a sound, something like a hiss, his eyes squeezing shut as his body seized without provocation. He clutched his torso and doubled over, clenching his teeth as he sank slowly to his knees, and as he fell forward on his hands he gasped, then bit back a cry, and Alizeh, who was watching this unfold with increasing horror, realized that Cyrus was trying not to scream.

She forgot herself.

She forgot her own tired body and shot upright in fear, her head swimming only a little as she stumbled, steadying herself as she rushed toward him. "What's happening?" she said, stricken. "Why are you hurting? Let me—"

She touched him and he jerked away, forcing out a single word: "Don't."

"But—"

Cyrus's head shot back in a sudden, violent motion, his eyes going wide as he paled, his skin taking on an ashen, sickly color. His body trembled, his chest heaving as he breathed, faster and faster, his face all the while frozen in a single, horrified expression. She knew then that he was seeing something.

That he was *hearing* something.

"No," he shouted. "*No*—"

He broke then, broke with an agonized sound as he collapsed forward, his shoulders shaking as he gasped for breath.

"I can't," he said desperately. "I can't, I'm sorry— *Please*—"

Alizeh bore witness to the torture in his eyes. She heard the low, keening sound he made as a single tear, then another, tracked slowly down his cheek.

She thought her heart might fail.

She understood, rationally, that Cyrus was guilty of bringing the devil into his own life, but she didn't know how to turn away from the suffering of others. She stood there and watched, horrified, while he begged blindly for mercy, as he flinched over and over like he'd been struck. Soon, a thin line of blood began dripping slowly from the crown of his head, then his nose.

Cyrus wept.

He pleaded even as he suffered, blood dripping into his

open mouth as he spoke. "Not the other one," he gasped. "Please, I'm begging you, don't take the other one—"

Cyrus would've died before exposing himself like this. Alizeh knew this, knew he would've willingly thrown himself off a cliff before betraying such emotion before her, and yet here he was, laid bare at her feet entirely against his will. She knew the mastermind behind this misery, and she suspected the devil was humiliating Cyrus on purpose—destroying him before her as a form of punishment, stealing from him his pride in the process, his privacy. She tried to avert her eyes, but how could she? When her pathetic heart snapped in half at the sight?

She was panicked, powerless in the face of his anguish, wishing stupidly that she might wrench him free from this trance, even as she knew any effort would be futile. For when Iblees invaded a mind, escape was impossible.

No, Alizeh knew better.

She was not naive; she understood that this episode had been orchestrated for her benefit. Iblees was torturing Cyrus in an effort to manipulate her sympathies. She saw her missteps quite clearly then, and with increasing despair, realized that she'd somehow betrayed herself.

She'd started to like Cyrus.

She'd begun to see him with complexity, with compassion. She did not, in fact, want to kill him. He was no longer a one-dimensional monster to her, but a perplexing character she hoped to understand.

She'd given Iblees this ammunition.

Indeed, Alizeh suspected she could put an end to this

torment right now if she said but one word: *yes.*

Yes, I'll marry him.

Oh, she was tempted. She'd been deliberating over the choice all day—and she'd felt herself leaning toward an answer in the affirmative more in every hour. But if she allowed herself, in this moment, to be strong-armed into making such an important decision, she'd only be proving to Iblees that her emotions could in fact be controlled by such dark tactics—and then he might never stop. Alizeh couldn't set such a dangerous precedent, certainly not now, when it was clearer than ever what misery she might face if she accepted Cyrus's offer. Her only hope of unifying her people came with a steep price; marrying Cyrus would lead her directly into the devil's arms, and she'd have to maintain a steely resolve in order to tread such treacherous waters. If she did not stand her ground now, where would this manipulation end? How many others would suffer? How many more lives would Iblees break before her in the pursuit of bending her will?

She released a shaky breath.

She could've prevented this. If only she'd been more guarded, if only she hadn't cared. If only Cyrus hadn't turned out to be so very, very human.

Slowly, Alizeh fell to her knees.

She took Cyrus's limp hand in hers, and, like a fool, she cried for him.

TWENTY-ONE

بیست و یک

ON PERHAPS ANY OTHER EVENING, a previous version of Kamran might've complained aloud at the inconvenience of changing for dinner, for it had always seemed to him a senseless tradition. As a young prince, he'd managed to avoid such rituals more often than not, for Zaal had been indulgent of his grandson, who'd once loudly insisted that he couldn't imagine the use in changing his clothes merely to eat a meal. He'd considered himself too practical for such nonsense.

In fact, just days ago he might've made some snide remark to his solemn valet about the waste of time, waste of fabric, waste of jewels. He'd thought himself above such *frivolity*, as he'd often described it. What was the point, he'd wondered, in such elaborate ensembles? What purpose did they serve?

For eighteen years, Kamran had been a fool.

A single day his grandfather had been gone, and already Kamran was beginning to understand that the hours the late king had spent in his dressing room were far from frivolous.

In fact, they were a small mercy.

While Kamran was being dressed, he could not be bothered. He was not asked to speak; he could not be questioned. There were no ministers to harangue him, no military maneuvers to put forth, no rivals to destroy. The enforced quiet was unexpectedly calming, the ritual requiring of him only to remain still, allowing his mind to prepare for the trials ahead. The clothes, too, were a gift, each layer like a bandage wrapped around his vulnerable body. He welcomed the weight: the heavier the pieces, the steadier he felt; the better armored for the hours he would endure, the physical and mental blows he would no doubt sustain.

Kamran even had the presence of mind to realize that this quiet window in the company of his unobtrusive valet might be his last for a long while.

He would savor it.

In any case, the prince's mind required silence to spin, for his apprehensions were tripling by the moment: he'd been unable to deduce Zahhak's intentions in his grandfather's rooms, and the unsolved mystery had left him uneasy. The problem was, Kamran had never been intimate enough with the late king's personal effects to know whether anything had been disturbed or rearranged. As far as he could tell, all was as it should've been, the glittering quarters as meticulous as always. And while some part of him knew he ought to have conducted a more thorough search, he'd lacked the fortitude to linger in the space any longer than was absolutely necessary.

It had been too soon.

His grandfather's scent had hung in the air not unlike a likeness of the man himself; his imagined form had been conjured from only sense and sensation. So powerful was this force that Kamran half expected Zaal to walk into the room at any moment, scolding him for the intrusion. Kamran had struggled to be surrounded by such potent memories;

his chest had ached as he toured the museum of his grandfather's life. The experience had affected him a great deal
more than he cared to admit, for it betrayed a weakness in
his character—a weakness of which his grandfather would've
deeply disapproved.

The prince closed his eyes on an exhale then, Zaal's
painful words reanimating, unbidden, in his mind—

"Enough," *his grandfather said angrily, his voice rising an
octave. "You accuse me of things you do not understand, child.
The decisions I've had to make during my reign—the things I've
had to do to protect the throne—would be enough to fuel your
nightmares for an eternity."*

"My, what joys lie ahead."

*"You dare jest?" the king said darkly. "You astonish me.
Never once have I led you to believe that ruling an empire would
be easy or, for even a moment, enjoyable. Indeed if it does not
kill you first, the crown will do its utmost to claim you, body and
soul. This kingdom could never be ruled by the weak of heart.
It is up to you alone to find the strength necessary to survive."*

*"And is that what you think of me, Your Highness? You think
me weak of heart?"*

"Yes."

Kamran's eyes flew open.

He felt his hands tremble and quickly curled them into
fists, struggling to restore his confidence. Kamran liked to
think of himself as a powerful, invulnerable force, but a single look at the last week of his life was enough to prove the
truth: he was too easily ruled by his heart, too easily manipulated by his emotions.

He was, in fact, weak.

The realization made him nauseous, a wave of self-loathing roiling in his gut. Kamran had been better in command of himself when he was distracted, when Hazan demanded from him a sharpness of mind and wit, when he was moving fast and making plans. But in the wake of Hazan's and Omid's departures—and after he'd dispatched a letter to his aunt—he'd spent the better part of the afternoon evading the stammering servants intent on delivering him hand-printed notes from Zahhak, all of which requested his immediate presence in one of the grand parlors.

Instead, Kamran had made himself scarce.

He'd flit from one darkened corner to another as a silver sea of Diviners slowly infiltrated his home; their long, liquid metal robes skimming the floor as they moved, the trained motions of their feet so unnatural they only ever appeared to glide.

He'd *felt* them as they arrived, each new presence striking him like a tap against a tuning fork, a low level hum of electricity buzzing along the distorted gold veins of his body.

It had frightened him, and like a child, he'd fled.

Kamran knew that a meeting with the nobles and Diviners would be explosive and absolute, for they owed him answers he was not yet ready to receive. There was more work he wanted to do before he was paraded before the priests and priestesses like a sick horse, assessed for worthiness and found wanting. He didn't want to hear them declare him unfit to rule; he didn't wish to be sentenced to a distant province, where he might live in an old, dilapidated holding of the crown, accompanied by a brooding cook, a miserable maid, and an unhappy valet, none of whom would've willingly left Setar to keep him company.

He was not yet ready for his entire life to change.

Instead, Kamran had pored over the enigmatic Book of Arya, which he kept clutched in one hand even now, loath to part with this essential piece of an enigmatic puzzle. Over and over he'd tried to get the book to give up its secrets, studying its skin for more hidden symbols, and pressing a pen to its pages without success, the paper proving impervious to ink. When he'd tired of that he'd filched food from the kitchens, filled skins of water, stocked empty crates with supplies they'd need for their weeklong journey—all of which he'd then hidden carefully near the stables.

The prince only deigned to dress for dinner in the interest of upholding a veneer of the status quo, for though he'd no intention of sitting down to a formal meal, he figured he might, at the very least, pretend to make an appearance before surreptitiously ducking out. Night had fallen upon Setar like a stroke of tar, and he meant to use the darkness to his advantage—for he still had to haul the hidden crates down to the dock.

"Thank you, Sina," he said quietly.

The valet drew back and bowed, straightening before saying, "As a reminder, sire, your cloak awaits you in your bedroom."

Kamran turned carefully to face the man.

There was no reason Sina should suspect the prince of needing his cloak, for he'd done nothing to betray his intentions of leaving the castle at this hour. "I shouldn't require my cloak," he said quietly, "if I'm only going down to dinner."

"Of course, sire." Sina lowered his eyes. "It's only that, earlier, one of the Diviners saw me passing in the hall and she bid me remind you that your cloak is hanging in your bedroom."

Kamran stiffened. "Why would she say such a thing to you?"

"Forgive me, Your Highness," Sina said, shaking his head. "I don't know."

Kamran's heart was pounding in his chest now. Once again, he seemed to feel the electric hum of the Diviners' presence, feel it spark along the glittering branches disfiguring his left arm. He didn't know what this new sensation meant, but he suspected that, whatever it was, it wasn't good.

"You may go," he said.

Sina retreated with another bow and without a sound—after which Kamran charged into his room, retrieved his hooded cloak from its hook, and stormed the halls of his own home.

He was perturbed.

Too many disturbing revelations and unanswered questions had finally unraveled his mind enough that it seemed, sometimes, like he was little more than a mess of nerves. He felt powerless in the face of so much uncertainty, and inaction made him uneasy. He felt he must do something or combust, and this was his sole thought as he flew down the grand staircase, heaving the cape around his shoulders as he went, the superfine black wool billowing about him like a pair of wings. He fastened the heavy gold latch at his throat before making certain the Book of Arya was tucked safely into his cloak, then assessed his escape options. He was determined to make an undetected exit from the palace and was just reaching for the chain mail mask in his pocket when he heard the distant, echoing sound of Omid's voice.

Omid, who'd failed him.

Night had fallen an hour ago, and the child had only now returned?

Inwardly, Kamran sighed.

He was going out to the stables anyway; he figured he may as well track down Omid and take him along, assign him a new role, make the necessary introductions to the groom. Not only would this give him an excellent pretense for leaving the grounds wearing his cloak, but Omid would then become someone else's charge, making him one less responsibility Kamran need worry about in his absence.

Resolved, the prince followed the muted resonance of the boy's voice, noting as he drew closer to the source that, even from this distance, Omid appeared to be deeply agitated.

Kamran frowned.

The boy was not, in fact, speaking; he was *arguing*, exchanging frustrations with what sounded like an angry footman—and no wonder. Omid was shouting in Feshtoon, clearly oblivious to the fact that most footmen in Setar would not be educated enough to speak the language of his southern province.

Kamran picked up his pace then, striding impatiently toward the front hall, intending to resolve the matter at once—when he heard something altogether more upsetting.

Miss Huda.

Her voice was unmistakable, and Kamran experienced a spike of alarm at the sound. He could neither imagine why Miss Huda had returned to the palace at this hour nor what she was doing in Omid's company, but the young woman was now screeching at the angry footman, her shouts growing only more shrill as she cried—

"I most certainly will *not* step aside—and don't you *dare* touch me—"

"Miss, please, you're not allowed to be here—this is a private hour for the royal household, the prince does not receive unsolicited guests in the evening—"

"But she's with *me*," Omid said in accented Ardanz before giving up and carrying on in his native tongue. "We're here on official orders! For the prince! You must let us pass!"

"Are you making any sense of this?" said a footman. "I can't understand a word he's saying—"

"What he's saying," Miss Huda interjected angrily, "is that we are here by order of the prince himself, and mark my words: my father, the Lojjan ambassador, will be hearing about this—"

Kamran thought his head might explode.

The audacity of this absurd young woman to invoke his name in the interest of her own immunity— Oh, he was already pitying himself for being forced to endure her company for the second time in the same day. He turned the corner too sharply, wishing he might leave these idiots to their fate when, suddenly, the entire abhorrent scene came into view.

Kamran stopped short, his body going slack in disbelief.

TWENTY-TWO

بیست و دو

OMID AND MISS HUDA STOOD center stage, both tall and too proud in equally awful, ill-fitting attire, shouting in different languages at a trio of stubborn footmen. In the wings stood Deen, the wiry apothecarist, and Mrs. Amina, the brutal housekeeper of Baz House; this unlikely duo stood silently side by side, each with a hand clapped over their mouths in horror.

Angels above.

Kamran had given the boy a *single* task.

He'd charged Omid with bringing in the apothecarist and the housekeeper for a round of questioning. After Miss Huda's unexpected arrival at the palace this morning, he'd been inspired to interview all others who'd known or conversed with Alizeh at length—and though Kamran had spoken once, briefly, with the apothecarist while incognito, he'd intended to ask the man more direct questions this time around.

Now, he knew nothing but regret.

"I'm sorry, miss," said a footman who didn't sound sorry at all. "I can't let you pass. I have no idea who this boy is"—he nodded to Omid—"and I don't care who your father is. So unless you're hoping to land yourself in prison tonight, step aside."

Miss Huda reared back, clasping a hand to her chest with no small amount of drama. "How *dare* you—"

"This is your final warning," said another footman.

"Oh, just you wait," she said, drawing herself up to her full height. "Just wait until I speak to the prince about this. My associate and I are here on royal orders—"

"Your *associate*?" Kamran said sharply, emerging from the shadows.

"Your Highness!" cried a chorus of breathless voices.

All bowed and scraped before him in an almost choreographed motion, all but Omid, the boy peeling off from the crowd to approach Kamran with wild eyes, his head shaking hard as he spoke in rapid-fire Feshtoon:

"I swear I would've been here before nightfall, sire— I swear with my whole heart I would've— I brought them just as you asked, except there was a mob gathered outside the palace gates—"

"A *mob*?"

"Yes, sire, the people are very angry, sire, and the guards were threatening to pull up the drawbridge to prevent anyone from coming through until Miss Huda told them who she was and finally we *did* get through the gates but then they wouldn't let us come through the front door because they said you weren't accepting visitors but then we finally got through the door and then they—"

"*Enough*," Kamran said.

Omid bit his lip and slunk back, looking suddenly like he might cry. The prince ignored this, his mind in chaos. He'd suspected the people would riot, so it wasn't a surprise, exactly, to hear that a mob had assembled—but it was devastating nonetheless.

Solemnly, he nodded at the footmen. "You may go."

"But— Sire—"

"Ha!" cried Miss Huda, jabbing a finger at the trio of young men. "I told you that you'd be sorry—"

"If I hear you say another word," Kamran said quietly, his eyes flashing, "I will have you barred forevermore from the palace."

Miss Huda fell back, two spots of pink appearing high on her cheekbones.

Kamran took a steadying breath, struggling to rein in his anger, his frustration, his myriad disappointments. He turned to the footmen, acknowledging them one by one. "Thank you for your efforts. I'll take it from here."

"Y-Yes—"

"Yes, sire."

"As you wish, sire."

And then, they were gone.

Finally Kamran was left no choice but to face his strange audience, the odd group staring at him now with terror. The prince knew he'd no one but himself to blame for this shameful turn of events, and wasn't sure then whether his anger was aimed more at himself, or Omid. Or perhaps even the infuriating Miss Huda.

Quietly, he said: "Someone explain to me at once what is going on here before I have the lot of you carted off to the dungeons."

Omid and Miss Huda, so loud only minutes before, seemed

incapable then of saying a word. Their mouths opened and closed as they shared frightened, uncertain glances, and Kamran thought he really might lose his mind when, finally, Deen stepped forward and broke open the silence.

"If I may, Your Highness"—he cleared his throat—"I'd only like to say that I, too, would love to know what is going on here, for I haven't the faintest idea."

Kamran raised his eyebrows. "How is that possible?"

"All I know, sire, is that the ruination of my day began when this young woman"—Deen nodded at Miss Huda—"barreled into my shop oh, about four hours ago and, without warning or even an introduction, began interrogating me—in front of my customers, no less—about someone I'd treated days ago, demanding all the while that I divulge confidential information to a complete stranger—which I feel I should point out is not only unethical, but illegal—and I was still trying to get the miss to leave the premises when this absurdly tall child"—he pointed at Omid—"barged into my store for the second time today, and this time demanded I follow him back to the palace or else hang at dawn for defying an order from the crown—"

Kamran made a pained sound.

"And then—and then these two hooligans"—Deen gestured vaguely at Miss Huda and Omid—"forged some spontaneous and no doubt *nefarious* alliance, after which they forced me into the back of a foul, rented hackney, where I was made to wait at least forty-five minutes before I was suddenly thrust into the very unpleasant company of the woman standing beside me now. I'm afraid I don't know her name"—he turned to Mrs. Amina and muttered an apology, which she ignored with a scowl—"but she spent the entire ride moaning about how angry her mistress would be upon discovering she'd gone, for her mistress was in terrible spirits and she couldn't be spared, especially not on such short notice—"

"All right," Kamran said flatly. "I think I've heard enough."

Deen nodded, then stepped back.

The prince was about to send the witnesses home, fire Omid on the spot, and bar Miss Huda from the palace grounds on principle, when Mrs. Amina suddenly cleared her throat. "I'd like to say a word, too, sire, if I may."

Kamran studied the woman—her beady eyes, her small nose, her ruddy cheeks—and couldn't help but feel a note of revulsion, even now. He'd never forget the bruises he'd seen on Alizeh's face, the threat of brutality this housekeeper had unleashed before his very eyes. Mrs. Amina was a cruel woman.

"You may speak," he said, watching her closely.

"Thank you, Your Highness," she said haltingly. "First, I'll preface this by saying that I realize now might not be the best moment to say my piece, but I feel I might never have another opportunity to stand before you, sire, and clear my name, and so I will say now in my own defense that when you last came to visit your good aunt at Baz House I fear you got the wrong idea of me, for I've read enough in the papers now to know I'd been right all along to discipline that girl, and in fact I think she could've benefited from a good beating, sire, for maybe then she wouldn't have gone on to cause such trouble—"

"Wait, what girl?" said Miss Huda, clearly forgetting her tacit agreement to be silent. "You don't mean Alizeh?"

Kamran flinched.

"Indeed, I do," Mrs. Amina said triumphantly. "I read the girl's name in the papers this morning and I knew straightaway when I saw it seemed familiar, and then I remembered how I'd heard that awful girl tell her name to this boy"—she pointed at Omid—"when he'd come to Baz House to hand her a dratted invitation to the ball, and which I see now I was far too generous to allow, and after the way my dear mistress came home last night, all affright over the terrible tragedy, I told her, I said to her—as I brought her a cup of mint tea to soothe her nerves—I said well how do you like that, milady, I've pieced it all together myself, the girl from the papers had worked here at Baz House all that time— And my mistress was ever so upset about the whole thing, I can't even describe her horror, for she'd begun thinking that you, sire, had known all along about the girl's deception and lied about it, for why else would you have defended her so ardently that day and again at the ball, but I assured her that the girl had likely bewitched you, Your Highness, and that you shouldn't be blamed for her wickedness—"

"*Mrs. Amina*, that is quite enough—"

"Forgive me," Deen said, frowning as he glanced around the group. "But were we brought in to be questioned about the same girl? The Jinn snoda who came to me for salve? If so, I cannot corroborate these stories, for I don't know her name, and I've no notion of her attending a ball or causing any kind of trouble—"

"She was no ordinary snoda!" Mrs. Amina cried. "Don't you see? I'd long suspected there was something the matter with her—she was always putting on airs, speaking all the time like she was some kind of toff—and I only blame myself, sire, for not exposing her sooner. I felt the darkness in her the first day I saw her, and when I watched her eyes change color right in front of me I should've known she had the devil inside her—"

"If anyone has the devil inside her," Omid said angrily, "it's you!"

"Vile girl," Mrs. Amina was saying, ignoring this outburst from the boy. "Never liked her. She never followed instructions, you know. Always sloppy with her work, cutting corners—"

"*Sloppy* with her work?" Deen cut her off, his eyes wide with shock. "The girl who came into my shop with hands so destroyed by hard labor she could hardly make a fist?" He shook his head, took a sharp step away from the woman. "You're the housekeeper who beat her, aren't you? Don't tell me you're responsible for that infected cut across her throat, too?"

"Oh, no, sir," Omid said quietly in Ardanz. "That was me."

Deen looked suddenly revolted. "Who *are* you people? Pray tell me, what crimes have I committed to deserve the great misfortune of your company? I merely treated a girl for her wounds!" He looked beseechingly at the prince. "Your Highness, will you not allow me to return home? I've done no wrong here—I don't deserve to have my name lowered by association with these heathens—"

"Hold a moment," Kamran said, considering Deen closely. "You can confirm that the girl's injuries were real, then? They weren't the result of an illusion?"

"An illusion?" Deen hesitated. "Your Highness, I can't imagine what reason she'd have to waste magic on torturing herself, but if for some inane purpose she'd managed to enchant her hands to ruin, I should think she'd have the ability to change them back. What need would she have of my salves if she could do such a thing on her own? No, sire, I don't believe her wounds were any kind of illusion." The apothecarist frowned then, appearing to remember something. "She did, however, discover in my presence that her body was able to heal itself at a more rapid rate than was normal, and removed her bandages after only days, instead of the week I'd suggested—"

"Heal itself?" Kamran repeated, going still. "Really?"

"Yes, sire." Deen blinked at him, surprised by the prince's interest. "Her skin recovered itself at a rather unnatural pace, which is not considered common even among Jinn—"

"A sign of the devil!" Mrs. Amina cried. "Here is proof!"

"Oh, do *shut up*," Miss Huda said irritably.

"You ignore the signs at your own peril, miss," Mrs. Amina countered sharply. "Jinn can make themselves invisible, not *blurry*—and no one was able to get a good look at the girl last night, almost certainly on account of the devil's influence—"

"There are possibilities other than the devil," Miss Huda shot back angrily. "The clothes she was wearing— Well, they'd been delivered with a note I couldn't read, but garments are all the time bewitched, particularly in battle, to

offer their wearer anonymity or protection, and her blur-
riness might've been the work of a fairly straightforward
magical enchantment—"

"*Dark* enchantments! Dark magic!" Mrs. Amina cried.
"Everyone knows that dark magic cannot be born without
the devil's interference!"

"This is utter rubbish," said Deen, rolling his eyes. "If
the girl had access to dark magic, do you really think she'd
accept a pittance in exchange for scrubbing scum from your
mistress's floors? You think if she had access to dark magic
that she'd willingly share a roof with a brutal housekeeper
who clearly took pleasure in beating her? *I should think not.*"

Mrs. Amina gasped in outrage, took a step back, and
promptly lashed out at the apothecarist, who rallied with
ease.

Kamran wanted to put an end to this madness, wanted
to clear these clowns out of his home, but he'd discovered
then—to his dismay—that he could not move. His pulse
seemed to be pounding in his head, his heart beating violently against his chest.

Bit by bit, he was being proven wrong about Alizeh.

Having now been personally subjected to Cyrus's manipulations of magic, Kamran could imagine that the southern
king possessed the skills necessary to have imbued her
garments with protections. Indeed it would make sense if
he'd magicked the gown to protect her identity from those
who wished her harm—for what else might explain why so
few people at the ball had been able to identify her? What
else would explain Cyrus's cryptic statement, his subtle

accusation that Kamran could *see* her?

Alizeh's gown had been incinerated, twice, as she entered and exited the fire. Perhaps in the process the frock had lost some of its effectiveness, blurring her from the crowd instead of blotting her out altogether. This might explain why Kamran's eyesight had failed him with such inconsistency, why she'd seemed to fade in and out of focus before him; as Alizeh's betrayals were revealed, he'd swung wildly between hatred and longing, wanting at once to kill her and save her.

The magic had perhaps reacted to his warring emotions.

If Alizeh had thought her identity was protected, this would explain, too, why she'd not felt the need to wear her snoda. It did not, however, explain why she'd physically assaulted the young man she'd—allegedly—agreed to marry.

Kamran grit his teeth; he felt then the onslaught of a powerful headache, pain gripping the base of his skull.

He didn't know what he felt most in the face of these reveals: anger or relief or confusion. Perhaps some mixture of the three. For while, on some level, these answers exonerated Alizeh, they also proved that she'd lied to him; she'd pretended not to know Cyrus while she was all the while allied with the Tulanian king. She'd accepted his help, his magic. She'd worn his gown; they'd *had a plan*. Kamran couldn't conquer the chasm of uncertainty yawning open under his feet, for there remained a great deal to doubt about Alizeh, including her betrothal to Cyrus, her alliance with the devil, and her escape from the palace on the back of a Tulanian dragon.

He felt at sea, drowning in doubt, and his frustration only intensified. This anger was directed toward himself, toward his grandfather, toward the circumstances that now defined his life.

That King Zaal had died at all had been reason enough for Kamran to rage, but it was the aftermath, he realized, that had broken him the most, for in the wake of his grandfather's murder, fear and grief had muddled the prince's otherwise inviolable instincts, causing him to question everything that'd felt so certain only hours prior. Once again, his emotions had overruled him.

Of all the trials ahead, Kamran was beginning to fear that his greatest obstacle would be overcoming himself.

"Your Majesty," came Deen's sharp voice, returning the prince to the present. "I beg you: please dismiss me from this circus. I should've been home for dinner by now, and my loved ones will begin to fear for my safety—"

"Loved ones?" Mrs. Amina made a sound of contempt. "You've got loved ones, have you? While the rest of us must marry our work, warm our beds with pain, and give birth only to bitterness—"

"*Enough*," Kamran practically roared.

In a hundred ways he'd been tested throughout his life—in battle and death and devastation—but there was something about being forced to stand still and listen to a pack of idiots speak nonsense in front of his face that made him want to self-immolate. "I don't want to hear another word," he said in a deathly whisper. "From *any* of you—"

The words died in his throat.

An eerie wave of sensation flared along his tortured skin as his heart thundered in his chest, the sound of his own breathing intensifying in his ears. He turned slowly, expecting to see a Diviner, and instead discovered Zahhak, the slippery man slinking toward him now with a cloying smile.

The defense minister came to a stop before him, clasping his hands as if in prayer. "I thought I heard a commotion," he said, taking in the broad details of the unfolding drama with no apparent interest. He returned his blank eyes to Kamran. "I've been waiting for you all day, sire. Perhaps now, we might finally speak."

Another tremor of sensation awoke along the prince's golden veins, just as three Diviners drifted suddenly into view.

TWENTY-THREE

بیست و سه

CYRUS WOULDN'T WAKE.

Iblees had tortured him until long after darkness had shed its skin upon the sky. Alizeh, who knew how to mark time with only her hands and the movements of the sun, had been able to estimate the time they'd lost, the hours Cyrus had been brutalized by the devil. The flower field, which had been so colorful and ethereal in daylight, was rendered a vast lake of pitch in the night. Alizeh did not know where they were; she did not know how to get back to the castle; and every time she closed her eyes for even a moment, she heard Cyrus screaming.

For what had seemed an eternity, she'd watched him suffer.

Bruises had bloomed and diminished all along his face and, she had to assume, his body, where the bluish stains occasionally spread just beyond his collar or cuffs; but the lesions never lasted longer than a minute. His ribs never seemed to break, though he'd clutched them many times in agony. His skin revealed no lacerations, though he'd bled for hours.

When Cyrus had finally stopped seizing, the moon stood high and bright in the sky, and Alizeh had held on to this miracle of light like a lifeline, terrified she'd succumb to her own fears before he even awoke.

Distraught, Alizeh had drawn Cyrus's heavy head into her lap, assessing up close the evidence of his suffering. His face was nearly unrecognizable in such a grisly state, but his clothes and coat, at least, had absorbed most of the evening's bloodshed. The moon occasionally threw into stark relief the damp stains glimmering across his garments, provoking in her each time a new wave of heartache. She'd mopped the remaining blood from his face with the skirt of her white dress, and used the wet of her own silent, unceasing tears to gently scrub the lingering stickiness from his eyes, his skin. Then, when none of this seemed to rouse him, she'd stroked his hair in careful, tender motions. Even then she marveled at the thick silk of his copper locks, the way they gleamed in the moonlight.

She'd begged him to wake.

He did not stir.

It'd been at least thirty minutes since the creases between his brows had smoothed and his body had stabilized, during which time Alizeh had lived with the terrifying likelihood that Cyrus might be dead. It shocked her to discover how much this possibility affected her. She should have rejoiced in his pain; she should have fled while he was unconscious; instead, she astonished herself by remaining firmly by his side, fearing for him, pleading with him to open his eyes.

These were feelings she did not wish to examine.

With a fumbling effort she'd discovered a weak pulse at his throat, giving her reason to hope; but alone in the expansive darkness her imagination was unkind to her. Her memories replayed the last hours on a sickening loop, and the more she turned over the devil's savagery in her mind, the more she felt a spiraling trepidation—a fear of what was yet to come.

Alizeh wiped desperately at her tears.

She watched Cyrus's closed eyes for any sign of life, but his rust-colored lashes rested heavily, undisturbed. Only then, when she was feeling quite desperate, did she dare to touch her trembling fingers to his face, drawing her hand down the stunning softness of his cheek. When still he was unresponsive, her motions grew more assured, more intentional. She caressed him with great care, brushed the backs of her knuckles along the sharp line of his jaw, grazed the elegant slope of his nose. It was strange to see him so defenseless, his expression so unguarded. The harsh edges of his tense and stoic expressions were smoothed away in sleep, the planes of his face rendered milky in the starlight.

She would never again deny that he was beautiful.

She whispered to him over and over, beseeching him to return to his body, to this present moment, and was again stroking the curve of his cheek when he caught her hand— weakly—and she went suddenly, deathly still.

Relief flooded through her even as her pulse sped up, for his fingers slowly closed around her own. He drew the back of her hand gently against his lips, and then, so softly she might've imagined it, he kissed her.

Alizeh's heart beat chaotically in her chest.

"Cyrus," she said, hating the broken sound of her voice. "Are you awake?"

He moved only a little, letting their clasped hands fall

against his cheek. He did not let go. He did not open his eyes. He tore open his mouth with some difficulty, wetting his lips before he drew a deep breath. On an exhale he said, "No."

Alizeh didn't know what to do.

She felt a bit mortified to have been discovered petting him, and she was more than a little unbalanced by the tenderness of his kiss. She sat very, very still in the dark, too aware of their held hands resting against his cheek, and waited for Cyrus to shake off the last of his stupor. She hoped her pounding heart was not audible in the silence, though she feared that it was.

"Touch me," he whispered.

Her heart beat only harder. "What?"

He released her hand, but only to press her open palm firmly against his face. For a moment his eyelashes fluttered, and then, quite contentedly, he sighed.

Alizeh realized, with a shock, that he was dreaming.

She knew she had to wake him—that the hour was growing only later; that her fear of the dark was growing only more acute; that she would eventually freeze to death even on this false summer night; and that, more important, they'd be missed—but she agonized over the decision, for he'd endured such brutality for so long she didn't think she could bring herself to disturb what appeared to be a truly restful sleep.

So she stalled.

Cyrus appeared to be in some in-between state of alertness, aware enough for speech, but too dormant to know he straddled two worlds. She would wait a bit longer, she told herself, to see if he'd find consciousness on his own. Alizeh didn't know why he'd fallen into such a strange stupor in the aftermath of his encounter with Iblees; but if Cyrus was still under the influence of dark magic, she worried forcing him to wake would end poorly.

In the interim, Alizeh gave in and did as he asked, caressing his face in careful, steady motions, occasionally drawing her hand over his hair, smoothing the strands away from his eyes. He soon made a soft, satisfied sound, so gentle and unaffected it made her chest ache; and then, like a child, he turned his head in her lap, sliding his hand up the inside of her naked thigh like it might've been a pillow.

Alizeh nearly screamed.

Earlier, she'd tugged up the hem of her frock, for she'd used her skirt to mop up Cyrus's blood, and had then knotted this heavily sullied hem in hopes of mitigating any further transfer of the red stain. And while, yes, she'd noticed that the dress had hitched above her knees—exposing several inches of bare skin beyond the lace trim of her stockings— she'd paid this small impropriety no mind, for the possible exposure of her thighs in almost perfect darkness had been the least of her concerns thirty minutes prior, when she'd thought Cyrus was dead.

Now, she could hardly breathe.

His hand was warm and heavy, his fingers splayed possessively across the innermost expanse of her upper leg, and worse, they were dangerously close to skimming the seam of her undergarments. Already the weight of his touch in so intimate a place had left her feeling a bit faint; if his hand moved even a little higher, she feared she might actually scream.

His head, at least, was holding her dress quite firmly in place—a fact she took comfort in remembering—but she didn't know what to do. If she were to fling his hand off her leg she would almost certainly—and jarringly—wake him. She'd not hesitate to do so under any other circumstance, but she still lacked the conviction to disturb him any further on so difficult a night, and worse, she didn't know what would happen if she did.

He exhaled heavily in his sleep then, his warm breath grazing her already sensitive skin, and Alizeh nearly whimpered. She was breathing too fast, alternately wondering whether she shouldn't just wake him and be done with it, and whether she might not be overreacting altogether.

He was *sleeping*, after all.

He'd not meant to touch her like this. In fact, she knew him well enough by now to speculate that if he'd any idea his hand was right now resting in such a scandalous place under her skirt, he'd be horrified. He only needed a little rest, she reasoned. Perhaps if his hand stayed exactly where it was, things might turn out just fine.

So when moments later he shifted an inch and his hand moved farther up her thigh, she nearly bit through her tongue to keep from making a sound. His fingers had much more than grazed the silky edge of her underwear, and Alizeh thought she might expire.

"Cyrus," she said, panicking. "Please wake up."

He said nothing.

"Cyrus—"

"Yes."

Her heart was beating too hard. "Are you— Are you awake now? Please tell me you're awake."

When, after a long beat, he didn't answer, she knew she had to do something; she couldn't sit here in the dark with the heat of his touch searing her; she feared the inside of her head would catch fire. Carefully, she hitched her skirt up a bit higher and prized his wandering hand off her thigh, but she'd hardly breathed a sigh of relief before her fears came at once to fruition. The abrupt motion startled him, and he immediately sat straight up with a gasp, looked around himself in an unsteady motion, and met her eyes. Even in the moonlight, she could tell he was disoriented.

"Cyrus," she said, overcome with relief. "You're awake—"

"Alizeh?" he whispered, exhaustion weakening his voice. "What are you doing here?"

"What do you mean?" She tensed. "We're in the flower field, remember?"

"No," he said, and he seemed to lose steam all at once, his head beginning to droop. "How did you"—he blinked very slowly—"how'd you get in my room? You're not supposed to be here."

Alizeh's relief became alarm.

"We're not in your room," she said, fighting back her panic. "It's just that the sun has gone down, and it's very dark now. And cold, actually, so if you wouldn't mind taking us back—"

"I'm so tired, Alizeh," he said, stumbling over the words. He sounded delirious. "Let's go back to bed, Alizeh."

"Cyrus—"

He laughed a little, like he was drunk. "I do say it a lot."

"What?" she said, going briefly still.

"Your name," he said, and closed his eyes. He nearly fell over, catching himself at the last second. "I didn't know your name for so long, angel. I love the way it feels in my mouth."

Alizeh's confusion was outweighed by the physical shock she felt at his casual affection, the endearment embedding in her chest, causing chaos.

"Cyrus," she said, feeling suddenly close to tears. "What's happening to you? Are you sick?"

"Oh yes." He nodded. "It's t-terrible."

"Is it magic?" Her fears ratcheted only higher. "Are you under a spell right now?"

"Mmmm yes always happens," he murmured. "Part of the cycle."

"What always happens?" she asked urgently. "What cycle? What are you talking about?"

He didn't respond; instead, he clapped a heavy hand against his cheek and frowned. "Did you wash my face, sweetheart?"

A new tenderness; another blow to her chest.

"Yes," she whispered.

"How?" His hand fell away, and he squinted into the darkness. "Did you call for a maid?"

"No." Her head felt strange. Overheated.

This time when he swayed, he fell.

Alizeh caught him with a soft *oof*, and his head landed with a gentle thud against her chest, where, without the heft of her golden necklace, the low neckline of her bodice was nearly indecent. Cyrus turned his head, pressed his face to the exposed skin of her breasts, and made a sound deep in his throat, something like a groan.

"You're so soft," he said, slurring the words. "So sweet."

Alizeh worked desperately to compartmentalize the torrent of sensation awakening in her body.

Something was very, very wrong.

"You feel so real," he whispered.

"Cyrus," she said. "You're frightening me."

He shook his head and took a deep, shuddering breath, unselfconsciously inhaling the scent of her. "Don't be afraid of me, angel. I won't hurt you. I'll never hurt you."

Alizeh's chest constricted, her heart frantic. He was a ton of dead weight; so heavy she didn't know how to get his head off her chest without shoving him to the ground.

"Listen, I know you're very tired," she said nervously. "But I need your help, sleepy boy. Can you do something for me?"

"Anything." He drew his nose along the swell of her breasts, kissing the smooth skin there once, twice, until she made a desperate, broken sound and he swore, low, under his breath. "Alizeh," he said, sounding drugged. "Can I taste you?"

She was shaking so hard the tremors were beyond her control now, and if Cyrus weren't half out of his mind she'd have been too mortified to speak. Her breath was coming in fast, in fits. She had to get herself in order or else she'd lose this struggle entirely.

"Listen to me," she said breathlessly, "I need you to get us back to the castle. Can you please do that for me, Cyrus? Can you use a bit of magic to return us to the palace—"

"Mmm," he said softly. "Yes, back to bed, warmer there—"

"No," she hastened to say, "*not* back to bed, *no* bed, just the castle—"

Alizeh bit back a shriek.

She went briefly weightless as the scene blurred, sounds merged, her stomach dropped, and she fell hard onto something soft and dense. The sound of crickets gave way to silence, the chilly darkness replaced by pools of warm, dim light that illuminated the shapes and contours of lush, decadent quarters she had to assume belonged to Cyrus.

And if this was his room, then she was lying on his bed.

TWENTY-FOUR

پچیست و چهار

FOR STRETCHES AT A TIME, Kamran would forget that his appearance had altered. He'd forget that his face was disfigured, that his eyes were different colors. He'd never been so vain as to linger before a looking glass, or even to catch a glimpse of himself in a reflective window, for of all the things he admired most about himself, his physicality was low on the list. Then again, he'd never *had* to care. He'd taken for granted his good looks. He'd long witnessed the effect he had on others; the way dilated eyes betrayed baser thoughts in his presence; the way young women trembled when he stood close enough. Kamran, like many people, was not insensible to a certain energy; he could feel a person's desire.

He could also feel their loathing.

Zahhak's animosity seemed to heat the air around them even as the minister smiled, his black eyes batting like the wings of a beetle, opening to reveal repellant insides for all of a moment before shuttering closed. Zahhak made no secret of his interest in Kamran's transformed face, tracking, with morbid fascination, the glimmering, fractured lines that disappeared into his collar.

"Are you quite well, sire?" he said, feigning concern. "You appear to be in a great deal of pain."

Kamran was careful to keep his expression impassive, even as the statement surprised him.

He was not, in fact, in *pain*.

This registered as a shock, for aside from the occasional discomfort he now experienced at the sound of Alizeh's name, and the odd hum he felt in the presence of the Diviners, the sharp, electric torment he'd more recently been suffering—the pain he'd, for days, ascribed to the discomfort of his clothing—had altogether subsided in the wake of his physical transformation. It was in fact the very lack of discomfort that kept him from remembering his new, grisly appearance.

He did not *feel* tremendously altered.

With a start, he remembered what Alizeh had said to him on the night of the ball—how she'd suspected, as his body had sustained wave after wave of torment, that he might've had an aversion to gold. She'd suggested, as a result, that he cease wearing clothing woven with the glittering thread. It had been an interesting observation, for the gilded stripe that once neatly bisected his chest and torso had all but shattered across his body in an almost reactive manner. But as he adjusted his sleeves then, stalling as he turned Zahhak's words over in his mind, he was reminded that even his mourning clothes glimmered in places with strands forged from the precious metal.

In that regard, nothing had changed.

His attire, designed and fashioned months prior, had not been relieved of its decorative goldwork; the glimmering raised embroidery iconic of his royal garb could be found along the ruffs, cuffs, and shoulders of nearly all he owned.

He struggled then to remember the first incident of this specific, physical discomfort, and the memory found him with the force of a shock: his mother slapping his hand away from his collar, telling him to cease scratching at his neck like a dog; him complaining that they couldn't find a capable seamstress in all the empire. But then, that wasn't entirely fair, for Kamran could not recall ever having such an issue with his garments prior to that morning—

The morning he'd met Alizeh for the first time.

All this he processed in but a matter of seconds, and as he lifted his eyes to meet Zahhak's beady gaze, a strange hypothesis had begun forming in his mind.

"I'm quite well," the prince said, finally answering the minister's question. "Though I thank you for your concern."

Zahhak hesitated, surprise widening his eyes before he clasped his hands, rearranging his expression. It occurred to Kamran only then that he'd likely never thanked Zahhak for anything.

"I've come to you now on a matter of great import," Zahhak said briskly. "In the wake of all this terrible, terrible tragedy, the nobles and I had resolved, among other things, to restore the magical protections of the empire with all possible haste. We assembled early this morning to issue a series of urgent summons to Diviners across Ardunia, but found our actions were redundant, for the esteemed priests and priestesses had begun delivering themselves to the palace before our messengers had even mounted their horses. They've been appearing at intervals all day, you see, having already foreseen the darkness befalling Setar."

"Minister," Kamran said sharply, sparing a glance at his four, wide-eyed onlookers. "As you can plainly see, we have the distinct displeasure of an unexpected audience tonight. Perhaps this discussion should wait for another time."

"I gave you multiple opportunities, sire, to have this conversation in private, but you ignored my every request. I've no choice now but to beseech you where we stand."

Kamran went briefly light-headed with rage.

"*Get out*," he said, spinning around to face his unwanted crowd. "Go home. All of you. *Now.*"

"Forgive me, Your Majesty," said Deen, holding up one finger, "for I would love nothing more than to leave, but I should require a carriage, for our hackney is long gone, and it isn't possible to hail a hansom cab from the palace—"

"*Out*," Kamran shouted, pointing at the door. "Get out and walk home, for all I care—"

"*Walk?*" Miss Huda gasped. "But it's at least half a mile just to cross the bridge, sire, and it's terribly dark and cold outside—"

"And there was a mob!" Mrs. Amina cried. "We might be set upon by bandits!"

Kamran dragged a hand down his face and cursed himself, his life, and this godforsaken troop of halfwits he'd never have known were it not for Alizeh, who'd so thoroughly transfixed him, and so completely possessed him, that he'd failed to notice she counted among her allies a murderous street child, a priggish apothecarist, an illegitimate miss, the demented king of Tulan, and possibly the devil himself.

Oh, he felt he was living through a surrealist nightmare.

Zahhak cleared his throat. "Sire, I know you are benevolent enough to understand the urgency of the situation. Perhaps you will not object to accompanying me now to more private quarters, for the Diviners have requested to meet with you at once. We cannot delay any further."

Kamran felt his blood pressure spike.

He wasn't meant to deal with this right now; he was *meant* to have carried the crates of supplies down to the dock; he was meant to have packed a satchel of essential goods for his journey. He was meant to have finished preparing for a swift escape—not be curtailed by a team of imbeciles, cornered by Zahhak, or reduced to ash by the Diviners.

"I've no doubt," Kamran said firmly, "that you can appreciate how much I've had to do—as you put it, in the wake of all this tragedy—and as I'm currently quite preoccupied, I'd prefer to meet with the Diviners tomorrow"—he offered a terse nod to the trio of priests standing silently to the side—"when my mind is better rested."

Zahhak's expression darkened a shade. "I'm afraid I cannot put them off any longer, sire. We have a new quorum assembled now, and they're ready to perform what they've deemed to be a critical ceremony—one that cannot, under any circumstances, wait another moment."

Now Kamran glowered.

He'd known this betrayal was coming and still he struggled to restrain his anger. "A critical ceremony," he repeated. "A critical ceremony for what purpose, pray?"

Once more, Zahhak's eyes lingered on the glittering

striations upon Kamran's face. "Surely you will wish to do whatever is best for the empire," he said, baring his teeth in a smile. "The Diviners only want to be certain. They bound this magic to your body at birth with a power that was designed never to be undone. There's no precedent for such a marking to mutate in this way, or for a body to reject it. You cannot be surprised by their interest."

Kamran became suddenly aware of a presence behind him, an impulse pricking, alerting him to danger.

He turned his head only halfway, spotting, out of the corner of his eye, the approach of the three Diviners—though how they managed to change positions so quickly, Kamran couldn't imagine.

He turned his gaze to the ground, struggled to remain calm. "You intend to take me by force?"

"During these dark times," Zahhak said silkily, "it is of the utmost importance that we pledge our allegiance only to the true sovereign of Ardunia. Else we cannot be certain to emerge victorious. Surely, you can understand this."

Kamran heard someone gasp at that, and was reminded, as renewed anger tore through him, of his unwanted onlookers.

Very well.

If Zahhak was going to intentionally humiliate him in front of an audience, Kamran would return the favor in full.

"I understand," the prince said darkly, "only that you've been eager to undermine me from the moment my father was murdered. You expected my grandfather to keel over shortly thereafter, didn't you? He was over one hundred years old—his death must've seemed inevitable. But my grandfather lived too long, didn't he? Just long enough to give me time to ascend the throne at a suitable age." Kamran watched the older man stiffen, and took a careful step forward.

"It must've been frustrating for you to see him live," he went on. "For had both my father and my grandfather died in quick succession, I might've been crowned king as a mere child, which would've been a perfect storm of tragedies for a power-hungry man like yourself. I offer you my sympathies," the prince said coldly. "It must've been a blow indeed, to have lost an opportunity to rule as regent."

Zahhak's nostrils flared, his anger surfacing only briefly before he regained control. Still, he spoke in an uncharacteristic rush when he said, "I've worked for this empire since before even your mother was born, sire, and to note the disparity between my sixty years and your eighteen would be to comment on the difference between a mountain and a grain of sand."

He, too, took a step closer.

"That you lack the intelligence and experience necessary to rule Ardunia is a generous understatement. There is no sense in allowing a child to inherit the greatest empire in the world simply by order of birth, and I will not scruple to say that I resent the reward you were dealt for the mere effort of being *born*, a feat accomplished by millions of others who live and breathe today.

"Your grandfather, on the other hand, was a great man and a great king, and I was proud to serve under him. But he destroyed his entire legacy by appealing, in a moment of weakness, to the most detested creature alive. Nearly a century he ruled our land, and now he will be remembered with only hatred and disgust. *Yes.*" Zahhak's eyes glittered with menace. "Your grandfather lived too long. And I can only hope he hasn't instilled the same terrible values in his grandson."

Kamran felt his chest heave with fury.

"Our king is dead less than a day," he said, his voice rising an octave, "and you dare to speak of him with such vitriol?"

Zahhak narrowed his eyes. "That you still hold him in such high regard is damning indeed, *sire.*"

"It is a comfort to me," Kamran said quietly, "to know that I was always right to loathe you."

"As it is a comfort to me," the minister countered, "to know that you will soon be returned to your truest form. Bereft of a crown, you are little more than a spoiled child, unseasoned and ill-informed, and altogether undeserving of the throne."

Unexpectedly, Kamran smiled.

"You take a great risk by voicing aloud your truths, Minister. With every word you put forth you walk yourself closer to your own funeral. Has it not occurred to you," he said quietly, "to fear for the possibility that my crown remains firmly fixed upon my head?"

Zahhak swallowed, his jaw clenching. "Seize him," he said.

Kamran had hardly opened his mouth to speak before his lips were sealed shut, his legs pinned together, and his arms bolted to his sides. His mind screamed in protest as he struggled uselessly against his magical binds, his eyes darting back and forth in a terrible panic. Alarm bloomed through his body, awakening inside him simultaneous fear and rage. For the second time in less than a day he was paralyzed— though this time at the hands of the Diviners, the priests and priestesses who'd always loved and protected him, and upon whom Kamran had relied all his life. This latest blow of another savage betrayal rattled him to his core.

He went suddenly weightless.

The prince felt, more than saw, that he hung in the air, experiencing a strange emotional and physical detachment as his body was shuttled through space. He thought he heard a familiar, insistent buzzing sound, but then came the clamor of voices—a thunder of shouts and cries—and the din faded into nothing as he was forced, floating and paralyzed, from the room.

TWENTY-FIVE

بیست و پنج

KAMRAN STRUGGLED IN VAIN.

It was not in his nature to give in under attack, and he could not bring himself, even immobilized as he was, to simply let go. His mind thrashed against the injustice of it all, against the breakdown of his life. Ardunia had been his to inherit from the moment he could form conscious thought; this was his home, his land—these were his people—and no matter his many qualms, and no matter the complaints he'd so often registered aloud, Kamran did not want to lose who he was. Even he, at this miserable juncture, could admit now that there was perhaps some truth to Zahhak's remonstrations.

Kamran *had* been a spoiled child.

He'd taken his life for granted; he saw that now. But never again would he be a child, and never again would he be cosseted. He'd been forced, unfinished, into this blistering kiln of change, and it had vulcanized him; it would continue to transform him. He could learn from his mistakes. He could adapt as the situation demanded.

And he did not want to lose his crown.

He listened, for a moment, to the sound of footfalls echoing through the corridor, the back of Zahhak's greasy head leading the way as they went. The trio of Diviners were close behind, and Kamran knew this only because he could feel them there, their presence as palpable as the cloak that still draped his body. Mercifully, the prince could move his eyes, and he was able to follow the path they forged through the endless halls of his home, which meant he soon realized, with mounting dread, that they were heading to the throne room.

The inevitable was finally upon him.

The prince was about to be dragged before a team of nobles who would flay him with their castigations, only to then force him before a halo of Diviners who would perform a ceremony that would strip him of his birthright.

On top of everything else he'd endured these last twenty-four hours, this seemed a bridge too far. He felt something break in his chest, something hollowing in the region of his heart.

In a single day, he had been decimated.

Even as it killed him to imagine it, Kamran held fast to a single hope: that, after they ruined him tonight, he might still have time enough to dash to the docks to meet Hazan. He was worrying over this, clinging now more than ever to the idea that, in the wake of his metamorphosis, he might at least become his own man, avenge his grandfather's death, and forge his own path—when, at a sudden split in the passage, Zahhak took a sharp left, and Kamran veered right.

A fresh wave of unease moved through him.

He couldn't turn his head to see for certain, but he had to assume the Diviners were behind this abrupt change in plan.

He was now going in an entirely different direction from the defense minister, and it was a minute before he heard Zahhak's surprised shout, his distant footfalls growing louder as he chased them down.

Kamran heard the minister's voice as if through water.

"Where are you going?" came his dull, warped cry. "You're meant to follow me to the throne room—we're all prepared—"

"Not tonight," said a Diviner.

They never stopped moving.

Hope took flight in the prince's heart, shook him from within. He had no idea where they were headed now, but this seemed a promising turn of events.

"What do you mean?" Zahhak said, his muted voice shaking with anger. "We had a plan— You agreed to perform the ceremony tonight—"

"We agreed only to test the boy," came the simple reply.

"Test him? Test him how? *Wait*— You can't go back on your word— You're incapable of lying—"

"We promised to determine whether the boy is fit to rule."

"There's no question but that he's unfit!" cried Zahhak. "The boy is mutilated! That has to mean something! The magic has clearly made a statement—"

"*Leave,*" said the Diviners in unison.

The word was spoken softly, but it hit Zahhak with a forceful gust, knocking him back several feet and keeping him there. The defense minister fought in vain against this unrelenting wind, crying out as they retreated.

Kamran's heart was pounding dangerously fast, for the hope that had so recently burgeoned in his chest had quickly evaporated.

We agreed only to test the boy.

The prince hadn't a single reasonable hypothesis for what might happen next—and he didn't have much time to theorize. Once Zahhak had been left behind, the Diviners propelled him through the castle at a breakneck speed, moving so swiftly the scenes around him blurred, so he had no idea of their location and could not guess at where they might be headed. His only clue arrived when he felt himself growing dizzy, and he realized, as his head spun, that they were spiraling upward, climbing floors. Of all the hints he might've received, this one was by far the darkest, for he knew most assuredly then that they were ascending the palace spires, and there was nothing good to be found here.

Still, he told himself not to overreact until he knew more—until he could be sure—

They came to a sudden, disorienting stop outside of an ominous, heavily rusted door—which blew open at the Diviners' behest—and Kamran began to panic. When he felt the icy air of the merciless winter night rush all around him, his panic wedded with horror.

This was the tower prison.

Infinitely worse than the dungeons, which were only temporary holding cells, the tower prisons were reserved for the worst transgressors—usually high-ranking criminals who required more time to be sentenced, and were in the interim doomed to wait out this period in the harshest form of solitary confinement, to make certain they didn't escape. Keeping prisoners was an exhausting, grueling, and inefficient business; his grandfather had never cared for it. He'd always encouraged Kamran to deal with criminals swiftly; once a judgment had been made, the punishment would be served, and the prisons cleared out. Inmates were, as a result, never kept for very long, and the worst of them were often beheaded shortly thereafter.

They hadn't used the tower prisons in years.

Even Kamran, who was fairly stout of heart, shook inwardly at the thought of such a fate. How the Diviners intended to *test* him with this experience, he couldn't know, and what he'd done to deserve this level of cruelty, he couldn't imagine. He only hung there, suspended in the doorway of his disgusting new home for the length of a truly terrifying moment. It was pitch-black but for the glimmer of the moon and stars, for the tower had a single open-air skylight, which loomed from on high, at least fifty feet above his head. He had no idea what carcasses he might be forced to share this room with, and it made him ill to imagine he might leave this place only to have his head removed from his body.

Fear awoke, untamed, inside his mind.

How was this wretched place meant to prove his mettle? If only he could speak aloud a single word then, he would've begged for quarter. *Why?* he wanted to shout. *Why are you doing this? What have I done to deserve such a sentence?*

Alas.

Kamran hadn't more than a moment to process this tyranny before his body was shuttled into the cell, the door slammed shut behind him, and he was finally, unceremoniously, released.

He fell to the icy stone floor with a pitiful cry.

TWENTY-SIX

پیست و شش

CYRUS STILL CLUNG TO HER, his cheek pressed heavily against her chest, but his effort to transport them appeared to have drained the dregs of his energy, for he'd fallen asleep once more. He did not stir; he said not a word; and she could feel his deep, even breaths against her skin.

Inch by agonizing inch she drew away from him, carefully disentangling their limbs. He resisted at first, making incoherent sounds of protest, but he soon accepted his empty arms even as he frowned in his sleep. She watched him shift a bit, trying to get comfortable, and soon his hand slid up the silk sheet of his pillow, just as he'd done with her leg.

A rush of air left her lungs.

Perhaps her overwrought nerves could finally recover. They were safely back in the palace, Cyrus was in bed, he no longer seemed to be in danger of kissing her, and now all she had to do was sneak out and slink back to her own quarters—which was much easier said than done, for this palace was enormous and terrifyingly vertiginous. Alizeh had no idea where her rooms were positioned relative to his, but compared with all else, this seemed a simple enough problem to solve. First, she'd need to figure out how to exit Cyrus's room without notice, and then she'd have to make certain to avoid running into Sarra, who'd no doubt want to discuss Alizeh's progress on the path to murdering her son. Should she manage all this, Alizeh would only need to ask a few nosy, gossiping servants for directions to her room, all the while hoping the uninitiated among them would neither question who she was nor ask about the bloodstain on her skirt.

Simple.

With a quiet groan, she surreptitiously slid off the bed, but then, glancing back at Cyrus, she hesitated.

She knew better than to think his intoxicated actions tonight were indicative of some larger shift in their relationship. Cyrus had told her quite plainly just hours ago that he *hated* her, and the nosta had confirmed this. They'd enjoyed some reluctant and surprising moments of friendship, but she didn't think it was enough to erase such passionate feelings of loathing, not when the agreement between them was meant to end with murder.

Still, Alizeh was too reasonable to deny that, despite her many practical objections, she was intensely *aware* of Cyrus; there was no questioning that she felt a baffling, magnetic pull between their bodies. Then again, that didn't mean she trusted him.

And right now, she feared for him.

For two hours the devil had put him through seven levels of hell, and apparently it wasn't his first time. She doubted it would be the last. And while she knew Iblees had taken notice of her concern for Cyrus, she felt there was nothing to be done for it; Alizeh didn't see the effectiveness in pretending to reverse what had already been set in motion; the devil was not stupid. She would never be convincing enough to trick him into thinking otherwise. Alizeh *did* care. Ice ran through her veins, yes, but it had never made her coldhearted. She'd sat there and borne witness to Cyrus's suffering. She'd cried for him.

And now, no matter the devil's machinations—no matter the incomprehensible state of things between she and the perplexing king—Alizeh was too tenderhearted to abandon his battered, brutalized body without a touch of mercy.

With a sigh, she walked over to his side of the bed, studying his strained expression, the dried blood caking his garments. Cyrus still wore his boots, his sword belt, his dense black coat. She saw the glimmer of a sheathed blade resting heavily against his leg and knew he must be terribly uncomfortable. Gone was the softness in his face earlier rendered by sleep; he'd been grumpy since she'd pulled away from him, and his shoulders had tensed all over again, even in slumber.

When she closed her eyes, she still saw him bleeding.

She could hear him weep.

Gently, she drew her hand along the vamp of one sleek, black boot, the craftsmanship of the maker displayed in every inch of the buttery leather. With careful movements, she tugged up the hem of Cyrus's dark trousers until she uncovered a swath of warm, golden skin dusted with his coppery hair. Focusing her eyes on the buckle she'd sought out, she unfastened the boot easily, then slid the supple article free from his socked foot, also black. Alizeh took the heavy boot into her hand and examined it, helpless to admire the careful, even stitches, the evidence of hours and hours of hard labor, even as she set it down. She repeated the process once more, on his other foot, and once done, she placed the sturdy pair neatly against the wall.

Then, delicately, she drew one of Cyrus's arms away from his pillow, and gingerly tugged it free of its coat sleeve. She intended to roll him onto his alternate side, hoping to replicate the action on his other arm, when he suddenly jolted. He drew a violent breath and sat up like a springy child's toy, startled just as he'd been in the flower field. This time, however, Alizeh knew what to expect. She knew he wasn't truly awake, and she would avoid being drawn into ephemeral conversations with him.

She doubted he'd remember much of this.

"Alizeh." He blinked blearily, studying her with red, glassy eyes. There was a desperation in his voice when he said, "Why did you leave me?"

His words were like a shot to the heart.

With effort, she pushed aside this aching sensation, knowing that what he'd provoked in her was the work of a ghost. Never would she have expected an uninhibited version of Cyrus to be so emotional or affectionate, but then—she didn't actually know what she was dealing with, or what, exactly, he was going through.

Whatever it was, *this* was not the real Cyrus.

"Will you help me?" she said instead. "I was trying to take off your coat."

He said nothing, just looked at her, then at himself, partly divested of his jacket. In stark, childlike motions he removed the rest of the article, then shoved the garment halfheartedly away from himself. It toppled, with a slithering sound, to the floor.

Alizeh promptly scooped this up into her arms, surprised by its weight, and draped it carefully on the back of a nearby chair. She turned around just in time to see Cyrus ripping off his shirt.

Like dew in winter, she froze.

He'd pulled the dark article up over his head, his face disappearing as his naked upper body came suddenly, shockingly into view, and Alizeh, who'd not realized how she was staring, did not stir until she heard the ragged sound of her own breathing. Good God.

Cyrus was *powerful*.

She didn't know how else to describe the sight of him, stripped down to his skin. She didn't know how to fathom into words the corded muscle that moved as he stretched, the sinewy lines of his body that snaked all the way down his torso. He gleamed in the soft light, the shadows carving him into a wonder so substantial she was disturbed by a sudden, stupid desire to touch him, to see what he might feel like under her hand.

Cyrus paid her no attention.

He pulled the shirt free, his hair suffering in the aftermath, and let the garment fall where it fell, not seeming to care for its fate. Alizeh watched him in a daze as he moved, riveted by the motions of his arms as he unbuckled his sword belt, marveling at the tension in the muscles flexing across his body, the tightly restrained power behind even his slightest movements. He let the precious holster and its weapon fall to the ground with a clatter, and Alizeh, who'd been in something of a trance, nearly jumped a foot in the air at the sound. But it was when he began unbuttoning his trousers that she turned sharply around with a stifled cry, covering her entire face with her hands.

Oh, she was ashamed of herself.

She'd been gawking at him brazenly, like an unprincipled deviant, her heart beating like the wings of a hummingbird, so fast it was making her feel ill. Heavens, but she'd forgotten herself. She was *not* an unprincipled deviant. She did *not* ogle the naked bodies of men under the influence of dark magic.

"Alizeh?" she heard him say.

She made an effort to moderate her voice, but did not turn around. "Yes?"

"*Alizeh*," he said again, this time softly scolding.

"Are you," she said tremulously, "are you decent?"

She heard the low rumble of his laugh. "Yes."

Terrified, she turned around in slow motion. She discovered him still sitting up but was relieved beyond reason to find that he'd pulled the blanket around his lower body.

"Hello," she whispered, lifting a hand in greeting, like the veriest idiot.

He only looked at her in response, looked at her with manifest desire, his gaze darkening as he watched her, like he wanted to devour her. His eyes raked her face and body until she felt a liquid heat roil through her, tension coiling taut in her stomach. She took an unsteady step back.

"Come here," he said roughly.

"N-No," she said, shaking her head. "I can't— I— Cyrus, you're very tired."

She watched his chest expand as he breathed, his eyes closing even as he fought it. "I want you," he said, weakening in that familiar, sudden manner. "Next to me."

"I'll come back," she lied, her heart pounding in her ears. "You rest here until I return."

He rolled his neck, stretching tense muscles as he sighed. He sank down a few inches, his head perilously close to his pillow. "Alizeh," he whispered, even as his lashes fluttered, his exhaustion proving unconquerable. "Don't lie to me."

She said nothing to this, not knowing how to respond. She only clasped her hands tightly against her stomach, feeling herself tying ever more tightly into knots.

Finally, like slowly sinking sediment, Cyrus's heavy body succumbed. He slid with a soft hush against his sheets, his head hitting the soft down of his pillow. He did not lift his weary arms to draw the blanket above his shoulders, but here was where Alizeh walked away, for the truth was she'd reached her limit the moment Cyrus had removed his shirt.

She swallowed.

It wasn't right to be so attracted to a man she was meant to kill. Besides, Cyrus had no idea what he was doing. He was out of his head, his common sense dimmed by something dangerous. If he had any idea of the things he'd said to her— If he had any idea how he'd been acting around her—

Just then came a sharp knock at the door.

Alizeh bit back a shriek, her heart resuming its desperate

pounding. She heard the soft call of a maid's voice, asking for leave to enter, and looked desperately at Cyrus, who didn't stir.

The servant called out again.

Alizeh knew what happened next. She'd *been* that snoda. For a brief window in the evening, during which time the occupants of a house were expected to be downstairs for dinner, a servant would come into a room to stoke the fire, refresh the linens, and attend to small tasks. The protocol was to ask permission thrice, waiting each time for a response before accepting silence as tacit consent to cross the threshold.

One more knock, and the snoda would enter the room.

The maid would almost certainly have a heart attack—and worry dearly for her job—once she discovered the undressed king lying in his bed, but it would be at least a minute or two before the snoda reached this chamber, Alizeh was realizing, for Cyrus, as sovereign, likely lived in the largest and most opulent wing in the castle. There had to be at least several large rooms between the bedchamber and the entrance.

Which meant she might have *just* enough time to hide.

Frantically, she whipped around.

Angels above, if she were discovered in the king's bedchamber—if she were even discovered in his *rooms*—the scandal would no doubt disseminate through the empire in under an hour. She'd either be expected to marry him or be denounced as a harlot; either way the repercussions would horribly complicate her life.

Alizeh had learned her lesson this afternoon: there were

Jinn working in this palace, and not only were they ready and eager to spread news about her, but she couldn't rely on her invisibility to help her now, for those efforts worked only on Clay eyes. Perhaps if she found Cyrus's dressing room, she might hide in his closet—

But when she heard the door open, a moment later, her mind went blank. She bolted down the hall and yanked open the first door she could find.

TWENTY-SEVEN

بیست و هفت

THE NIGHT WAS BLISTERING.

Kamran clambered to his feet and dusted off his cloak, taking a moment to calibrate after having been so incapacitated, and only moments later he was shivering. The stone floor underfoot was icy in places, frost having recently chased the rain. The silence was serrated by the devoted chitter of crickets, occasionally stirred by the hoot of a hunting owl; terrible gusts howled and battered the tower skylight, the wind not knowing how to navigate the narrow opening.

Kamran looked up.

This small, distant window, he was realizing, was both a blessing and a cruelty in this dire place, for while it provided what was no doubt a welcome light during the day, it also exposed its prisoner to the elements at night—proving to Kamran once again that pleasure and torture were often delivered in the same blow.

It made him think of Alizeh.

It was impossible not to think of her then, to be reminded of the linchpin of the tragic story that had become his life. Alizeh, who'd awoken in him emotion he'd never before experienced, who'd opened his eyes to a kind of glorious madness he hadn't even known was possible—and then, with a tender smile, so delicately snapped in half his entire world.

She'd risen up from dust, come to life on a breeze, and left a trail of perfumed flowers in her wake as she ushered in the fall of a king who'd ruled the greatest empire on earth for nearly a century. The true wonder was how she'd done it. Without lifting a finger—without even raising her voice—

She'd simply stood tall, and his world had collapsed.

She spoke, and the Diviners had been slaughtered; she spun, and his grandfather had been murdered; she laughed, and his body had been disfigured; she breathed, and his mother had vanished; she sighed, and his aunt no longer spoke to him; she *left*, and his own people had turned on him. Kamran could not even hear her name without taking it like a shot to the chest.

Even then, he wondered whether he'd ever see her again.

With great effort he forced himself to clear his mind of her, and, as his gut twisted, he felt a quiet gratitude for the icy chill that braced him, for it was an excruciating blessing: this cold was likely the only reason Kamran could breathe through the stench of his revolting cell. He was afraid even to move, for his foot had a moment ago brushed against a soft heap of what had to be a stock of dead animals. The feathered among them he could not explain, but the furrier beasts whose carcasses littered this floor had no doubt fallen to their deaths from the lip of the skylight. He supposed he'd know more about his rotting inmates upon sunrise; until then, he was left with only the curse of his imagination, for it painted him a terrifying picture of his days ahead.

Still, he was not without a sliver of hope.

For some perplexing reason the Diviners had not stripped

him of his weapons before locking him in the tower, and he wondered whether he might not, in daylight, be able to use his daggers to scale the stone wall; he could perhaps wedge his blades between bricks bit by bit, carefully levering himself up the steep incline. It would place an excruciating demand upon his body, one he wasn't sure he was capable of, but even the possibility of escape granted his lungs the necessary inch they needed to expand, and finally, he was able to draw breath.

If only he could survive this brutal winter night, he might overcome this. He would break this tower apart brick by brick if he had to; he would not be left here to rot; he would not be dragged from this pit to an unjust execution.

He *swore* this to himself.

And then he wondered, as he shouldered the weight of his present failure, how long Hazan would wait for him at the docks tonight before giving up. He wondered whether anyone would ever realize where he'd gone. It was then, as he had this grim thought, that he seemed suddenly able to hear them.

Or hear something, anyway.

The sounds of the world around him dimmed in a disorienting, unnerving sea change; a hush soon filled his head in incremental, staticky fits and starts, this warbling birth of sound and vibration generated as if from nowhere, and which haunted him then in that eerie darkness. The white noise evolved into whispers that stroked cold fingers along the inside of his head, making him want to tear his skin from his body; the soft tremors grew steadily louder, crawling forth from an unformed, senseless hush into a swarm of voices that clamored in his eardrums, attacking him with a forceful resonance, shouting and fighting to be heard all at once—

Kamran clapped his hands over his ears, falling hard on one knee as his head exploded.

"—have any idea that the nobles were reconsidering his right to the throne? How cruel—and in the wake of his grandfather's murder—"

"I don't know, miss, his grandfather wasn't a very good person—"

"Oh, I only meant that it must be hard for him, you know, to deal with all these revelations—"

"Where is it?! I know you know where it is, and I demand you tell me—"

"I can't believe I'm helping you hooligans. I was supposed to be at home hours ago—"

"Kamran, you idiot. What have you gotten yourself into now? Come along then, pet, thank you for telling me—"

"—can't just leave him in there! Omid, do you remember which way they turned after that?"

"—already searched the king's rooms! I couldn't find it!"

"At least that horrid housekeeper is no longer with us—"

"Yes, miss, I followed them all the way up—"

"—didn't see you? How did you manage that?"

"—a long time, sir, being a street child means learning how to disappear in plain sight and I—"

"Hazan!"

"Oh, thank goodness you're here—"

"Why are you protecting him? Where did you take

him? Why are you willfully jeopardizing the future of this empire—"

"—the hell are you two doing here? And—aren't you the apothecarist?"

"Your cloak weighs heavy tonight, sire."

"Yes, I'm an apothecarist. Who are *you*?"

"—saving the prince!"

"It's my duty to assume control of the throne! You must tell me where it is! It's my right! It's my—"

"You should turn out your pockets, child, and unburden yourself."

"—what have you done with it? *Where did you put it?*"

"Turn out your pockets, child."

"Turn them out."

"Turn out your pockets."

"*DO IT NOW—*"

With a rising, whistling shriek that nearly took off his head, the voices were suddenly ripped out of his mind, leaving in their absence only a lingering scream that all but blew out his eardrums. Kamran was on both knees now, fighting back a cry of agony as his chest heaved, and his head ached, and his ears rung painfully as the sounds of the world slowly regenerated around him. He soon heard the trill of crickets, the call of a nightbird, the wind sweeping a scatter of dead leaves toward his feet. Still, he struggled to regain his strength. In the aftermath of this strange episode Kamran was left shaking, his limbs trembling. He felt an unexpected warmth of moisture at his ear and lifted an unsteady hand to inspect it, his fingers coming away smeared with blood.

Kamran's heart was pounding.

He didn't understand what'd just happened, but he was aware enough to fuse together what seemed the most likely theory: that this experience could only have been crafted through the use of magic, which meant the Diviners must've been trying to communicate with him.

Turn out your pockets.

These cryptic words made no sense. There was nothing in his pockets save a bit of gold, Alizeh's book, and his chain mail mask, and last he'd checked, none of these things was a sledgehammer, which was the only item he truly cared to possess at the moment.

Nevertheless, he was too curious to ignore such a direct command, and he clumsily patted himself down, turning out his pockets even as his head swam, his frozen fingers fumbling. The usual suspects were all here, all accounted for, and there was nothing else to—

Kamran's hands stilled, then, as he felt the shape of something unfamiliar in his interior cloak pocket.

Carefully, blinking to clear his blurry vision, Kamran withdrew a small, rectangular package from his pocket. It was a slim box wrapped in brown paper, tied with simple red twine. He recognized the gift at once, the significance hitting him with an astonishing blow. His understanding of the moment was indeed so powerful, so fiercely unsettling that he felt his eyes prick with emotion.

The late Diviners had given this to him days ago.

Before they'd been murdered, before his home had been invaded, before his grandfather had been killed, before he'd

ever known the satin of Alizeh's skin. It was because of this
package that he'd arrived at all in the Royal Square; the
Diviners had summoned him for a visit that day despite the
fact that he'd never announced his return to Setar. He'd awoken early to avoid the crowds that would inevitably swarm
the streets, and was making his way to the Diviners Quarters
when he was stopped in his tracks at the sight of what he
thought was a grown man about to murder a servant girl.

This moment.

It had changed the course of his entire life.

Later, after the pandemonium had settled, and after
the Diviners had taken in the street child to care for him,
Kamran had finally gone to see the priests and priestesses to
whom he still owed a visit. He'd checked in on the boy while
he was there, but Kamran had been so distracted by the out-
come of his infuriating meeting with Omid that he hadn't
paid much attention to the gift the Diviners had pressed into
his hands on his way out the door. The prince, who'd been
by then accustomed to receiving small gifts on occasion from
both Diviners and commoners alike, merely tucked the parcel into his cloak pocket, meaning to open it at a later, less
chaotic moment.

It had remained here ever since.

Now he stared at it with shaking hands, but he did not
delay any further in unwrapping this package. He tore it open
like a crazed man, tossing the scraps to the filthy ground,
and carefully lifted the delicate lid of a simple wooden box.
A wisp of paper fluttered out at once, and which he caught
in a desperate motion with his unbloodied hand. Then, his

heart pounding in his chest, he looked inside the box, within which he discovered a single black feather, resting in a bed of linen.

At first, he did not understand.

He scrambled to unfurl the paper, which he quickly held up to the moonlight, and in the distant glow he was able to discern that the scrap was but a piece of a much larger document. It was a small slip of paper with torn edges, and its pale skin had been printed upon in the neat, careful script of his grandfather.

It read:

> leave this feather to my grandson, to use only when all else seems lost, when his tragedies feel insurmountable, and hope feels impossible. He will need only to touch it to his own blood, and Simorgh will come for him, as she once did for me. I also leave him my

There, the message was cut off, and Kamran's heart sped up to a truly frightening pace; suddenly he could hear nothing but his own breaths, the harsh sounds echoing between his ears, his mind spinning as the world around him seemed to fracture and reassemble, fall apart and resurrect.

Still, he did not hesitate.

Kamran pressed the feather into his bloodstained hand and, with a shaky, terrified breath, he closed his fist.

IN THE BEGINNING

در آغاز

ONE NIGHT WAS BORN
   a royal child
   Windows shattered
   the rain was wild

   The queen rejoiced
   The king ran inside
   He looked at his son
   his eyes went wide

   The baby had hair
   the color of milk
   His body was healthy
   soft as silk

   Still the father was frozen
   He did nothing but stare
   at the white of his lashes
   and the white of his hair

   You've birthed an old man
   was all he could say

This child is cursed
and he tore him away

The mother then cried
The babe did, too
He cried in the way
babes often do

Amid protests and screams
that terrible king
strapped the child to his back
and did a terrible thing

He climbed a mountain
his arms growing stiff
Left the baby to die
at the top of a cliff

The wind was screaming
the child was, too
He screamed in the way
children often do

when their parent
is vile
and stupidity reigns
when delusion
wins
and intellect wanes

From on high watched a beast
who didn't like what she heard
Simorgh, Simorgh,
a magnificent bird

Her heart was unmatched
her magic unknown
She snatched up the child
to raise as her own

With four other chicks
the boy grew in her nest
He was happy and loved
and knew he was blessed

She warned him that
one day
he'd have to return
to a life he'd not known
to a role he'd not learned

He rejected this warning
but Simorgh insisted
His destiny was written
it could not be resisted

News reached him one day
that a woman still cried

That an empire was failing
that his father might die

Simorgh brought him finery
that he wore without joy
to return to the palace
he'd not known as a boy

He said his farewells
with an ache in his heart
to the family he'd chosen
whom he'd loved from the start

Then he seated himself
on his mother's back
and she tore through the sky
with a deafening crack

Color exploded
when she took flight
She landed at the palace
in a shower of light

None would forget
the day Zaal had returned
The way the world brightened
the way his father had burned

Zaal took the throne
he was always meant to claim
But he would never forget
his true mother's name

TWENTY-EIGHT

بیست و هشت

ALIZEH WAS TRYING NOT TO breathe. She dared not make a sound. She didn't even know where she was. In her panic she'd not merely yanked open the closest door, she'd inadvertently *broken* it, shattering the lock with unplanned, wretched preternatural strength. The hefty trio of engaged bolts had torn through the solid frame, and now the blasted door wouldn't latch, her panic only escalated, and she feared that, when the real Cyrus awoke, he'd renege on his promises and actually kill her for this appalling invasion of his privacy.

She leaned heavily against the broken door, trying to catch her breath as she held the substantial panel closed. For the moment, at least, she was safe, for Alizeh suspected the maid would know better than to poke her head in a chamber that was usually locked. Still, her mind was racing; she'd hardly had time to register that Cyrus kept a bolted room in his own private quarters before she'd been blindsided by its cozy interior.

She realized only then, as she looked around, that she'd formed no expectations at all of Cyrus's personal tastes. He never wore anything but black; she'd not assumed he had any interest in color or comfort, and was stunned to discover that he'd hidden away such a beautifully appointed space. She stood then in a well-worn sitting room anchored by a rug of astonishing detail, rendered in vivid shades of blue; the space itself was furnished with cozy, lived-in seating, floor-to-ceiling shelves stocked with tattered books, and a titanic fireplace before which stood a colossal, weathered desk stacked with papers, pots of ink, and various bell jars through which gleamed specimens of crystallized rock, each neatly labeled.

There was so much to look at she hardly knew where to rest her eyes. Her nerves calmed incrementally as she looked around, praying all the while that the room might present her with a secret exit, or a closet, or even an accessible window.

Instead, she saw evidence of Cyrus everywhere.

An empty cup of tea, a half-eaten apricot, and a slim leather volume with a visible bookmark sat together on a dusty end table; dozens and dozens of loose pages crammed with lines of steady, even script had been bound in twine and left stacked on one of the faded velvet couches; aged, yellow maps of terrains she didn't recognize had been annotated and pinned to the wall; a half-toppled tower of patterned rug pillows trembled beside a stack of unopened crates; a gleaming ox-headed mace rested against the slightly singed arm of a reading chair; a dark coat and a top hat hung from hooks adjacent to the fireplace; a bottle-green, thick-bristled hairbrush sat upon a low table beside a sleeve of long-stemmed matches and a solid bar of perfume; and there was a single, brilliant sword, the gleaming copper blade of which had been planted into the wood floor beside the desk chair.

Alizeh wanted then, possibly more than she'd desired anything material in a long time, to open drawers, lift cushions, leaf through pages, and look around—even as she knew it would be treacherous to snoop. Nevertheless, she managed to restrain herself not because she was virtuous, but because if she stepped away from this door, it would yawn open, and she couldn't risk—

She heard a startled scream.

Ah, the poor servant had discovered Cyrus, then. Alizeh heard the pounding of the snoda's panicked footfalls as the girl bolted from the room with a terrified cry, and then, as the front door eased shut with an audible *snick*, her own petrified heart began pounding anew.

It really hit her then.

She had *broken* his door.

She clapped a hand over her mouth, not knowing how she'd explain this. She couldn't hide the evidence of what she'd done, and she didn't know whether he'd believe the truth.

From afar, she looked unambiguously guilty.

Even she could see how it looked: any who doubted her would assume she'd taken advantage of Cyrus's torture— and subsequent torpor—to trick the king into bringing her into his private rooms, whereupon she'd forced him into bed only to then break down a locked door and rifle through his personal belongings.

It made her seem fairly diabolical.

She bit her lip. Such a story was false, of course, but she could not deny an urge to be just *a little* diabolical, for the desire to rummage through his things was agonizing. This room was a veritable museum of wonders, dotted not merely with fascinating artifacts of Cyrus's life, but with evidence of his state of mind, his current pursuits and interests. She felt certain there were answers here—clues to a series of mysteries she might otherwise never be able to solve—

And then, with a start, she saw the cabinet.

How she'd overlooked it initially, she did not know, though perhaps because it was fairly unattractive: large, dark, weathered, and looming from its position against the wall, adjacent to the fireplace. It was a sort of cabinet of curiosities, something more likely to be found in an apothecary than a sitting room, with many little doors and drawers, each with an individual keyhole.

Temptation sunk its teeth in her.

She drew inches deeper into the room, feet moving toward the chest almost without her permission. The broken door groaned quietly open behind her, but she paid it no mind, for the maid was gone, the wing was quiet, and she felt quite certain Cyrus was asleep. She clasped her hands to keep from touching anything, but as she approached the cabinet, she felt her fingers flare with heat, proving a deliciously strange sensation for a girl with ice in her blood. The closer she drew, the more Alizeh felt almost tethered to this odd piece of furniture, as if she were compelled to approach it, as if it contained something that belonged to her—

Slowly, the cabinet began to tremble.

Alizeh felt her pulse pick up and advanced toward the unit now with haste, the old wood rattling with increasing fervor. It was making a terrifying racket, the tremors so intense they disturbed the walls and floors of the entire room. She understood, dimly, that she would pay for causing such a clamor, that the din might wake Cyrus, that this could land her in a catastrophic amount of trouble, but at the moment, it seemed worth the risk.

Alizeh was transfixed.

She drew a fortifying breath as she pressed her heated hands against the old, shuddering exterior of the cabinet, the reverberations beginning to crescendo. She was waiting for something, even as she knew not what, and only when the vibrations had built up to the strength of a small earthquake did one of the small doors finally snap and swing open.

Alizeh hardly dared to breathe as she peeked into the deep, gleaming compartment—and in an instant, her mind came unraveled. The heavy furniture had not ceased its shaking, the tumult growing only more frenzied, but Alizeh found she no longer cared to be quiet.

She wanted to scream.

She felt betrayed and confused, her heart pounding wildly in her chest. Carefully she reached inside, her hand glowing so hot it hurt, and attempted to retrieve what was hers, what she'd worried she'd lost—and the door snapped shut so quickly it nearly took off her fingers. The cabinet went eerily still.

And Cyrus, damn him, was fast.

To be fair, Alizeh had been preoccupied and the room had been rattling, but that he'd approached her with this degree of stealth—such that she'd not even sensed his presence— was truly impressive. She could not know how he'd done it; she had no idea what he'd seen or how, exactly, he'd spun

her around and cornered her. She knew only that Cyrus was
about to show her exactly why so much of the world feared
him, for she was pinned against the wall, and there was a
sword pointed at her throat.

"*What,*" he whispered, his eyes glittering with barely
restrained fury, "are you doing in here?"

Even then, even when she'd begun to hate him again;
when, his promises aside, she truly believed he'd not hesitate
to kill her— Even then, she was relieved he'd managed to
put on a pair of pants. He was not, however, wearing a shirt.

Alizeh dropped her gaze, stared at the blade. She was so
much shorter than him that she could see her reflection in
its shine.

"Why," she said, lifting her eyes to his, "do you have my
book?"

He faltered at the murderous look on her face, his anger
fracturing as warring instincts inside him fought for domi-
nance. She could see his inner conflict—could see his twinge
of remorse even as his resentment percolated. Alizeh was not
without an imagination: she saw why he might think she'd
betrayed him when faced by ample evidence that she'd broken into his locked room—and she did not blame him for
doubting her. How could she, when she understood how he
felt? Of course he didn't know whether he could trust her.

But neither did she know whether she could trust *him.*

His blade was beginning to dig into her throat, and she
worried, for a moment, that he might actually hurt her.

"Cyrus," she said. "I asked you a question."

"I stole it," he said quietly.

The nosta warmed against her chest.

"When?" she said, her heart failing. "Why—?"

"Days ago," he said, his halting whisper betraying his guilt. Still, he did not lower his weapon. "I replaced it with a decoy enchanted to look identical."

"You went through my room at Baz House," she said, astonished. "You searched my things—"

"Yes."

"You *lied* to me."

"Technically," he said, "I did not."

"Don't you dare speak to me like you're an idiot," she said angrily, the blade cutting her just a little as she spoke. "You understand very well what I mean."

"Stop moving," he said, furious. "This sword is devastatingly sharp—"

"Then lower your weapon, you scoundrel!"

He did, but only enough so it was no longer touching her. "Are we back to this, then?" He swallowed, staring at the cut at her neck. "Insulting each other?"

"You dare mourn the loss of my goodwill," she whispered, "even as you hold a blade to my throat."

"And you," he countered, his voice dropping an octave. "You have the audacity to rebuke me, when I've discovered you doing the same detestable deed, breaking into my rooms to search my private belongings—"

"I didn't mean to break the door!"

"You *chose* to ransack my things," he cried. "Meanwhile I was forced to rummage through yours!"

Slowly, as if heavy cataracts were clearing her eyes, Alizeh began to see what Sarra saw.

It's not that I do not care, the woman had said. *It's that I no longer believe him. For the last several months, my son has blamed all his bad decisions on the devil. Never does he take accountability for his actions. He's always begging me to understand that he has no choice—*

Alizeh felt suddenly, dangerously ill.

She did not ask Cyrus how he'd done the hateful deed, for he'd accomplished things far more complicated than breaking into her unlocked, humble closet of a bedroom; it had likely taken him minutes to accomplish this trifling chore.

She only stared at him then, her heart slowly atrophying in her chest. She ached at the betrayal, at her own stupidity, at her idiotic weaknesses that had led her to be kind to him. She hated herself for ever admiring him, for crying for him as he'd screamed, for mopping up his blood and all but tucking him into bed. He'd bought her a piece of bread and her charity had been so easily purchased, her porous heart so easily moved. She'd really thought perhaps they could be something like reluctant friends.

Oh, she was a fool of astronomical proportions.

He would never be on her side, she was realizing. No matter his occasional moments of humanity, Cyrus was in bed with the devil.

Still, even as her heart hardened against him, she could not condemn him as Sarra did. She'd seen what Iblees had done to him tonight, and she could not deny that Cyrus suffered greatly at the hands of his merciless master. But she reminded herself once more that Cyrus had *summoned* Iblees into his life; this copper-headed king had been offered something in exchange for his torment, and while she didn't know what he'd received, or why he'd done it, she could not, by definition, call him a victim.

Steadily, she met his eyes.

She saw an intensity in his stunning irises, something desperate straining against his control, and she swore in that moment she could almost feel his soul pressing against hers.

Even then, he was breathtaking.

Some quiet, foolish part of her wanted to rest her bones against his powerful body, feel the weight of his arms around her. She wanted to stroke his cheek one last time.

"Cyrus," she said softly. "Give me back my book, and I give you my word I won't hurt you."

It seemed like an eternity before he said, thickly, "I can't."

The nosta flashed hot against her skin.

"Very well." She lowered her eyes. "I just want you to know, in advance, how sorry I am. You've already been through so much tonight. I really don't want to do this."

"Alizeh—"

She moved in a flash, striking his sword arm before throwing a kick to his side in a rapid combination that briefly unbalanced him, even as his blade nicked her throat, drawing a thin line of blood. This she paid no mind, for she'd forced him to drop his arms a nanosecond, which was all she needed to knock the sword from his hand, after which she landed a hard kick to his chest, sending him stumbling across the room just long enough for her to lunge for the copper blade she'd earlier seen planted in the floor. She lifted this sword as she spun around and found Cyrus standing there, his own recovered weapon clenched in his right fist. With his free hand he rubbed absently at the angry red mark she'd left on his heaving chest, looking at her with a fiery expression she couldn't decipher.

"You *kicked* me," he said angrily.

"You cut me," she countered.

Something awoke in his eyes at that, a moment of misery there and gone, before he carefully lifted his blade, meeting her challenge. Quietly, he said, "Do you intend to fight me?"

"Are you going to prevent me from retrieving what is rightfully mine?" she asked, lifting her chin. "If so, yes."

"How did you even know it was here?" he asked, advancing slowly. "How did you know to come searching for it?"

"I had no idea it was here," she said indignantly. "I already told you, I broke down your door by accident—"

He laughed, darkly. "And you snapped open the lock on my cabinet by accident, too?"

"I didn't even touch it. It opened on its own."

"What?" He stopped moving. "What do you mean?"

"Maybe you should first explain to me why you even have a *locked* cabinet inside of a *locked* chamber," she said angrily, "in your own *locked* wing of the castle!"

"You ask this even after you've destroyed my door?" he said, losing control of his temper. "It's obvious to me now that I should invest in even greater levels of protection, for there are demented Jinn running around breaking into my quarters and rifling through my things!"

She gasped. "I am not a demented Jinn, how *dare* you—"

"I am going to ask you one more time," he said, marshaling his patience, "to tell me how you knew it was here, Alizeh—"

"Or what?" she said. "Or you're going to kill me? I thought you weren't allowed to kill me."

For some reason he flinched at that, awareness awakening in his eyes. His looked away and Alizeh wondered whether he was thinking of the devil, perhaps remembering his earlier encounter—except that his reaction was incongruent to the experience. Cyrus seemed weighed down, suddenly, subdued by what looked suspiciously like grief.

"What did you mean," he said, still staring at the floor, "that the cabinet door opened on its own?"

"I meant exactly what I said."

"But that's not possible." He shook his head at the ground. "The cabinet is heavily enchanted—you would've had to break the many tiers of security—"

"That book," she said, incensed, "is mine. Mine by birth, by order of the earth. It knows me. I felt its presence when I approached the cabinet, and it unlocked itself to reach me—I did nothing but—"

"Unlocked itself?" He looked up sharply. "You mean it displayed some kind of power on its own?"

Alizeh laughed then, finally understanding. "Poor, tormented Cyrus," she said, her voice softening. "All this time, you've been trying to make it animate, haven't you?"

"Yes."

"You will fail."

"Why?" he said urgently. "Why can't I open it?"

"Aren't you meant to wield great power?" she parroted

back at him. "How is it you're so unschooled in the workings of magic?"

"Alizeh—

"More important, why would you think I'd ever tell *you*?"

Cyrus was breathing hard now, staring at her with something like desperation. He dropped his sword to the floor with a sudden, terrifying clatter. "Please. Tell me."

"I will not," she said, narrowing her eyes. "Unlike you, I'm not bound to share my secrets with Iblees. Now give me back my book, or pick up your weapon."

"I won't fight you." He shook his head. "Forgive me. I never should've lifted my sword against you."

"Why not?" She bristled. "You don't think me a worthy opponent?"

"You," he said ardently, "have always been too worthy. I will not hurt you."

The nosta burned against her skin.

Alizeh fought back a shock of feelings then, her heart convoluted, impossible to parse. Struggling to clear her head, she said, "You don't need to worry about hurting me. I'm quite capable of defending myself."

"Alizeh," he whispered. "I would destroy you."

This made her mad.

She lunged at him with an angry cry, slicing her sword through the air with brute strength and speed and still he dodged this and dove for his mace, which had been resting against a nearby couch, and spun around in an instant to meet her next blow, her sword crashing against his staff with astonishing violence. Again she advanced, swinging her blade in a diagonal arc, and again their weapons collided, the sound of metal clanging in her ears. Over and over she attacked; he retreated. She lunged; he evaded.

Alizeh had the advantage of fleet-footedness and strength and still Cyrus parried her every move. True, she hadn't used a sword in several years, and as a result her skills were rusty, if not a bit outdated, but her preternatural gifts should've given her an edge; instead, they only seemed to balance the scales. She didn't understand how Cyrus was so capable or swift, or how he seemed to anticipate her actions. Worse, he did not seem to tire, and he never lifted his weapon except in defense.

It was infuriating.

Finally, angrily, she held her ground and glared at him. She'd funneled so much effort into the exchange that she was now exhausted, her arms shaking a little, and had to resist the urge to stomp her foot like a child.

"Give me back my book," she cried. "It belongs to me!"

Cyrus shook his head slowly, staring at her in wonder. His chest was heaving slightly, his voice only a little breathless from his recent efforts. "Marry me," he said.

Alizeh tightened her grip on her weapon, her eyes widening in outrage. "You think this is funny?"

"I'm not joking."

"Give me my book right now, or I swear I'll tear this room apart."

"Alizeh," he said, shaking his head. There was a warning in his voice. "Please don't test me."

"Why not?" She was sincerely asking the question. The

longer she stared at his heated eyes, the more she lost confidence in herself. "What are you— What are you going to do?"

"Touch my things," he said softly, "and I will physically remove you from this room."

"You wouldn't dare," she said, but weakly, for she didn't know whether he would. "Would you?"

When he only offered her a grim smile in response, Alizeh felt a bolt of fear, which she forced aside with great effort.

Calmly she walked over to his desk, and for a moment she studied the many bell jars he'd neatly organized, tiny labels reading things like *Cryptocrystalline silica* and *Hexagonal scalenohedral mineral*. Then she placed her hand on one of the glass domes. Very politely, she said, "Please give me back my book."

He made a sound, something like a growl. "I can't," he said, frustrated. "You know I can't."

Alizeh held his eyes as she knocked the specimen to the floor, where it landed with a crash, glass shattering everywhere. She reached out to knock over another when he said, in a low, lethal voice—

"Stop."

She knocked over the second one.

"*Alizeh.*"

He said her name like an epithet, the sound lancing through her like a blade. She looked up in time to see that he was advancing toward her now with a fiendish gleam in his eyes, like he was going to pick her up and throw her over his shoulder and—and do something, she didn't know what, and she quickly spun around, swinging her sword toward him, pointing it in his direction to keep him where he was.

"Don't take another step," she said, panicking just a little.

There was something terrifying, yes, but also glorious about Cyrus as he stood there, shirtless and unrepentant, without a weapon, entirely unafraid. She was actually trembling a little.

He did not strike her as the kind of person who bluffed.

"You forgot," he said softly, touching his hand to the blade she pointed at him, and making it disappear. "That I don't fight fair."

Alizeh stumbled back and stared, in astonishment, at her empty hands, and then up at him. Cyrus wasted no time closing the distance between them, moving now with unrelenting determination. She hurried backward desperately.

"Don't you dare pick me up," she cried, her heart racing in her chest. "I just want what's mine! It's not polite to pick people up against their will!"

Inches away, Cyrus came to a halt.

"It's not *polite*?" he said, stunned. "Alizeh, it's not *polite* to break into people's private rooms. It's not *polite* to tear down people's doors and destroy their things—"

"For the hundredth time," she said, exasperated, "I broke your door by accident! I was only trying to find a place to hide before the maid walked in!"

This gave him pause.

"The maid?" He frowned. "You mean the snoda who entered my room," he said, pointing in the direction of his room, "and screamed so loudly in my face she woke me up?"

Alizeh nodded. "When she knocked, I didn't know what to do. I knew I couldn't be found in your bedroom or it would cause a huge scandal, so I yanked open the first door I found—"

"Yanked it open?" he cried. "You practically tore the door off its hinges!"

"I know that, and I'm sorry! Sometimes—not often—but sometimes, when I'm in a panic, I forget how strong I am, and I break things, and I'm very sorry." She was wringing her hands now. "I swear, I'd fix it if I could, but I've never been any good with carpentry; though I did once, in one of my other positions, have to mend the legs of a chair I'd accidentally snapped off, and which I managed to repair, luckily, with a rather powerful adhesive before the housekeeper found out—"

At that, the fight seemed to leave his body.

"Alizeh," he said, turning away with a sigh. "You don't have to fix my blasted door."

"Nevertheless," she said, swallowing. "While it should be noted that I'm still *furious* with you for stealing what's mine, I swear I didn't enter this room with malicious intent."

He looked up at her then, a slight line forming between his brows. "You really mean that."

"Of course I do."

"So you didn't"—his frown deepened—"you didn't come here tonight with the express purpose of retrieving your book? Or rummaging through my things?"

"No."

"You have no intention of triple-crossing me?"

"What?" She almost laughed. "No."

He shook his head, as if trying to clear it. "Then what on earth are you doing here?"

"I already told you, I was running from the maid—"

"*Here*, Alizeh," he said patiently. "Not this room. What are you doing *here*, in my wing of the castle? All this time I've been operating under the assumption that you snuck in when the maid opened the door, but now I'm just . . . confused."

At that, Alizeh went still.

She was quiet for a long, tense moment before she said, finally, "You don't remember *any* of it?"

TWENTY-NINE

یستونه

CYRUS STARED AT HER, HIS confusion transforming into something like fear. "Remember any of what?"

His stricken expression inspired a pang in her heart, for the insensible organ had no brain and could not be reasoned with. Alizeh was *angry* with him, and still she softened.

"You don't remember," she said, "what happened in the flower field?"

There was a long beat during which Cyrus averted his eyes, his throat working. "I do remember," he said finally.

"What's the last thing you remember?"

"What do you mean?" He did not look up.

"Well, do you remember talking to me?"

"Yes," he whispered.

"And then?"

"And then," he said, and sighed, looking suddenly, intensely uncomfortable. "Then, I experienced some pain."

She hated the way he said it, hated the way his voice hollowed out. As if his suffering were something inconsequential and fleeting, as if it weren't actual torture, as if she hadn't sat there and watched as blood dripped down his closed eyes and into his open, screaming mouth.

"I think it was a fair amount worse than that," said Alizeh.

"I don't know what you saw."

"A great deal," she said quietly. "I saw a great deal."

He nodded, a muscle jumping in his jaw. He still wouldn't look at her. "Interesting," he said flatly. "I didn't realize you'd seen anything at all."

Alizeh hesitated at his tone, not knowing how to interpret his words. "I'm sure," she ventured, "that I couldn't even begin to imagine the depth of what you suffered. But I was there, I saw everything—"

"You," he said, attempting a wry smile, "were *not* there."

Alizeh actually flinched, she was so surprised.

She didn't know whether to react to the fact of his statement being patently false—or whether to wonder at the undertone of an accusation in his voice. That he thought she'd abandoned him was strange enough—but that he was *upset* about it?

Had she somehow managed to hurt Cyrus's *feelings*?

This, she struggled to fathom.

"Don't misunderstand me," he went on, studying the middle distance. "I don't blame you for leaving—in fact, it's quite understandable, considering the circumstances, for it must've been not only an unpleasant viewing, but an excellent opportunity to be rid of me—"

"You have it entirely wrong," she said with some heat. "I was there the whole time."

Finally, he looked up, perplexed even as he shook his head. "Why would you challenge this? Alizeh, when I came to, you were gone. I brought myself back to the palace alone—"

"How would I have left?" she asked, cutting him off. "We

were in the middle of nowhere."

"I don't know," he said dismissively, as if this were a trivial point. "You are not without your own resources. You have supernatural speed—clearing a couple of miles wouldn't take you very long, and if you walk far enough through the field, there's access to the main road. The castle is quite visible in the distance. I assumed you snuck back in here only to retrieve your book before running away."

Alizeh drew a deep, steadying breath.

She knew now that she'd have to prod his memory, and while she suspected that the truth would hurt him, *this*— him thinking she'd abandoned him in that state—struck her as far worse. If nothing else, her pride couldn't handle it.

"I never left you," she said, steeling herself. "I sat there for two hours while you suffered, and I used my own dress to wipe the blood from your face. I begged you to wake up. I begged you to bring us back to the palace—"

"No," he said, "no, you . . ."

His voice trailed off as he looked at her—*really* looked at her—his eyes fixing upon the knotted red stain on her gown. Alizeh saw him visibly stiffen, the blood draining from his face.

"Cyrus," she said. "I didn't leave you there."

He was breathing hard now, his body turning to stone before her. He seemed paralyzed by this revelation, astonished into speechlessness. Finally, he said, "That wasn't a dream?"

"No," she whispered.

"Fucking hell." He pushed a hand through his hair and looked away, his body so tight with tension she worried he might break.

"What— What did you think happened?"

"I thought I was in bed," he choked out. "I thought I was sleeping—"

"But how did you think you got back to bed?" she pressed. "Who did you think took off your boots, or your bloody coat?"

He shook his head. "In the aftermath of these— experiences—I always"—he hesitated—"I often sleep for a time, because it takes me a while to recover. Still I somehow get myself into bed. No matter the circumstances, I manage, in the end, to take care of myself, even if I can't always remember doing so. It didn't seem important *how* I got myself in bed—only that I *did* get myself in bed. I didn't question it."

"I see," she whispered.

"You were in my room," he said thickly, "because I brought you there."

"Yes."

"And you—" He looked up, distraught. "You took care of me. You washed the blood from my face."

This was the second time he'd fixated upon this latter point; once while delirious, and now again, fully alert. Alizeh wasn't sure why. "Yes," she said. "I used my skirt to mop up the—"

"No," he said, and shook his head, as if he was remembering something. He lifted a hand to his cheek, his confusion growing only more apparent. "No, you *washed* my face."

Alizeh frowned. "You seem preoccupied with this detail."

"It's impossible not to notice the difference," he said, dropping his hand. "Even when I manage to wipe away the worst of it, I wake up from these incidents with my eyes all but sealed together by the dregs of dried blood."

Alizeh absorbed this admission like a punch to the gut.

It was the casual way he said it, the nonchalance with which he described something so gruesome, that revealed so much about him. It was confounding to her, how he didn't seem to care about the blows he took, that he could speak so easily about his own torture.

"I just don't understand," he was saying. "How did you wash my face when we had no water?"

At that, Alizeh felt the prickle of something like embarrassment. How could she put into words an explanation that, when spoken aloud, sounded melodramatic to the extreme? At the time she'd seen only a person in need; she'd not questioned the impulse to assist; she'd not thought she might be overreacting. Now she wasn't so sure.

Nervously, she clasped her hands.

"I did use my skirt to mop up most of the blood," she said, fixing her eyes firmly on the floor. "But then— Then I used the moisture of my tears to scrub away the sticky residue."

Cyrus was silent for a frighteningly long beat.

When he finally spoke, his voice was soft, his astonishment palpable. "You cried for me?"

"It has been noted," she whispered, "that I perhaps cry too much."

"You used your own tears," he said, all but broken, "to wash the blood from my face?"

To this, Alizeh had no glib response.

The earlier prickle of embarrassment had become a full-body mortification as she stood there, her head heating as she listened to him take inventory of her earlier actions.

She couldn't bring herself to meet his eyes.

"Alizeh. Please look at me."

She shook her head at the floor. "This is quite humiliating for me, Cyrus. I won't look at you."

"Why is it humiliating?"

"Because I was *stupid*," she said in a sudden burst. "I was kind to you only to discover that you'd been lying to me all this time—that you'd stolen my book and refuse to give it . . ."

The words died in her throat.

Alizeh had lifted her head as she spoke, anger burning away the worst of her unease, but she was stopped short by the look on Cyrus's face. The anguish in his eyes struck a bolt through her chest.

"Why did you do it?" he said, his voice strained. "Why were you so kind to me? I'd heard someone crying, but I thought the sounds were part of a dream, or a hallucination. God, the way you touched me—" He cut himself off, his expression tortured. He shook his head, dragged a hand across his mouth. "Alizeh, my own mother has never touched me with such tenderness. I didn't think there was any chance you could be real."

She didn't know what to say.

Her heart was beating so hard she could hardly hear her own thoughts. Cyrus had looked at her many times since she'd met him, and always with varying levels of intensity, but never quite like this. Never like he wanted to fall to his knees before her.

She heard her voice shake a little when she said, softly, "I believe the words you used to describe me were *quite charmingly pathetic.*"

Cyrus exhaled so hard she watched his chest cave a bit. He looked devastated. "I deserve to be shot for saying that to you."

She managed to smile, but there was no life in it.

"Will you tell me what was happening?" she said instead, hoping to somehow dull the fire in his eyes. "You told me that this always happens to you, that it was part of a cycle."

"Yes," he said, but the word was raw, worn out. "It's a medicinal sleep. It always puts me into a strange fog. Afterward, it's the only way to keep me alive."

Alizeh paled. "You mean Iblees tortures you nearly to death and then brings you back from the brink—just to do it again?"

"Yes."

She thought she might be sick. "Does he do this often?"

"Yes," he said softly.

"How often?"

"It depends." He swallowed. "Sometimes twice a week."

She clapped a hand over her mouth and made a sound, something like a sob.

Cyrus only looked at her, looked at her with the same,

unremitting heat in his eyes and said nothing. A heavy silence descended between them, the quiet thick with things unspoken. Something had changed in the wake of these revelations, and Alizeh wasn't sure she could define it. She knew then only what she saw, and what she saw was a version of Cyrus she'd never seen before.

He seemed shaken.

What's more, he had touched her—drawn his hands down her body, pressed his lips to her skin—and now they both knew it. Alizeh hadn't really allowed herself to think about what'd transpired between them, for she'd filed away his delirious words as inadmissible testimony; she'd not thought it fair to consider his drugged actions as evidence of overarching feelings toward her. But the longer he stood there without speaking aloud a retraction—without issuing an apology or denial—the more she wondered whether he stared at her now not with fear, but with longing.

He moved slowly then, shattering the silence with his quiet movements, closing the inches between them until the memories of him came back to life with a fever that seared her. She could still hear the crickets, could still see the moonlight on his face. She doubted she'd ever forget the desperate way he'd asked if he could taste her, the sound he'd made when he pressed his face to her breasts.

Suddenly, she couldn't breathe.

He was close now, his eyes bright, burning. She'd never seen such tightly restrained emotion in his face or in the lines of his body. His desire was so potent it was intoxicating; she felt herself tremble under the weight of it. He wanted to touch her—she knew this, she saw it in the rigid control he maintained over his hands, in the stiffness of his stance, in the way he moved incrementally closer until she saw nothing but him. His eyes dropped to her lips and his own lips parted, drew breath. He exhaled shakily.

She worried that if she said a word, she might combust.

"I touched you," he said softly. "Do you remember?"

Alizeh's heart was pounding so hard now she actually felt a bit faint. What could she say to his question? The truth was a single word easily delivered and yet this answer seemed desperately, desperately fraught. She felt it, felt it even as she said, *Yes, I remember,* against his throat. Even then she knew she was pitching forward into madness.

He whispered, "And do you condemn me for it?"

He tilted his head, his lips almost grazing her cheek, and the harsh sounds of her own shallow breaths grew only more desperate. She didn't know when he'd gotten so close, but he now occupied her senses entirely: the heady scent of his skin; the sight of his naked chest; the sound of his beating heart. She lacked only touch, only taste, and she ached for it. Her mind was gone; she couldn't even remember her own name standing this close to him. She knew, dimly, that this was a bad idea, that she was playing with fire, but Alizeh had survived an inferno once, and she thought she might survive such a blaze again.

"No," she breathed.

She saw a shudder move through him, a heavy exhalation that rocked his frame. He made a desperate, broken sound as he closed his eyes, but still, he didn't touch her. He wouldn't put his hands on her, wouldn't put an end to her torment, and she was far too conflicted, even then, to claim him for herself.

"Alizeh," he whispered. "Let me make you my queen."

It was a cold, sharp snap of reality.

Alizeh stiffened and drew back, her head cleared in an instant, alarm roaring through her body.

"Did you—" she said, panicking. "Are you trying to seduce me? To get me to marry you?"

Cyrus looked like he'd been struck.

He stared at her, his chest heaving, his eyes so plainly devastated she was overcome at once with regret.

"No," he said, exhaling the word.

The nosta warmed.

"I'm sorry," she cried, shaking her head, "I'm sorry, I know it's a terrible accusation, but why did you— Why would you—"

"Why are you acting like this is a surprise?" He was recovering slowly, his pain calcifying, heating before her eyes. "I made my intentions clear from the beginning, Alizeh, I want to marry you—"

"The *devil* wants you to marry me," she exploded. "That's not at all the same thing! How can you not see—"

"Marry me," he countered, "and you get your crown, the devil is briefly sated, and I'm discharged, in great part, of my debt. We all get something we want. Why is that so wrong?"

"It's one thing," she said angrily, "to enter into a false arrangement in the pursuit of our own interests. But this— Cyrus, this wouldn't be false, and it would complicate everything. What were you going to do? If I kissed you? What would come next?"

"I would marry you," he said, stepping closer again, coming dangerously within reach. "I'd marry you tomorrow. And then I'd take you to bed. For weeks."

She felt her face heat, her heart pounding recklessly. It was a shocking thing to say, but more shocking was the way her body reacted to his pronouncement, with a flare of desire she struggled to extinguish.

"And then?" she said, failing to steady her voice. "You expect me to kill you?"

He hesitated. "That choice is yours to make."

"You're unbelievable," she breathed. "How can you be so cavalier? This is a deathly serious situation—"

"And what was *your* plan?" he said, his eyes flashing. "How did you think this would end?"

"I don't know," she said, and shook her head. "I wasn't— I wasn't thinking—"

"And now you're thinking too much."

"You're being cruel—"

"And you are needlessly shocked. You've known from the first that I am yoked to a ruthless master, that in fact I sought you out under his orders, that I disrupted my life and disordered my home and tore myself open at his behest, all for you." He swallowed. "All for you. Do you really not see what you've done to me? In a matter of days you've stripped me down and upended my world. My hours are in disarray, my future is in chaos, and my head—my head—"

He turned away and grimaced, his fists clenching, and

Alizeh thought her heart might stop.

"And instead of being angry," he went on, "instead of driving you away—instead of wishing we'd never met—I keep staring at that fucking cut on your neck, Alizeh, and I want to die."

"Cyrus—"

"It's my own fault," he said, and dragged both hands down his face. "I have only myself to blame. I knew better; I knew you were dangerous. You've had the upper hand from the moment I laid eyes on you. I saw you and saw right away that I was in hell, and I hated you for it, because I realized even then that you would be the end of me."

"What are you talking about?" she asked, alarmed. "You speak as if I harmed you—"

He laughed then, laughed like he might be coming unhinged. "Of course you don't know. Why would you? How could you possibly know the truth? That you've been haunting me for so long—tormenting me every night—"

"Cyrus, stop it," she said. "You're not being fair— I never even *knew* you—"

"You don't understand," he said, tortured. "I've been dreaming about you for *months*."

The nosta flashed hot against her skin, and Alizeh went still. "What?"

"I didn't know who you were," he said, shaking his head. "I didn't know your name. I thought you were only an achievement of my imagination. Some kind of conjured fantasy."

Alizeh felt stricken. Disoriented. Her pounding heart was a disaster. "What— What did you dream about me?"

He only looked away, said nothing.

"Are you not allowed to tell me?"

Cyrus laughed a bleak laugh. "Oh, no, *this* story I'm free to share. I just don't want to."

"Why not?"

"Alizeh," he whispered, still refusing to meet her gaze. "Spare me a bit of mercy. Don't make me say these things out loud."

"Please," she said urgently. "I don't mean to make you suffer. But I need to understand— If the devil has been planting my likeness in your mind, I must know how he's using me. What did I do to you? Did I hurt you in your imaginings?"

It was a moment before Cyrus said, now staring at the wall, "Far from it. I always thought you were some kind of an angel."

She drew a sharp breath.

That word, again. He'd called her *angel* in his delirium, and now she thought she was beginning to understand.

"It was a long time before I suspected Iblees had anything to do with my dreams," Cyrus was saying. "I see now, of course, that I should've doubted sooner, but you always struck me as far too lovely to be associated with him. So generous, so sweet. So beautiful I could hardly look at you, even in my dreams. I thought my mind had magicked you to life as an antidote to my nightmares. I never dared to believe you might exist in real life."

The nosta continued to substantiate his words, and Alizeh grew only more unsteady as she listened; she worried she wouldn't survive this speech.

"When I saw you for the first time before the ball," he went on, "I finally understood. You have no idea how you unbalanced me then. How could you know how it terrified me to look at you when I realized the devil had done this to me on purpose? That he'd taken a reverie I'd come to cherish and twisted it, tainted it with his darkness?"

"I don't understand," she said desperately. "Why does Iblees torture you so much? Why would he do such a thing?"

Cyrus finally looked up, meeting her eyes with a force of emotion so intense Alizeh felt the nosta burn against her skin, verifying something he hadn't even spoken aloud.

It shocked her.

"I made the devil the only oath he would accept," Cyrus said softly. "The terms of which are damning, indeed. If I renege on our agreement at any point, in any way, my life will be his to control forevermore. Often I think he made me this bargain because he felt certain I would break under the weight of it. Iblees would much prefer the convenience of an utterly loyal subject—for either way, he'd get what he wanted from me. I think it's why he so often torments me, pushing me too far. He'd planted you in my mind with the express purpose of destroying me emotionally, undercutting me, stripping me of my defenses so that I'd be unprepared when we met." He laughed, and the sound was bitter. "No doubt he hoped that, upon discovering your identity, I'd release you at once, and in the process, lose everything."

Alizeh's eyes burned with tears as he spoke. There was no other way to describe it: her heart was breaking.

"I didn't trust you," Cyrus said quietly. "How could I trust you? You were a vision conjured by the devil, designed to ruin me. I hated you for being real, for coming to life only to personify torture, to be another trial to endure. In fact I *wanted* to hate you. I wanted to discover your faults, your flaws. I thought you'd never match up to the figment of my dreams, and I was wrong. You are far more enchanting in real life. Far more exquisite." His voice shook just a little when he said, softly, "It is excruciating to be in your presence."

Again, the nosta seared her skin.

Alizeh wanted to sit down; she wanted a glass of water; she wanted to submerge herself in a cold bath.

She could only bring herself to say his name.

"I knew, somehow, that it would come to this," he said, looking away. "I just thought I was stronger. I thought it would take longer. Instead, you've managed to sever me in half with astonishing speed."

"You're being unfair," she said, forcing herself to speak, her heart beating painfully in her chest. "You act as if I'm intentionally cruel. As if I'm indifferent to you."

"Aren't you?"

"No," she whispered, her eyes filling with tears. "Of course not."

Cyrus stared at her from where he stood, his chest heaving with barely leashed intensity. He devastated her with that look, even as he seemed planted in the ground, immovable. "Then be with me," he said softly. "Let me worship you."

"Oh, don't do this," she said, wiping angrily at her eyes. "This path is too perilous already, and we both know it. Don't speak of things you cannot give me."

"You have no idea what I could give you," he said, his own eyes blazing. "You have no idea what I want. I have been in agony for *eight months*, Alizeh. Do you know how hard it's been to pretend I don't know you? To pretend I don't want you? To act as if I haven't known every inch of your body in my dreams? To learn that your heart has been entangled elsewhere? I look at you and I can't breathe. In my mind, you are already *mine*."

"Stop," she said, struggling now to catch her breath. "Don't talk to me like this— This is dangerous, Cyrus—"

"Then why tell me you care?" he countered. "Why tell me you feel something only to dismiss me? Do you think it's easy for me to stand here before you and speak so candidly? Do you think me a masochist? Do you think I enjoy this pain?"

"How can you be so self-pitying?" she said miserably. "How can you blame me for the movements of your own heart? How can you hold me accountable for your misfortunes even as you hold hostage my belongings, as you plot and murder under the orders of a despicable beast?

"I understand your turmoil, Cyrus, really, I do. I am not without compassion. I saw enough of your suffering tonight to imagine how wretched you must be. But how can you ask me to trust you with my heart when you still keep secrets from me? When you are beholden to the darkest creature alive, forsaking all others for him, placing his wishes, his demands, above all else?" She shook her head. "No, I could never be with you," she said. "Not because I am indifferent, but because you could never be faithful to me—you could never choose me first—and you should not blame me for my fears."

He went quite still then, doing nothing to mask the agony printed upon his face. "I might, one day, be free."

"Maybe," she allowed. "Until then, you could not know what he might ask of you. You might break me just to please him."

When he did not deny this—when he only looked at her, looked at her like he wanted to drive a dagger through his chest—she had her answer.

"Where does this leave us, then?" she whispered. "Will you rescind your offer of marriage?"

He laughed, and it was tragic. "How I wish I could."

"Then I need you to know," she said, summoning her courage, "that despite everything, I might still accept. In the interest of my own future."

Her words nearly broke him.

She saw it in his eyes, in the sudden fall of his shoulders, in the way his arms fell heavily at his sides. "After all this— after everything I've shared with you tonight—you would become my wife," he said, his voice ragged, "in title only?"

"Yes," she said quietly.

"You wouldn't touch me. Or laugh with me. You wouldn't share my bed."

Her heart was beating in her throat. "No."

"Alizeh, you would make me the most wretched man alive."

"I'm sorry," she said, shaking her head as she spoke. "I'm desperately sorry." Her feeble heart was splintering in her

chest and she fought frantically against the ache of it, struggling to hold her ground. She, too, had a path she was meant
to follow.

"It's just that your arguments," she said haltingly, "your
reasoning— The picture you drew— It was undeniably compelling. I've been turning over the possibility in my mind all
day, and while I haven't made my decision yet, I know that if
I ever hope to have a chance of leading my people, of fulfilling my destiny, I will require an empire—"

"And then?" he said softly. "Will you kill me then? Is this
the order in which you intend to annihilate me? Will you
tear out my heart first, rip off my crown next, and end my
life only when I'm on my knees, begging you to end my misery?"

"*Cyrus*," she said desperately. "*Please.*" She was losing the
battle with her tears and struggled to fight back the flood.
"I never asked for any of this—all I ever wanted from the
world was to disappear. *You* brought me here. *You* made me
this offer. *You* gave me the opportunity to see what I might
be, and I can't willfully blind myself to the possibility now,
not now that I know there are people out there waiting for
me—not when I, too, have a duty—"

"I am well aware," he said, lowering his eyes, "of how I did
this to myself. You need not bury the blade any deeper." His
voice quieted then to something less than a whisper. "But
will you promise me something, angel? When you do decide
to kill me, will you tell me how you intend to do it?"

"Cyrus—"

"*Enough*, I beg you." He shook his head. "I am only a man,

Alizeh, I can only withstand so much torture in one day. Please," he said, his voice breaking on the word. "Leave me. Leave me to what's left of my godforsaken life."

She stood there a moment, frozen.

"And tomorrow?" she said quietly. "Who will we become then? Are we to be enemies once more?"

He said nothing, his body trembling almost imperceptibly as he stared at the ground, and when he finally parted his lips to answer, there came a sudden, urgent pounding at the door.

THIRTY

سی

CYRUS STIFFENED, BUT HE DID not move; neither of them said a word. Alizeh was still staring at his mouth, wishing the world beyond these walls would drop dead just long enough for her to know his answer, but her hopes were soon dashed.

There was another round of relentless pounding at the door, and finally Cyrus closed his eyes and swore, drawing away from her with palpable anguish.

Alizeh stood there, paralyzed in place, her mind spinning, her heart broken. She heard his footfalls as he strode to the entrance, heard the whine of the old wood as he opened the door.

Sarra's voice was unmistakable.

"*Where have you been?*" she screamed. "I've been searching for you everywhere! Your valet said he'd come up earlier to dress you for dinner but he claimed you weren't here—and then you never appeared downstairs and neither did the girl, who isn't in her room, and I had no idea where to even *begin* looking for you, for the last place I expected you to be so early in the evening was lying unconscious in your bed like some kind of profligate, not until my maid told me she'd heard about the most miserable snoda sobbing her eyes out in the kitchens, fearing for her job after finding you asleep in your chamber—"

"*Mother.*"

"—and why aren't you wearing any clothes? Heavens, but you look worse than death—have you been ill? Is that why you were abed at this hour?"

"Yes."

"Your timing," she said angrily, "is disastrous. It's just like you to go and get yourself sick when you're actually needed, begging off when everyone else has to deal with the fallout of your demented actions—"

Alizeh was astonished.

She knew the grim extent to which Sarra loathed her son, and within the context of the woman's injured mind Alizeh could indeed understand her emotional conflict, for she rightfully blamed Cyrus for the brutal murder of her husband. Still, even knowing this, it was shocking to hear her hatred animated thus. It was unnatural to listen to a mother berate her son for falling ill, never bothering to ask whether he was okay. There was something so painful about the exchange that it was hard to hear.

"Will you not get to your point?" Cyrus was saying, his voice clipped. "What is it you need from me?"

"I need that girl!" Sarra shrieked. "Where is she? Where is Alizeh? What have you done with her?"

Alizeh felt a sudden spike of alarm.

"What have I *done* with her?" Cyrus laughed, but it sounded angry.

"Don't take that tone with me, as if I haven't every reason to doubt you! The girl is not in her rooms! What else am I supposed to think? No one has seen her in hours, no one save every Jinn in Tulan," she added hysterically, "who've been arriving in terrifying hordes from every reach of the empire, and who stormed the castle an hour ago—"

Alizeh felt her heart stop.

"What?" Now Cyrus sounded alarmed. "What do you mean? Are they being violent?"

"Yes, they're being violent!" she cried. "What on earth can you think I mean? There are thousands of them, Cyrus, and they're threatening to break down the door lest she show herself."

"I don't understand," he said, his urgency escalating. "Why are they angry? I thought they loved her—"

"Then you knew?" she said, overwrought. "You knew who she was? You knew she meant something to them? Oh, Cyrus, how could you?" Sarra sounded truly broken then. "Of all the stupid and terrible things you've ever done— You told me she was of royal blood, but you didn't tell me she was *this*—this *messiah*! She's going to tear apart the empire!"

Alizeh felt dizzy now, her breaths growing only faster, more labored. She couldn't believe this was happening. More than that, she couldn't believe, after all these years, that it was happening like *this*.

It was a disaster.

"What are they demanding?" Cyrus asked coldly.

"Why did you bring her here?" Sarra said, and practically sobbed. "Why have you wrought such havoc upon our home? Do you not see what will become of us? More Jinn will hear of her and they'll come for her—they'll crawl out of every dark corner of the earth"—she gasped—"and we'll have to wage war against our own people—"

"Mother," he said sharply. "Get a hold of yourself."

"You are a blight upon this family," she cried. "You are a stain upon the earth—"

"What do they want from her?" he said, his voice shaking with fury. "What are their demands?"

"They want proof that she's real! And they want to know she's unharmed. Most of all they want to know whether she's come here to marry you, whether she will take the throne."

Alizeh gasped, clasped a hand to her throat.

Cyrus was briefly silent. He was subdued when he said, finally, "Do they *want* her to marry me?"

"I don't know!" Sarra exploded, sounding unhinged. "All I know is that they're threatening to set the city on fire if she doesn't show herself soon—and I can't find her anywhere—"

"I'll find her," he said roughly, and even then Alizeh knew he was protecting her. Cyrus knew she hadn't wanted to be found in a compromising position with him, in his bedroom, and the small gesture meant a great deal to her. But she was slowly realizing there was no use. She could not hide forever.

"Where are you going to find her?" Sarra shouted. "You know where she is? You've known this whole time and you've just been torturing me?"

"First," Cyrus said, ignoring his mother's outburst, "you must get them to calm down. I can't let her stand before this mob until I'm sure she can be safe."

"*You* ask them to calm down," Sarra shot back. "You think I haven't been trying? They won't listen to me!"

Her reputation be damned.

Alizeh could no longer stand there silently. These were her people, and they were her responsibility. And she knew that if her parents were here, they'd tell her to come into the light.

They'd tell her not to be afraid.

Her heart pounding desperately in her chest, Alizeh held her head just above the rising waters of terror, and stepped out of the shadows.

THIRTY-ONE

سی و یک

KAMRAN HAD BEEN STANDING THERE for at least twenty minutes already, staring at the sky with a fragile, fracturing hope. He'd tucked the scrap of paper back into the box, and the box back into his cloak pocket, but the feather, now marred by his blood, was still clutched in his fist. His mind was a maelstrom of warring emotions, upended by the inconceivable evidence that his beloved Diviners had known, days and days before they were murdered, not only that King Zaal would die, but how Kamran would suffer.

It made his heart ache.

He marveled at how certain the priests and priestesses had been of his movements and actions. Kamran was now in possession of a piece of his grandfather's will, and had he opened this parcel but a day sooner, he would've been shocked, yes, but also confused and devastated. He might've used the feather too soon, or at the wrong time. Worse: the slim box could've been easily lost. Misplaced. Handled incorrectly.

And yet, the Diviners hadn't worried. All had happened precisely as they'd foreseen.

He'd mistakenly assumed that the new crop of Diviners had betrayed him by tossing him into the tower. He saw now that they'd been protecting him—locking him somewhere

Zahhak might not reach him, and leaving him high enough in the sky so that Simorgh might come to him easily.

What he didn't know, of course, was which part of all this was meant to be a test. He didn't know what, exactly, he was meant to prove, or how he might prove it—but he saw now that they had known his plan. They must've known he was heading to Tulan, for the gift of Simorgh—the exalted character he'd heard so much about in childhood, about whose kindness and generosity Zaal had told endless stories—was a gift of transportation and protection. Kamran knew he could ride upon her back, that she would carry him where he needed to go, that she would offer him her armor and her companionship.

Simorgh was beloved by many, but especially Ardunians, who believed she still lived here with her family but who hadn't been spotted since the day Zaal was returned to the palace in a triumphant moment, blazing through the sky on the back of this brilliant, ethereal creature.

And now, here stood Kamran, presented with a possible exit from the madness of his life—an opportunity to ally with the most legendary magical beast in the history of his world—and he didn't even know whether Simorgh would come. Kamran had no idea whether he'd done the deed right, or how long it might take the magnificent bird to find him.

Hours? Days? Would he freeze to death until then? Was she even alive, after all this time?

It occurred to Kamran that he might keep warm by searching the floor of this filthy tower for a pair of rocks he might strike together against a pile of dead leaves; and while he wasn't beyond searching the decrepit depths of this cell with his bare hands, he did hesitate at the thought, hoping then for a third option, preferably something more like divine intervention, or—

He heard the sudden thunder of harried footsteps, the swell of agitated voices.

"Kamran? Kamran, are you in there?" There was a violent pounding against the metal door, and the prince was so stunned by this unexpected clamor that he struggled to rouse himself from his thoughts; indeed he'd hardly a moment to gather his wits before he saw a soft, gleaming light fall steadily from the sky above him. He'd been so consumed by silence and strangeness all this time that he thought, for a moment, he might be imagining things—just until he heard a growing buzz as the soft light approached, the little glow flickering as, without warning, it bopped gently against his face.

Hazan's firefly.

Kamran was overcome. He'd never felt such elation or relief. He thought he might fall to his knees with the heft of it.

Instead, he said, quite calmly: "What took you so long?"

Hazan, in response, broke down the door.

The rusted metal panel made a deafening groan as it was knocked free from its frame, the hinges screeching as they were torn apart. Kamran moved quickly out of the obstacle's path, the entire cell shuddering as the weighty door hit the ground with a reverberant crash.

Once he felt it was safe, Kamran moved forward to clasp

hands with his friend—to thank him for what he'd done—
and instead, he recoiled so intensely he nearly tripped over
the rotting lump of something extremely dead.

"Your Highness?" Miss Huda peered through the open
doorway. "Are you quite well?

"He's alive!" Omid cried, and tackled Kamran in a show
of affection for which, just days ago, he might've been sentenced to death. "You're alive!"

"Good God," said Deen, roughly yanking Omid away from
the prince. "Extricate yourself at once, boy. What are you
thinking? One does not simply hug the prince of Ardunia—"

"I'm sorry," Omid said breathlessly. "I'm terribly sorry,
sire, it's only that I'm just so happy to see you—I thought
for sure the defense minister had done something terrible to
you—"

"Oh yes, he's spitting mad," Miss Huda added, nodding
eagerly. "He's going around screaming at everyone, even the
Diviners— I've never seen servants so spooked, and that's
saying quite a lot, for Mother can be unforgivably harsh with
the staff."

Kamran stood there, staring at this circus in a state of
shock.

He'd heard their voices in his mind earlier; he knew that
they'd been discussing him, wondering about his whereabouts; but he hadn't thought they'd make up his rescue
party.

"What," he said, hardly able to speak, "on *earth*—are you
lot doing here?"

"Obviously *I* came to save you, you idiot," said Hazan. "I was fairly close to the castle—stockpiling weapons to crate for the journey—when my firefly found me. I'd left her at the palace to keep an eye on things in my absence, and she alerted me to your situation as soon as Zahhak showed up. I came as swiftly as I could."

"I'm not asking about you," Kamran said dismissively. "Of course *you're* here—and I'm very glad about it, thank you for coming, really, I mean that—I'm asking about *these* three—"

"Oh," said Hazan, and Kamran heard the frown in his voice. "Yes. Isn't it sweet? They insisted on helping me rescue you."

"What? *Why?*"

"Well, we saw that you were in danger, sire," said Omid. "It was a terrible betrayal— I didn't think the Diviners would ever use such awful magic on you—"

"And we weren't going to stand there and let the rightful king be dragged away," cried Miss Huda, "so that some serpent of a minister could steal your crown! My father *detests* Zahhak, and I know this for a fact because when Father is in his cups he often lists the people he loathes, and the defense minister numbers high on that list, which is fairly long, actually"—Miss Huda frowned—"I hadn't really thought about it until just now."

"And you?" Kamran turned on the apothecarist. "What's your excuse?"

"Oh, I haven't the faintest idea, Your Highness," said Deen, looking about the tower with a visible revulsion. "That awful housekeeper was horrified by the idea of taking part in any of this—and I was stupid enough to agree with her out loud. She then demanded I be a gentleman and walk her the half mile down the bridge so she might hail a cab on a busier corner in town, the fare of which she suggested we share." He sighed. "I think I might've said yes to these blockheads"—he nodded at Omid and Miss Huda—"simply to avoid being alone with her, though, with all due respect, sire, I find I'm regretting that decision now."

"I see," said Kamran, frowning.

"Come on, then," Hazan said, clapping the prince on the shoulder. "Let's get you out of this hellhole. We'll have to make a run for it straightaway; Zahhak is on a rampage. He's tearing apart the castle looking for you—and for something else—your grandfather's will, it sounded like—"

Kamran felt a bolt of fear.

"And I suggest we head to the docks without delay. There's a great deal I need to tell you, and then we need to come up with a plan—"

"A great deal you need to tell me?" Kamran's alarm intensified. "About what?"

Hazan almost smiled. "I ran into your mother."

"*What?* Where?"

Hazan nodded toward the exit. "Never mind that now. We'll have plenty of time to talk and plot while we're on the water."

"On the water?" said Miss Huda, her head swiveling between them. "Are we getting on a boat?"

"*Not you,*" said Kamran and Hazan at the same time.

"Hazan," the prince said, shaking his head as he glanced again at the skylight. "I can't leave yet. I have to stay here at least a while longer."

"What?" Hazan recoiled. "Why would you want to stay here? You're standing next to a matted pile of rats—"

Miss Huda shrieked.

"Oh God," Deen whispered. "I think I'm going to be sick."

"They're not rats," said Omid helpfully, in a broken accent. "Well, they're not *only* rats. There's also a possum, I think, and, um, the other one, I can't remember the name in Ardanz—"

Miss Huda shrieked again.

Kamran paid this no mind; he was about to hold out his hand to Hazan, to show him the feather clutched in his fist, the parcel tucked into his pocket, when suddenly the night was torn asunder by a beautiful, terrifying cry.

Kamran could not see her, not at first, for the astonishing bird was blocked from view by the mostly enclosed roof, but he felt his bleeding hand heat against the feather he still clutched, and he knew in his bones that she'd arrived. The tower prison shuddered as she alighted, and he was struck by the force of her power, the strength she wielded even now, when he couldn't see her. He saw the shadow of an enormous talon through the skylight, and in a series of violent, elegant motions, she crushed the roof of the prison with her claws. Pulverized rock came raining down on their heads, and the group of them bolted from the room to avoid the catastrophic shower, returning only when all was quiet, and when, through the clearing dust storm, Simorgh appeared as if out of a dream.

She was magnificent.

Kamran moved forward as the others drew back, and he fell on one knee before her. Broad and gleaming, Simorgh spanned the width of the entire room, her downy, glimmering feathers a muted starburst of color in the moonlight. She canted her head and regarded him with dark, inky eyes a long time before she finally nodded in a simple acknowledgment that set Kamran's heart to flutter. She made a sound, a warble soft and tender, then dropped to her knees so that he might scale her back.

Kamran felt his breath catch in his chest.

"*Simorgh*," Hazan whispered.

"Heavens above," Deen gasped. "I never thought, in all my life—"

"Am I dreaming?" said Miss Huda. "I think I might be dreaming."

"Yes, miss," said a dazed Omid. "You are."

Hazan stepped forward and bowed before the bird, who only studied him curiously. The former minister rose incrementally, his body rigid with astonishment as he turned to the prince. "Kamran, how did you—?"

"I promise," said Kamran. "I'll explain everything later. But if the situation is as dire as you say, we better get going."

"Get going?" Hazan's eyes widened. "To Tulan, you mean?"

"Yes."

"With *Simorgh*?"

"Yes."

"Oh my goodness, we're going to Tulan?" cried Miss Huda. "Are we going to save Alizeh?"

Again, Kamran flinched at the sound of her name. He didn't dignify Miss Huda's question with a response.

"Take these," Hazan said to the prince, pulling a strap over his head. "I grabbed a few weapons from the stockpile before I left—I didn't know if I'd need them. But if we'll be entering Tulan from on high, best to have them at the ready, just in case." He tossed Kamran a quiver of arrows, and then a bow, both of which his friend caught easily, and slung quickly over his back.

"Thank you," said the prince. "Truly."

Hazan only looked at Kamran a moment, then responded with a firm nod.

"Could I have something, too?" said Omid, who was approaching Hazan with an eagerness Kamran found unnerving. "I don't have any weapons, and I'd like to be armed—"

"Oh, and I as well!" cried Miss Huda. "Do you happen to have any throwing stars? I'm quite good with throwing stars—"

"You can't be serious," Kamran said, horrified. "The two of you are *not* coming with us."

"Three." Deen cleared his throat, sounding suddenly quite peppy. "There are three of us, actually."

"I thought you had to get home?" Kamran said darkly, turning to face the apothecarist. "I thought you said you had loved ones waiting for you. That you had no idea what you were doing here."

"That was before I knew I was going to meet Simorgh," said Deen, who quickly bent in half when the bird turned to look at him. "My loved ones will understand. If they even believe me." He stared at the bird in wonder. "I can't go home now."

Kamran shook his head. "Are you all blind?" he cried. "There are *five* of us. We can't all five of us fit on the back of the same bird—"

Simorgh made a call.

It was a gentle, melodious sound, but it carried nonetheless, and in a moment Kamran realized they were not alone. Simorgh had brought others—the children Zaal had known in youth, whose nest he'd shared as a babe.

Four more magnificent birds alighted at the top of the tower, the group of them peering down into the dark, trilling softly.

Briefly, Kamran closed his eyes. "Oh, for heaven's sake," he muttered.

Deen whooped.

"If you choose to come, you're coming under your own command," Kamran said sharply. "Get yourselves killed and I won't be bothered. Is that clear?"

"Yes," cried Omid, pumping a fist in the air.

"Get ourselves *killed*?" Deen frowned. "I didn't realize we might die—"

"No, sire," said Miss Huda, shaking her head. "With all due respect, Your Highness, I don't think that's very responsible of you, for we shall require a leader, and you were quite literally born for such a role—"

"*Hazan*," Kamran said, pinching his nose.

"Miss Huda," his old minster said quietly. "You may rely upon me should you require anything."

Simorgh launched upward then with a resonant cry, landing heavily at the broken lip of the tower, which trembled under her weight. She then chirruped to her children, who landed one at a time in the round cell, loading passengers one by one.

Miss Huda first, laughing through her tears; then Omid, who hugged his bird like the child he was, unselfconsciously kissing its feathered face; then Deen, too proud to betray more than a small, delighted smile as he mounted, even as he fought an obvious swell of emotion; and then Hazan, tall and dignified, he took his seat with the humility and grace befitting a knight, nodding just once at Kamran before he ascended, with a great flap of wings, into the sky.

When finally the others were settled among the clouds, Simorgh landed once more before the prince, and Kamran approached the beautiful bird in awe. He drew his hands along her silky feathers with great reverence, then mounted the incredible creature with care.

She took off at once.

Kamran was forced backward as they ascended, and quickly hooked his arms around the bird's graceful neck as they rose higher and higher up the destroyed spire, and once they loomed above the palace Simorgh made a cry that wrenched open the night, flapped her powerful, shimmering wings, and assumed her place at the head of the pack.

There was a thunderous *crack* as she took off, and a shower of color streaked across the sky, painting the heavens in an otherworldly phosphorescence.

The sight filled him with a complicated joy.

Kamran looked back as they vanished into inky skies, wondering, with a quiver in his heart, who he might be if he ever returned.